THE MERLIN PROPHECY: BOOK ONE
Battle of Kings

By M. K. Hume

The Merlin Prophecy: Battle of Kings
The Merlin Prophecy: Death of an Empire
The Merlin Prophecy: Hunting with Gods

THE MERLIN PROPHECY: BOOK ONE

Battle of Kings

M. K. HUME

ATRIA PAPERBACK

New York • London • Toronto • Sydney • New Delhi

ATRIA PAPERBACK

Atria Paperback
A Division of Simon & Schuster, Inc.
1230 Avenue of the Americas
New York, NY 10020

Copyright © 2011 by M. K. Hume

Previously published in Great Britain by Headline Review, an imprint of Headline Publishing Group

First Atria Paperback edition January 2013

ATRIA PAPERBACK and colophon are trademarks of Simon & Schuster, Inc.

For information about special discounts for bulk purchases, please contact Simon & Schuster Special Sales at 1-866-506-1949 or business@simonandschuster.com.

The Simon & Schuster Speakers Bureau can bring authors to your live event. For more information or to book an event contact the Simon & Schuster Speakers Bureau at 1-866-248-3049 or visit our website at www.simonspeakers.com.

Designed by Dana Sloan

Manufactured in the United States of America

10 9 8 7 6 5 4 3 2 1

ISBN 978-1-4767-1512-4
ISBN 978-1-4767-1513-1 (ebook)

This book is dedicated to David Hill, a kind and gentle
man, who departed this life on 30 September 2009,
after a long and courageous battle with cancer. David was a
family man to his bootlaces, and he was devoted
to his caring wife, their five sons, and their partners.
Through David's guidance and influence, his sons display
admirable qualities of their own because, like all
good men, they are reflections of their father. No higher
praise can be conferred on any man.
Ave, David.

MARILYN HUME

THE MERLIN PROPHECY: BOOK ONE

Battle of Kings

PROLOGUE

On the brow of the storm-torn headland, where the steel tines of the ocean wind combed the long grasses into smooth ringlets, the girl-child looked down upon her new home and sighed.

Grey stone rose coarsely out of the green flanks of Tintagel, where the leaf-shaped spearhead of land jutted into the Hibernian Sea and the wild waves smashed themselves to foam on the eroded cliffs below Gorlois's protective wall. The girl shuddered at the cheerlessness of the small, conical cottages which clung to the cliffs below the fortress, linked by steep, winding paths that tethered them to the paved courts above. Beyond the narrow steps, one hundred feet below, the sea crushed the cliffs into pebbles and gnawed its way into the peninsula in a long, narrow inlet.

The girl turned slowly in a circle, holding her waist-length hair out of her eyes as the wind tore her luxuriant locks into rags of russet and mahogany. No trees grew at Tintagel, nor on the land around the fortress, so the long grass was the only hiding place for small hunted creatures. Although the wheeling, circling gulls preyed on the small fish and living shells of the shallows, other predators waited above, wings riding the invisible currents of the air and hungry eyes watching for the slightest movement in the long tangles of green grass below.

The girl bit her lip as a merlin dropped from the sky like a stone, its wings folded and its talons outstretched. Its scream of triumph drowned out the small cry of a young rabbit that found itself snatched up in the raptor's cruel claws. Tears appeared in the girl's clear eyes as she followed the flight of the huntress.

"My lady." A deep rumbling voice disturbed the girl's moody thoughts. She turned too swiftly and, for a moment, the sky wheeled around her in a dizzying parabola. As her startled eyes rose to meet a pair of warm black irises in a broad, sunburned face, she felt a sudden chill of premonition that froze her tongue.

"Are you well, child? Perhaps you've been too long in the sun?"

The girl's vision narrowed until all she could see was the greatly magnified face of the warrior who stood over her. A dull roaring sound filled her ears as she watched the smiling mouth, so close to her own, open slowly to release a viscous flow of dark blood. The sun had dazzled her frightened eyes, but she was sure she could see a terrible, sucking wound that opened across the warrior's strong, thick neck.

"You are unwell, Lady Ygerne. Please allow me to help you back to your maid."

Her legs folded, and as she slid into a dead faint Gorlois swept up the frail body of his betrothed who had been so newly delivered to Tintagel by her father. Concerned, the tribal king assessed the violet shadows below her eyes and the childish shape of her long lashes as they rested upon her pale cheeks.

"She's so small—and so young," he whispered to himself as he hefted her slight form in his arms, taking care not to drop the reins of his horse in the process. I hope she's not sickly, he thought guiltily, even as he ordered his servants to ride ahead and prepare a hot, sweetened drink for her. He'd already lost one young wife to childbirth and, although his heart had not been given to the delicate little princess who had carried his stillborn son, he remembered the shrill desperation of her childbed cries with a sick dread. But his position demanded a wife and, more urgently, an heir, so he longed for a woman who could survive in his harsh and wildly beautiful domain.

"She's but ten years old, you fool!" Gorlois told the wind as he climbed back onto his horse, still pressing her insubstantial length against his barrel chest. "She's frightened, she's lost, and she's far from her home." He was still searching her face with an expression of kind concern when her eyelids fluttered open.

"There you are, my lady. I'll soon have you back in a cozy room with a warm rug to cover your knees. You'll feel better for a cup of hot milk from my kitchens. Tintagel is a wild place, and very isolated, but I have fairer houses in Isca Dumnoniorum that you will find comfortable and beautiful. The winds are warm and mild there. Tintagel is my country's heart, so my wife must understand what makes it beat, but she need not love it, as I do." He smiled in a fatherly fashion as he observed her obvious confusion. "Never mind, pretty sweetling! When you have rested, perhaps my home will not seem so grim."

Above his head, the birds continued to wheel as they squabbled in the wind-torn sky. Ygerne's pale lips smiled tremulously, and she watched another falcon as it rode the thermals in the bright sky. She could imagine its golden eyes, seeking and seeking, and wondered if the bird could see her or would acknowledge her presence.

Without understanding her vision, the threat of the bird, or the childish invitation in her actions, Ygerne turned her face and snuggled into the broad chest of Gorlois. She felt safe and loved for the first time in that long, strange, and painful day. And as Gorlois felt her hair and her warm flesh pressed against his body, the fragility of her lovely face wound itself around his heart.

Myrddion's Map of Pre-Arthurian Cymru

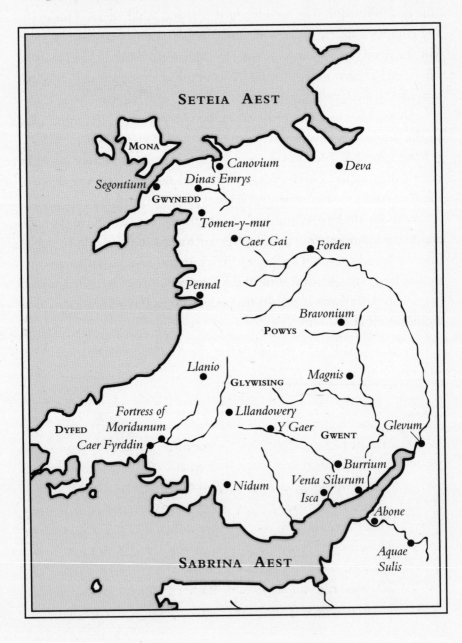

SETEIA AEST

MONA

Segontium
GWYNEDD

Canovium
Dinas Emrys

Deva

Tomen-y-mur
Caer Gai

Forden

Pennal

Bravonium

POWYS

Llanio

GLYWISING

Magnis

Fortress of
Moridunum

Lllandowery

Y Gaer

Glevum

DYFED

GWENT

Caer Fyrddin

Burrium

Nidum

Venta Silurum

Isca

Abone

SABRINA AEST

Aquae
Sulis

Chapter 1

FROM MONA

Why should the worm intrude the maiden bud?
Or hateful cuckoos hatch in sparrows' nests?
Or toads infect fair founts with venom mud?
Or tyrant folly lurk in gentle breasts?
Or kings be breakers of their own behests?
  But no perfection is so absolute
  That some impurity doth not pollute.

—SHAKESPEARE, *THE RAPE OF LUCRECE*

"Daughter?" An angry, masculine voice bellowed from the forecourt of the old villa at Segontium. Disturbed farm birds squawked and squabbled as they scrambled away from the huge horses. "Olwyn! Come out at once! Explain yourself!"

The sounds of nervous horses and a series of shouted orders, all delivered in a stentorian, impatient voice, forced Olwyn to put down her spindle, smooth her hair and woolen robe, and hurry out of the women's quarters towards the atrium of an ancient house where a tall, grizzled man was stripping off his fine leather gloves and woolen cloak, dropping them negligently over the nearest oaken bench.

His garb was careless, but his leathers, the well-tended furs, and the embossed designs of hawks on his fine hide tunic indicated wealth and power. The heavy golden torc that proclaimed his status and a collection of brass, gold, and silver arm rings, wrist bands, and cloak pins were worn with such negligent grace that Melvig radiated the authority of a king. Even more telling were the disdainful eyebrows, the heavy lines of self-indulgence that drew down his narrow lips and a certain blunt directness in his stare that spoke of a nature accustomed to giving orders. On this particular afternoon, above a greying beard, his eyes were stormy and promised that squalls would soon come to her door.

"Father! How nice to see you. Please, sit and be welcome. May I order the wine you like so much?"

Melvig ap Melwy made a grumpy gesture of assent and threw himself into a casual slouch, his long, still-muscular legs outstretched and his fingers tapping the armrest of his chair with ill-concealed irritation. Olwyn turned to her steward, who was hovering nervously behind his mistress. "Fetch the last of the Falernian wine that came from Rome. And some sweetmeats. I believe my father's hungry."

"Hungry be damned, woman! I'm cross. And it's your infernal brat who's the cause of my upset. A man ought to be able to ride with his guard to see his daughter without risking assassination."

Olwyn's brow furrowed. Her father had always been a tyrant and a blusterer, but she loved him despite his faults. As the king of the Deceangli tribe, he often risked death from impatient claimants to his throne and ambitious invaders. But, so far, he had proved to be an elusive target and a vengeful survivor.

"Idiot woman! It's that daughter of yours. More hair than brain, I say, and thoughtless to a fault. She ran across the path right under the hooves of my horse. Only good luck prevented me from being thrown . . . and I'm too old to risk my bones."

Olwyn smiled with relief, noting that her father showed no concern for the health of his granddaughter. Melvig was utterly egocentric.

"You're not very old, Father. You're only fifty-two years by my reckoning, and you're far too vigorous to be harmed by a twelve-year-old girl."

"Humpf!" Melvig snorted. But he was pleased, none the less, and accepted the fine goblet of wine and ate every sweetmeat on the plate that was offered to him by Olwyn's fumbling, nervous steward. When he had licked the last drops of honey from his huge mustache and drained the last of the wine in his cup, he fixed his daughter with his protuberant green eyes.

"Olwyn, my granddaughter is near as tall as your steward, but she still runs wild through the dunes with her legs bare where she can be seen by any peasant who cares to look. When did she last have her hair brushed? And when did she last bathe? She's little more than a savage!"

"You exaggerate, Father. She's high-spirited, and too young to be cooped up indoors. Would you take her from me? She's all I have."

"And whose fault is that?"

But Melvig's eyes softened a trifle, as much as that dour man was able to express feelings of sympathy. He remembered that Olwyn had lost her husband to a roving band of outlanders in her second year of marriage. Since Godric's death, she had steadfastly refused to remarry, and preferred to live with her servants and her daughter on the wild stretch of coast below Segontium. In Melvig's opinion, his daughter was too young at twenty-five summers to have turned her face away from life. She still had all her teeth, her skin was unlined, and she had proved that she was fertile. If she had any loyalty to her clan, he thought with another spurt of temper, she would have given him another grandson years ago.

But Olwyn's hazel eyes were slick with unshed tears, so Melvig was moved to pat her arm awkwardly to show his understanding of her fears. Although he was an impatient father, this particular daughter had always been a favored child, for in all the details that mattered Olwyn had been obedient and circumspect.

"I'll not take her from you, daughter, so have done with all this fussing. But you must be aware that she's as wild as a young filly and as heedless as a foolish coney that dares the hawks to strike. Would you have her stolen and raped? No? Then you must see to her education, Olwyn, because I'll be searching for a husband for her at the end of winter."

Olwyn's heart sank and a single tear spilled from her thick, over-long lashes to roll down her pale cheek. Melvig used his large, cal-loused thumb to wipe away the salty trail with affectionate impatience.

"May the gods take thee, woman," he whispered softly. "Don't look at me as if I steal your last crust of bread. I'll not take her yet, but the day will come soon, Olwyn, so you'd best be considering how you are to spend the rest of your days. Now, where are my traveling bags?"

Too wise to waste time in fruitless argument, Olwyn saw to the comfort of her father first, and then sent her maid to find her moon-mad daughter.

Segontium wasn't a large town, but it bore the stamp of the Roman occupation in its small forum, brick and stone buildings, and sturdy wall. Once, over a thousand Roman troops had been quartered in the surrounding fields, allowing Paulinus, and Agricola after him, to smash all resistance by the Ordovice tribes. Above a pebble-strewn shoreline, Segontium looked towards the island of Mona where, forever after, all good Celts would remember the shameful slaughter of the druids, young and old, male and female, as they faced their implacable enemy on the ancient isle of sacred memory. Rome's predatory legions had known that the druids held sway over the tribal kings. During the rebellion, leaving Boudicca to rage around Londinium, Paulinus had hastened north to rip the living, beating heart out of the Celts on Mona rather than bring the Iceni queen to heel. His desperate plan had suc-ceeded, for few druids had escaped the bloody massacres, and Paulinus had crushed the superstitious, suddenly rootless Celts. In one final insult, the Christian priests had decided to take root on Ynys Gybi, a tiny isle huddled against Mona's flanks.

Segontium bore its taint of blood, while something heavy re-mained in the Latin name to cause the least superstitious man to fur-row his brow and make the sign to ward off evil. The dark shores in winter, the screams of gulls, and the sea-tainted air that was softened by the earth and trees of Mona warned its neighbors to beware.

Olwyn had come to Godric's house with joy, in full knowledge that her man had no Roman blood in him. Their ancient home was cobbled together from a ruin, using stones taken from Roman villas and the conical houses of the Celts, but Olwyn felt no taint in the clean winds that scoured the corridors of fallen leaves and the sand whipped into corners by storms. Situated a little to the south of the shadow of Mona, their snug house suffered the vicious blows of the Hibernian winds, but Olwyn was content. Even the worn floor tiles, with their alien designs of sun, stars, moons, and constellations held no fears for her. Wind, clean sunshine, driving rain, and freezing snow combined to drive any sour humors from the house and purge it of the Roman poison.

But Godric had ridden away to protect his uncle's fields from tribal incursions, and when he returned he was tied over his horse's flanks, wrapped in greasy hides and pallid in death. Olwyn had been too numb to weep, even when she had unbound her husband's corpse and exposed the many wounds made by arrows in his cold, marbled flesh. A stump of shaft protruded from the killing injury over his heart, and Olwyn had been so lost to propriety that she had struggled to tug it free.

Eventually, after she had used a sharp knife to slice the flesh that held the cruel barbs of the arrowhead in place, the small length of shaft had seemed to leap out of Godric's breast with an ugly, sucking noise. In a daze, she had washed her husband's flesh, oiled his hair, and plaited it neatly before dressing him in his finest furs and a woolen tunic. Finally, she bent to kiss his mouth, although the faint, sickly odor of death almost made her vomit. Blessedly, her tears began to fall.

All the comforting obsequies of death were observed but only one duty consumed Olwyn's waking moments. The arrowhead was separated from the remnants of its shaft and Olwyn labored for many hours to drive a narrow hole through the wicked iron barb. Then, after months of toil, she hung the arrowhead round her daughter's neck by a soft plait of leather.

Melvig, her father, had been repulsed by the gesture, but Olwyn was a strange, obsessive creature who lacked his sturdy practicality, so he said nothing. If he had been honest, Melvig would have confessed that his stubborn, self-contained daughter frightened him a little with her intensity. Like all her kin, Olwyn was wild and strange. Melvig often wondered why he had taken a black-haired hill woman as his second wife, although her blatant sexuality had certainly stirred his loins. The gods were aware of his frustration when she produced no sons, only daughters, and all of them peculiar!

Melvig ate in a petulant, reflective manner and scorned to use the old Roman divans, choosing instead to experience the solid service-ability of an adze-formed oak bench and table. His daughter served him mead with her own hands, although she wished privately that the Deceangli and Ordovice tribes were still at war so that her father would be forced to stay in his fortress at Canovium to the north. Still, she smiled in that distant fashion that always aggravated her father's temper. Even as he accepted her excellent wine, he fought a desire to box her ears or to slap her pale cheeks until she cast off her impassive-ness to weep and curse him. Anything but that empty face, the old man thought impotently, but managed to save his irritation for the belated appearance of his granddaughter.

Conscious of the gulf between them, Olwyn tried to bridge that yawning space without touching him, which she knew would not be acceptable to the irascible old king.

"How go your borders, Father? I know your friendship with King Bryn ap Synnel is as strong as ever, but the Picts still raid our lands in the spring." She was conscious that she was gabbling, but that gulf . . . She bridged it in the only way she could, with hurried words, hoping to deflect criticism from her wayward daughter. "I know you are in alliance with the Cornovii king, but the Brigante aren't very friendly, are they? I do wish you had time for more peaceful pursuits."

Melvig frowned. He was uncomfortable with *woman's chatter*, as he called it, and was unwilling to discuss political matters with anyone, including his son, Melvyn.

He ran his hand through his beard and scratched his chin to cover his awkwardness. As an affectionate but distant father, he had never known how to discuss anything of importance with his daughters, faring better when he was issuing peremptory instructions in a gruff voice. He patted his daughter's head clumsily, and tried to deflect any personal revelations.

"You don't need to worry your head about the Picts, or those Brigante bastards. They've got a new king who's more amenable to reason than his predecessor. It's the south where the true dangers lie, but there'll always be someone to keep you safe, girl. You don't need to be afraid."

"I'm not afraid, Father. Whatever will happen, will happen. We all stand in the hollow of the Mother's hand."

Melvig cleared his throat, and Olwyn knew he was embarrassed by any reference to the Mother, whom all sensible men feared to their very bones. Regretfully, Olwyn patted her father's shoulder in passing and went to wait for her daughter.

When she finally arrived, the girl came at a run, with scant regard for her wind-torn hair and grass-stained skirts. Melvig noticed that Branwyn's feet were bare and dirty, and that one sunburned hand clutched her sandals behind her back.

As if he wouldn't notice!

"So, my young barbarian, you've decided to honor us with your presence at last. What do you have to say for yourself, eh? Don't you realize how foolhardy you are to run across the path of galloping horses? The gods must have protected us both, for you weren't trampled to death and I didn't fall from my horse."

Branwyn stood resolutely before him with her dirty feet slightly apart. Her eyes were cast down modestly, but Melvig wasn't deceived.

"Are you half-witted, girl? Give me a fair answer, or by my oath I'll have you locked in your room. And there you will stay for six months, even if I have to leave a guard to enforce my wishes."

"You're frightening her, Father!"

"Her?" Melvig snorted derisively, and waved a chicken leg in his granddaughter's direction. "She's afraid of too little for her own good."

The object of his disapproval was a tall, slender girl just approaching womanhood but still possessing all the awkwardness of a young

11

animal. Her skin was startlingly pale, for Olwyn and Melvig both tanned easily, and were always a warm, golden hue. Her eyes were inherited from Godric, and were brown and lustrous, but they were harder and more willful than those of her noble father. Her mouth was generous and naturally red, but her nose was too long and narrow for feminine beauty, and her lips always appeared to be smiling at something vaguely unpleasant. Her mahogany-brown hair with its highlights of bronze was an odd frame for her pale flesh and dark eyes, and with that imperious nose coupled with brows that rose upward at the outer corners the child possessed an alien, disconcerting sexuality. Melvig felt his palms itch with the desire to slap her pale face. Even Olwyn, a doting mother, was a little repelled by her daughter's indifference to the opinions of her elders.

"I beg your pardon if I frightened you, Grandfather," she replied meekly. "But I like the sand and the gulls, and I don't really notice anything other than where I'm going when I'm freed from my lessons."

"You'll discover just how frightened I am, young lady, if you run under the hooves of my stallion again," Melvig spluttered, but his mouth curled in grudging appreciation. She was a spirited vixen, although she irritated him mightily. "You'll feel the flat of my hand!"

"Father!" Olwyn protested, her eyes finally registering concern.

"Go to your bed, girl—without your supper," the king ordered, gazing off into the distance to indicate that he had made an irrevocable decision. "Perhaps a time of fasting will remind you to take more care in future."

"There's a storm coming, so all sensible folk will be seeking shelter for the night," Olwyn added. "You could easily have been caught in the elements of the gods through your foolishness, Branwyn. The storm clouds come from over Mona, where the druids tended the sacred groves. They tell us that the spirits are angry when the winds blow fiercely from the island, so any sensible person knows to pray to their household gods and keep their head down."

The girl bowed low to her grandfather with a gravity that was totally false. Olwyn saw the girl's lips quivering with scorn, and felt a frisson of fear at her daughter's arrogance. Then the girl was gone, leaving behind the smell of sunshine and seaweed, as well as a small scattering of sand granules.

"Mark my words, Olwyn, that little vixen will bring trouble to your house. Your Godric was a good, decent man, and apart from your failure to remarry for the sake of your family you've always been a dutiful daughter. But what can be made of Branwyn? She's willful, disobedient, and completely unprepared for marriage. That's your fault, daughter! She's not even particularly beautiful," the old man added, combing his beard with irritable fingers. For the first time, he had felt the child's blatant, unconscious sexuality and he was disturbed by its wild strength. "What is to become of this plain, fractious, and peculiar child?"

Having voiced his opinion, he considered that the discussion was closed. Oblivious of the offended expression of his daughter, he stamped off to his quarters in a much-improved humor, while behind his receding back, Olwyn seethed. She regretted her gender and the intense, inward-looking nature that robbed her of the ability to voice any argument or complaint. Whenever her father invaded her quiet world, she felt impotent, frail, and alone. Olwyn accepted that her daughter was reckless and even heedless of others, but Branwyn was so like her grandfather that the child sometimes overwhelmed her mother.

A distant rumble of thunder intruded into Olwyn's turbulent thoughts and she moved to the heavy wooden door of the villa. Her manservant was waiting to bolt the doors for the night, and Olwyn felt a surge of guilt that she should keep this good man from his bed. Uncharacteristically, she remained at the entrance to her house after ordering him to retire, because, like her mother before her, Olwyn couldn't resist the lure of the approaching storm. Wild weather fascinated her and made her believe that real blood raced through her quiet veins.

The storm gradually blotted out the last, numinous light of the long evening. Black clouds marched across the sky in the vanguard of the tempest and were laced with bruised purples and livid greens as if the gods had struck heaven's face in a jealous rage. Behind the leading edge of the boiling storm clouds came an ominous denseness that seemed more palpable than air. Periodically, lightning lanced out of the darkness and struck the sea or the island like a crooked staff of incandescent energy. The air smelled of ozone, salt, and the breathless sweat of a dead afternoon.

Olwyn clutched herself and shivered. Something was angry: not the gods, precisely, but something older and more primal that barely deigned to notice, for the most part, the small irritants of humanity. Now, that indefinable "it" had been stirred and, in its sudden temper, was tearing the sea to shreds of foam and eliminating the stars that had filled the sky.

Superstitiously, Olwyn backed through the wooden doors and slammed them shut behind her. As she lowered the heavy bar into place, she heaved a sigh of relief that the villa was locked against whatever sought to smash it into fragments of brick, wood, and tile.

"When Poseidon pounds his trident and Zeus throws his thunderbolts, all sensible people cover their heads and pray that they will see morning," the steward, Plautenes, told the cook, a fellow transplanted Greek who was shivering with fear in their narrow bed. "Don't fret, Crusus. The gods have no use for men like us. As the old saying goes, they've got other fish to fry."

Perhaps Plautenes was right, for the villa was shaken to its strong foundations by peal after peal of rolling thunder. Tiles were dislodged by the wild, gusting winds and several trees in the orchard were ripped out of the ground.

Throughout the terrifying evening, only two people in the villa were completely at peace. Melvig slept soundly, for he was a hardheaded realist who refused to fear the demons of the air that existed only in the imaginations of the foolish. Under the fine linen covers of his pallet, he slept dreamlessly, to wake at dawn without any memory of the storm or the dangers it had presented.

After prayers to the Mother and an invocation to Grannie Ceridwen to save her household, Olwyn fell into the dreamless, untroubled sleep of the truly innocent, trusting that her mistresses would save her from the terror of the darkness.

In her small room, before a narrow, shuttered window, Branwyn gloried in the havoc that played out before her wondering eyes. In the face of such elemental power, she found herself unable to be frightened when the pyrotechnics of sheet and forked lightning limned her narrow and limited view of Mona with lurid color.

"It's wonderful!" she whispered to the storm with a childlike glee. "Tomorrow anything might happen, for the gods have wrought the sea and the air anew. How exciting it is!"

When she finally fell asleep in a wild tangle of long limbs and unbrushed hair, the stillness that descended over the villa held no fears for her. Branwyn, daughter of Olwyn and grandchild of Melvig ap Melwy, had yet to learn the smell and taste of terror.

Chapter II

UPON THE TIDE

Before the kitchen fires were lit, before Olwyn stirred from her narrow pallet, and even before her grandfather opened one eye to enjoy the rise of a newly minted sun, Branwyn was awake, dressed, and abroad. Wise to the fury of storms, she knew that the tide would have delivered up a rich treasure in broken and whole shells, sea-polished stones, seeds, and the skeletal, grey wood that the waves deposited along the high-water line. With the ghoulishness of a child, she reveled in examining dead fish that had been cast up from unimaginable depths and were stranger than any fisherman's catch. Iridescent jellies quivered on the white rime of deposited sand that softened the piles of uprooted weed, black silt, and shiny grey stones.

Nothing could keep Branwyn away from such marvels.

The sky was barely lit with the first flush of dawn when the girl cast off her rough leather sandals on the tough grass foreshore, tied her skirts into makeshift trousers between her legs, and picked her way down to the tide line.

Her head scarf was soon employed to serve as a collection bag. Shells, complete and beautiful, were popped into the cloth. Spiral horns, like the fierce weapon of a centaur, were placed into the folds of linen. A strange, translucent cone, shaped like a whimsical hat, followed her other treasures, and this booty was soon joined by stag horns of tide wood, two pebbles the color of ripe apricots, and a fragment of weed that was firm yet pliant, entrancing Branwyn's imagination with its strange beauty.

Soon, she had rounded the point and was picking her way through a tangle of dark grey rocks, peering through the early morning light into marooned rock pools where small balls of spines tried to hide in crevices. Tiny fingerlings danced away from her questing fingers as she stirred the salty, crystalline water into miniature whirlpools.

Then an alien sound, a groan, stopped her movement and evaporated her inner peace. Wrenched from salt-burned lungs and a seared throat, the sound was as harsh as a crow's cry against the perfection of an idyllic dawn. Like the wild thing that she was, Branwyn crouched low and scanned the wet rocks that surrounded her at the water's edge.

There!

Above the suck of the waters, a huddled shape was wedged between two fangs of greyish stone. Whatever it was, the contorted form was large, black, and menacing.

Branwyn almost left it to die. So close! Like any startled animal, she was poised to run back the way she had come. So easily are kingdoms made, and lost, then made again, on the courage of a girl not wise enough to understand the texture of fear.

Branwyn crept cautiously towards the huddled shape. When she was a spear length from the body, she saw the outflung, open hand that was as white as new bone against the coarse grey rock. The fingers were long, with nails so clean and well tended that Branwyn wondered if a woman lay supine where the sea had thrown her body.

Carefully and warily, Branwyn knelt beside the huddled shape, which appeared to be tangled in heavy, wet wool. Every sense was alert as the girl pulled an edge of the still-sodden cloth away from the head. She gasped in shock.

The body was male and the face was beautiful. The man's nose was long, narrow, and straight with sensitive nostrils that flared, even now, as he struggled to breathe. His eyebrows were perfect, black semicircles

18

above closed eyes that were fringed with long, curling lashes. The eyelids appeared bruised and tender, so that Branwyn's heart gave a sudden little skip as if something pressed down hard on her chest.

"It's the face of a demon!" her rational mind argued, for Branwyn was aware of the legends that spoke of fair seals in human form that sometimes came out of the night to steal away the souls of unwary girls.

"He's a gift to me from Poseidon!" she said aloud. "The storm has given me a present, for no one so beautiful could possibly wish me any harm."

She was suddenly determined to save the injured man, and immediately set about putting her desire into action. With much tugging and grunting effort, she stripped the clinging, heavy cloak from the inert body, dragging the man out of the crevice in the process. A long cut on his side was revealed through his torn tunic and an equally livid wound marred the perfection of his white forehead. The movement caused his injuries to bleed sluggishly, and Branwyn felt a twinge of alarm that she might cause him to suffer further harm.

"If I leave him here, the sea will have him again," she told herself loudly to invest her words with confidence. "This time, he'll surely drown!" Branwyn spoke to herself often, having grown without other children to provide her with company. "And anyway, he's mine, to do with as I wish," she murmured childishly.

The stranger began to mumble in a strange language. His eyes slowly opened and she discovered that they were black and quite insensible. He flinched away from her touch and would have struck her, had she not drawn back as she would from any wounded animal.

Branwyn was willful, but she was no fool. This stranger was delirious, injured, and he could easily die if she didn't find shelter for him. But where could she take him? And how?

Just above the shoreline, she could see a ruined cottage that, for the large part, gaped open to the elements. Except for one corner, most of its thatched roof was gone, and two shale walls had tumbled in under the dual ravages of wind and icy winters. But part of the structure was still protected from the elements if she could find a way to bring her prize to its doubtful shelter.

Branwyn realized that the stranger was watching her intently, although she couldn't guess at what he saw. Schooling her voice into the tones of the cook when he was being most autocratic, she began to issue orders.

"You're hurt, sir. Come, no argument or foolishness. You must rise so I can help you to safety." The man's unfocused eyes looked up at her blankly, while his marble forehead furrowed in an attempt at concentration.

"Get on your feet," she ordered, although she willed her mouth to smile sweetly. "I'll help you, if only you can stand for me."

As a child will obey the voice of an adult, even when they are fretful and ill, the young man stirred and slowly attempted to climb to his knees. Branwyn lent him her meager strength to support him as he struggled to stand upright.

"Very good, Triton," she muttered, when at last he leaned heavily on her thin shoulders with one shaking arm. "Now we'll try to get you to walk."

With indrawn hisses of pain, her gift from the sea obeyed her commands. Together, they struggled into the sharp, wiry sea grass, where his knees crumbled like broken kindling, taking Branwyn to the ground with him. A sharp elbow caught her in the stomach and winded her, leaving both man and girl lying prone under the rising sun until Branwyn managed to struggle to her feet and continue the arduous task of bullying her charge. Slowly but inexorably, they climbed the slope that led to the ruined croft.

Over an hour had passed by the time she released her charge at last and permitted him to collapse in the shade of the rock walls. Above him, sufficient thatch remained on the roof to protect his supine body from rain. Carefully, Branwyn spread out his cloak to dry and weighted it down with stones lest it should flap in the wind and draw attention from some passing peasant. The girl wanted no witnesses to her adventure. This man was hers.

Gently, she stroked his forehead and found that his skin burned with the beginnings of a fever. His lips were cracked with thirst and she regretted that she had neglected to bring a water skin.

"Never mind. I'll go home, I think, and beg some food from Plautenes. He always gives me what I want."

Her dark, cat's eyes gleamed impishly. Plautenes might profess to love his plump Greek cook, Crusus, but Branwyn knew that the steward wasn't impervious to the female sex. He had never laid so much as a finger on Branwyn, but she understood from his hot brown eyes that he nurtured illicit thoughts about her. Branwyn wasn't entirely sure what these thoughts entailed for, unwisely, Olwyn had neglected this part of her daughter's education. Little did the mother understand how curiously her daughter's imagination dwelt on the mysteries of sex.

Yes, Plautenes would filch bread, cheese, and goat's milk for her from the kitchens, she decided as she returned to the villa, where her unexpected return was greeted with incredulous pleasure by her mother.

"You're back, Branwyn? Good girl! Your grandfather would never leave if he thought you were wandering off again after his complaints. He's already broken his fast and is in an expansive mood, so be nice to him and we may return to our normal routines once he's gone."

Olwyn pinched her daughter's cheeks to induce a little color into their pallor, then tamed the girl's wild mahogany curls with her own bone comb and straightened her crushed robe.

"Off with you, sweetheart! Your grandfather loves you, but he's used to having his own way and has no patience with the interests of his womenfolk." Olwyn had no appreciation of the irony in her words. She failed to recognize that both Branwyn and herself were much like her arrogant father in their separate, eccentric fashions.

Branwyn endured several homilies and lectures from her grandfather, sat on his knee, and kissed his cheek with charming, youthful giggles. She made a great many promises that she had no intention of keeping. Although she smiled winningly and assured Melvig that he was the best man in the whole world, her mind remained fixed

21

on the ruined hut and the plight of its injured occupant. Her last sight of her trophy as he had lain, feverish, coughing, and curled into the cool sandy sod, added a sense of urgency to the brilliance of her laughter.

Once she was released and had plundered the kitchen for food and clean rags, she headed for the stables. Branwyn knew her mother would ask questions if she requested salve for the stranger's wounds, and she had no intention of sparking Olwyn's curiosity. Fortunately, she knew that the stables would provide her with a vile-smelling ointment used to treat swellings on delicate hocks or to cure cuts and abrasions on horses' legs. Her grandfather's stable lad was too stupid to question his master's granddaughter, so she took a thick compress of moss and some mysterious, pungent oil wrapped in a grimy length of oilskin. Melvig would be long gone before he discovered she had been helping herself to his horse salves—if he ever did.

Despite her best efforts, noon had come and gone by the time Branwyn returned to the ruined cottage. The sky was miraculously clear and seemed newly washed by the storms of the night. A few clouds scudded in from the sea and gulls squabbled on the foreshore as they hunted for dead fish and shellfish torn from the safety of their rocks. With the feel of sandy grass beneath her bare feet, Branwyn sensed her quiet life was trembling on the brink of change.

Within the purple shadows of the hut, the stranger continued to sleep fitfully. He stirred irritably when Branwyn forced milk between his lips and when she inadvertently knelt on his right arm as she applied the horse salve to his temple and ribs. The ointment stained his delicate skin an unhealthy sanguine, but the girl knew that the smelly mess would cause him no lasting harm. Then, with strips of rag, she bound the stolen compress to the wound on his side and fastened it securely in place.

His hairless, defined torso made her stomach feel strange. Unused to the manners of epicureans, Branwyn couldn't know that his body had been plucked clean of body hair. Caught in the throes of her first experience of lust, she was mesmerized by a male beauty that was

22

so different from the greasy complexions of the villa servants or her grandfather's ancient, rough masculinity.

She sat beside him throughout the long afternoon, watching as he twisted and turned in his fever, and tried to understand the odd words that exploded from his well-shaped mouth in spasms of delirium.

For her, it was enough simply to watch him as he breathed.

As dusk fell, Branwyn left the water skin close to his hand, along with the food she had brought, wrapped in a piece of rag. His woolen cloak, now dry, did double duty as a blanket that she tucked around his slim form, flushing when she inadvertently touched his thigh. Then, regretfully, she returned to her mother's house.

The night dragged as Branwyn longed for morning. Had Poseidon sent him to her only yesterday? Would he love her as the gods had decided he should? Every foolish love story told by the maidservants flitted through her dreams until her twelve-year-old imagination had turned her stranger into a hero, cast into the storm by the jealousy of the queen of heaven, whom he had rejected. Seamlessly, Branwyn included herself in her wondrous fantasy, the true love of his heart for whose sake he would defy the gods and carry her away to his gold and ivory palace.

Only an indulged, protected child would have been so foolish. Branwyn had always been the center of her small world and she couldn't imagine why anyone would choose to cause her harm.

At first light, excitement lent speed to her feet as she ran the mile or so to the ruined cottage. Anticipation flushed her cheeks with handsome color and caused her eyes to sparkle with a luminous joy. Had the stranger opened his eyes, he would have seen the woman in the child clearly revealed through all of her tremulous vulnerability. But he continued to sleep.

In his fever, the stranger had cast off the cloak and his hair had broken free of the leather thong that had kept it from his eyes. His hair was not particularly long, but it was glossy black and exceptionally fine, with the first strands of white appearing on the right side of his forehead.

Branwyn shivered.

His pallor had warmed during the night so that his skin appeared rosy where his cheek rested against his hands. Carefully, so as not to waken him, Branwyn eased herself down onto the sod until she lay against his long, bare spine.

He didn't move. His shoulders rose and fell gently with his steady breathing, while Branwyn yearned to rest her hand on his breast and feel the long, slow beat of his heart. Her romantic imagination fueled by her innocent desires, she watched the clouds scud overhead through the smashed roof. In her content, she must have fallen asleep, for she was awakened, suddenly and shockingly, by a heavy weight across her thighs and a rough hand clamping off her throat.

Branwyn mewed with surprise and looked up into the flat black eyes of the stranger, who was examining her with all the casual disinterest of a king—or a god.

"Where am I? And who are you?" he demanded in a very bad approximation of the common speech. "I'll break your pretty neck if you scream, so nod if you understand what I'm saying."

Branwyn nodded, all dreams of love, heroism, and romance swept away by a flash of something atavistic and cruel in his glacial stare. Then the pressure on her bruised throat was eased.

"I am Branwyn, daughter of Godric of Segontium and grand-daughter of Melvig ap Melwy, king of the Deceangli people." She attempted to capture some of her usual arrogance, but her voice broke with emerging fear.

"Another jumped-up savage crowing over his petty dung heap." The stranger rolled his eyes derisively. "So I'm at Segontium, I suppose?"

Branwyn nodded.

"And you're responsible for this thing?" He indicated the poultice with a twitch of his nostrils. "If I'm not mistaken, your remedy smells of horse liniment."

Branwyn spat at him, her temper outweighing her fear as he sneered at her and her family.

"Quite the little savage, aren't you?" He smiled down at her. "Still, you saved me from the sea, so I suppose I owe you something."

The weight on her hips was released as the stranger raised himself until he was kneeling and began to pull off his boots. "Gods, but they're ruined," he muttered to himself in disgust as he upended each boot carefully onto his cloak. Two soft leather pouches fell free and Branwyn heard the unmistakable, gentle clink of gold coins.

"So even a little savage knows what gold is. It's handy that you didn't think to rob me when you had your chance."

"You're a horse's arse!" Branwyn swore crudely, conjuring up the worst insult she could imagine. "I'm not a thief!"

He backhanded her negligently with one graceful hand, but the force of the blow belied its casualness. For a moment, Branwyn's senses darkened.

"What delights are you hiding under those rags?" the stranger murmured reflectively as he began to strip and search her. He stroked her immature breasts appreciatively before bending to lick a line of sweat from her cheek with his tongue. She flinched away from the ugliness of the action as he lifted her birth talisman with an elegant finger.

"You've nothing of value, my dear, except this amulet. It's pretty, but hardly worth confiscating. Perhaps I might allow you to keep your pretty toy as a reward for keeping me safe when I wasn't quite . . . myself?"

His fingers played with the golden chain on which hung her father's only gift to her, a small gold and ivory figure of the goddess Ceridwen, lying beside the iron arrowhead between her breasts.

"I wish I'd let you die!" Branwyn hissed, then shrieked when he cruelly twisted one of her nipples.

"You will be nice to me, little one. I'd hate to be forced to cut off your breasts."

The stranger showed her a thin, deadly knife that he drew from a sheath inside his boot. As he watched her eyes flare with fear, he twisted her nipple again, even harder this time, until tears filled her eyes.

"Please?" He smiled down at her gently while tapping his forehead with one finger. "I must have scrambled my brains on the rocks, my pretty. Will anyone come looking for you if we stay here till I'm ready to resume my journey?"

"If I'm not home by the noontime meal, my mother will send out her menservants to find me. They'll catch you . . . and you'll regret treating me so cruelly."

"I think you're lying, my little poppet. You've brought bread and cheese for us, so you expected to be out here for many hours. I think I'll be long gone before they realize you're missing."

The tears began to spill out of Branwyn's eyes, but she scorned to cry aloud or to beg like a child. Her cozy dreams of love and devotion had vanished, leaving her frightened, angry, and mortified. The roil of her emotions expressed itself through the contempt in her eyes, which the stranger recognized immediately. He slapped her once more, hard enough this time to leave a handprint on her downy face.

"I'd forgotten how boring children can be," he said. Yet he smiled, as if he offered her a priceless compliment. "Maiden tears and shy manners are the dreary companions of pretty faces and lissome bodies."

"Then let me go and I won't tell anyone where you are," Branwyn replied as persuasively as she knew how. Her natural courage kept her voice steady, but they both recognized that the bravado in her words was false.

"I don't think so, little one," he said. "Open your mouth!"

Branwyn locked her lips firmly together as he thrust a piece of cloth towards her mouth.

Pitiless, he moved with the speed of a serpent.

Her arms were pinned by his knees so his hands were free to pinch her nose closed.

"Open your mouth, bitch!"

Choking, she was forced to open her mouth to gulp in air, and the man rammed the filthy rag between her teeth. Although she gagged and retched, she still managed to bite his forefinger, drawing blood in the process.

"You harpy! I'll scar from that bite!" he snapped, as he lashed her hands together with part of her own tunic. Trussed so tightly that she could scarcely move, Branwyn hoped that he would leave her and make his escape while the day was still young.

But her captor was sadistic and she was at his mercy. As a cat toys with a helpless bird for sport alone, so he reveled in a terror that she couldn't banish from her eyes. Her resistance had annoyed him, so he was determined to make her pay a huge price for her struggles.

Branwyn had never known such violence or scorn. She'd never imagined that any man would contemplate rape of the kinswoman of the king. Her mother had dedicated her life to the worship of the goddess once her husband had lost his life, so the daughter was accustomed to the reverence that her mother's sacrifice merited. Nothing in her experience had prepared her for the rough male hands that forced her knees apart and stripped the cloth from her genitals as the stranger began to assault her immature body, drawing blood and inflicting a growing shame that turned her eyes black with horror.

The stranger took his time, leaving Branwyn to stare blindly at the fluffy white clouds that seemed so close and so achingly pure. Gulls circled above the ruined hut and she struggled to lose herself in their squabbling, raucous cursing as they jostled for position on the foreshore where the tide was already beginning to peak. In truth, she wanted to separate herself from the sweating, set face above her, wishing herself elsewhere as he defiled her with his body and a constant stream of ugly oaths. She knew nothing of men and now she desired to live apart from that accursed sex until she was dead.

Eventually, he spent himself inside her and she felt her gorge rise behind the makeshift gag. His blind, self-absorbed face sickened her and made a mockery of all her daydreams. How could her mother have loved a man with her entire body and soul? Branwyn was no longer surprised that Olwyn had dedicated herself to celibacy after his death. If her father had been half as brutal as this animal, then surely his end must have been a blessing for Olwyn. No wonder she had chosen not to remarry.

"He might kill me now, to ensure he escapes unscathed," she thought, more calmly than she would have imagined possible. Simultaneously, she saw the thought and the pleasure of it flit through his eyes and come to rest on his smiling lips.

Think, Branwyn, think!

"Thank you, my lord," she murmured through the gag, the sound muffled and warped although she tried to mouth the words clearly. "Thank you!"

His curiosity was stirred. Rapists are rarely thanked for their attentions.

She could tell that he was a vain man, one used to compliments and accolades. She endeavored to smile through the gag and to make her eyes dewy and soft. To emphasize her capitulation, she raised her numbed, bound hands to stroke his damp hair away from his forehead.

His puzzlement deepened. Instinctively, Branwyn could tell that this was a man who must understand everything and her salvation might lie in her lack of predictability.

He tore the gag from her mouth and eyed her suspiciously, his body still pressing her painfully into the grass and sandy soil.

"What tricks are you trying to play, my little she-cub?" His voice held no trace of empathy or apology, so Branwyn reasoned that this man never counted the cost of the fulfillment of his desires.

"It's not a trick, my lord. You have saved me from a life of dedication to Ceridwen and the fate of spending my days in lonely contemplation and prayer. Celibacy is all my mother has ever desired for me."

The stranger stared at her intently as he searched for any sign of deceit in her childishly worshipful eyes. Branwyn was an accomplished liar, having practiced the art daily to enjoy her life as she chose without the strictures of chaperones, constant questions, and curfews, so the stranger was unable to pierce her mask of deception. Yet he wouldn't permit himself to trust her.

"Thank you, my lord," she said again. "I hadn't expected to be initiated into the holy rites by a grown man, least of all by a stranger of note from a far-off land. You've insulted me and my kin, but I know the sea sent you to me to save me from my mother's plans, so I can forgive your arrogance."

He pinched her cheek harshly in punishment and she winced at the sudden pain, but she schooled her traitorous eyes to remain open and admiring.

"You didn't act like a grateful girl. And you fought and spat like a whore. How can I know if you're telling the truth?"

"You took me by surprise, my lord. I'd have freely given you anything you asked, but you chose to use your hand. I'm not a slave, or a peasant who can be taken by force. What would you have me do?"

The stranger laughed, but he did not untie her hands. Despite his pleasant voice and attractive features, he'd survived to full adulthood because he lacked trust in others and could conceal his viciousness behind a bland countenance.

"Such pretty words, Branwyn, daughter of Godric and granddaughter of Melvig ap Melwy. I don't trust you an inch, but at least I'm spared maidenly hysterics. You're an unusual girl and, if I let you live, I have no doubt that you will make your mark upon the world. But why should I permit you to survive if you could inform on me?"

Despite her fear, Branwyn picked up the bald challenge that he had flung down so casually before her. As Olwyn often bemoaned, she was Melvig's granddaughter. Every word she spoke was cunning and chosen with care to disarm him, to flatter his ego, and to win his admiration.

"I'm only a girl, my lord, and I'm tolerably certain that I couldn't hurt you in any way, even if my hands were unbound. Nor could I free myself easily if I attempted to do so. Besides, I don't know your name, or where you have come from or your reason for being on this coast. How can I do you harm? In fact, a day might come when we could be allies, as I believe that I am in your debt. I'm no threat to you." She smiled at him. "Now that you've awakened my body to the mysteries, why should I choose to repay you with danger and pursuit? You've freed me from the unpleasant prospect of dedication to the goddess, a role I know I would hate. In fact, my lord, I would welcome further instruction before you leave me."

Although her actions sickened part of her soul, Branwyn squirmed until her groin was pressed against the naked thigh of the stranger. She rubbed herself against him suggestively although she was almost too terrified to speak.

"Your words are pretty, little vixen, but I have fond memories of your teeth." He sucked the small wound on his forefinger.

"As I said, you took me by surprise, master. When the sea dumped you on my shore, I thought you were a special gift from the gods. Perhaps you are! I ask that you don't kill me—for I promise not to tell a soul that you were here."

The stranger laughed and smoothed her slightly swollen cheek with one negligent hand.

"You're a liar, but you're entertaining and quick-witted far beyond your years. Now, tell me how I might safely leave this place. How might I reach Glevum and the roads that lead to the south? Who knows, but perhaps I'll leave you here in safety if you answer me fairly."

Branwyn thought furiously.

Unlike most of her sex, she had a curious nature that had led her to examine her father's scrolls and maps. She'd not received sufficient teaching to be able to read and she'd been unable to explore the wonders of her father's scriptorium, but his maps had called to her with their siren song of travel and she had studied them in detail. It seemed she was still under the protection of the goddess, and she thanked her father for the scrolls that might save her life.

"There's a track that leads to the south beyond the dunes," she said softly as she gazed unflinchingly into the stranger's eyes. "It was originally used by the Romans, but it's now overgrown. If you're determined, you can make your way along it. Follow the track along the coast until you reach a fishing village called Pennal. The road from the village will take you across the hills to Y Gaer, then Burrium, Venta Silurum, and, finally, the port below Glevum. From there you can take ship to anywhere in the world."

The stranger eyed her narrowly with an expression that suddenly reminded her of a stoat, so cold, calculating, and predatory was his stare.

"You could order mounted men to be at my heels before nightfall."

"I could, if anyone listened to a girl. But I would have to explain to my mother that I've lost my maidenhead. And then she'd happily imprison me in our villa for my own good. She wants to keep me a child forever so she tries to protect me from all threats. As for my grandfather, he would order me to be strangled, for I have lost my bride price. You know I speak the truth, just as you know I'll be silent."

The stranger rolled off her body and gathered up his cloak, the package of food, and the water skin. Then he looked down at her speculatively and placed one large hand around her slender throat. Branwyn closed her eyes submissively, although her heart leapt in her chest. She had tried—and she had failed.

His thumb pressed down on her voice box, creating sudden, lancing pain. Her body bucked instinctively, but she pressed her lips together so she made no sound. He wasn't the type of man to be swayed by tears or pleas. Perhaps courage could persuade him? Perhaps not.

"That was just a taste, little one, for I'll hunt you down and kill you slowly if your warriors should pursue me." He gave her a final, calculating stare. "I'm going to leave you to release yourself from your bonds," he whispered. "Remain here, quietly, until after darkness falls if you know what's good for you, and then you may do as you choose. I'll be long gone by sundown."

Branwyn's mind scurried through a number of options designed to make him pause. As she considered them one by one, she decided to present the face of an avaricious child, eager to profit from the morning's events and hoping to disarm him by acting like an unpredictable whore-child.

"May I beg for a memento, my lord, something to remember you by?" She managed a smile. "I'd like a reminder, something to prove that I've not dreamed this whole meeting."

He snorted with amusement. She was terrified that he might still change his mind, or be affronted by a request that was, on the face of it, such an unlikely reaction to rape. Cunning mimicked greed as she pouted.

"Perhaps I want something to hate. I don't know, but I would like a gift—anything at all. I like pretty things."

"Why?" he asked flatly, as his doubts of her sincerity resurfaced with a vengeance.

"Perhaps I'll bear a child," she replied and masked a shudder of revulsion. She tried to smile but was unsuccessful, her lips merely twisting into a grimace. For a moment, the stranger's brow furrowed in confusion, then his arrogance reasserted itself and he stripped a small amber ring from his thumb and tossed it at her.

"This ring belonged to my mother. She was a lady of considerable charm, vivacity, and traitorous deception. I took it from her dead hand after I poisoned her. You and I are well met, Branwyn, daughter of Godric, for we are much alike, but you may rest assured that our paths will never cross again."

As he sauntered out of the ruined hut, she lay on the sod floor with the ruins of her robe pulled up to her waist. When she was sure that he was gone, she permitted herself to sob quietly. She'd struggled hard to hide her terror and convince him that she was no threat, so she'd taken little time to consider her myriad small hurts. Now, as the drama came to its conclusion, humiliation flooded her abused body and almost overwhelmed her calculating brain.

"I hope he dies slowly and in terrible agony! The gods gave me no gift when they sent a demon to murder me. But I'm not dead and I won't die, no matter what happens."

Part of Branwyn's agile mind accepted the truth that she had brought her rape upon herself. Childhood's end comes to all girls, but Branwyn felt a sense of guilt from the dual whips of foolishness and selfish arrogance. She gnawed at her rag bonds, tearing at both cloth and tender flesh with her teeth. Suddenly, she felt so befouled that she could scarcely bear the thought of the filthy stamp he had placed upon her, both within and without.

No matter how she worried at the knots with her sharp young teeth, an hour passed before she was finally free. She staggered to her feet and struggled to return circulation to her swollen fingers, so that she could wrap herself in her torn robe. As an afterthought, she swept up the amber ring and drew it onto her index finger, which it fitted perfectly.

Under a late afternoon sky of particular brilliance, she ran blindly for the sea as if her tormentor were in hot pursuit. Careless of broken ground that snatched at her feet and caused her to fall, and oblivious of the acquisition of many new scrapes and bruises, she plunged into the waves and immersed her whole body in the salty water. She sat in the wavelets as tears streamed down her face to join the brine that beaded on her pale skin.

For a long time Branwyn sat, rocked, and cleansed herself in the sea that washed the scent, the blood, and the sweat of him from her body. Only the screaming of the gulls repeated the keening that echoed through the vaults of her skull.

In truth, Branwyn thought of nothing: not of the rape, not of the stranger, nor even of her family. In some secret, atavistic part of her consciousness, she knew her doom had come upon her and the sun would never shine on her again.

Chapter III

A TRICK OF FATE

Such is the protection they [the Celts] find for their country
   (It [the invited Saxon horde] was in fact its destruction)
That those wild Saxons, of accursed name,
Hated by God and men, should be admitted
into the island like wolves into folds,
In order to repel northern nations.

—GILDAS

Week had followed dreary week, although the summer sun shone brightly. The sea glittered and frolicked in the blue day and the gulls were comical counterpoints, always squabbling like argumentative children over live shells, dead fish, and the occasional scavenged scraps from the villa's kitchen. The trees in the orchard ripened with fruit, the menservants were kept busy smoking fish and tending the vegetable patch, and the world of Segontium was fair, sweet-smelling, and peaceful.

Yet Olwyn fretted, night and morning, for Branwyn no longer roamed far and wide during the day and expressed no interest in the seashore or long rambles through the wonders of the foreshore.

The child's dark eyes were turned inwards and her voice had been silenced. Olwyn longed for the willful, disobedient girl who had been so filled with raw enthusiasm for life. The changeling who now imprisoned herself in her small plastered room rarely smiled, never laughed, and spent hours on her bed or staring out towards the isle of Mona.

Olwyn flinched at the thought of that blessed isle. She had lived for years in its shadow, and so much blood stained it that perhaps the gods had been angered by Branwyn's joy of life, and were punishing the child for her hubris. Perhaps Olwyn had not been dedicated enough in her prayers to Ceridwen, and now the Old Ones sought to take her only child to sharpen her devotion. Olwyn prayed long into the night, begged the Mother for mercy until her knees were raw and her hands were bloody from striking the tiles in her piety, but Branwyn remained as emotionless as a small effigy in petrified wood.

Would Olwyn have continued to watch her cuckoo child without daring to shatter the illusion of calm and peace that Branwyn's silence evoked? Perhaps. Or was she sufficiently frightened of the child's new timidity to have ultimately chosen storms and tempers above this eerie obedience?

As it happened, Olwyn's maidservant brought word of Branwyn's illness.

"She can hold nothing down in her stomach during the mornings, my lady. Nothing! And she can scarcely move from her bed for weariness. I know it's impossible, but Mistress Branwyn acts like my daughter when she's breeding. She almost dies of the sickness for the first four months and then, when the babe begins to show, she becomes well again. But Mistress Branwyn is scarcely twelve years old, and she's never lain with a man."

The maidservant made the ancient sign against the chaos demons and Olwyn felt her cheeks leach of color. Could Branwyn be pregnant? Such a condition would certainly explain her change of mood. But how could it have happened? With some trepidation, Olwyn decided to ask her outright, regardless of what bad news she might discover.

When she entered her daughter's room, Branwyn was still abed with the covers pulled up to her chin and an old, cracked bowl close to hand in case of nausea. Olwyn was sure she had never seen a more woebegone face than the one that thrust itself deeper into the sheets as if to avoid her mother's sharp gaze.

"I'm not well," Branwyn moaned, her words muffled by the enfolding cloth.

"I know, daughter," Olwyn replied softly. "Gerda told me as much. She thinks you quicken with child."

Two spots of bright red color emphasized the pallor of her daughter's face.

"No! I can't be with child!" Branwyn surged upright in response to her mother's bluntness. "I *won't* be with child! I'd rather cut my wrists and *die*!"

Olwyn reached out one hand, a gesture that her daughter ignored.

"Have you lain with a man, Branwyn? Don't fear to tell me, for no blame will attach to you. You're only a child."

"No! No! No!" Branwyn's expression was both mutinous and revolted. The child was talking herself into a state of hysteria, and when she began to retch weakly into the bowl, Olwyn held her hand solicitously and wiped the flushed little brow. "You must believe me! How could I have lain with a man when only Grandfather and our house servants are here? They are all old and ugly."

It can't be true. Branwyn must be sickening for something, Olwyn told herself, although her sleep was disturbed by terrible nightmares and the goddess seemed to turn her face away from Olwyn's prayers.

As the slow months followed, Branwyn's health slowly began to improve. But Olwyn couldn't blind herself to the swelling in her daughter's belly. Rightly or wrongly, Branwyn had lied, and now she was surely with child, one that swelled so grotesquely on her slight frame that it seemed that the unborn infant was an incubus sucking out her daughter's life. Branwyn wouldn't tolerate questions, willfully choosing to deny the evidence of her eyes in favor of some fanciful imaginings. At her wits' end, Olwyn was forced to consider her own inaction.

Autumn had fled, and winter had come to the northern coast of Gwynedd. Sea and sky were grey, while sleety rain fell daily and blanketed Olwyn's mood with gloom. She leaned on the door frame and watched the northern road, clutching a heavy woolen shawl tightly around her shoulders. Soon, Melvig ap Melwy would ride down that path, flanked by his warriors in breastplates of oxhide and bronze, and Branwyn would be forced to reveal her sin. Granddaughter and unborn child could die if Melvig so desired, for the old king wouldn't suffer Branwyn's silences and denials. As the paterfamilias, he had the right to order Branwyn's death.

A chill wind stirred the last dead leaves that were banked against the wall of the villa, disintegrating in the rain to brown and sanguine skeletons. Olwyn shivered as the breeze snatched at her plaited hair, loosening a few long tendrils with its cold fingers. Her father would not feel a moment's compunction, nor listen to Olwyn's pleading. He would follow his own road, as he always did, even if he later regretted the rashness of his decisions. The babe would be left in the open to die when it was born and Branwyn would be cast off forever.

Whom could Olwyn turn to? Her brother, Melvyn, was a grown man with a son older than Branwyn. He would never choose death in the old ways for his niece and an infant, for Melvyn was softer than his father although he was the Deceangli heir. But to reach Melvyn, Olwyn must travel to Canovium, and once she was in her father's city Melvig would soon learn the details of his granddaughter's sin.

No, her brother could not help her, even if he dared to defy his father.

The leaf mold twisted in a sudden, vicious gust of cold air, as the last traces of summer were swept away from the villa walls and dispersed in the orchards beyond the house. Olwyn began to shiver in earnest. Her daughter was far from perfect, but she was all that Olwyn still possessed of Godric, whom she had loved so passionately that the Old Ones had been angered by her ardor. Yes, Branwyn must be saved, even if the babe was doomed.

Olwyn looked around the warm, comfortable house that had once resonated with Godric's laughter and Branwyn's childish enthusiasms and tantrums. Mother and daughter must leave quickly, before Melvig decided to make another sudden visit, but the reason for their departure must be plausible or her father would assume some kind of plot was afoot.

How? What could she do?

Then, as if the Mother relented and showed her the way, Olwyn remembered her sister Fillagh, a willful girl who had married a very unsuitable man from Caer Fyrddin far to the south. Olwyn had been separated from her sister for thirteen years, but blood called to blood, and Fillagh would welcome her if she went to visit. More importantly, Fillagh would give sanctuary to Branwyn.

Melvig would not be happy, but he wouldn't choose to pursue her, having sworn never again to gaze upon the face of his wayward daughter Fillagh. For a time, Olwyn and Branwyn would be safe.

But a southward journey was fraught with danger. The murderous Vortigern reigned in the south and styled himself the High King of the Britons. Even Melvig considered an alliance with Vortigern was the only means to protect his kingdom, for the High King had slain his lord to gain the throne. A regicide would be untroubled by the murder of women who unwisely crossed his path.

Rumors had trickled northwards of Vortigern's Saxons, who had been invited into the south to act as the High King's bodyguard. Olwyn had listened to a conversation between Melvig and a guest only a year earlier, as they cursed the regicide for his treason towards his own people, a charge that Olwyn only imperfectly understood.

Traveling south had its dangers, but Olwyn had little choice. Fillagh and her Roman husband offered a chance of life for Branwyn, provided that Olwyn had the courage, the wit, and the strength to deceive her father, something as foreign to Olwyn's nature as the quick anger that fueled Melvig and his difficult granddaughter.

Energized by a solution of sorts, Olwyn instructed her steward to find a reliable manservant to head south on a suitable horse. He would also be required to journey north to her father's home once he had returned from Caer Fyrddin. Several hours were devoted to teaching the man the full text of a message to her sister, and another to her father, for the servant couldn't read. Then, with the dice irrevocably cast and the traveling wagons packed, Olwyn informed Branwyn that they were embarking on a journey to Caer Fyrddin.

The wintry sky and the slow, melancholy rain were as nothing to the reaction of her daughter, who flatly refused to budge.

"Then you will surely die, as will your child," Olwyn told her baldly.

"I'm not pregnant!" Branwyn shouted.

"You are! The child moves within you as any fool can see, and Melvig ap Melwy is no foolish young man to be flummoxed by your lies. He has nine living children and countless grandchildren. He will recognize your condition at a glance."

Some spark of the old, reckless Branwyn stirred in the child's dark eyes. Her mouth set in a thin white line that made her appear far older than her twelve years.

"I had no lover, I swear. A creature came from the sea—a demon or a selkie, I know not which—and sought out my bedchamber. He marked me as his own and took me in my sleep. I dreamed that he would kill me if I resisted him."

Olwyn sighed gustily with exasperation. "Who do you suppose will believe such a farradiddle of lies? Melvig is well aware how babies are quickened, and demons lack the flesh to plant the seed. Don't be foolish, daughter!"

"Then who, Mother? What strangers had come to this lonely place at the time when I conceived? Do you suspect old Plautenes? Do you suspect Melvig himself? I tell you, a vile creature of the darkness, disguised as a beautiful man, defiled me as I slept. Doubt me if you must, but let me sleep."

Stretched to breaking point by anxiety, Olwyn was weary of pandering to her daughter's sulks and caprices. In an indulgent mother of many years, such a sudden lack of empathy was, perhaps, explicable only because Olwyn was terrified of her father's ire. Rudely and forcefully, she dragged the covers away from Branwyn's curled body and threw a fresh tunic at the girl's gaping, startled face.

"Get up and assist your maid to pack! We're traveling south to my sister, so don't think to sulk or to argue. If you won't rise of your own accord, I'll order the servants to carry you to the carriage in your disarray. Shout, cry, and pout all you want, but this time you will obey me."

"You don't believe me!" Branwyn's lower lip quivered as she swung her thin legs over the side of the bed. For the first time, Olwyn recognized the calculation that waited below the sheen of tears in Branwyn's eyes. Even now, pregnant and threatened, Branwyn was attempting to manipulate her mother's love. Once again, Olwyn's palm itched to slap her daughter's face.

"What does my opinion matter? Melvig won't care what I think, and he won't tolerate a pregnant granddaughter who is unwed. The only way to avoid disaster is to leave our home."

Reluctantly, Branwyn obeyed this new, more obdurate mother who examined her with eyes that were hard and unresponsive. For the first time, she began to understand the peril that threatened.

Much chastened, and silent with apprehension, Branwyn joined her mother in the traveling carriage, a vehicle that was only a little more graceful than the heavy cart used to transport grain and firewood to and from the villa. Another wagon carried the supplies that Olwyn considered vital for a protracted visit away from the north. The huge wooden wheels, each with a band of iron on the rim to give it strength, seemed to find every rut on the old Roman track that headed towards Pennal, but at least a leather cover kept out the worst of the weather. With every jolt, Branwyn felt more nauseous and she longed to complain at the hardness of the plank seat and the sand that seemed to envelop them with every stride of the horses. But one glance at Olwyn's face was sufficient to shrivel the words on the girl's tongue.

Olwyn was rigid with anxiety. Would Melvig follow them? This road was thick with brigands. Were the two stout fellows who controlled the straining oxen sufficient to protect them?

The coastal road snaked over hills and river valleys, although it always remained within sight or scent of the sea. The land was largely wild and empty, for the winds blew strongly here, and twisted the trees into stunted pathetic forms that seemed to flinch away from the shore. The winds intruded into the leather tent on the traveling cart, and although the women were mostly dry, sand turned their eyes gritty and their feet were chilled to painfulness, regardless of the piled furs that surrounded them. Sleep was difficult in such stuffy quarters, and even when the pallid sun shone and the leather cover was removed, mud made the journey equally unpleasant.

Eventually, after three long days, they arrived at Pennal. Conical huts clustered around a curved bay where muddy silt and black weed made the air rank with a rotting sea smell, and the odor of fish seemed to permeate the only inn. Olwyn and Branwyn slept under a reed roof and discovered the discomforts of straw bedding.

"There are lice in the beds, Mother. I think I'd rather sleep on the wagon," Branwyn complained as she scratched her pale arms to bloody stripes with her nails.

"We're all suffering, daughter. But tomorrow we head inland, so the air should be sweeter. I'll not rest easily until we are under Fillagh's roof. I left a message for my father telling him that I wish to spend the night of the solstice at Caer Fyrddin, where a special pyre is lit. I've never told him falsehoods in the past, so perhaps he will be deceived. Pray that he believes my lies! If not . . ."

Olwyn's voice trailed away, leaving her daughter to consider a number of unpleasant possibilities. Branwyn lay in her crude, prickly bed and cursed the ocean's gift that had made everything go so disastrously wrong.

At that inauspicious moment, the child decided to move in her belly, hands and feet turning, pushing, and kicking. Branwyn grimaced and tossed abruptly, careless of any discomfort to the babe.

"I hate it! I hate it! I hope it dies as soon as it's born," she snarled aloud. "No demon's child is entitled to life. Its father was a prince of evil, so no good can come of this accursed creature."

Olwyn was appalled and struggled upright so that she could gaze at her daughter's angry face. "Don't tempt the gods with your pointless threats, Branwyn. If the gods really permitted a demon to quicken your womb, they have a purpose that neither of us can understand. The Old Ones will not be mocked. Nor will they be bargained with, nor lied to. Most of all, they'll not tolerate our pitiful defiance. If the child is born, you must raise it whether you care for it or not."

As Olwyn sank back into her verminous bed, Branwyn thrust her fist into her mouth to stifle her sobs. No! Though the seas might boil and the gods might smash the earth to bloody dust, she'd never love nor care for this child. Let her mother raise it, for Branwyn had learned that the goddess was cruel and had no love for women and children. She killed them often enough, didn't she?

"I wish the stranger had murdered me outright, for he killed everything else," Branwyn whispered into her folded cloak, which took the place of a pillow in this filthy little room.

Olwyn had been struggling to sleep but her senses suddenly felt unnaturally sharp. She heard her daughter's muffled words and her heart stopped for one agonizing moment.

May the gods protect us! She was raped!

She listened to her daughter's breathing as it gradually slowed. The girl drifted off into a shallow sleep, disturbed by nightmares that racked the tender, fragile body. Olwyn swore that she would do anything, and forgive everything, if her daughter would only learn to laugh again.

For the first time, Olwyn wondered if perhaps it would be best for everyone if Branwyn's bastard were to die in childbirth. Then, in penance, she begged Ceridwen and the Mother to forgive her for the impiety of her thoughts. The gods would decide.

• • •

THE TRACK TO Llanio was difficult for oxens, servants, and travelers. Once the sea was behind them, the lightly forested hills, perilous with scree and black ice, rose steeply. The wind howled constantly and only Olwyn's willpower drove the little group onward to their destination. The journey wasn't far as the crow flies, but four long days passed before Llanio hove into view.

The Demetae tribe was very different from the peoples of the Ordovice and the Deceangli. The High King's mother was Demetae, and he spent half of every year in the south where the air was softer, the coastal beaches were heavy with white sand, and the river valleys provided rich silt that encouraged successful farming. With such resources, the Demetae should have been well fed, satisfied, and content with their lot.

The reason for sullen faces and a general feeling of gloom, even in a backwater like Llanio, originated from the actions of King Vortigern. A man with an iron fist and an even harder mind, Vortigern had ruled Gwynedd, Powys, and other, smaller states since his youth. He had even made incursions into the lands of the Cornovii and the Dobunni and had, until recently, been undisputed High King of the united tribes of the south. Then Ambrosius the Wise had returned and had stamped out any small fires of rebellion within his lands.

Ambrosius and his younger brother had crossed from Brittany, where they had sought shelter after Vortigern murdered their brother, Constans, who was the High King at the time. For years they had roamed the Roman world, but now Ambrosius had returned to Venta Belgarum and lit a beacon in the south. At Llanio, Olwyn heard news of the return of the legitimate king that ran on the wind like storm clouds, a potential threat that chilled Olwyn's heart.

Vortigern would not forsake his entrenched position in Cymru, regardless of Ambrosius's ambitions, for the west endured as the seat of his power. Nor would Ambrosius risk banishment again by loosing his followers against the regicide before the time was ripe. Rumor hinted that Ambrosius played a waiting game and left Vortigern to hold the west until circumstances and old age brought his enemy within the reach of his sword. So the small world of the Britons waited on a knife's edge in an illusion of peace and prosperity.

The Demetae and the Silures ought to have reveled in their good fortune, for they lived in an age of security under the firm hand of a wise king who had reached his fortieth year but was still hale and vigorous. Vortigern had two youthful sons to rule after him and no enemies threatened his reign. Yet, beyond logic and custom, he had taken a Saxon woman, Rowena, to wife. Her yellow hair, cerulean eyes, and smooth golden skin inflamed his blood and addled his kingly wits.

At first, the Demetae lords were amused by their king's passion. They eyed Queen Rowena's long legs and sniggered behind their hands at the thought of Vortigern imprisoned by those smooth, golden limbs while in the thrall of passion. Unfortunately, Vortigern feared the growing strength and cleverness of his older sons, and Rowena fed his paranoia with subtle warnings of threats and treachery. She begged him to take her own kin as bodyguards, and, dazed with lust and nervous of his sons' ambitions, Vortigern agreed.

So the Saxons had come to Dyfed, to be welcomed by their new master. But Vortigern's subjects remembered the barbarian raids of the past, the gutted churches and burned villages of the east coast, and they seethed inwardly.

But when a king commands, who dares to argue? Each day, more and more Saxon families arrived in Dyfed, using their height and their favored position to lord it over the native population, who were forced to bide their time. Many resentful eyes watched the king and his dangerous wife with envy and concealed fury. When Rowena bore a son and became pregnant again, the Demetae began to fear a new threat: a half-Saxon king who would change their ways forever. In hope, they looked towards the young Vortimer, the king's son by the Roman Severa, who suddenly seemed the best of a bad choice of wives.

Olwyn neither knew nor cared how deeply anti-Saxon fever ran in Llanio, although she observed a demolished Roman villa where the stones had been pulled apart and left to lie in the fields while a building of crude logs took its place. When she asked her manservant what the structure was, he told her that a Saxon had arrived with his house carls and had built his timber hall on the heights where the Roman administrative center had once stood.

"What fool would tear down a stone building to erect so crude a structure in wood?" she asked.

The man shrugged expressively. "The Saxons distrust all things Roman and destroy any traces of the legions rather than use them. Too often in the past, the Romans have defeated them in pitched battles. For all that they are the favored friends of King Vortigern and act as his personal guard, they are brutes at heart, barbarians, with cruel, angry gods and strange, uncivilized ways."

Olwyn examined the alien, threatening building through the flap in the leather tent as the carriage lumbered past on the path leading down to the village.

"That hall has an overbearing aspect, for it dominates the high ground so that only fire could destroy it. Still, Vortigern may come to regret his choices, especially if he's tardy in his obedience to the goddess. She's older and stronger than any of the Saxon gods."

"Yes, my lady," her servant answered, but he feared the long, iron swords of the Saxons that could kill the serpents of the goddess just as easily as the Roman legions had slain the druids on Mona. He was a thoughtful man who knew the world was changing, and the changes weren't for the better. He also feared the Saxon warriors, who stood a head taller than most of the tribal warriors.

The track from Llanio to Moridunum, also known as Caer Fyrddin in the common language, was in good condition, and well traveled. Mounted warriors, the occasional farmer laden down with trade goods and produce, a priest, and several Saxons shared the journey with Olwyn's carriage. The road was very steep in places, forcing mother and daughter to walk beside the wagons so the oxen could climb the

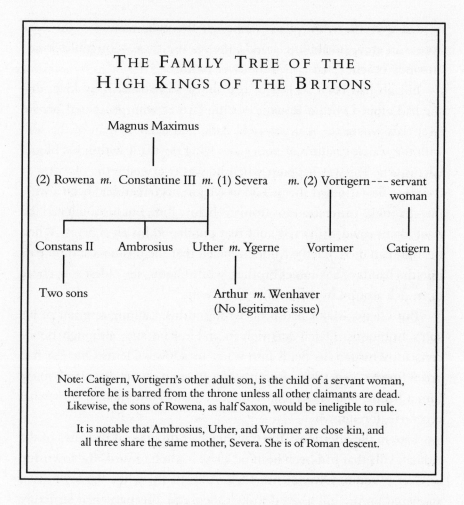

THE FAMILY TREE OF THE HIGH KINGS OF THE BRITONS

Magnus Maximus

(2) Rowena *m.* Constantine III *m.* (1) Severa   *m.* (2) Vortigern --- servant woman

Constans II   Ambrosius   Uther *m.* Ygerne   Vortimer   Catigern

Two sons   Arthur *m.* Wenhaver
(No legitimate issue)

Note: Catigern, Vortigern's other adult son, is the child of a servant woman, therefore he is barred from the throne unless all other claimants are dead. Likewise, the sons of Rowena, as half Saxon, would be ineligible to rule.

It is notable that Ambrosius, Uther, and Vortimer are close kin, and all three share the same mother, Severa. She is of Roman descent.

dangerous incline. The journey was no less uncomfortable than in the north, for cold rain still fell drearily and thick mud impeded their progress.

Weary to the bone and pinched with cold, the travelers arrived at Moridunum. The Roman name conjured up thoughts of doom and madness, but Olwyn had been told that the town was situated some way inland on a broad, sluggish river, and possessed a pleasant aspect. Above and beyond the houses, the old Roman fortress that had given the town its name commanded a tall hill, one of a small chain that beetled over the river valley. Although the gulls rose over the dark houses in grey, squabbling clouds, the sea itself was some miles away, on sandy beaches that lipped the river mouth.

Fillagh had been so lost to reason, or so bedazzled by love, that she had eloped with a Romano-Celtic farmer who prospered on the river flats where the soil was rich, dark, and deep. A man of the soil, with the warrior nature of both races lying dormant within his blood, Cletus One Ear was happiest when he was overseeing the plowing or counting his fat-tailed sheep. Cletus Major, his father, had been a wine merchant like generations of Romans before him, but his son hated the trade that provided the red gold that purchased his river acres. When the old man died, Cletus Minor decided that the business should pass into the hands of a younger brother, while Cletus, the eldest son, chose to "muck around in the mud like a peasant."

But Cletus Major had been wrong in his scathing opinion of his son's ambitions. Dyfed was rich in arable land and, although floods constantly turned his fields into water meadows, Cletus One Ear had green fingers. Vegetables, fruit trees, even grain on the drier land, made him a happy, contented man with an equally contented, if somewhat eccentric, foreign wife.

Late in the afternoon, the traveling cart drew up at the gates of the Roman villa that had been built on a rise leading towards the township of Caer Fyrddin. Olwyn's heart fell. Admittedly, while the town itself staggered up the hill like a drunken shepherd, this particular structure was well maintained, but instead of tiles the roof supported crude thatch, and Cletus had not whitewashed his walls, so they presented a dun-colored face to the world. Chickens and several ducks had taken ownership of the forecourt and, although the villa's gardens were laid out in efficient rows, there was not a single flower or ornamental shrub to be seen. Winter vegetables, blackberry canes, fruit and nut trees dominated the villa's landscape in well-weeded, straw-protected phalanxes.

Olwyn scarcely had time to set foot on the crazy stone paving at the villa's entrance before a tall, corpulent man with a florid face, a wide, gap-toothed grin and a shiny bald pate enveloped her in a bear hug. Lifted off her feet by this apparent madman, Olwyn was completely breathless by the time he had squeezed her vigorously, kissed her on both cheeks, and then deposited her back on her feet.

"Welcome, Sister Olwyn! Welcome! On my oath, but you're a tiny little thing. No meat on your bones. Well, my cook will soon remedy that problem. And this little maid must be Branwyn. Welcome, child, and come out of the wind. Little ones in your delicate condition should be warm and cozy, with a special spiced wine and a lovely bowl of fresh stew to toast your chilled fingers."

Swept into the villa with the assistance of a plump arm and hands the size of small hams, Olwyn could only guess that this tornado of a man was her sister's husband, Cletus One Ear. The fact that the lobe of his left ear was missing, along with most of the side cartilage, seemed to verify her assumption. Branwyn, who had mastered passive resistance during their long journey to the south, gaped in consternation at the huge man and realized that he would undoubtedly have carried her inside if she hadn't decided to enter on her own two feet.

"Olwyn! Branwyn!" a high-pitched voice squealed delightedly, and Olwyn found herself enveloped yet again, this time in the plump, matronly arms of her younger sister, Fillagh.

Thirteen years had wrought much change in Fillagh's appearance. Although she was a year younger than Olwyn, Fillagh could have passed for a decade or so older. Her plentiful black hair had a faint sprinkling of grey, while multiple childbirths had thickened her once-tiny waist and widened her hips. Extra weight pillowed her small form so that her cheerful, open grin and widespread arms reminded Olwyn of her long-dead mother.

"Let me look at you, sweet one," her sister cooed as she released Olwyn and scanned her slight, willowy form from head to heels. "You're not eating well? We'll soon fix that, won't we, Cletus?"

"Without a doubt, my pet," her husband answered as he raised one of her work-scarred paws to his lips.

"Thank you, Fillagh!" Olwyn whispered. "I don't know how to

repay you for your kindness in allowing us to visit you. I had to remove my daughter from Father's reach, and had you not offered us sanctuary I don't know how we would have fared."

Olwyn spoke almost by rote, voicing all the courteous pleasantries she could unscramble from her scattered wits. Fillagh had been a slender, black-haired twelve-year-old with a vivacious eye, pert breasts, and an unpredictable temper when she had first met the son of the wine trader, Cletus Major, and recognized something in him that even his father had never seen. She saw his courage and his irrepressible joy in ordinary experiences, as well as a passionate understanding of all things that grew out of the earth. Cletus could turn the life cycle of a flower into a vast and exciting epic of creation. Fillagh discovered that idle compliments and the slavish devotion of young men seemed shallow when compared with the earnest dreams espoused by awkward, shambling Cletus. Perhaps it was the miracle of the attraction of opposites, but Fillagh discovered that she wanted no other man.

So, on a soft spring night, she left her father's house in Canovium and followed Cletus Minor on the road to the south. Melvig caught them not far from Segontium and Cletus lost part of his ear defending Fillagh from the wrath of her sire. When she vowed that she would marry no one but Cletus and cursed her parent for inflicting her lover's bloody wound, Melvig washed his hands of her. With that inauspicious day, her joyous existence had begun.

Now, in her noisy, unattractive villa on the flanks of Moridunum, Fillagh saw herself through her sister's eyes. Being quite without artifice or vanity, she burst into a peal of amiable belly laughs that set her double chins quivering.

"Bless you, Olwyn! I know I'm not a bag of skin and bones like I used to be. Love's put meat on me and I'm all the better for it. Father would never have countenanced a farmer as my husband. But you can see how well it's turned out. He chooses not to speak of me, I know, but I have survived his rejection. Aye . . . and we've flourished." She shook her ample hips for emphasis.

"You have children, Fillagh?" Olwyn managed to murmur as she was hustled into a huge kitchen and seated at a plank bench while a large earthenware bowl of stew materialized in Fillagh's plump hands. A spoon of battered silver, huge in size, was produced with a flourish.

"Aye, we have seven sons! My man tells me I have enriched his farm with every birth. My eldest has learned his letters and is now discovering how to work our lands under the tutelage of our steward. Two sons are fostered with good families in Venta Silurum, where they'll learn useful skills for the farm. The others run wild like all little savages, except for Elric, who's only six months old." Fillagh examined Olwyn's waist critically. "You've never remarried, sweetling? Ah, well, true love is hard to find, I'll grant you. Still, it must have been lonely for your Branwyn as she was growing."

Olwyn flushed at the unintended criticism, and Branwyn paled a little. Fillagh's quick eyes saw that the child couldn't eat the tasty stew that Olwyn had devoured without even realizing it.

"The babe drains you, little one," she said, one of her hands pressing Branwyn's belly while the other stroked the girl's aching back. "Yes, he's a big, vigorous child who is determined to grow fat on his mother's strength, bless him."

Branwyn paled even more, until her eyes appeared like dark holes burned into a piece of linen.

"It leeches off me and I wish it were dead. It'll cause disunity all its life, the poor demon-spawned thing," she whispered faintly.

"What are you saying, sweetling?" Fillagh asked, all practical common sense. "No child is evil . . . and demons cannot breed."

"A demon in the guise of a beautiful youth raped me in my sleep," the girl whispered through bone-white, dry lips. "I swear it! He threatened to kill me if I made a sound."

One trembling hand sought out a pocket tied over the swelling of her belly, searching through her hidden treasures until Branwyn found what she sought and removed her small, clenched fist.

"The creature left me this ring, taken from the finger of the mother it poisoned." Branwyn's hand opened hesitantly, and the two sisters could see a large amber bezel set in a delicate gold ring. Inside the rich stone, a spider was trapped, perfect and fragile, in a frozen moment that had become eternal. "The demon laughed, and promised it would do the same to me if I told anyone."

The sisters exchanged glances, while Olwyn took the ring from her daughter's unresponsive fingers. "This thing has no place near you, daughter. It's vile and ugly, and it isn't a gift that was given with good intentions."

"No, pretty Branwyn! Your demon is a cruel creature if it has harmed you so, and left you with such a loathsome memento," Fillagh added, and enfolded Branwyn in her warm arms. She pressed the girl's tired head against her large breasts and stroked the thick brown hair. "Aye, child, he was a monster for sure, for only a demon would harm a little girl. He was strong, wasn't he?"

Branwyn nodded and began to weep in response to her aunt's kindness. Her thin shoulders shook, and Olwyn felt a spasm of jealousy. Her child was weakened, blighted, and unlike her dancing, reckless self, but she could turn to Fillagh when she rejected her own mother.

"Cletus, stir your fat rump, and carry this poor little darling to the guest room. No, missy, no arguments, for your feet won't touch the floor while I have a strong husband to lift you." She turned and smiled fondly at her husband. "Could you send my maids to undress her and make her comfortable, my dear? While they're at it, they can prepare Olwyn's bed as well, and provide her with one of my tisanes to give my niece strength. She carries a heavy burden!"

Cletus may have been the master, but his wife was the true ruler of the villa. In no time, her commands had been obeyed. Then, with a promise that they would speak in the morning, Olwyn too was ordered to bed, where she found Branwyn already asleep, her hair tousled and a little color returned to her cheeks.

On a pallet stuffed with lambs' wool, under rugs of fine homespun, and with a floor heated by a functioning hypocaust, Olwyn lay and listened to the sounds of the villa as it ground to a halt. Night had barely fallen, but the villa kept farm hours and the oil lamps were soon extinguished. Outside, a faint wind blew up the river valley so that a sound, almost like the sigh of a woman, tried to wend its way into the warm room. A night owl called and Olwyn's blood cooled with superstition. A thousand creatures were waking to hunt in the darkness and Olwyn responded with overt sensitivity to the small scuffling of fear that seemed so close to the secure walls of the villa.

One thing was certain in this mad world of change and peril. No demon would disturb her daughter's sleep tonight, nor would any intruder threaten the peace that enveloped the child like one of Fillagh's woven blankets. Olwyn had found sanctuary for them both; the goddess had finally decided to smile upon two of her suffering daughters.

Myrddion's Map of Pre-Arthurian Southern Britain

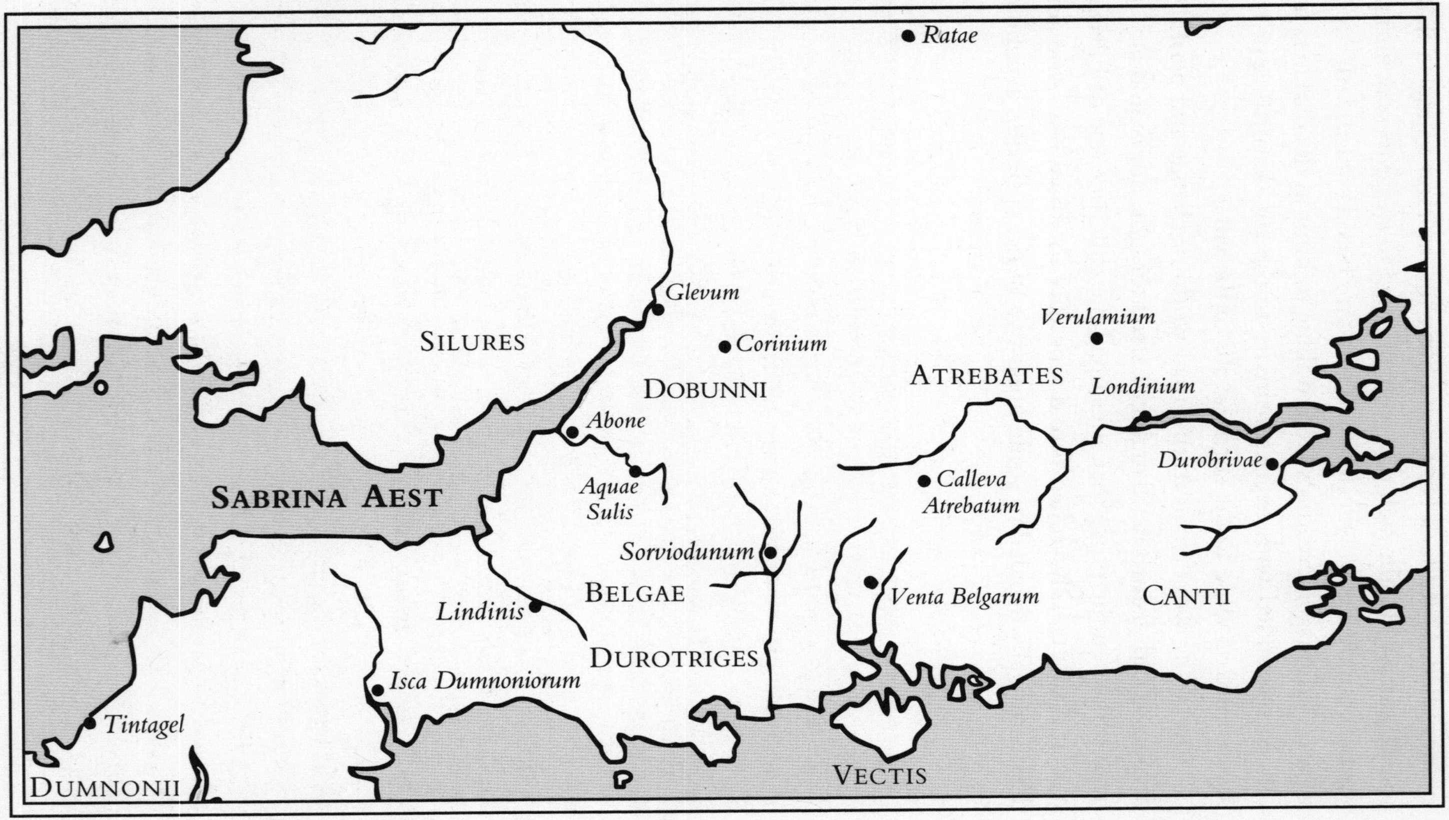

Chapter IV

AN INAUSPICIOUS BIRTH

In faraway Tintagel, Lady Ygerne stared out at the many shades of grey that defined sea, sky, and land as, in the grim room behind her, men decided her fate. Her father had ridden the weary miles from Lindinis to attend this meeting, but his grey eyes were now stark with concern for his only daughter. Her unnatural pallor and her long, poignant silences overrode his pride that his child was poised to become the queen of the Dumnonii tribe, and unconsciously he flexed the muscle that ran along the line of his jaw as he stared down at the documents of betrothal. Ygerne couldn't see his distress from her position near the slit window, but she could feel the radiating waves of his concern.

Beside Pridenow of Lindinis, Gorlois and his young nephew, Bors Major, looked down at a crude map and a messy sprawl of documents that lay on a bench, lit by a vile-smelling fish-oil lamp. The final agreement between the great tribes was coming to fruition and, in a dim corner, Gorlois's scribe turned plain men's speech into the eloquent, complex sentences of the betrothal agreement. Offers of land, gold, slaves, and livestock were promised and formally accepted. Just beyond the light, a five-year-old boy, Bors Minor, watched the official rituals of betrothal with a child's wide-eyed wonder. Meanwhile, the young Ygerne comforted herself with the knowledge that she was learning her true worth in the world's wealth. Gorlois had made huge concessions in order to cement the marriage agreement, which was unusual in that, as the bridegroom, the king of the Dumnonii could ask for a fortune in gold from any prospective father-in-law.

Ygerne had dwelt at Tintagel for two strange and confusing years. Ordinarily, the betrothal documents would have been signed before she left her father's house, but Pridenow was a fond parent and Ygerne was a beauty although she was only ten years of age. Accompanied by a chaperone and servants, she had been delivered to Gorlois so that Pridenow could satisfy himself that his darling would be happy with the Boar of Cornwall.

From their first meeting, Gorlois had been entranced and had rediscovered his boyhood in her presence. He had forgiven her strange fits of fancy as being part of her charm, and had proved to be a patient and an assiduous lover. Even Ygerne, frightened as she was by a life that was stern and hard, had found security in Gorlois's strong arms and velvet brown eyes. While he remained more father than lover, she found that the secret parts of her heart were opening to the gentle person who dwelt within his hulking, muscular frame. And Gorlois had demanded nothing sexual of the child-woman, recognizing that she was frightened of physical contact. A considerate man, Gorlois understood that patience would succeed where the assertion of his rights would alienate Ygerne forever.

So here they were, and the betrothal had been sealed. Ygerne looked over towards her betrothed and, feeling her eyes on his face, Gorlois looked up and smiled with such warmth and affection that she felt embraced from her head to her toes.

He loves me. How strange, for he barely knows me.

Ygerne's thoughts ranged out over the darkening sea, empty of even her favorites, the gulls, with their comical cries and ebullient natures.

"A storm is coming, puss," her father whispered, as he joined her in staring out at the empty scene. "See that line of black cloud against the last of the sun? We'll feel its full force within hours."

"Is the storm bad luck, Father? Is my betrothal cursed?"

"Nonsense, puss! Storms come to Tintagel so frequently in winter that the trees don't grow—else they'd be blown away by the winds." He lifted his daughter's fair, frail face. "Now smile, my pet. Gorlois is the best man in these isles, save for Ambrosius, and even I dare not look so high for your future husband. You will be happy within your marriage."

Ygerne shivered, although she was swathed in a thick woolen shawl. The storm marched towards the fortress like an army of invasion and the rolls of thunder in the distance mimicked the rumble of marching feet.

"The light is almost gone, Father. I long for sunshine and soft days."

"You will be very happy after the consummation of your marriage in the prescribed two years, puss. I promise you! A good husband makes any weather soft and fair."

Her father's eyes glowed with subtle, lambent fire in the lamplight. His grey eyes were the wonder of his tribe, but their stare could be as cold as the sunless sea, except when they gazed on the face of his daughter.

She took pity on him then. Her father was desperate that she should be happy, and she worried at his increasing thinness and the lines that scored his smooth skin from nose to jaw. A hint of illness gave his flesh a trace of yellow in the nacreous light.

"Are you well, Father? Does something ail you?" Ygerne asked, suddenly afraid as the center of her life stuttered in its smooth, circular pattern.

His expression lightened and a wide smile split his handsome face. "Of course, puss, and in the days to come I'll smile often to think that my darling now lies under the protection of the Iron King of the Dumnonii."

But his fingers quivered in hers, and Ygerne schooled her face into passive compliance so her father wouldn't recognize the terror that coiled in her heart.

• • •

IN THE MONTHS that followed their brutal journey, Olwyn had cause to bless her sister and her good-natured husband. With their laughter, simplicity, and sweetness of spirit, they began to bring Branwyn back from the far, cold silences that had enveloped her. Cosseted and spoiled, she was encouraged to sit in the sunshine or fuss over the old farm bitch who was long past her frolicsome youth. Branwyn sang a little, and even spoke of how blue the sea glittered from their hillside, although she refused to travel to the sands to breathe in the salty air.

The winds were not so strong, here near the entrance to Sabrina Aest, but the gulls sported their white breasts and grey-barred wings with pride and argued as vigorously over fingerlings and broken shells as they had done at Segontium. Branwyn smiled as she watched the cheeky birds steal grain from the hens, and one day she was enchanted by a loud verbal battle over stale, milk-soaked bread between an optimistic gull and an old gander with a bad temper. The gander won the skirmish, having a significant weight advantage.

During spring, the women saw little of Cletus and his half-grown sons, although the little ones squabbled as noisily as the gulls. The fields called, with their insistence on constant labor, and Cletus worked cheerfully from sunrise to sunset before returning to the villa in the evening, covered with thick, brown loam. As the master, Cletus need never have touched a clod nor pushed a plow, but he loved the aroma of the earth and was worshipped by his servants for his devotion to them and to his fields. But he never lost an ounce, for all his physical labor.

As the days became warmer, and the furrows bore fast-growing shoots of vivid green, peace seemed to have come forever. Fillagh set Branwyn to work at small tasks, but the girl's condition limited her usefulness to shelling peas or stirring the huge pot of stew that hung on the oven hob. Never for a moment did Fillagh refer to the unborn babe as a girl. When asked why she was so certain of the child's sex, she shrugged and replied that her instincts told her that the boy would be large and strong.

And then Branwyn's waters broke.

Terrified, the girl told no one, and when her maidservant found her in her room she was rigid with pain and desperate to prevent the birth of the child at all cost.

Fillagh's sympathy was lessened by the hysteria in the eyes of her niece. "It's easier to stop the tides, Branwyn, than to prevent this babe from being born," she ordered brusquely. "So you can stop fussing right now. The child demands to be born, and you have no choice in the matter."

Privately, though, she was worried. She whispered her fears to her sister. "She'll damage herself if she can't be calmed, Olwyn. I know it can hurt the child, but poppy juice may relax Branwyn so that she'll stop fighting the birth pangs. But the boy might die, I warn you, so the choice must be yours. I can't take such responsibility on myself."

"Branwyn is my first concern," Olwyn replied. She almost wept, but she felt her husband's shade pressing against her back and lending her courage. "The child must be a secondary consideration, Fillagh. I wish I knew what to do for the best. I'm only good for prayers and I'm a useless mother to allow my daughter to face this awful danger. Father was right all along. I should have remarried and fulfilled my duty to our family."

"You'd marry without love, Olwyn? Shame on you! You were the one who taught me that marriage is true joy when the heart is engaged. I'll save Branwyn, and the boy, if only because I owe my whole, lovely life to your example."

The birth was long, hard, and terrifying. For hour after agonized hour, Branwyn sweated, screamed, and cursed, fighting her own body to the point where the women believed that her frail, abused spirit would die. Olwyn promised the goddess whatever duty was required of her if only Branwyn was allowed to live. Even the optimistic Fillagh almost despaired that the girl's fierce, desperate will would ever permit the child to be born alive. But, finally, as spring rains began to drench the night sky, the child tore his way free from his mother's body. In blood, distress, and pain, the infant took his first, lusty breath.

The women clustered around Branwyn, staunching the sudden

rush of blood. They pressed her abdomen to expel the afterbirth and bathed her face in cool water while Fillagh saw to the welfare of the infant. When her bloody hands touched his squirming, slippery limbs, a shock ran through her fingers and centered on her brain. Fillagh had never been overly religious and she didn't believe in the Sight, but now she found that disconnected images invaded her unwilling imagination.

Visions of blood on stones, dead children with splayed limbs mutely begging for help, and crowns drenched in gore spiraled through her mind. A pair of brilliant blue eyes suddenly loomed so large that Fillagh lost her balance. She almost dropped the infant, but Olwyn steadied her with one hand and, with the other, took hold of the babe. As her sister had already discovered, the child's impact was immediate.

No prophetic revelations stirred Olwyn's instincts. Instead, she felt a rush of love so visceral that she almost forgot to breathe. Some wary part of her brain warned her that she couldn't possibly love a child so completely and with such speed. But the real Olwyn was deaf to reason. She scooped up the infant and held him to her breast, regardless of the blood and mucus that streaked his sturdy little form.

Fillagh gripped her sister's arm. "You felt it? You saw the child's power? You must love him, sister, for he could easily become a monster. Love alone can defeat him and make him human, and I fear that Branwyn will never accept him."

"I felt nothing but love from the babe." Olwyn smiled like any new mother, obsessed with her first child. "He's a beautiful boy! Look, I can see Godric in his little face. I'll love him enough for Branwyn, sister. How could I not do so?"

Fillagh glanced narrowly at her sister and wondered at the magic of attraction. One touch had captured Olwyn's guarded heart, and she knew that Ceridwen protected this strange and wonderful child. "He will live on and on, regardless of the enmity of the world," she whispered to Cletus. "Ceridwen has chosen him, and the goddess always has her way."

"Then Mithras help him," Cletus swore, for the goddess terrified all sensible men. "Let's hope that she gives him knowledge from her cauldron."

But Branwyn refused to suckle the child and turned her face away from the babe when he was shown to her.

"Take it away! The very sight of it makes me feel sick," she wailed fretfully and, because she was so weak and exhausted, Olwyn took the boy into the next room. Quickly bathed, wrapped in a swaddling shawl, and tucked firmly into the crook of Olwyn's arm, the infant stared up at her with black eyes that already seemed able to focus.

While they waited for the wet nurse to arrive from the nearby village, the sisters examined the face of the perfect, beautiful child. Full-term, pink, and large in size, the infant was unusually still and silent. There were no tears, no signs of fear, and not even the normal struggle of limbs constricted by the swaddling cloth. The boy gazed up at Olwyn's face and she would have been prepared to swear that he could see her.

When she handed him over to the rosy-cheeked peasant woman whom Cletus had hired as wet nurse, the babe protested a little until the woman presented her breast to him. Even then, he fed reflectively without greed or fuss, and fell asleep before he had finished. Yet when Olwyn took him back into her arms, his large, almond eyes opened and he stared at her with milky content. Olwyn thought her heart would burst with love.

THE NEXT MORNING, Cletus showed concern in every line of his body as he paced up and down his broad, flagged courtyard.

"The child should be acknowledged and be given his *bulla*. How else can he be safe from the wrath of the gods?"

The sisters glanced at each other with affectionate impatience. The bastard child was under greater threat from his great-grandfather, who would be quick to order his exposure to the elements if Melvig learned that such an embarrassment lived and thrived.

As usual, Fillagh had a practical suggestion. "Why don't we show the child to the sun, who is the father of us all?"

Olwyn felt a little foolish as she carried her grandson out into the bright spring morning, where the air was sweetened with the smell of wild broom, lavender, and a faint tang of sea salt. The breeze was mellow, soft, and warm as Olwyn bared the babe's body and raised him towards the light of the sun. She expected wails of infant protest, or signs of distress, but the child simply closed his eyes to the unaccustomed dazzle of light and waved his rosy limbs in ecstasy. When Fillagh asked the lord of light, Myrddion, to accept this child who was touched by darkness, the boy crowed with pleasure. Olwyn experienced a sudden flash of inspiration as she lowered him and rewrapped him in his swaddling clothes.

"I name him Myrddion Emrys after the lord of light who is our father! Ceridwen will protect him for she has told me so, but the lord of light will always be part of his spirit. Let his name remind us that darkness is not his birthright."

Fillagh laughed a little at her sister's serious face, for the farmer's wife was made for joy, not sadness. Then she sobered and clutched her husband's hand.

"Myrddion is a good name, sister, and a strong one that is worthy of such a beautiful boy. Bless you for your thoughts, Cletus, but I fear the sun won't give a bulla to young Myrddion to protect him."

"We will let the gods decide," Cletus said quietly. "If Myrddion wants him, then he'll send a token to keep the boy safe."

Both women stared at the stolid, unimaginative farmer who would seem to lack even a trace of poetry in his soul, except for his love of green and growing things. Fillagh was constantly surprised by the sensitivity that survived in her husband's plain, heavy body.

"Aye, Cletus!" she sighed. "It does no good to fuss, so let's see what bulla presents itself to the boy. It's certain Branwyn will reject him, so the god and the Mother must take the place of his parents anyway."

"I will become his mother!" Olwyn averred, her voice as rigid as her daughter's had been. "This child will be cared for until he is a man. I have nothing to give him, but the goddess will surely provide."

"Aye!" Fillagh added with a little shiver of apprehension. "This child will find a way to grow and prosper, because the goddess will help him to find his destiny." She said nothing of her insights into the future, fearing that the child carried too much weight on his baby shoulders already without bearing her odd, superstitious presentiments.

BRANWYN'S HEALTH SLOWLY improved in the months that followed. At first, she ate sparingly, but as her appetite increased, color returned to her cheeks and flesh began to clothe her slight frame. Then, hesitantly, she ventured out into the farm, chasing her cousins as they ran between their rows of carrots and cabbages until her feet and the hems of her gowns were black with soil. Still later, as she felt her youth once again stir in her blood, Branwyn took to walking by the river and finding polished stones discarded by the tidal surges. But, regardless of her flushed cheeks and smiles, she avoided the beaches and the waves that nibbled at the sands with their memories of shameful pain.

For three months, the infant Myrddion had no bulla or charm. Nor, in truth, did he have a mother. Branwyn fled in a swirl of skirts if she saw the wet nurse feeding her son, or came across Olwyn singing to the babe in the early evening. Not that Myrddion seemed to care. He wound his chubby fingers in Olwyn's hair, pulling so gently that she hardly realized that he was begging for a kiss. He grew in grace and beauty, in spite of his birth mother's deep and unrelenting hostility.

Cletus One Ear remained hopeful that the gods would send a gift to the babe. He had almost weakened several times, and had considered purchasing a golden bulla himself and burying it in his fields to create a fiction of godly intervention, but each time he decided to wait a little longer. Perhaps the gods did intervene. And perhaps chance is a rare and a wondrous thing, for Olwyn, Cletus, and Fillagh knew that

Branwyn would never consider searching out a charm that would save her hated son from harm.

Whatever the answer might be, Branwyn discovered Myrddion's birth gift when she picked up a particularly large clod of clay with the intention of miming a throw at Selwyn, one of Fillagh's sons. As she pressed on the damp, pliable earth, it broke apart in her fingers and she dropped it with an exclamation of surprise.

"Look, Branwyn!" Selwyn crowed, one finger pointing at a trace of gold amidst the lump of soft clay. "There's something in the soil."

Branwyn picked up the piece of clay that glistened with a sliver of yellow gold. Wonderingly, she brushed the metal with her fingers and then attempted to scrub it with the bottom of her dirty skirt. As they moved towards the villa, Branwyn continued to scrape the earth from the golden object until she reached a crude water bucket, into which she plunged her prize.

Cletus wandered over to join his niece and together they washed the small token until long-packed clay finally released the pure metal within. What the muddy water revealed, winking softly in the filtered light, caused Cletus to clutch his own bulla in surprise.

A golden ring lay inside the wooden pail, a man's ring meant for a large, strong finger, and Cletus couldn't help but scoop it up to examine it in the noonday light. A large red stone was set inside a heavy mount of gold that was roughly scored to resemble the rays of the sun.

"It's ugly!" Branwyn snapped. "I wish I'd never found it, for I can tell that it will bring nothing but ill."

Cletus ran his powerful, broad thumbs over the heavy shoulders of the ring. The gold felt buttery and glowed with a rich orange color that indicated the purity of the metal. "No. It's very old, maybe going back to the Seven Hills when the Republic was still young, but it's a fine example of early Roman craftsmanship."

"Well, I don't like it! And I don't even want to look at it!" Branwyn hurried into the villa, where she almost knocked Olwyn off her feet in her haste.

Cletus tossed the ring into the air until it reflected the spring sunshine in the heart of its stone with a brilliant flash of blood.

"What has upset Branwyn?" Olwyn asked. "If I hadn't minded my step, she'd have knocked me over in the doorway. She looks ill."

"She found this ring among the vegetables, buried in a clod of dirt. I don't know why she took such an instant dislike to it, but I'm almost certain it's a ring from old Roman times when the fortress kept this whole valley safe from harm. See? The maker carved the gold so that its rays of light fan out from the central stone. Do you understand, Olwyn? We now have our miracle. Branwyn, of all people, has found us the god's gift for little Myrddion."

Cletus handed the gem to Olwyn and she placed it on her index finger. It was so loose that a careless movement would have caused it to fall, but she saw the crude workmanship, and noted that the ruby had been cut with confidence so that a small fire burned in its heart.

"It's perfect!" she murmured. "It is just what is needed for Myrddion's bulla. I have a suitable thong, and when he is older a chain will keep it safe round his throat. I hope he'll want to wear it one day."

"Branwyn wasn't pleased," Cletus warned.

"No. But my boy will be protected by his bulla. I'll call for the priest tomorrow and Myrddion will be promised to the sun, and to Ceridwen, who is my ancestor. Perhaps, between both of the deities, we can keep him safe."

Cletus loved dispensing hospitality, so Fillagh couldn't convince her husband to curb his generous spirit. The next evening, several cronies and their wives came to the dun-colored villa bearing birth gifts for the babe, eager to see the sun priest welcome the latest child into the life of the family.

Of necessity, the priest was paid lavishly to give the simple ceremony a cachet of legitimacy, because Branwyn refused to attend the rite. As Fillagh pointed out to her sister, the fiction of Olwyn as Myrddion's mother was even more firmly imprinted on the lives of the residents of Moridunum. Olwyn, however, couldn't be happy with the situation. Her daughter continued to insist that her son did not exist, when she wasn't cursing the child with all manner of terrible fates. Cletus heaved a sigh of relief when the ring was finally tied around Myrddion's neck on a narrow thong.

Even more frightening for Olwyn was her fear that Branwyn might ensure that the infant did, indeed, disappear into the shadows of death. Late one afternoon, as Olwyn stitched a tiny robe contentedly in the atrium, she was alerted by a sudden, affronted, and lusty cry from her grandson, which was immediately muffled. Leaping to her feet and running pell-mell to the room she shared with Branwyn, Olwyn found her daughter bent over Myrddion's wicker basket. A small lambs' wool pillow was clamped over the infant's face and his plump legs and arms were pumping like waterwheels in his distress.

"What are you doing, Branwyn?" Olwyn asked sharply, one hand wrestling for the pillow.

Branwyn raised her dreamy eyes to meet those of her mother. "Nothing. The child was crying, and I wanted him to stop."

"Will I be forced to constantly watch you, daughter? The child may cause you to remember a time of pain and torment, but he's never done harm to you."

Olwyn's face was wide with shock and dawning horror as she considered the difficulties that would lie ahead if she needed to keep her grandson safe from the murderous instincts of her daughter. The late afternoon sun slanted through the room's wooden shutters and barred Branwyn's face with lines of light and shadow. Something secretive, sleepy, and sly on that face almost stopped Olwyn's tongue.

Myrddion cried fretfully, as if he understood that his world was dangerous and poisoned with hatred. Olwyn picked him up and cradled him close to her breast, while her darkened eyes tried to pierce her daughter's dreamlike calm.

"You must stay away from the babe, Branwyn. You may even consider him as your brother if that fantasy eases your heart, but infanticide is a dreadful and unforgivable crime. You would be killed out of hand and I couldn't save you. Please, daughter, stay away from the child!"

Branwyn smiled distantly and curled up on her pallet, pulled the woolen coverlet over her folded body, and fell quickly into sleep.

Olwyn sought out her sister. She was obsessed with a sense of impending disaster.

"What am I to do, Fillagh? How can I watch the babe every moment of the day? Nor can I cast Branwyn off, for she's been raped and is a little mad. Perhaps Ceridwen protects her by clouding the truth in her brain, but whatever justification she has, I must protect my grandson from her hatred."

Always tender-hearted, Cletus bustled off to organize some spiced wine for the women. Fillagh used her thumb to smooth away the tears that came so easily now to the eyes of her sister.

"After the solstice, you must return to Segontium, Olwyn. You've been gone for nearly a year now, and Father will be at your door as soon as you return."

Olwyn blanched and tightened her arms around Myrddion while the child twisted his body to examine her face with his lustrous black eyes.

"What will I tell him? How will I keep my boy safe from his anger?"

"Tell him the truth, silly! Father will sniff out lies like a starving dog. He'll know if you try to fool him, so make him your ally. You know how he loves to be consulted for his wisdom."

Olwyn nodded, but she stroked Myrddion as if he was under threat. "Branwyn must be married off. Father will insist on it, for the sake of his honor. Then Myrddion will be safe, for she will be forced to live with her husband. Perhaps it's just what my poor daughter needs to leave the past behind her. Perhaps she'll forget the ugliness of her ordeal when she holds another babe in her arms."

Cletus returned, bearing with exaggerated care a tray on which goblets and a bowl of sweetmeats balanced precariously.

"Thank you, husband." Fillagh smiled triumphantly, as if she had solved some dreadful problem with minimal effort. "You always reward me so well for my best ideas."

"But what of Myrddion?" Olwyn whispered. "Father will kill him for sure!"

"Just look at the babe, my dear," Cletus interrupted. "What man wouldn't welcome such a strong youth into his family? Myrddion is a beautiful boy." He smiled fondly and Myrddion rewarded his uncle with a brilliant smile, while both women looked at the burly farmer with barely concealed incredulity. "What? Have I said something peculiar?"

"You only met my father once, but surely you realized, perhaps as he was cutting off your ear, that he's not overly sentimental. He won't care what little Myrddion looks like." Fillagh gave her husband's vestigial ear a little tweak.

"Then tell him that the boy's the child of a demon. I'm certain that Branwyn would swear to the truth of that if Melvig tortured her. Perhaps he's superstitious."

Both women sighed gustily. As a plan, it was as good as any other, but neither woman placed much trust in the mercy of their cantankerous sire.

ONE FURTHER INCIDENT marred the quiet weeks before Olwyn and Branwyn left the sanctuary of Caer Fyrddin. Olwyn owed much to the goddess, she felt, so she and Fillagh took the infant Myrddion to a Roman temple that had originally been dedicated to the earth goddess. Now it had become the temple of the goddess of knowledge and, beyond her, of Don, whose name should not be spoken, the Mother of the Celts.

The building was small and much damaged by time. Several columns had collapsed and had been dragged away by provident farmers for use in other projects. The portico was ruined and had collapsed. The tiny, whitewashed building had no windows and only a single wooden door, before which were placed several bowls of rancid milk for the snakes that were permitted to inhabit the temple. As winter now held the land in its iron grip, the reptiles were safely in hibernation.

At first, Olwyn had been dismayed by the dingy little building, and had been convinced that Ceridwen and the Mother would reject such a mean place of worship. But then, during a regimen of earnest prayers, Olwyn had sworn she felt the touch of the Mother in her mind, so now she faced the mud-colored walls and the silvery spiderwebs lurking in its darkened corners with more faith. Still, as she laid Myrddion down on the sun-warmed stones at the entrance to play with a small ball of cloth, she longed to take a birch broom to clean and sweep fresh air into the sanctuary.

Olwyn and Fillagh had barely begun a long chant in Ceridwen's honor when Myrddion began to giggle loudly. At first, the sisters continued with their worship, but the child's laughter rose in happy chuckles that intruded into their prayers.

With a sigh of irritation, Olwyn rose to her feet and grinned apologetically at her sister. She moved quietly to the forecourt, and would have lifted the child into her arms had she not been warned by a sibilant hiss that caused the hair to rise on her arms. She halted, catching her breath.

"What ails you, sister?" Fillagh asked, her eyes saucer-shaped as she stared at Olwyn's rigid, terrified body.

"The serpents!" Olwyn hissed herself. "The serpents have come into the sun!"

Hardly daring to breathe lest she should alarm the snakes, Olwyn shuffled round the doorway until she faced the laughing infant. Somewhere behind her, she sensed the presence of her sister and heard indrawn breath as Fillagh absorbed the scene before them.

Myrddion sat on the flagstones with the ball on his lap forgotten. Bright as bronze coins with the sunlight glittering on their scales, two serpents coiled about his arms and kissed his baby face with their flickering tongues. The child clapped his hands and Olwyn almost fainted with horror. Surely the serpents would strike at him, alarmed by the sudden movement.

"Mother, bless us!" Fillagh breathed, and Olwyn felt her feet swept away from under her. On her knees, she stared at the startling tableau with tears pouring down her cheeks.

The serpents sensed the vibration in the flagging as Olwyn fell to her knees, and turned their flat eyes towards her. Curling their bodies sensuously about the child's arms, they dropped their heads towards his legs, their tongues testing the air as they moved. Then, with final kisses to Myrddion's sensitive feet, they slithered away into apertures in the paving, leaving the child and the sisters alone on the temple forecourt. The weak sun disappeared behind a bank of cloud and the humans shivered in a sudden rush of cold.

Released from her terror, Olwyn staggered to her feet and snatched up her grandson. He squirmed in her tight embrace and began to wail thinly at the loss of his playmates.

"The child is blessed—or cursed!" Fillagh whispered. "What woman can understand such portents?" Her eyes were wild with nervous tension and she stared at Myrddion as if he had suddenly grown two heads.

"He's only a baby, Fillagh, so how could he be cursed?" Olwyn retorted with desperate urgency. "The sun has accepted him."

"But so have the serpents of the goddess. What man can dwell between the day of the warrior and the night of the Mother? How may such a thing be, unless Branwyn is correct and his father is truly a demon?"

"No more, Fillagh! Say nothing further that will lie between us like a curse in the years to come. You should be thanking Ceridwen that she saved Myrddion from the snakes, not blaming him for being unscathed."

Fillagh looked out over the wild valley where she could see the river rushing towards the sea and the fat sheep that grazed on the green flanks of the hills. The sun was a weak, white ghost in the winter haze, but its warmth eased the chill of the earth that rose through the flagstones and upwards into her chilled feet. She felt her sister's hand rest on her plump shoulder, as gentle as the caress of a mother.

"I love you, Fillagh, and I owe you so much for the shelter and protection that you have given to my family. I cannot remain angry with you, even for five minutes, so forgive me if I have insulted you. Perhaps you're right . . . but little Myrddion is important for reasons that I do not understand, yet feel in my heart to be true. And I love him, Fillagh, more than I ever loved Branwyn."

So, with much regret, and floods of tears from Fillagh, the small family left Moridunum as another spring came slowly to the river valley. Cletus One Ear was miserable and hugged Branwyn again and again, promising her a warm welcome if she returned.

When the oxen took the weight of the carts, strained a little and then began to move along the rutted road leading to the north, Olwyn and Branwyn waved until Cletus and Fillagh were small black specks in the distance. Even then, Fillagh's boys ran alongside the wagons for several miles until, puffed and tired, they stopped, shouted final farewells, and turned back towards the ugly villa and its endless wells of love.

Olwyn set her eyes upon the northern sky and ignored Branwyn's sullen complaints. She played with Myrddion, who was already trying to speak, and practiced the words she would use to placate her father on her return to her home.

Chapter V

A CHILD DENIED

Melvig stalked up and down Olwyn's forecourt, his boots making clipped, staccato snaps as his leather heels struck the tiled floors. A picture of righteous rage, his face was drawn down into a sullen, infuriated mask, and Olwyn tried not to flinch when he raised his reddened eyes to look at her.

"So! Daughter!" Melvig snarled. "Explain to me where this infant came from. Is the boy yours? Have you betrayed your family name, Olwyn? I heard the rumors before you'd been back a week."

Back and forth, back and forth, Olwyn watched the movements of her father's pacing feet as he strode across the room. Even when he stopped and brought his angry, old man's face only inches from hers, Olwyn stood her ground and said nothing.

"As a widow, you may do as you choose. But don't think to come to me for any assistance when the people of Segontium turn their faces away from a dirty whore."

"Father!" Olwyn exclaimed, and clapped both hands to her flaming cheeks. "I am no whore! I am a priestess of Ceridwen and I serve the Mother, so I belong to no man. No man! Not even yourself! You have no right to accuse me out of hand."

"If I choose to call you a slut, who will gainsay me? Or is it Bran-

73

wyn who has been making the two-backed beast with a lover?" Melvig shouted, his temper fraying as she watched his face redden. "Don't you *ever* contradict me, woman, for I am not one to countenance your insults."

"My insults? Mine? You call me a slut and accuse my daughter of behaving like an evil whore and *you* are insulted? You go too far, Father. I have never said a word against you, nor raised my hand towards you, but you shame us all by your outbursts."

Melvig's lips twisted and he swore with sudden crudity. One huge, age-spotted hand reached out, almost covering her face with his extended fingers, and he thrust her away from him so that she stumbled from the force of his anger. She struck her head against the wall as she fell.

"Owlwa!" a small voice screamed. "Leave Owlwa 'lone!"

Melvig paused in his instinctive warrior's crouch over his daughter's body. He felt a sting in his calf and swung one huge hand to swat away the annoyance even as he turned . . . and faced an angry, red-faced toddler.

Bemused by the child's combative stance, and irritated further by the small eating knife that had been driven into his lower leg, Melvig's expression wavered between the extremes of indignation and indulgent amusement. The boy, Myrddion, was poised to throw his sturdy body at the shaggy old king, although a child of such tender years could barely control his own bodily functions. Olwyn shook her dazed head and struggled to rise.

"Myrddion? Come here, darling boy. Come to Olwyn!"

She opened her arms wide and the child brushed past Melvig and threw his slender body against her breast.

"The child in question, I see," Melvin snapped, although his anger seemed to be seeping away with the slow trickle of blood that was running down his leg from his wounded calf. "So this is the bastard? At least he's got balls, considering he lives in a household of women and Greeks."

"This is Myrddion Emrys, who was presented to the sun god after his birth and accepted by the Mother's serpents before he could walk." Olwyn spoke as formally as she knew how, hoping to give Myrddion an illusion of status. "As you can see, he is a fine boy."

"But whose boy is he? When will you answer me, woman?" Then her father's face grew crafty around the eyes. "You're not a coward or a liar, and you would speak out in your quiet way if he was your child. So the boy must be Branwyn's son!"

The finality in Melvig's voice made Olwyn's blood run cold. Perhaps her father would stay his hand if he believed Myrddion was her child, but his granddaughter's bastard son? Never! He would demand his right to avenge this offensive slight on his honor.

Even as she began to beg her father to be sensible, he shouted for her steward, Plautenes, who came running immediately.

"You! Find my granddaughter and bring her to me at once. Understand? I don't want to be left cooling my heels while I wait on that young woman's pleasure. Drag her here if you must."

When Plautenes nodded and turned to leave, Melvig shouted out for wine and food, and Olwyn saw a flicker of annoyance slide across the servant's smooth, unlined face. Melvig saw it too.

"Why do you keep these nasty little pederasts around your house?" he muttered as the slave left the room. "Surely there are more than enough Ordovice to serve you."

Olwyn lifted her chin a little, held Myrddion close, and tried to answer her father without inflaming his temper any further. When the king of the Deceangli was thwarted, he often made decisions that he regretted after he had time for reflection.

"Please, Father, Plautenes isn't a pederast. Nor is Crusus. They do not consort with children, but love each other like husband and wife. There is too little love in the world, Father, and they take very good care of me and mine."

Olwyn could see her father beginning to formulate a stinging rejoinder when Branwyn entered the atrium from the colonnade, approached her grandfather, and bowed her head in respect. The effect was spoiled by a slight, ironic smirk that caused Melvig's brows to furrow.

"Explain yourself, Branwyn. Where did this babe come from? Who was your lover?"

"He's not a babe!" Branwyn glared at Melvig, and sparks flew as stubborn, egocentric wills clashed. "He's the child of a demon, and he's accursed. I'll not touch the creature, so you may kill him if you want, Grandfather. I'll not pine for him."

"Branwyn!" Olwyn cried, aghast.

"You're unnatural, girl!" Melvig snapped.

"Unnatural? A demon in the guise of a beautiful young man crept into my room and raped me. He spoke a devilish language, so I cannot even tell you his name. I hate the creature as I hate the seed he planted in me. If I am unnatural, what does that make that . . . thing that my mother loves more than me?"

Mother, save us all, for Branwyn is demented and consumed with hatred. Olwyn's thoughts were chaotic, but she was also appalled at her daughter's callousness and icy control. The girl was a stranger who seemed to blame her mother for some betrayal that Olwyn would never understand.

"A demon!" Melvig pronounced scornfully. "I'm surprised they have the equipment to breed."

"More than sufficient, Grandfather. The demon was cruel and determined to destroy me through his son. Doubt me if you will, but this child will bring bad luck to Segontium."

Suddenly, Melvig laughed. "Your son has already done his best to kill me. He's got a strong arm for a little one—and a bold eye. I could almost like the little bastard."

"He was trying to protect me, Father," Olwyn tried to explain, as she pleaded mutely with her daughter to provide some kind of aid. "Myrddion had no idea what he was doing. He's only a baby, Father, and I swear there's no evil in him."

Her father chortled with amusement, and Branwyn smiled coldly from behind the back of her hand. The boy furrowed his brow and twisted in Olwyn's arms so that he faced his accusers, and even Melvig felt the child's wide, black eyes as they fixed themselves upon him. The infant's gaze was so direct that the king felt that he had been thoroughly examined and found wanting in some essential element of his nature. As for Branwyn, the child's gaze narrowed with dislike and something akin to contempt towards her, if a child of less than two years was capable of such complex emotions.

A cautious knock on a door across the colonnade warned them that the servant had returned with wine, ale, and the small honey cakes that Melvig loved. Sensitive Plautenes read the unhappiness that lay behind his mistress's full mouth and dark eyes, and hurried back to the kitchen as soon as he had set down his tray.

"I heard raised voices, Crusus, and the mistress was on the verge of tears. I swear that the young mistress was almost gloating at her mother's terror. Agh! She's as cold as a witch's tit, that Branwyn. We'd all be better off if she'd died in childbirth."

Crusus clapped his hand over his lover's mouth with a moue of horror. "For the sake of the gods, Plautenes! Have a care. The king is none too fond of either of us, and if he hears your opinions he'll order you to be throttled. I only hope my pastries soothe his temper."

Crusus was a gifted cook, so the sweet delicacies were quickly washed down Melvig's maw with beakers of Olwyn's best wine. He smacked his lips enthusiastically and even smiled at Myrddion when he thought no one was looking.

Once he had paced a little and drunk a few more glasses of wine, he came to his decision. It was a judicious ruling that pleased nobody else, but solved all his problems.

"Well, Branwyn, I've decided that you are telling me the truth, so I will ensure that your tale of inhuman rapine is spread where it should be known. We shall let the world believe that the bastard is the child of a demon—for so you have sworn. Therefore, as you are soiled but

77

guiltless in this matter, I will find you a suitable husband before the summer. You will accede to my wishes or face death, do you understand?"

Branwyn's face was wiped clean of any triumph or mirth she might have felt when her grandfather sanctioned her story of a demon rapist. Her expression became blank and formless, as if her personality had been leached away by the thought of her impending marriage. Melvig saw her lips begin to shape a refusal and beat her into speech.

"You will deny me at your peril. Never believe that I'll have you killed, for I'll not punish you so lightly for disobedience. How would you fancy a lifetime of imprisonment? Or, better yet, perhaps I'll banish you with only the clothes on your back. Rape by a demon will seem kindly by comparison with life as a friendless, poverty-stricken female."

Olwyn's eyes pleaded with her daughter to be silent. Branwyn dropped her mutinous gaze and bowed low.

"As for you, daughter, I am hurt by your subterfuge. As a widow, you've lived your life pleasantly and willfully, but those days are over. I'll present you with a choice of suitable husbands in recognition of your blameless life in the past, but you will marry again, whether you like my choices or not."

Wisely, Olwyn bit her lip and said nothing. She cuddled Myrddion closely and the tired child, who had begun to suck his thumb in distress, wound his small arms around her neck.

"As for the bastard, he may live . . . but only because he shows courage, which amuses me in a young man. Let all men and women in this villa know his ancestry, so they will be alert to any threat directed towards the souls of the pious. If he should grow to be wild, willful, or wicked, then he will be put to death for the safety of the people. Now! Where's your cook?"

As Melvig ambled off to terrify the kitchen servants, Olwyn sobbed into Myrddion's shoulder. The child smelled sweet and fresh, like cut grass after evening rain, with a hint of warmed milk. She breathed him in as if she could hide him in her ageing womb for safety, while Branwyn echoed her cry of pain.

"Oh, Branwyn," Olwyn wept. "It won't be so very bad, my dear. My father can be stern and ruthless, but he's not cruel. He'll find you a man who'll treat you well, and perhaps you'll come to like him a little, given time. I had never met your father when we wed, but I found that he was gentle and understanding. I couldn't help but love him so much that, even now, the thought of marrying another man makes me very sad."

Branwyn's head swung up. Her eyes were venomous, and Olwyn flinched away from the obvious dislike her daughter cast at her in that glance.

"I'm not you, Mother. I will marry no man!"

"You'll have no choice." Olwyn sighed. "Why are you so angry with me?"

"Where were you when I needed you?" Branwyn began in a quiet, relentless voice that gradually rose in volume and passion. "Did you notice that I was upset after the demon raped me? No! And why did you take me to Aunt Fillagh's house? To save yourself from Grandfather's anger. Then you champion that twisted product of the demon—that thing! That hateful creature! You love it! You care more about it than you do about me. I hope it kills you, the way it has murdered me."

Olwyn could only stare mutely at her daughter. She had never understood Branwyn, but she loved her with a depth of feeling that was almost blind. Almost. As she gazed into the handsome, twisted face of her daughter, she was struck by how little she liked Branwyn under the layer of love she felt.

Let her go, Olwyn thought as she hugged Myrddion close to her. She knew she had irretrievably lost her daughter, but the goddess had given her a second chance through the quiet, loving eyes of her grandson.

"Oh, Branwyn, you will suffer for your arrogance and the ugliness that lives inside you. Hate me if it makes you feel better, curse me if your life is easier with someone to hate, but until you love something or someone more than you love yourself, you still belong to your demon."

Six months later, Melvig basked in early spring sunshine and stared out over the strait towards Mona. The sunlight loaned his face a little warmth so that his complexion shone and his grey and white hair appeared reddish in hue to match the streaks of color in his beard. He was feeling expansive and successful, having negotiated the stormy waters of family without drawing blood.

Branwyn had required force.

She had cursed him, using words that Melvig could hardly credit a fifteen-year-old girl could ever know. She had spat and kicked, but neither her intended husband nor her grandfather had been swayed. The young warrior who had been chosen to wed Branwyn had seen the possibilities of his position instantly. His family was impoverished and a child that was a direct descendant of the king of the Deceangli would cement his wealth for his lifetime.

"Let the silly little cow rave and swear," he had told his mother after his first, inauspicious meeting with his betrothed. "She will belong to me soon enough, and then I'll school her in the duties of marriage. I will need your help, Mother, for this girl's been spoiled all her life."

His mother had been as ecstatic as her son.

"Remember, Maelgwn, that this girl has been raped by a demon, or so the gossip goes. Of course she'll be tainted. How could she not? I'll help to teach her the duties that she owes to her husband in his house, of course, but you must be firm, if you understand me, son. You must treat her like a horse, and force her to accept the bridle."

From the beginning, Branwyn had been terrified under her spitting, scratching violence. In Maelgwn, she saw something of the man who haunted her nightmares. In certain tricks of the light, he seemed taller and his eyes and hair blacker, so that Triton came towards her once again, with an outstretched hand that promised pain and mortification. She heard Maelgwn's voice through the veil of a more melodic memory of terror, so that the broad, plain face of her betrothed writhed and shifted to Triton's features . . . then back to his own, in a dizzying, mad, shape-shifting horror.

Ignorant of his granddaughter's growing madness, Melvig was very pleased with the arranged marriage. Maelgwn had wed Branwyn, although she was bound and gagged during the ceremony with her husband's permission. Later, she had been carried off to Tomen-y-mur where Maelgwn had a rather run-down estate that would keep the king's granddaughter occupied for years to come. Melvig rubbed his palms together with approval as he thought of how the fractious Branwyn had finally been forced into obedience.

Maelgwn was not a monster, only a mother's boy who had never cut himself loose from her cloying love. The first night of his marriage was a grotesque travesty of love, for Branwyn had fought like a woman possessed. His mother had warned him that Branwyn would not be gentled until she was with child, so the bridal bed saw one rape after another, although Maelgwn vomited away the rich food of the marriage feast after he had been forced to bind her arms then prise her legs apart.

By day, she was forced to labor like a kitchen maid on the orders of her mother-in-law until hatred was deeply carved into her inflexible nature. Branwyn waited, knowing that the demon and his seed had brought her to this pass. She knew, with the utter certainty of the crazed, that her day of vengeance would come.

As for Olwyn, she had accepted the youngest suitor presented to her by her father. Eddius was a younger son, and his family was notable for a Roman strain that made him less eligible than his fellow warriors. Melvig presumed, incorrectly, that Olwyn had chosen the younger man because she would hold the whip hand in status, wealth, and experience.

But her father was wrong. Each suitor had been carefully assessed on one criterion alone—his response to Myrddion. Only Eddius had grinned at the toddler and swung him up into his strong arms. Only

Eddius had tossed the boy high into the air until Myrddion had dissolved in a peal of giggles. Olwyn was won over without the need for a pretty word or an empty promise.

As for Myrddion, the whole world now knew the ancestry of this strange great-grandson. Melvig grinned appreciatively. Branwyn and Olwyn had been clever with their lies, for who would willingly antagonize a demon by killing its son? But who would follow the child of a demon, or raise a sword in his defense? Melvig had ensured that Myrddion would never trouble the legitimate kings of the Deceangli or the Ordovice, simply by averring that Myrddion's mother had spoken the truth concerning his antecedents.

Branwyn was now pregnant again, as was her mother, and Melvig congratulated himself on his cleverness.

"So that's the end of this little drama," Melvig said aloud to the wind. "With luck, Olwyn and her brood won't cause any more trouble while I remain alive."

Slow years followed, season blending into season, and Myrddion was drawn to the shores near Segontium just as Branwyn had been. Storms covered the sands with sea wrack and a treasure trove of shells, fish, strange twisted wood, and the detritus of broken ships. Like his mother before him, the boy dreamed large fantasies with himself as the hero as he sought solace from his aching loneliness. Olwyn had given birth to a son, soon followed by another, and with two infants to care for she had little time to spare for her grandson, although she never ceased loving him.

Little escaped Myrddion's clever, lambent gaze. His great intelligence formed barriers between him and the world, and these walls sometimes resisted even Olwyn's huge capacity for love. The boy's constant questions and his sharp insights dumbfounded her and Eddius, leaving them worried that the boy would wither without companionship to stimulate his growing intellect.

Nor could Myrddion join in the games and mock battles of the other children of Segontium. From the time when he was first able to reason, he was forced to understand that he was different and frightening. The village children would chant insults at him until he felt the blood surge up into his head.

"Bastard! Demon seed! Bastard! Demon!"

When he looked into the pails of water left for the horses and saw his dark visage surrounded by a wild tangle of black hair, Myrddion was so distraught that he broke the reflection with his hand.

Ugly! Ugly and damned!

With her usual sensitivity, Olwyn noticed Myrddion's uncharacteristic silence and black depression. With a sinking heart, she recognized the signs of a growing rage and she remembered Fillagh's warning, and Olwyn's subsequent oath.

"Love alone can defeat him and make him human," Fillagh had exclaimed, her eyes pregnant with warning.

Olwyn had vowed that she would love Myrddion so much that Branwyn's desertion wouldn't matter. Now, it seemed, it did matter.

"Myrddion, sweetheart, come to Olwyn."

The sturdy little boy barely hesitated, but Olwyn's instinctive antennae picked up that momentary doubt. Then she spread her arms wide as Myrddion ran into them and pressed his face against her warm breasts.

"Why are you troubled, my darling? I know you are, by those frowning black brows of yours, my darling boy." She cuddled him and felt his body begin to relax.

"I'm ugly!" he wailed in a muffled voice, and Olwyn could feel his tears through her peplum. "The Mother and Grannie Ceridwen will reject me, and I will be lost forever."

He paused and lapsed into miserable intensity.

"What's a bastard, Olwyn? Why do the other children hate me?"

Olwyn sighed and kissed her grandson's thick and lustrous hair. With an aching heart, she sought for words that would show this strange child how much he was really loved.

"You're not ugly, Myrddion. You're beautiful. The village children envy you because you're taller than they are, and so much stronger and more comely than they will ever be. How could the Mother reject you when she holds all of us to her heart because we belong to her? And Grannie Ceridwen loves you because you are her boy. The children think that they can hurt you, and that is why they shout these lies at you." She released him a little so she could see his doubtful, mutinous face. "A bastard is someone whose father is unknown, sweetheart. Your father is unknown, it's true, Myrddion, but don't be so foolish as to listen to silly gossip. Olwyn will always tell you the truth."

So Olwyn explained to the child how deeply Branwyn had been wounded—and why. In simple language, the rape on the shoreline was explained, while Myrddion questioned the reasons for his natural mother's lack of love towards him.

"You know how your chest feels, darling, when the village boys say cruel things to you? Imagine that feeling, only greater, as if it were pressed on your chest for every minute of every day. Then imagine you had been badly hurt, and someone asked you to love another person who looked like the evil person who had originally caused you so much pain. Your mother couldn't bear to remain fearful forever, so she doesn't want to see you—and refuses to love you. Your poor mother has been driven a little mad by her memories of a very bad man, Myrddion. She can't help what she feels."

Olwyn wrapped her arms about her grandson once more and heard Myrddion's tiny sigh of comfort and acceptance.

"So you see, my darling, you are not to blame. An evil man made you, but so did I, and so did Branwyn, and Grandfather Melvig who is a king. And, at the very beginning, so did Grannie Ceridwen, who came with the Mother and her snakes, to show how much they both loved you. Look in the water and see what is really there, not what other people say they see. Never forget, my sweet boy, to look below the surface and not judge another person by what they say. What we do and what we are is what really counts."

So Myrddion learned his first and greatest lesson, while Olwyn deflected the most dreadful consequences of the lie that lay at the heart of Myrddion's birth.

But Myrddion was more than just a sufferer of fear and loneliness. He was also an angry child, especially when he was pushed into a corner. One day, after months of chanting and ridicule, the angry creature that coexisted with his rational self surged out of its dark hiding place like an attacking wolf. Eyes reddened with fury, Myrddion flung himself at the largest boy, both fists pumping to strike at whatever bare flesh was near at hand.

The smaller children screamed and ran away from the whirlwind that Myrddion had become. With feet, hands, even his teeth, the boy attacked the largest of his tormentors with an animal's ferocity. Of course, the larger village boys landed more blows than they received, and Myrddion was soon covered in scrapes and blood. Even when one lout, four years older than his six-year-old assailant, deliberately broke the smaller boy's thumb, the enraged Myrddion still struck him a stinging blow with his damaged hand. Although he was soon buried by a kicking mass of arms and legs, Myrddion showed no signs of submission until Eddius waded into the twisting melee of children and dragged the young boy up by his torn tunic.

"For shame, lads! For shame! Five against one hardly seems fair odds, and him half your size," Eddius chastened the village boys, who scrambled to their feet and hung their heads in embarrassment at the intervention of an adult.

"He started it!" the largest boy muttered as he wiped a long streak of blood from his mouth. "He loosened my tooth!"

"How old are you, Brynn? Ten years? Eleven? This young wildcat is only six. For shame, Brynn! Your father should keep you occupied at his forge if you can't act like a good Celt. And you, Fyddach, your father is a warrior at Canovium. What would he think if he saw you beating a boy half your size?"

Most of the accused lads shuffled their feet and hung their heads in humiliation, but Fyddach was made of sterner stuff and lifted his chin pugnaciously.

"He's the son of a demon, lord, and everybody knows it. He's got no business pushing in around his betters, so he should stay away from us. We don't want him, and we don't like him. We've told him to stay away from us, so he can't complain if we call him names that are true. He is a bastard, and he is the son of a demon. Even the king says so."

Eddius sighed with exasperation and tightened his grip on Myrddion's tunic. The child's eyes were narrowed and red with fury and hurt.

"Listen, you young fools. Myrddion is better born than any of you, and shows twice your courage. How will he treat you when he is a man and has won his sword? Did you think of that, you sons of blacksmiths, fishermen, and traders? No, of course not. And if his father was a demon, imagine what he could do to you once he learns how to master his powers. You certainly didn't think of that! Now, run away, boys, and if I ever catch you harming my young ward again, I'll tan your hides with the back of my sword."

Gratefully, the boys ran, but words of derision still drifted back to Eddius and Myrddion on the morning breeze.

"Now, lad, let me look at the damage. Ah, but your gran will clout me proper for the bruises you bear, you silly boy."

Clucking his teeth and shaking his head, Eddius dragged Myrddion to the communal well, thrust him down onto a slate step, and used a scrap of the boy's tunic to clean his many cuts and bruises. "Idiot!" he murmured smiling. It was hard to stay angry with Myrddion. Something charismatic and attractive in the boy's face drew people to him.

"You could have been badly hurt, Myrddion. As it is, I'll need to take you to the healer to set that broken thumb. And one of those boys must have had a knife, because something has cut deep into your arm. Olwyn will worry."

"I'm sorry," Myrddion answered guiltily. "I lost my temper when they were shouting at me. What's so wrong with being a bastard, Eddius? Gran explained that who my father is doesn't make me either good or bad, for I am the only one who can choose what sort of person I'll become. But how can I be sure that my father wasn't a demon? Ouch!"

"Yes, your thumb is broken. Come on, Myrddion! Hold this pad against your arm and try not to cry. Tears always make bullies even worse."

Myrddion's lips certainly quivered, but he bit down hard on his tongue and his tears disappeared behind the pain. He looked up at Eddius, who seemed so tall and strong that Myrddion wished the young man was his father.

"You're still not telling me the truth, sir. Why don't people tell the truth?"

"It's easier to lie, lad. Sometimes, when you are caught doing something bad, and you know it's bad, the temptation to make an excuse is really strong, so that no one remains angry with you."

Eddius was twenty-nine, two years younger than his extraordinary wife, and every day he thanked the gods for the lucky chance that made her his spouse. Her grandson was so likeable and mature that it was easy to treat him like a little adult. Eddius ran one sun-bronzed hand through his sandy hair and eyed Myrddion with affectionate exasperation. He knelt next to the boy beside the well, oblivious of the stares of a gaggle of women who were, ostensibly, drawing water, but were actually eavesdropping for all they were worth.

"According to your mother, she was raped by a demon who had disguised himself as a beautiful young man. She eventually told your gran of her ordeal, admitted she had lied, and revealed that the beast could barely speak our language. All that Branwyn did wrong, apparently, was to disobey her mother and go alone to the beach where she found her rapist. She knew she shouldn't. But to answer your question, you'll never know for sure that your father isn't a demon, because there are many, many wicked men in the world. To this day, your poor mother hates all men, even her husband, and refuses to take care of her two daughters—all because of one wicked man."

Myrddion's eyes were teary and very sad, so Eddius gave him a quick hug to show that he was loved.

"Inside the gold shell you wear round your neck is your father's ring. Your mother gave the ring to your grandmother, and said the demon had given it to her. Apparently, it had belonged to his mother, whom he had murdered. Yes, I know—if your mother spoke the truth, then your father was a most unpleasant creature, although I can't say if he was a demon or not. As well as the demon's ring, there is another special, very ancient ring inside the shell. This ring was found in your great-uncle Cletus's fields, and served as your bulla when you were dedicated to the lord of light. When you are a man, I hope you will wear that Roman ring with its sun-fire stone, for you were named for Myrddion of the sun. You may be a bastard, but your birth and your bloodlines mark you for greatness." Eddius draped his heavy arm over Myrddion's shoulders. "And we love you, boy, as does everyone who knows you. What do village children matter?"

The day had almost reached noontide.

The sunlight fell on the boy's dusty black hair, which retained a high gloss like a raven's wing, and a hint of blue was revealed in the merciless light. The boy's eyes especially caught at Eddius's sympathetic nature. They were wounded by what he had been told, and now the child struggled to understand the cruelty of that long-ago violence. Wise beyond his years, Eddius accepted that Myrddion understood the concept of rape and murder, so the boy must have felt increasingly soiled by his background.

"As a child of the gods, nothing of this story should cause you to feel any guilt for the actions of your parents. Perhaps, one day, you will eventually find your father and discover your ancestry."

Myrddion nodded with an adult's gravity. "So the village boys didn't lie. I am the seed of a demon."

"Do you believe yourself to be wicked? Could your dear gran love a cruel, evil creature of chaos? No. You are Myrddion, and you are loved." He smiled down at his young ward. "But we must now go to the healer so Olwyn doesn't beat me with her iron pan until my head rings."

Myrddion laughed politely as, shakily, he took Eddius's proffered hand and rose carefully to his feet.

"You were very brave today, Myrddion," Eddius added softly. "I was proud of you."

"I lost my temper," Myrddion whispered. "I could have hurt one of the boys and that would have been wrong."

"You're the one who's still bleeding," Eddius retorted with a wide grin. "You were outnumbered, so fair's fair."

Eddius and Myrddion walked through the narrow, cobbled streets that led to the outskirts of the township. At the end of a dirt track, a single, conical hut was separated from other dwellings by a brackish pond surrounded by hazel trees and thick flowering gorse. A thin trail of smoke rose from a hole in the center of the sod-covered roof, but no other signs of habitation were obvious to Myrddion. At the front of the cottage, which was sealed tightly with a heavy door, a series of large, wheel-thrown pots contained a range of plants and weeds, while many herbs, familiar and strange, grew in a neat garden off to one side of the unmortared slate walls. A drying rack held several hides that had stiffened and cured in the sun and Myrddion's sensitive nostrils recognized the aroma of smoked fish coming from a small sod hut behind the cottage.

"Look, Myrddion. The healer keeps beehives. The little people give her their honey in return for the stout homes in which they live."

Eddius pointed to two conical hives made out of plaited and woven straw that were set on little tables above the ground to protect the hives from predators, both large and small. Myrddion's curious eyes spotted more vegetable gardens, tubs of geraniums that loomed in small riots of scarlet, apple trees, several nut trees, and a small enclosure where a cow and a newly born calf were cropping the grass before a lean-to that offered them protection. His twitching nose told the boy that somewhere pigs grunted and rolled in mud, while chickens squawked and searched for grass seed behind the cottage. Even the sound of ducks came from the pond, and Myrddion's eyes grew even rounder with amazement as someone puttered out of a narrow path between the thick gorse and the brambles.

"Well, Eddius, what brings you to my door, boy?"

The lilt of the voice alone indicated that the figure making its careful way towards them was female. The voice was melodic, sweet and light, rather like new honey, and Myrddion's jaw dropped at the pleasure of its music. The healer's hair was very long and was full of leaves, twigs, and bits of straw so that the face under it was almost obscured. The wild tresses were iron grey, like the clothing that was layered over the roly-poly form. The healer tottered forward on impossibly small feet and patted Eddius's arm with equally tiny, plump fingers.

"Come in! Come in! I can see the young sir has been in the wars, so to speak. We'll soon put that right, won't we, Boudicca?"

Myrddion shook his head in confusion. Who was Boudicca? As if in answer to his unspoken question, a large mongrel bitch galloped out of the brambles to stand, panting and grinning, next to her mistress.

"Boudicca, this is Eddius, Master of the Strait of Mona," the healer stated with utter seriousness. "And this young man is, I believe, his wife's grandson, Myrddion, who has come to us to be healed."

The dog appeared to nod to her new acquaintances and tentatively licked at Myrddion's free hand. Myrddion flushed and risked patting the large red hound on her broad, flat forehead. The dog wriggled ecstatically.

"Boudicca likes you." The healer smiled happily, and began to jiggle a piece of string through a hole in the door until it opened to reveal the dark interior of the one-roomed cottage. "Come in! Come in!"

The healer began to shed layers of woolen garments while she stoked a central fire, stirred the contents of a large iron pot that hung from a tripod over the red-hot coals, and pointed at a bench stool that was set before the fire. As each layer of clothing was removed, more of the healer's face became visible, even though the hut was quite dark after the brilliant sunshine of a late spring noontime.

"Now, young Myrddion! Let's be seeing what you've done to yourself."

Myrddion must have looked as startled as a young fawn caught in the light of the hunter's fire.

"But I've not introduced myself to you, have I? Faith, but I'd be losing my mind if it weren't safely locked inside my skull. My name is Annwynn, which is a very noble name for such an ordinary woman. I've no treasure, nor a cauldron of plenty, and I'm no kin to the goddess, Ceridwen, although legend has it that you are, young sir. No, Annwynn's just a healer—and happy to serve as I can. Now, strip down to your loincloth, lovey, and stand near the fire so I can easily see you."

Myrddion looked at Eddius for confirmation, and the warrior nodded with a slight smile. As the boy undressed, Annwynn bustled about the small room collecting pottery and wooden jars, a small pearwood box, soft rags, and a beaker of something that smelled wonderful, especially when she added hot water from an odd, spouted container that hung from a hook attached to the tripod over the fire.

"Sweet, hot mead," she explained economically, handing the mug to Eddius, who sipped it suspiciously. The broad smile that leapt to his lips as he savored the taste caused Annwynn to laugh delightedly. "Some folk say old Annwynn has magic in her fingers. Others call her a witch. But she makes good mead, doesn't she, brave sir?"

"It's very good," Eddius replied, stretching his long legs before the fire.

"And now for you, young Myrddion. You're a fair lad, I see, but you've hurt yourself. It's a good thing that I've a good eye for my stitchery."

Although Myrddion was young, he wasn't foolish. He raised his eyes to look at Annwynn's face at the thought of his arm being stitched together like the seam of his tunic, and all his doubts fell away.

Annwynn looked down at him, and Myrddion imagined that she smelled like a ripe apple. Her face was almost completely round under the mop of hair that she was now tying back from her face with a colorful strip of cloth. Her cheeks were rosy and rounded under low cheekbones, and even her eyes seemed too blue and protuberant to be quite real. Her brows were thick semicircles of black hair that gave her expression a permanent cast of surprise. The ingenuous kindness of those wide-open eyes was immediately disarming.

91

Annwynn's nose was short and snub and ended with a distinct ball of flesh that caused anyone who looked at her to hide a smile. Below that clownish nose was a delicate, full mouth that was naturally moist and red. Even her small, regular teeth were unthreatening, as a gap between the front two added to the overall effect of harmless humor and gentleness. A dimple in the center of her rounded chin and others at each corner of her mouth finished off the attractiveness of her face. She made people smile, even when their hearts were heavy with pain and loss.

Annwynn was in her middle life, somewhere over forty years, which was a very respectable age for a woman, but no citizens of Segontium could tell the curious anything about her past. She had appeared in the town some twelve years earlier, and had quickly become invaluable for her herb lore, her jollity, and her skill as a midwife.

She took a needle out of an oiled piece of leather, put it into a small bowl of hot water, and hunted for another mysterious packet in her pearwood box. With a little cry of triumph, she lugged out a ball of very fine thread that was made from animal gut. Myrddion's eyes grew wider as she revealed a narrow rod of iron, not even as wide as a feather quill, from her packet and thrust it into the fire.

"Are you brave, young Myrddion? Must I give you the juice of the poppy? Or can you stand firm while I cauterize this cut? I don't know how clean the blade was that caused your wound, but if a village child held it, then it is very dirty. Wounds rot if they aren't perfectly clean, so I'm washing yours now with clean water. She smiled down at Myrddion. "Good boy, for you didn't flinch! Yes, it has bled freely, but I must be sure. Otherwise you'll be a very sorry young man."

"I can be brave," Myrddion whispered. "As long as I understand what you're doing."

Annwynn laughed until her belly shook.

"Why, he's old beyond his years, Master Eddius! He speaks like a little magistrate and not like a boy at all. Oh, it's wonderful!"

And she laughed until all her flesh jounced and bounced and Myrddion watched her body, mesmerized by the sight. He didn't realize she had removed the iron rod from the fire until he felt a sudden, agonizing burn on the wound. He would have flinched away, but Annwynn had gripped him with her other arm so that his body was immobilized against her rolls of fat. The cauterizing was quick, but Myrddion felt it all, and watched it all, his eyes drawn to the cherry-red iron rod as it probed the wound.

"Why do you caut . . . cautersize?" Myrddion struggled to find the right word.

As she lifted away the iron rod, Annwynn freed the boy's arms. "The word is cauterize. Do you know your letters, child?"

Myrddion nodded.

"It's used to burn out any evil humors that can cause the flesh to rot. Many healers don't believe in these humors, but I do, and my patients almost always live. My teacher was an old Jew who said he was born in Damascus, wherever that is. He could read his letters as well, but I can't read them because girls were never taught where I come from."

While Annwynn spoke, her hands were busy, and Myrddion realized that she had pulled a needle threaded with gut through his flesh, drawing the edges of the wound together by tying a small knot. Although she hurt him, Myrddion was fascinated.

"Where do you come from, Annwynn?" he asked without raising his eyes from her busy fingers.

"Me? Why, I come from far to the south, from Portus Lemanis where the trade ships come from Gaul. It's a place where the whole world comes and goes by sea. Gracious, child, but you get me talking like no other. There! That's all done now. Just three little stitches, neat as can be. I fear you'll have a tiny scar, but you'll not care for that."

Annwynn found a wooden jar that held a thick, brown substance with a strange smell. Using a small wooden paddle, she smeared the cream liberally over the wound and then, still without touching the flesh any more than necessary, she bound the arm with a clean length of old rag.

Myrddion eyed the makeshift bandage suspiciously.

"Don't be thinking that the ill humors will find entrance to your wound from a dirty cloth. You can be assured that I boil these rags for half a day over the fire, and I dry them in clean sunshine. Does that explanation make you happy, young sir?"

Myrddion blushed.

For half an hour, Annwynn spread her brown cream on assorted grazes and growing bruises, covered cuts where necessary, and then splinted Myrddion's broken thumb. She hurt her young patient quite a bit, but he was fascinated by everything she did and bit his lip if her ministrations caused him discomfort.

"You'll have a very uncomfortable night, so I am giving Eddius just a little poppy juice in mead that will help you to sleep." She patted his cheek, and helped him to dress because of the awkwardness of his splinted thumb. "You must come back in two days, just to check that your wound is still clean and healing."

Boudicca accompanied them to the doorway and Myrddion winced as his abused muscles complained when he reached out to scratch her ears. Meanwhile, Annwynn searched madly through the contents of a chest in the corner. With a cry of elation, she snatched up a small object, bustled to the doorway and pressed it into Myrddion's hand.

"This is for bravery, sweet chick! It is the owl of the goddess, and represents the hunter and wisdom. That is you, young master."

Myrddion looked down at the stone that filled the palm of his hand. Someone had taken time to chip out two semicircles in the object that met to form the suggestion of a beak. Within the two semicircles, smaller circles were chipped out to mimic rudimentary eyes. White pigment outlined the inscribed pattern to accentuate the likeness of an owl.

"Thank you," he said. "I'll keep it forever."

"No, you won't. But the owl will protect you and will never leave you," Annwynn answered enigmatically, then called her dog and closed the cottage door behind her.

As Myrddion followed Eddius along the path leading to the villa, the boy struggled to order his thoughts. He was weary and hurting, and the sharp, long grasses that grew above the beach caught his sandals and tripped him, causing him to fall. Eddius saw that the boy was suffering as he tried to regain his feet, so he swept him up in his strong arms. Against his will, Myrddion felt his head begin to droop. Long before the villa came into sight, Myrddion was sound asleep on Eddius's shoulder.

Olwyn's husband smiled as he strode along, bearing Myrddion's slender form without any difficulty. He had two sons of his own and he loved them with a kind of madness, so deeply and viscerally did his passions run. But Myrddion connected strangely with Eddius's brain and the warrior admitted to himself on that sandy track overlooking the beach that the boy was likely to eclipse even his great-grandfather, the king of the Deceangli. There was some quality in the boy that promised greatness.

Eddius sighed.

The bay was a wide sweep of sand, lacy waves, and the deep, dark waters out of which the island of Mona rose, wreathed in rain clouds and its own bloody history. Would Myrddion make his way here, in the shadow of tragedy, or would he travel further than Eddius had ever imagined?

Eddius shrugged and shook the boy awake as his sandals slapped against the flagstones of the villa's forecourt.

"We're home, Myrddion. It's time to explain ourselves to Olwyn."

Far away, Ygerne screamed in the final agonies of childbirth. In a rush of blood and mucus, a baby girl with a caul over her face was expelled into a cruel, uncaring world. When the child was washed and swaddled, Ygerne raised her arms to claim her firstborn daughter with tears of purest joy.

"Morgan! I shall call her Morgan, for she is all my happiness and my hope." Ygerne wept, her tears mingling with the sweat of her labors. "Now, take her to her father, to King Gorlois, and tell him he has a fine daughter who will bring distinction to his house."

The servant women ran to obey her, but the old midwife remained behind with her patient and examined the child's caul. She shuddered at the strangeness of this aberration of nature. Children born with such a mark suffered from the gift of prophecy and, according to superstition, could not drown. The old woman had not liked to touch a child so drenched in woman's magic.

"Take care of this hood of skin, lady," she told Ygerne. "The legend says that if a caul should fall into the wrong hands, its owner will die or, at the very least, be under the power of the caul's possessor."

Ygerne took the ugly thing and hid it among her pillows.

"Be very sure I will see it safely hidden, good midwife. For I swear that nothing will harm my child. Not in this life, or the next. Thank you, good woman, for your assistance and for your advice."

"It's nothing, Lady Ygerne, nothing," the midwife protested, but when she left the castle the next day, she felt released as if from a prison. She swore with her whole heart that Tintagel would not feel the weight of her shadow again.

Chapter VI

THE APPRENTICE

Two years passed quietly, full of the small triumphs and tragedies that all families experience in the daily trials of living. Olwyn bore another child, a third sturdy boy, but the birth was hard and taxed her body sorely so that she almost perished when she bled copiously after he was born. Annwynn labored hard to save her life, using her full repertoire of herbs, heavy binding across Olwyn's flaccid belly, and a ruthless refusal to accept that her patient would die. Against all the odds, Olwyn survived, although she was very weak and would never regain her strength.

Once mother and son were safe, Annwynn drew Eddius out of the birthing room to speak to him seriously. Myrddion had been terrified during the ordeal, so he hid unseen behind a column to eavesdrop on their conversation.

"Your wife mustn't bear another child," Annwynn warned. "I can't tell you why, for I don't fully understand what the body demands, but I can promise you that Mistress Olwyn will bleed to death if she goes into labor again. I have seen her condition many times and the outcome is always death for the mother, and usually for the child as well."

Eddius's face screwed up with physical pain and he knuckled his weeping eyes like a small child. "I'll avoid her bed. I'll do anything you say, for I'll not risk Olwyn. I love her, and I can't imagine life without her."

As he wept without shame, Annwynn reached across to pat his unshaven cheek.

"Lad, you may swear that you will shun the marriage bed, and mean it, but the lusts of the body are strong. Better to avoid the pregnancy. Should Olwyn ever be with child again, you must inform me as soon as she knows. I have a potion that will kill the child, while saving the life of the mother. It's sad for us to do, I know. But if your love is true, it's better the babe dies rather than the mother."

"Aye! Anything you decide. I'll do whatever you say."

"How is Myrddion? He must be terrified, for he loves his gran beyond reason. I sometimes fear that he would go mad if anything happened to her."

Eddius smiled damply. "Once Olwyn promised him that he could learn some of your skills as soon as he had mastered his Latin, he turned into an excellent scholar. Even his tutor's exacting standards are satisfied, and if you have no objections we will send the boy to you for five days a week for training and toil. Subject to your agreement, Olwyn asks that we should pay two pieces of red gold per annum for his apprenticeship once he turns nine years. It's only two months, so I warn you that he'll try to wheedle his way into an early start, now that we owe you so much."

Annwynn smiled enigmatically. "You owe me nothing but my fee, Master Eddius. And you may tell Myrddion he may come at any time. These old bones ache more fiercely in the winter, so a pair of sharp young eyes and a strong back will be very welcome."

In the way of fractured families, Olwyn had heard little of her daughter until she received a brief and rather curt message from a courier informing her that Branwyn's husband had died of a fever and that he had been buried, as was his wish, where he could hear the sea. As his son was only five years old, Branwyn had called for her husband's younger brother to take his place in the running of his estate.

As no further messages were received, Olwyn was forced to accept that Branwyn desired no help from her mother and had no interest in the safety and happiness of Myrddion. Had Olwyn known the truth, she would have been alarmed, rather than disappointed.

Gentle, well-intentioned Maelgwn had succumbed to a lung fever in a state of mind very similar to relief. Life with Branwyn was a turbulent sea of trouble, fear, and threat. More than once, Maelgwn had woken in the dead of night to find Branwyn missing from the marital bed and crouched close to him like a predator stalking its prey. On one occasion, she had been hiding a large kitchen knife behind her back.

Branwyn had been given no choice other than to accept Maelgwr, Maelgwn's brother, into her bed. The second son had none of his brother's consideration, albeit he wasn't unduly under his mother's influence. The first time Branwyn attacked him, he beat her until her face and arms were black with bruises.

As for her feelings towards her eldest son, Branwyn's animosity had not abated with the passage of time. All infants, regardless of their sex or relationship to her, were in danger from Branwyn. But as they grew, the troubled woman seemed able to accept them, and even play with them like the child she still was. But hatred eats away at the soul, so Branwyn could love nothing and no one, having retreated into a wholly egocentric obsession with old wrongs.

The day after his ninth birthday, Myrddion rose early in his small plastered room, dressed with great care after washing in cold water, and brushed his long hair until it shone. Using a chewed twig and charcoal, he cleaned his teeth vigorously, for Olwyn followed the Roman concepts of cleanliness although in all other ways she was a true Deceangli. Once Myrddion had checked his reflection in a pail of water in the kitchen, he packed a hasty meal of bread, cheese, apples from the root cellar, and several slices of cooked meat sliced off the bone, to take with him on the journey to Annwynn's house.

Now that he was fluent in Latin, both written and spoken, and was able to turn the sounds of the common language into his own form of written translation, the boy filled his satchel with a smooth piece of slate that he often used to take notes, some coarse pieces of chalk, a precious piece of much-used hide that had been written upon and scraped clean so often that the leather was almost too thin for use, ink made of ground charcoal and gum, and a stylus pen made from a sturdy quill. Like all budding scholars, he also carried a sharp knife to trim his quill and scrape away any errors, and a worn piece of sea sponge that would clean his slate.

Then, armed for a new, much-anticipated experience, Myrddion grabbed two chunks of bread, slapped a piece of meat between them, and quietly left the villa, eating his hasty breakfast as he went. The morning was an answer to a dream. He would start to learn the art of healing, and he would discover what life held in store for him.

Somehow, the rising sun was brighter and more beautiful than Myrddion remembered it. The villa was clean and white in the growing light, while the trees with their new, lime-green growth almost hurt his eyes with their brilliance. The sea caught the rising sun and turned the foam to lacy gold as if the attendants of Poseidon had dressed themselves in cerulean blue and pearl. Myrddion was so taken with this metaphor that he imagined how he would dress Poseidon, should the god be disposed to ask advice from a boy. Chuckling at his thoughts, he traversed the winding shoreline paths, kicking at clods of earth and tussocks of sea grass as he went.

Segontium was only beginning to stir when Myrddion hurried through its streets. Servants opened shop fronts and shook out mats to place on the thresholds, while others brought wicker baskets of fruit and vegetables or bundles of birch brooms and other wares to tempt the passers-by. Kitchen fires sent out plumes of grey smoke, and as he moved through the town the rising sun seemed to encourage the citizens to hang out washing on lines strung between trees, while the low hum of noise vibrated as villas, cottages, and two-story wooden and stone dwellings came to life. With his feet stirring a faint memory of frost on the grass, Myrddion's heart lightened as he saw Annwynn's cottage, its pond, and its many outbuildings at the end of the dusty road.

Boudicca was already out, teasing the hens and frolicking in deep drifts of clover that were already buzzing with bees. The greying dog gave a bark of greeting and went back to her ecstatic rolling in the dark green weed. Annwynn was using a short paddle of wood to stir the steaming contents of a large copper cauldron that had been placed over an outside fireplace. As Myrddion watched, she wound a hot, wet mound of boiled rags around the paddle and heaved the sodden mass out of the huge pot and into a willow basket. A makeshift line that stretched between her apple trees was already festooned with cloth hung out to dry in the strengthening sunshine.

The healer looked up, wiped her sweating brow with her forearm, and noticed her visitor.

"Well met, young Myrddion. Welcome! The day is half-done already, so we must hurry. Have you eaten, lad, or are you too shy to dine in a witch's kitchen? Do you want a drink of cool water or one of my herb infusions? Are you warm enough, or can I find you an old cloak?"

Myrddion laughed self-consciously.

"Do you plan to let me answer, Mistress Annwynn? I've already eaten, but I'd love some more food. Gran says that I'm growing, so I'm always hungry. I'd really enjoy one of your herb ... er ... whatever you called them, and I'm warm enough, thank you. I'd never call you a witch unless I had decided to name my grandmother as one. She's a priestess of the goddess and she swears that one of her mother's ancestors was kin to Ceridwen. Gran works with herbs and simples too, but she wouldn't teach me, for she thought that if people knew I was learning about such things I'd be damned as evil because of my father. But I'm babbling on like a fool, mistress, so please forgive me. I'm nervous so I want to make a good impression on you."

Annwynn narrowed her eyes against the sun's rising glare and shaded her face with one forearm. The boy stood easily, with a tall lad's natural grace that had no gawkiness in it. His hair was uncut and fell below his shoulders in a straight, glossy curtain. At his right brow, a few strands of pure white marred its blue-black glossiness and Annwynn felt a shiver of concern to see the thumbprint of prophecy marked on the boy.

In all other ways, Myrddion was a beautiful specimen of youthful masculinity. Although he was slender, Annwynn's keen eyes picked out the long muscles that sheathed his arm and leg bones and promised strength and resilience. His brows turned up at the outer edges, giving his face a quizzical and slightly devilish cast, but his dark, almond-shaped eyes nullified any negative effects. The womanish lashes that accentuated the beauty of those eyes added to the softness and purity of his face, with a mouth that was delicately modeled and quick to smile. Even Myrddion's teeth were perfect and Annwynn felt a moment's resentment towards a child who was so bountifully blessed by nature. As a child, Annwynn had been plump, awkward, and plain, so she had been judged as useless for any task other than the endless corrosion of hard, physical labor leading to an empty future.

Ah, Annwynn, you're being unjust! The boy can't help his good looks any more than you can change your plain features. It's what's inside that counts, and this lad is passionate to learn my craft. From me! And he speaks and acts like a young man rather than an immature boy.

Annwynn's thoughts scurried back to her usual, sunny view of the universe. Dumping her basket of steaming rags onto a nearby tree stump, she ambled over to Myrddion and threw one heavy arm over the boy's shoulder to usher him into her cottage.

Gazing around at the fascinating array of drying herbs, jars of mysterious objects, and warm, colorful weavings, Myrddion realized that nothing in Annwynn's cottage had changed since his last visit. The boy sighed happily.

"Sit you down, Myrddion. Do you like mint? Yes? Then you shall try my mint tisane. But first I must explain your duties, for I will be your mistress and you must accord me the respect due to your teacher."

As she spoke, she bustled around the fireplace until she found two beakers, spooned some odd, dried something into each one, and then poured hot water over the shriveled, chopped leaves. The steam wreathed around her plump face, which had developed a network of new wrinkles around her twinkling eyes as she smiled.

"I will obey you in all things, mistress," Myrddion replied earnestly. "I am grateful that you consider me fit to be your apprentice."

"And you are only . . . eight . . . nine, isn't it? Your gran has taught you courtesy, but the gods alone know where you got your brain. You sound like a little man, Myrddion, but you don't need to pretend with me."

"Mistress, I'm not pretending, truly I'm not." He sipped carefully from the beaker of mint tea while he tried to decide what to say. "People laugh at me behind their hands because they believe that Gran has trained me like a pet dog. Yet this is the way I am, for good or ill. I talk this way naturally." He looked down at the beaker in his clenching hands. "I wish I didn't. I would like to be like every other boy . . . but I'm not, and I can't change the way things are."

The boy looked so forlorn that Annwynn changed the subject and began to explain his duties. Each day, he would arrive before dawn and collect herbs for drying, boil the rags used to bind wounds, and clean the tools that Annwynn used as part of her trade. Then he would collect the eggs, milk the cow, sweep the cottage, and weed the vegetable gardens. At midday he would eat. In the afternoon, if Annwynn had no patients, she would show him how to make the various poultices for sprains, breaks, cuts, and boils.

As he became more able, he would help his teacher with patients and learn the more complex problems of internal diseases and their treatments. Annwynn welcomed note taking, and if he wished to assemble a scroll on her medicine, then she had no objections.

And so Myrddion's apprenticeship began.

Although Olwyn worried about his extreme youth, the children of the peasantry commonly began training for a life of labor at an even younger age. Toil was the natural and inevitable lot of the poor, and a bastard like Myrddion could not expect to inherit anything from his mother, his grandmother, or the king of the Deceangli. He had been made aware from the cradle that he must earn his own bread, so he went happily to Annwynn's cottage every morning, with only the occasional holy day when he could completely relax and play.

The boy loved the early mornings best. He enjoyed hunting for mandrake root, edible and poisonous mushrooms, and fungi of such brilliant colors and interesting textures that they resembled exotic night flowers. Annwynn was a master of herb lore and her knowledge of the properties of plants was so extensive that Myrddion begged his grandmother to provide him with some fine hides that could be used to construct a series of scrolls. Ambitiously, the boy planned to immortalize the whole of Annwynn's vast knowledge. So, although each day consisted of hard labor, he spent his nights hunched over a small table scribing every newly learned detail of plant lore onto his scrolls by the light of an oil lamp. Many years later, when he was a very old man, the scent of fish oil, pungent and slightly rancid, reminded him of the flanges of the vivid yellow and red fungi that grew in the forests outside Segontium.

"Different parts of the country host different plants, depending on the weather, the trees that predominate in the forests, and the richness of the soil," Annwynn explained. "In other countries, especially those that have a warm climate, the flora will be totally different from what we have here. Oh, lad, I sometimes wish I could travel just to discover all there is to know about everything that grows. How wonderful it would be to find plants that are unknown, and to discover what properties they have in the preservation of health and life."

Annwynn's eyes would glow with enthusiasm and her whole face be transformed when she considered such wonderful propositions. At those times, Myrddion truly loved his mistress, not for her kindness or for her generosity of spirit, but for the avid breadth and depth of her mind.

Eighteen months passed happily and productively, while Myrddion grew like a weed and his mind stretched and expanded with the exacting challenges of his position. At first, the villagers distrusted the touch of the demon child, but Annwynn suggested that his ancestry was an aid to her medicines, for Myrddion had chosen to follow the human half of his blood, rather than the temptations of wickedness. As a further incentive, the boy had a delicate touch and rarely caused pain, no matter how terrible the wounds might be. And then came the night of the fire at the Blue Hag Inn.

Segontium had several taverns, but the Blue Hag was by far the largest establishment of its kind in the town. Although it had a flag-stone floor, the inn was of two-storied timber construction, with a gimcrack series of rooms above the more sturdily built ground floor.

How the fire began would remain a matter of conjecture, but its outcomes were tragic and would set Myrddion on a life path that would cause him to become an extraordinary man.

THE FIRST WARNING that Myrddion received of the fire was a ruddy glow in the distance from the direction of the township. Eddius pointed out the bloody haze to his wife and the other children, while the Greek servants set up a caterwauling of fear and distress.

"Cease that dreadful noise, Crusus!" Eddius ordered crisply. "The villa isn't alight, so call out the field hands and we'll try to assist the citizens of the town."

Olwyn clutched her skirts with whitened knuckles. "Be careful, husband! I've always been fearful of fire in towns where whole streets can be destroyed in minutes. May the goddess save the people from too much loss of life."

"I must go to my mistress," Myrddion decided and ran to find his satchel.

"No, Myrddion, you might be hurt . . ." Olwyn wailed after him, but Myrddion scarcely heard her. She turned back to Eddius. "If you need somewhere to bring casualties, husband, we can open up the ser-vants' quarters for the injured. Take care, my love."

Eddius paused only to stroke his wife's cheek affectionately and then began to lope towards the site of the fire, his long legs soon leav-ing Myrddion far behind. The boy struggled on, his senses acute in the darkness of the late evening. Autumn had just come to the land and the night air had an edge of cold, but Myrddion could smell the acrid stink of burning along with a sweet reek that reminded him of cooking meat. His child's mind rebelled while the older, cooler part of his consciousness reasoned that Annwynn would be desperate for help, even the ham-fisted efforts of a half-trained boy. He ran on towards the red glare of the fire.

The site of the blaze, the Blue Hag, was a small slice of the Christian hell. Flames had engulfed the lower floor of the inn and were now stretching out fiery tentacles towards the stables and the upper story of the main building. The shrill screams of horses confused Myrddion at first because the beasts sounded like frightened women. A girl at an open window on the upper floor was shrieking as well, and Myrddion turned away as she leapt from the open shutters with her woolen tunic already smoking.

"Annwynn? Has anyone seen the healer?" Myrddion shouted, but the men who were passing water from hand to hand in any buckets available took no notice of the wide-eyed boy. Only when Eddius saw him, as he threw a wooden pail of water over the roaring maw of the inn's public bar, did Myrddion receive any kind of answer.

"She's down the street outside the wool trader's establishment," Eddius roared, then applied himself to the hopeless task of preventing the fire from spreading. As Myrddion hastened to find his mistress, he saw frightened ostlers trying to drag maddened horses away from the blaze while other servants and visitors alike continued to throw themselves out of the windows of the second story.

"By the gods! Nothing can live in those flames!" Myrddion muttered, and raced over the slick cobbles until he reached the makeshift area that Annwynn had set up for the injured.

Women from the village had dragged pallets out into the street and woolen rugs were employed to cover those survivors who were shaking with shock. Myrddion stared aghast at the bubbled skin, burned hair, and charred clothing that seemed welded to shining and swollen flesh.

"You're needed, lad! I've brought some unguent for burns in my satchel but it won't last long. I also need at least one fine, sharp blade— you know the one I use! I'll need more unguent, and you can fetch all the poppy juice that I have to hand. Move! Oh, and I'll need more bandages and splints, and my pearwood box. I'll also need my stocks of mandrake and henbane seeds, and a mortar and pestle. Hurry, for love of the goddess! You know how to open the door."

Myrddion raced towards Annwynn's house, fleet-footed with the urgency of his mission. Only a few seconds sufficed for him to bypass Annwynn's safety measures at her door, and he began filling baskets with everything that he thought might be useful, as well as those items on his mistress's shouted list. Boudicca looked at him nervously, but Myrddion begrudged the time even to pat the head of the old dog.

"On guard!" he ordered her, and began the long run back to the fire, which had already spread to adjoining houses. Racing towards his mistress with the first basket of supplies in his arms, he heard Eddius screaming.

"Ignore the inn! It's lost, and there's no help for it. Start wetting down its neighbors! Stop the fires from spreading, or the whole town will burn to the ground."

Cinders were already flying on the light breeze and several thatched roofs were beginning to smolder. Men used makeshift ladders and woolen blankets to batter out the smaller flames, but where one fledgling fire was defeated three or four more sprang up in its place. The reek of burning houses, the stink of death, even the roar of flames and the screams of the terrified humans and animals, combined to create a gruesome assault on the senses until Myrddion was forced to shut everything out of his mind except for his duty to his mistress.

"To me, boy! We save only those who can be treated."

Then Annwynn put him to work.

Without pausing to record the faces of the injured, Myrddion smeared unguent over burned heads, limbs, and torsos. Where large areas of the body were affected, Annwynn simply shook her head and called for the poppy juice. On clean wool, and without a stitch of clothing on their agonized bodies, the worst injured then slipped into a deep sleep from which there would be no return. The dying were left on the street, while those who had some chance of survival were moved,

107

pallet and all, into the store to be out of the noise, smoke, and stink. Annwynn used too much of the poppy to permit the terminally injured to survive, and Myrddion could find no words to fault her, for those less injured continued to twist with limbs that were still smoldering.

Myrddion learned many lessons on that dreadful night, the most important of which was the care necessary to assist both the living and the dying. He watched the women who sat with the suffering as, inside the wool store, they talked gently and optimistically to the wounded. These women took care to give their patients careful descriptions of their injuries, while explaining Annwynn's prognosis for their recovery and calming them with cool water, common sense, and gentle words.

In the street, kneeling on the hard cobbles, older women sang lullabies, took on the roles of mother, wife, child, and lover, gave solace to the frightened, and stroked unblistered skin without showing a flicker of shock at terrible wounds and burns. Men, women, and children died gently, their path to the shades eased by the courage and love of strangers. As he watched such actions with deep humility, Myrddion vowed that he too would be a healer who cared for the dignity of the dying, as well as those lucky ones who managed to survive.

The night seemed endless. Myrddion was trusted to apply splints to broken limbs, for many poor souls had thrown themselves onto the flagging rather than burn to death. He had watched his mistress treat broken limbs of all kinds, and as long as the skin was unbroken Annwynn trusted him to pull the bone into place and bind it tightly with straight pieces of wood on either side of the affected limb. Myrddion grew used to hurting patients very badly during his ministrations, and his own body was soon blackening with bruises after kicks and blows from flailing fists or legs, even though he was assisted by those elderly men who were unable to endure the physical demands of the bucket line. Regardless of the pain, he worked on until the fire began to die under the force of the rain that had begun to fall just an hour before dawn.

As the sky lightened and the last of the wounded were finally moved into the wool merchant's store, Myrddion stretched his aching back and searched for Annwynn. She was surrounded by a group of sober-faced women as she explained the care that would be needed for more than twenty seriously injured patients. The healer badly needed to sleep and to replenish her supplies, but fortunately there was no shortage of wives and daughters who would labor for hours to ease the pains of the suffering. For the first time in what would be a very long life, Myrddion wondered at the generous natures of women.

Feeling his gaze, Annwynn looked over at him and smiled maternally.

The wool merchant's storage area had been roughly swept and bales of wool had been thrust against the walls to free a large central area where the pallets had been laid in rows. Sufficient space had been left between the pallets to permit the women to move around the occupants. Men and women in various stages of undress were laid on the makeshift beds. Splinted and bandaged limbs, salve-smeared burns, bruises, swellings, and all the horrible litany of a disaster of devastating proportions stretched out across the room so that Myrddion was forced to see only injuries, not people who had laughed, loved, and enjoyed life. To accept their humanity was to be crushed by the sadness of the whole night. In the darkest recesses of the barnlike space, other women plied their needles and sewed pitiful, twisted corpses into makeshift shrouds. Myrddion counted over thirty neatly laid-out bodies.

Annwynn stroked a shoulder here, or patted a cheek there, as she moved to the spot where Myrddion stood, awkward and lost, near the doorway of the store.

"You've worked hard, Myrddion, and probably saved many limbs during this dreadful night. Go home now and sleep for a few hours, and then I'll expect you back at the cottage, for I'll need you to prepare more unguent for the burns and boil up whatever rags we've used. I'll remain here for a while, and go home as soon as I can." She glanced along the rows of moaning, feverish bodies and their quiet attendants. "Many will die, Myrddion, no matter how hard we try. Do you understand why?"

When Myrddion shook his head slowly, Annwynn took the trouble to explain, although she was almost numb with weariness.

"You've seen how burned limbs can swell and split. Sometimes I cut the skin myself to relieve the agony. But our skin seems to protect us from evil humors that live in the air and on every common object around us, and when it is breached the humors find their way straight into our flesh and blood and the wounds putrefy. Some burned ones do live while others die, but I can't predict who will lose the battle. I have learned that if a third of the body is blistered, then the person cannot survive, but some patients seem to be on the road to recovery until their body heat suddenly rises and they die very quickly. I cannot even begin to guess what causes their deaths. Gods, we know so little of what happens with these wounds."

Annwynn shook herself vigorously, patted Myrddion on the head with sad affection, and told her apprentice to ignore her mood and hurry off home.

Myrddion closed the wool storage door behind him carefully and quietly and gazed along the street towards the spot where the Blue Hag had once stood. As he walked past the corner and down to the crossroads, the ruins came into view.

In addition to the inn, three other buildings had burned to their foundations, while others had been partially destroyed in the conflagration. Although the fires had been extinguished, wisps of smoke still rose from collapsed rafters and piles of ash. Warriors were searching among the ruins and a row of bodies lay on the cobblestones in a light drizzle of rain. For the first time, Myrddion saw the pugilistic stance of a cremated human being, arms raised as if to fight in a rictus caused by flame. As he walked along the row of corpses, he noticed that many of the skulls had exploded and, although his eyes were sickened by the blackened flesh and fused facial features, his brain was already seeking answers to these strange physical responses to burning.

"This charnel house is no place for you, young Myrddion," Eddius ordered, as he appeared out of the dissipating smoke like a black scarecrow, streaked with soot. Eddius was covered with the smuts of the fire that now ran in black rivulets down his cheeks and arms in the cold rain. The warrior had a slightly boiled look, and Myrddion realized that the fire had scorched those who had fought it so fiercely. Eddius's eyelashes and parts of his eyebrows, his beard and even the hair on his arms and legs had been singed and seared away by heat.

"Aye, Lord Eddius. I'll tell Gran that you're safe and will be home shortly."

"I'll return when I'm sure the fire is truly dead," Eddius agreed, and clapped his adopted son on his back. "You did well, boy. I don't know that I could look closely on such burns as you dealt with during the night. Fire is our dearest friend, but when it turns on us it becomes our most destructive enemy. I'll never again take a naked flame for granted."

Myrddion raised his eyes as he swore wholeheartedly, "Nor I, my lord! I swear never to treat fire incautiously again, now that I've seen what it can do."

"Good lad! Now, off with you. Get you home and rest for a few hours, for I've no doubt that your mistress has chores for you once you've slept and fed. Don't keep the healer waiting."

As Myrddion shuffled along the sea path, his sandals barely lifted out of the damp sandy sod through weariness, he looked at the turgid waves below him with new caution. Water and fire! Necessities if a man were to live. But the gods had provided each of these blessings with a nasty sting in the tail. With every gift, the gods created a curse.

When the villa came into view above the dunes, clean and white in the rain-drenched light, Myrddion's childlike heart wanted to weep at his homecoming. The familiar old walls promised safety and love, while the landscape around it, full of freshening sea wind, darkening clouds, and slow, heavy waves, threatened his comfort and existence.

Was anything as it seemed?

"I'm too tired to think now," Myrddion said to the rain as it struck his wet body with hard, little gusts. "I'll work it all out later."

Chapter VII

THE BROKEN TOWER

In the forbidding, slate-grey mountains, King Vortigern pursed his lips with disgust as he stared up at Dinas Emrys, his ruined fortress, where workers crawled all over the great stones, shaping and moving them until some semblance of order could be reimposed on the chaos of fallen walls.

"The work goes well?" he asked his steward without turning his head.

"Aye, lord," the steward replied impassively. "As the prophecy demands, Dinas Emrys will return to life."

"The prophecy!" Vortigern snapped vindictively, recalling his chief sorcerer, Apollonius, who had sworn that the gods had told him that the king would perish at the hands of his sons if Dinas Emrys did not rise again. Vortigern had cursed Apollonius and his convenient dreams, but he had ordered the reclamation of the fortress anyway. With prophecies, a wise man always chooses to be certain.

Dinas Emrys had originally been built on a large shelf of rock overlooking the river valley that spread out below it like a green quilt. This narrow, arable valley, and the wealth that came from rich soil, had obviously merited protection in ages past, although Vortigern's strong right arm and the strength of the tribal kings now maintained peace in the land without the need for an impregnable fortress.

But the king had decided to stir himself and restore Dinas Emrys to its original strength. Any sensible subject obeyed King Vortigern without question, for he was a man of volatile moods and a willpower that was famed for its inflexible, unyielding stubbornness.

In appearance, Vortigern was neither tall nor short, standing at a thickset five feet eight inches. His shoulders were very wide and his neck was thick and muscular, so that his head jutted forward like that of a pugnacious bull. The similarity was accentuated by flaring nostrils and a broad forehead that bulged over thick, black brows that almost met above the nose.

Vortigern's hair was very curly, so he chose to keep it cropped close to his skull. Once coal black, his curls were now iron grey and still as plentiful as ever, except for a bald patch on the crown that Vortigern disguised as best he could. In fact, the king was a very hairy man who sprouted white hair in tufts from his ears and nose, and in swirls and curls across his broad back and his barrel chest. His body slaves regularly trimmed this excess, for Vortigern was also very vain, especially of his smooth skin and unlined eyes, which were green and set wide apart. Beside his obvious strength, one feature warned even the innocent and the unwary that Vortigern was a dangerous man. His mouth was very small and his lips were red and as full as those of a fair woman, carrying the suggestion of a smile that persisted even when he was annoyed. When rage consumed him, that mouth became ruby red and glistening, as if the choler in his temper lent his lips a semblance of seductiveness. His tongue darted repeatedly between his small white teeth, as if he tasted something pleasant and wished to enjoy its sweetness constantly. His enemies likened this action to the flickering of a serpent's tongue, implying something reptilian in Vortigern's nature. More than one victim had been deceived by that voluptuous half smile, as the cruelty of Vortigern's justice belied his womanish mouth.

The High King of Cymru was irritable and homesick, so his retainers stepped cautiously in his presence. Vortigern missed Rowena, his queen, and he cursed the prophecy of Apollonius that had brought him to this cold, barren place of flint and granite to oversee the restoration of his fortress.

Rowena's yellow plaits, so long and thick with their heavy lacings of golden cord, besotted the king. He loved to loosen those plaits, running his fingers, comblike, through the sword length of hair as it sprang free of its tight constraints. Rowena's hair was a wonder, a marvel here in the west of Cymru where redheads and dark-haired folk predominated. Her blue eyes were quite different from the Celts' as well, in that there was no green or gold in their ice-blue depths, only a circle of indigo around the very edge of the pupils. The blue eyes of the people of Cymru were more interesting, but Saxon eyes were hypnotically pale and cold, like northern skies or saltwater.

Sighing despondently, Vortigern sawed on his horse's tender mouth with the reins and headed back towards his camp. With his personal guard thundering behind him on huge heavily muscled steeds that were more suitable to the plow than to hill country, the king and his warriors set the flintstones flying as they crashed back towards kinder country. Vortigern's guard, one and all, were huge Saxons who could only ride the heavier farm beasts, and they gripped the reins with a fierceness born out of an inward terror of their animals rather than good horsemanship. Given a choice, Saxons never rode at all.

As protection, and to underscore his authority, Vortigern had rammed an iron cap over his curls. The helmet was decorated with a pair of bronze wings spread wide from its sides, as if gulls' wings had been turned to red metal. Most of his countrymen were offended when they saw that helmet, for the wings turned a serviceable tribal cap into a piece of Saxon body armor. Under the shadow of the helmet, the king's face revealed a lifetime of decision making and authority through its deep furrows between the eyes, the long creases that ran from each nostril almost to his chin, and the parallel lines that drew down each corner of his mouth. The king's irises seemed to trap the light so that no luster escaped to give them any pretense of geniality. His eyes reminded most men of the frozen earth, caught in the first frosts of winter when life has burrowed deep into the soil to preserve itself from the cold.

"Find Apollonius and Rhun! I'm growing impatient and summer will be done soon enough. Once winter comes, the fortifications at Dinas Emrys will be too wet and cold for repair. We must hurry!"

As AUTUMN CAME sweeping in across the mountains, Segontium shivered in its russet and amber cloak of leaves. Myrddion was still a boy of ten, long of leg and sharp of eye, but already he had seen suffering enough, and his joy was clouded by his knowledge of the dangers of the world. Olwyn often caught him looking at her young brood with eyes that were narrowed with caution and fear.

"What ails you, precious?" she asked him, as Myrddion watched the two smaller children chase chickens in the forecourt of the villa. She stroked his glossy hair back, and saw a growing number of white hairs over the right temple. Her hand checked its gentle caress for a heartbeat as she recognized the mark of the far-sight, as the peasants called it, before her love overcame her superstition.

"Why do we have to die, Gran? If the Mother and Grannie Ceridwen know so much, why do they permit everything in the world to be born, only to die so pointlessly? It's so wasteful, Gran!"

Instead of laughing at him, as many women would have done, Olwyn took Myrddion's fears seriously and answered them in kind. "No one can know the mind of the Mother, my boy, not even one of the priestesses, and wisdom isn't mine just because Ceridwen is a distant ancestor. I can only guess at their reasons. But I believe that nothing dies, not completely. Our bodies are fragile shells and we can be snuffed out so easily. You saw our frailty at first hand during the fire at Segontium not so long ago. But what happens when flowers die during the winter?"

"They appear out of nowhere during the spring and the summer," Myrddion replied slowly, with darkly knit brows.

"Aye. The flower becomes a bulb or a seed that lives under the soil, regardless of how much snow is piled above it. Then, when the winds blow warmly and the snow is gone, the bulb shoots and the flower bursts forth again. If flowers can live, die, and live again, then so can we."

A slow smile grew as Myrddion absorbed this simple concept. As usual, he took Olwyn's idea to the next logical step.

"If we are correct, the bulb that looks dead and is hidden in the soil is our soul—the center of our being. I sometimes wish I could cut open a dead body and try to find this soul that is the most important part of all of us. I will do it one day, but I'm afraid that our spirit is like the warm wind. I think it is invisible, and can grow in another body and allow us to go on and on, like flowers and trees and grasses that live forever."

Although Olwyn felt a little queasy to think of her grandson defiling a corpse, she understood his need to know, so she convinced Myrddion that he shouldn't try such a dangerous experiment until he was older and safe from the superstitions of the uneducated.

"Remember, Myrddion, that the sun and the moon rule you, which is very strange and miraculous. You have a great destiny, for all that you are distrusted by foolish people who believe in demons. One day you might meet your birth father and learn that he is a cruel man, but not a supernatural being. For now, you must understand that wickedness is more terrible and terrifying than a thousand demons or a dozen necromancers. They have no power to harm you, for magic is only a charlatan's trickery. Walk with an unbowed head and know that I'll always love you."

Myrddion was enjoying a wonderful relationship with the healer Annwynn, his teacher and second mother. Since the night of the great fire, the young man had been full of questions that she had struggled hard to answer. Sadly, although Annwynn had the experience necessary to be a great healer, her illiteracy barred the scrolls of the ancients from her understanding forever, and she recognized this lack in her knowledge. Therefore, not long after Myrddion's eleventh birthday, she decided to give Myrddion the most precious thing she owned.

Myrddion had labored hard that day. He had harvested the last of the herbs from the kitchen garden, bound them in neat bundles, and hung them, upside down, from the smoke-stained rafters of the cottage. In the afternoon, he had gone into the vestigial forest to hunt out any roots, wild parsnips and radish, mandrake, mushrooms, moss, and lichen that hadn't already been harvested during the summer months.

He had returned to Annwynn's cottage with several full baskets of bounty, his face smudged with dirt, his hands filthy, and his feet shuffling with weariness. But, by the shine in his expressive eyes, Annwynn knew that the boy had seen things that had given him enormous pleasure. He was eager to share his experiences.

"I saw a merlin as it took a rabbit, Annwynn! Such a large victim! I could scarcely believe the bird could lift it, least of all take to the wing with the coney in her talons. The merlin's wings were barred with white as if winter were here already, and her claws were particularly long and hooked. I couldn't believe the strength and grace of her, especially as she flew off towards the mountains."

Annwynn smiled down at her young charge. "At this time of year, the birds have young who are not quite ready to leave the nest and need to be fattened up to survive the winter. Needs must, Myrddion, my lad. The female merlin must give her chicks the best chance of survival, so she'll perform huge feats of strength because instinct and circumstance drive her onward. I have known women who've moved heavy stones to rescue injured children when, normally, they could never have hoped to budge such a weight. Love lends strength to all of us, but we don't know how such miracles come to be."

"We know very little, mistress, when all is said and done. So many people die of quite simple things. The blacksmith's son died of a toothache last week, and I couldn't believe that a tooth would be capable of killing a healthy young man."

Annwynn recognized the fervor of intense curiosity that fired Myrddion's large eyes. She smiled indulgently and tried to explain.

"You were here and you saw what I did to ease the boy's pain. Aye, I cut into his gum with a sharp, clean knife and the boy fainted with the shock and the pain. We could see the results. What happened, Myrddion? And why?"

"There was very little blood, mistress, but a rush of yellow and green pus poured out of the wound."

Annwynn nodded.

"I watched closely as you cleansed it. Afterwards, the cloth smelt rotten, as if something had died in his mouth. The stench almost made my stomach empty."

"That nose of yours is the healer's greatest tool, for we can smell putrefaction. Then what?"

Myrddion frowned and winced at the memory. "You packed his mouth with raw flax and the poisons continued to seep. The tooth was broken close to the gum and his whole mouth reeked. You cleansed the wound every few hours, applied hot packs to draw out the poison, and gave Rhys poppy juice so he'd sleep and not disturb the wadding—but he was still restless and in pain. Even when the wound stopped oozing pus, his jaw and his temples began to swell, and he started to rave in his sleep. His body grew hotter and hotter, so we wet him down, over and over, to cool his flesh. But nothing worked. He seemed to burn up from inside until he died in the early hours of the morning."

"Aye," Annwynn replied sadly, for Rhys had been fifteen years of age and was only newly wed. "The poison went to his brain and killed him. A simple toothache defeated me. For all my experience, I could do nothing to save him."

Annwynn looked so disconsolate that Myrddion made her a beaker of her favorite mint tea. He bruised the leaves a little in her mortar to release the fresh scent and taste quickly, for he knew that his mistress was troubled. She gulped a mouthful of the hot liquid, put down the beaker, and then clenched her hands together as if deeply in prayer. Having come to some kind of decision, she crossed the room to her thick woolen pallet and threw back one corner at its foot, revealing a heavy box some twenty inches high and at least three feet long and wide.

Myrddion goggled at the simple, undecorated container. The wood was strange and unfamiliar, and it possessed a pleasing aroma that Myrddion had never smelled before.

"My old master said the wood was called sandalwood, and insects would avoid the contents of such a box. I had never heard the name, but it is true that no moths or vermin touch any of the things he stored within it, and the perfume has lasted for forty years."

Myrddion stroked the surface and discovered that the wood was as slick as the finest imported cloth. He breathed in the heady, exotic scent and found that it lifted his spirits with its heavy opulence.

"Well? Open it then," Annwynn said, her face split with a wide, proud grin. "The box—and what's in it—is yours."

"Mine? Why would you give this lovely box to me, mistress? Your master left it to you and I'm no kin to be worthy of so fine a gift."

Despite his instinctive response, however, Myrddion continued to stroke the smooth, unblemished wood as if it were a living thing.

"The box isn't important, Myrddion, but the contents will be of vast use to you." Annwynn flipped open the brass catch and threw the lid back to reveal scroll cases and sheets of vellum, hide, and something that looked like pulped woven reeds. Where the individual sheets were visible, Myrddion could see close, small writing that covered every inch of each page. His breathing stopped for an instant with shock and amazement.

"What? Who? Er . . . I don't understand." Myrddion breathed in the heady scent of old scrolls, dust, and age, feeling his blood quicken in awe and disbelief.

"My master traveled all over the Great Inner Sea and served many important personages with his healing skills. He came to Portus Lemanis at a time when he was old and tired. I was his last apprentice, and he taught me all he could, but I couldn't read or write, so the scrolls were useless to me. My master knew he lacked the time to teach me, and asked me to protect the box and its contents until I could pass them on to a suitable healer. He was also trying to protect me, for women are distrusted if our mastery of medicine is too great." She sighed. "There've been many times in the past when I've lamented my inability to read. It may well be that the cure for an abscessed tooth might be found in these scrolls, and had I been able to understand it the blacksmith's son might have survived his illness."

Annwynn stared at her hands, and Myrddion sensed her deep and unceasing regret for the limitations of her skills.

"I could, perhaps, have learned to read all those years ago, although I was twenty years old and needed to earn my living. It was easier to put away my master's box after he died and promise myself that I'd learn to read the scrolls at some distant day in the future. As you know, I never did."

She lifted her eyes then, and suddenly her whole face was wreathed in smiles and merriment, leaving her pupil puzzled and off balance.

"Then a beautiful young boy with a broken thumb and a questioning mind became my apprentice. He had worked hard to master Latin and he took notes of everything he learned from me. My master would have liked young Master Myrddion, not least because he was rumored to be some kind of demon, for my dear old friend believed that all healers are touched by the gods in a special way. So! I've decided that the scrolls are now yours."

"You can't give them to me, mistress. They're too valuable—and too old."

"I can do as I please, Myrddion. And I do. You will use my master's knowledge and extend mine, because I expect you to explain anything you discover in the scrolls that might save some of my patients. Young men like Rhys make me feel a failure. So, take home my gift and study it well. Can you carry the box, or shall I send one of my neighbor's farm workers to carry it for you?"

Myrddion was forced to admit that the box was far too heavy for his journey along the soft, sandy paths near the villa, so Annwynn smiled her approval at his honesty and called for a farm worker who lived just outside Segontium. For a few copper coins, the man agreed to carry the sandalwood box to Myrddion's home.

That night, by the light of an oil lamp, Myrddion examined his windfall. Most of the scrolls were in Latin and covered a variety of topics, including battlefield surgery, infectious diseases, the plague, and simple wounds. For Myrddion, their potential was incalculable, and the boy couldn't wait to experiment with the information written so clearly on the soft doeskin in spidery black ink.

But the real wonders were the scrolls written in Greek.

Of course, Myrddion was as ignorant of the contents of these scrolls as Annwynn, for Greek was as foreign to him as Latin was to her. However, when it was unrolled, the very first scroll contained diagrams of strange body parts with descriptions in Greek and a translation into Latin. What a miracle!

Annwynn had understood that Myrddion would use his knowledge of Latin to learn Greek, and she blessed the day when a broken thumb had brought the boy to her door.

AGAINST ALL THE odds, Dinas Emrys raised its grey, looming tower over its halls, courtyards, and thick walls. Somehow, through threats, promises, and the expenditure of a small fortune in gold, the ruined fortress had returned to a semblance of life. With much panoply and blowing of rams' horns and the long brazen trumpets favored by the Roman legions, Vortigern came to Dinas Emrys with his lords, the Saxon thanes, and his extraordinary wife, Rowena.

The Great Hall at Dinas Emrys was small by comparison with many of his forts, and the walls of flint and bluestone were unmortared and drafty, as well as dreary. A roaring fire improved the ambience of the room, filled as it was with warriors, hounds, noise, and laughter. Drinking and eating, boasting and tricks from his chief sorcerers, Apollonius and Rhun, filled the early hours of the night until king and queen went off to a simple bed. His warriors burrowed drunkenly into the straw with their hounds for company to scratch and mutter through the night.

Vortigern was awakened from a deep sleep when the earth began to shake. With eyes half-blinded by sleep, he watched a huge crack appear along the corner of the walls. Leaping naked from his sleeping pallet and dragging Rowena with him, he pressed himself into the farthest corner of the small room, opposite the tearing stone. Dust filled the air, while a sound like an avalanche of flint and scree echoed and vibrated under the flagging. Then silence fell.

Hearing the shouts of his warriors and the barking of panicked hounds, the king dragged up his crimson cloak and wrapped a woolen blanket around his wife. Warriors burst into the room with drawn swords and escorted the royal couple down to the paved forecourt in case the earth should shake again. Men milled and shouted, horses screamed, and still more warriors fought a small fire that had been started by a fallen oil lamp in the stables. Dusty, smutted with soot and smoke, hair tousled and wild, the warriors sought invisible enemies with drawn swords and many pungent oaths.

Vortigern looked towards his great watchtower—and then he knew! Where stone had stood on stone and blotted out the view of the stars, a pall of dust now rose turgidly into the night air. The tower had collapsed as it tore itself away from the rest of the fortress, until now it lay in ruins below the cliffs that surrounded Dinas Emrys.

"To me!" Vortigern roared, the rage in his voice bubbling to the surface like hot lava. His tower had fallen and all his efforts at Dinas Emrys had come to nothing. As his warriors encircled him, Vortigern swore that he would know what had destroyed his tower, or every worker on the site of the fortress would be executed.

When the grey dawn stole over the hills, the sun picked out the broken ruins of the tower that had fallen, so that the shattered walls looked like a set of rotten teeth. Stones had tumbled and rolled down the hillside, and one side of the fortress gaped open in the cruel, unflinching light.

Vortigern rode away with his warriors and his wife trailing in his wake. Although the ravens rose from the woods in spirals of black rags, Vortigern scarcely noticed the portent. He did not draw rein until his troop clattered into the town of Forden, their horses half-dead with weariness. Yet no one, not even Queen Rowena, raised a voice in censure, for Vortigern was angry that he had been humbled by the revenge of the gods.

And so Dinas Emrys lay in abeyance, its stones scattered and its furnishings already looted by the hill people who seemed to grow out of the ground like mist wraiths as soon as the first signs of darkness crept up the valley. Vortigern's warriors had set sentries to guard the fortress and its breached walls, but to no avail. Small stones vanished, hangings from the hall that told of Vortigern's campaigns were stripped away, and even the new straw that had been laid down for the first banquet was stolen during the nights that followed. Despite the guards' best efforts, Dinas Emrys was picked clean, and the superstitious among the stoneworkers whispered that perhaps the gods were angry with Vortigern for welcoming barbarians onto Celtic soil, so that he had earned the wrath of the earth golems. Blessed Ceridwen had used her knowledge to tear these dreaded creatures from the earth, using fierce monsters to cast down Vortigern's pride and bring his dreams to mud and rubble.

But the workers whispered cautiously, for they all knew that the mud of Dinas Emrys smelled of old blood, so the wiser men among them understood that words spoken loudly sometimes tempted the gods to crush the unwary babbler.

Under the autumn rain and grey skies, they waited for the king to consider his options and make up his mind.

Chapter VIII

THE SONG OF THE SUN

onths before, and far away in Segontium, Myrddion was so happy that he feared such pure joy would cause the gods to be envious of him. The box had been polished clean, inside and out, and beeswax had been liberally applied to raise the grain and glow of the sandalwood. Myrddion experienced a sensuous pleasure every time he touched the surface of the healer's box and so he stroked it often, as if it possessed a soul and tangible flesh of its own.

The scroll cases had also been cleaned, repaired, and polished. The loose leaves of strange materials were preserved in the finest hide pockets that Myrddion could fashion, bleached and engraved in patterns of exquisite beauty. Even Olwyn was fascinated by Ann-wynn's gift, and puzzled over the sheets of strange fabric until her father came visiting in the summer, accompanied by his scribe. This worthy Greek had taught Olwyn what letters she knew, for Melvig had no love for learning and recognized no necessity for warriors, or women, to be literate. Only through great persuasion had Olwyn convinced Melvig that young Myrddion should be taught Latin five years earlier, so his scribe, Democritus, had found a suitable tutor for the boy.

Olwyn and Myrddion stepped away from the box and asked Democritus to give them his expert opinion on the scrolls and the loose sheets within it.

As the old Greek began to read the first script, he felt his knees begin to shake and his hands visibly trembled.

"Here? Here? In Segontium, of all places?" he muttered. "How can such books be here, in a place as primitive as this town of nothing and nobody?"

For an old man, Democritus was remarkably quick to drop to his knees and lift more of the scrolls reverently from their cases. His breath caught in his throat as he unrolled the brittle leather and saw two more blackened scripts, punctuated by drawings.

"By the heavens, boy, do you know what this is? Have you any notion of how precious this scroll is to any scholar?"

Myrddion shook his head. "It's valuable to me because I can read the Latin and I will become a healer."

"This tract is ascribed to Hippocrates, the most able of the Greek physicians and healers. This is a kingly gift."

Before Democritus could launch into another paean of praise about long-dead scholars, the boy broached his most urgent need.

"Sir, could you write down the Greek alphabet for me alongside the Latin version? I intend to teach myself Greek from these texts, but your help would make all the difference."

Democritus waved away the boy's request as if it were an uninteresting and trivial interruption. "Yes, yes, young Myrddion—before I leave. But look! Here's another! And yet another! All the great minds of Greek medicine have found their way here, into this humble box. Gods above!" he cursed reverently as he untied the shell-decorated lacings on one of the folders of loose pages. "Dear Hippocrates himself wouldn't be too proud to own this papyrus. It's Egyptian, my boy—Egyptian! It has been written in hieroglyphics and translated into Greek. This is a treasure trove indeed. I could spend what is left of my life willingly transcribing these wonderful relics. Any man who mastered the knowledge of these scrolls would become a very great healer indeed."

"Such is my intention, Master Democritus. I am apprenticed to Annwynn of Segontium and she has taught me herb lore and many of her skills, although I am not so arrogant as to believe that I have learned all that I need from her. She is a true healer, but she cannot read. Annwynn gave me this box, which once belonged to her master who died at Portus Lemanis many, many years ago. In return, I am to share my knowledge of what I read with her."

Democritus rocked back on his heels and peered carefully into the boy's open, shining face. He shook his head as if he doubted what he read in those transparent dark eyes and that eager expression. Then, sighing as if he had suddenly remembered his great age, he used his tall, twisted staff to drag himself to his feet. Shakily, he swept his grey hair out of his piercing eyes and combed his long, black-streaked beard with his free fingers.

"Mistress Olwyn, your grandson has received a princely gift that is far too valuable for a boy of . . . what is he? Eleven? This box should belong to someone more able to care for it."

Myrddion's eyes darkened and snapped with sudden understanding. His quick intelligence had already realized Democritus's intentions.

"Annwynn gave the box to *me*, Master Democritus. It is *mine*, because I am sworn to use the knowledge within it to hone her skills, as well as to learn myself. From what I have read, sir, the scrolls teach us how to cure illnesses, contagions, evil humors, and the wounds of battlefields and farms. They aren't meant to be studied by scholars, but were written to be put into practice so that healers could save the lives of the sick and the wounded. You must believe that I am sworn to do these things."

"Your boy is impertinent, Mistress Olwyn. You must confiscate the box and give it to someone more worthy of these venerable objects."

"You, for example," Olwyn said baldly. She had not forgotten his scathing remarks about Segontium.

"In the absence of any other scholar in this place—yes," Democritus replied blandly, his face smug with expectation.

Olwyn recognized trouble when she saw it. Excusing herself, she instructed Democritus to remain with her grandson while she found Melvig and demanded that her father mediate in the dispute between Myrddion and the old scholar. The king would decide who should possess Annwynn's box and scrolls. Olwyn felt her nerves twitch, for she was taking a calculated risk, trusting that her father would see that justice was done.

Unwillingly, Melvig accompanied his daughter back to Myrddion's spartan room, for he could see no reason why he should comply with Olwyn's demands. However, he soon balked once he was bombarded by arguments from Democritus, demanding that Myrddion's box should be confiscated. Normally, the king would have sided with any older person against the wishes of Olwyn and her hell spawn, but on this occasion he chose to take umbrage at Democritus's high-handedness.

"Where did you get this box from, Myrddion?" he demanded irritably. "Why would anyone want a box of scrolls?"

"Lord," Myrddion said softly as he bowed low to the king, "my mistress, Annwynn, gave me these scrolls concerning the art of healing as a part of my apprenticeship. She cannot read, and she expects me to translate them for her."

The answer seemed perfectly reasonable to Melvig, so his ire began to rise at this unseemly disturbance of his morning's rest. His time was being wasted to satiate the greed of an elderly scholar, a creature of no account in Melvig's prejudiced view of humankind.

"This box clearly belonged to the healer, Democritus, and she should be permitted to do with it as she wishes. If she has given it to Myrddion, I cannot see why it shouldn't remain in his possession. Why should you have it? I presume you want it, although you've avoided stating your intentions."

"Such precious knowledge from the ancients shouldn't be in the hands of an illiterate healer and a boy apprentice," Democritus retorted pompously, making his first serious mistake. "Someone who appreciates the knowledge within the scrolls should possess them."

For all his faults, the Deceangli king loathed intellectual arrogance. He grinned like an old grey staghound.

"These wonderful scrolls could be damaged by blood on a battle-field, or heaven knows what else if a village disaster should occur. Think of it, lord! The words of the great thinkers marred by pus or dirt. It would be wrong to risk such a storehouse of wisdom for the sake of a few lives."

Melvig drew himself up to his full height of five feet and nine inches. His mustaches bristled with indignation and his plaited hair would have stood on end had it been capable of movement.

"A few lives, man? In battle, my warriors often die hideously, and I'd be the very first to swear that any tool that saves them from suffer-ing should be used. Stained with blood, Democritus? So what, if men live when they might have died? No! Don't say another word! You'd pore over these scrolls for the sake of knowledge alone, and keep all the wisdom for yourself. At least this boy proposes to share his knowledge with all our people. I have decided that the healer is free to give her possessions to anyone she wants."

"But she's a woman!" Democritus wailed, making his second mis-take. "And she's illiterate!"

"And you're a pompous ass whose only talent is writing my let-ters," Melvig retorted, his face flushed with anger. "So get out of my sight, old man, or you'll find yourself begging for your bread."

Olwyn and Myrddion were effusive in their thanks as Democritus backed out of the room, but Melvig waved away their protestations of eternal obedience.

"Don't bother to make promises that we both know you won't keep," he told them, his humor much improved by their flattery. "Myrddion will be in and out of trouble all his life, long after my old bones are at rest. He's a lodestone for disaster! And you, Olwyn, will always take his part so that I offend more old servants. Yes, you will, girl, although I'll own you're more obedient than most of your sex."

As he left Myrddion's quarters, little larger than an alcove, Melvig turned back to proffer one last piece of advice.

"You should arrange to keep that box somewhere safe, boy, for Democritus is not above hiring ruffians to steal it. In his place, that's exactly what I'd do, if all other methods failed, so I advise you to conceal it carefully. You should ask Eddius for advice. That lad has admirable common sense."

WHILE MYRDDION WAS poring over his scrolls, painstakingly working out the Greek alphabet that Democritus had spitefully refused to give him, Vortigern fumed impotently in faraway Forden. Everyone suffered under the stings of his temper and his mood swings, even the previously inviolate Rowena, who found that for once the lure of sex had no power to soften the king's fury.

After two days of brooding, during which time he ordered a body servant to be beaten to death for dropping a rare glass beaker, Vortigern came to a decision. He must know the truth about his tower, even though Hecate, Ceridwen, or the Gorgon might pursue him, and even if the Wild Hunt of his ancestors found him abroad when next they howled through the sky.

For a heartbeat, his heated flesh cooled as he imagined a huge, antlered man-form as it strode through the wind-torn clouds, bloody eyes glowing like fiery pools, gigantic hounds and dim riders following in its wake. Primal, atavistic superstition almost overwhelmed him, forcing him to square his shoulders and still his suddenly shaking hands.

"Let come whatever chooses," Vortigern whispered, then turned to his manservant and bellowed, "I want Apollonius and Rhun. Bring those damned sorcerers to me. Now!"

The largest room in Forden's principal Romano-Celtic structure was neither spacious nor impressive, being constructed of a coarse plaster daubed over unmortared stone, with willow and lath subwalls. Their uneven surfaces created highlighted areas that danced and rippled in the uneven glow of aromatic oil lamps. Vortigern had discovered that the lamps were filled with fish oil when he had first arrived at Forden, and his anger at the stench had sent the citizens of the township into fits of panic. The wealthier shopkeepers of the town had soon found sufficient precious oil to sweeten both the air and Vortigern's foul mood.

The floors of this modest hall were at least flagged, unlike all but the Roman-influenced public buildings, for many of Forden's citizens lived on floors composed of packed sod, so iron hard that they could have been stone, except for a persistent patina of dust. Vortigern listened to the sound of his iron-tipped boots on the flags as he marched from one end of the long room to the other. Two wooden bench seats were set before a long, narrow table, laden with fresh fruit, nuts, bread, a whole wheel of cheese, and jugs of ale and cider. Grunting, Vortigern threw himself onto one of the benches, poured a mug of ale, and sliced off a hunk of heavy, yellow cheese.

A soft susurration of wool over stone caused the king to turn his head, the cheese halfway to his lips. Rowena smiled at her husband through full lips that were always soft and pillowy. Usually, her mouth captured her husband's full attention when they were alone, but now he turned away from her and bit savagely into the hunk of cheese in his hand.

"Sit, woman! I've ordered those charlatans that you've foisted on me to join us. My personal guard are ensuring that they are prompt in their attendance."

"You're being rash, husband," the queen murmured. "Apollonius can read the entrails of a suitable sheep for you and we will see what evil dwells below your tower. Should Apollonius fail, then my countryman will read the runes and he will know. Have no fear. Would I welcome frauds and cheats into our court? Would I imperil the strength and security of my husband's throne?"

Vortigern stabbed an apple with a narrow, delicate knife, whose silver handle was expertly molded in the likeness of a fish, scales and all. With elaborate precision, he began to peel the fruit in a long, continuous spiral, keeping his attention wholly upon his busy hands.

"Enough, Rowena! Oblige me by remaining silent. I don't welcome advice that weakens my position with the servants, so remember your place."

Flushing with embarrassment and anger, Rowena sat down stiffly, with a flounce of her long, ornately plaited hair. However, although her generous mouth was narrowed into a thin line of humiliation, she remained wisely silent. The king dissected his peeled apple into thin slices and chewed them into pulp before he swallowed.

Suddenly, with a great clatter of bronze armor plates, hard-shod heels, and the unmistakable noise of spear shafts striking the stone, Vortigern's guard entered the makeshift hall. Although there were only twenty of them, their size and discipline suggested a larger force. Young, ardent, and fierce, they dropped to their knees before their king.

"The sorcerers are here, lord," their captain stated, his ice-blue eyes and red-blond hair proclaiming his Saxon heritage.

"Where is Vortimer?" Vortigern asked as he waved a hand impatiently to bring the guard to their feet. "Where is my son?"

"He's in the south with his brother, lord," the captain replied neutrally.

A crafty smile flitted across the king's face, almost too quickly to be interpreted by an onlooker. "Keep me informed of Vortimer's movements, Hengist. I want to know at once if he attempts to leave Gwent for the southern lands held by Ambrosius."

The king swiveled his body to stare down at Apollonius and Rhun, who had entered silently and abased themselves until they were merely colored puddles on the dusty floor.

"Rise. I give you fair warning that I'm not happy with either of you. You come to me with talk of murder in the night and nameless treasons committed by my own blood. Then you promise that my fate can be averted if I rebuild Dinas Emrys. So, I rebuild Dinas Emrys—and then the damned tower falls down around my ears and almost kills me. Why didn't you predict that the tower could have caused my death? Or are you paid to organize my assassination?"

Apollonius was a portly Greek, ostentatiously dressed in robes of many colors that were decorated with arcane symbols. He lifted his face, and Vortigern could see that the man's brow was beaded with sweat. His double chins jounced nervously. Vortigern grinned sardonically in response. Let the fat fool beware, for he was sick of half-truths, innuendo, and being led around like a straw king on a stick.

"Lord of all Cymru, I swear the signs were clear. How could we know that a more powerful master of the dark arts was waiting for you to visit Dinas Emrys? He blinded our senses to his presence and his foul spells caused the earth to cast down your tower."

"Plausible, Apollonius! But your words cannot be proved, so I wonder at your response."

He turned to the second servant. "What do you say, Rhun?" The slanting black brows drew together in irony, or craftiness. "Do you ascribe to the theory of a master sorcerer who is out to murder me?"

Rhun was unable to read the king's face, so he shrugged impassively. "I cannot tell, lord. How could I, if I have been ensorcelled? But, if you choose, I can cast the runes and give you a solution. No necromancer can control the runes."

A dangerous man! Vortigern examined every inch of the northerner who stood so calmly in his presence. Rhun was tall and very thin, almost as if he starved himself. Consequently, his cheekbones jutted out as sharp as knife blades and his nose was avian in its beak-like prominence. By comparison, his eyes were sunken deeply into his skeletal face and his mouth was a humorless slit seamed by wrinkles, as if a cruel torturer had stitched his lips together.

"I so choose!" Vortigern said tersely, although he felt a cold finger trace its imaginary nail over the back of his neck.

"Then I will cast for you immediately."

The runes were small tablets of whalebone or walrus ivory that had been marked with a hot iron, the marks then accentuated and blackened by charcoal to form symbols that Vortigern didn't understand. Rhun threw them onto the flagged floor where they scattered, bounced, clicked like finger bones, and fell into patterns that were incomprehensible to the king.

Rhun stared at the shapes they made with a kind of sick horror. He sighed and began to mumble under his breath. Vortigern grew impatient.

"Well, Rhun, what do your gods say? Speak up and tell me what you see."

"I fear you will become angry at the message and strike me down in your rage," Rhun murmured, his voice reedy and thin.

"I'll strike you down if you don't speak. Immediately!"

Rhun gathered the small ivory tablets together and placed them in a leather bag that he looped over his belt. Then, once the tools of his trade were safe, the sorcerer straightened to his full height and began to speak.

"Your tower is ensorcelled and I don't have the power to lift the charm that causes the stones to fly apart. Only you, Lord Vortigern, can bind the stones of Dinas Emrys together. Only you can find the child of a demon, sacrifice him, and, seal the stones with a mortar mixed with his blood."

Vortigern leapt to his feet and his beaker of ale toppled and spilled over the tabletop.

"A demon child? Where in this world would I find such a creature? You have found an answer that cannot be refuted and so think to keep your head. Have a care, Rhun, for I am not a fool—and I'm not a man to cross."

Rhun was silent for a moment, but then he gathered together his courage and used the sorcerer's old reply, half charlatan and half prophet.

"Only you, King Vortigern, can establish the truth buried inside the runes. Only you can seek out the Demon Seed. But beware, my king, for you may meet your doom when you find this child. Should the Demon Seed live, he will ensure that everything you have built is burned away. At Caer Fyrddin, where the runes say he was born, the Demon Seed will conjure a wind that will blow throughout these lands and scour away the last of those who love you. So, ask no more, King

Vortigern. I cannot read the runes any further, for they have closed themselves to me. Please, lord, ask no more."

Vortigern scratched at his chin with his forefinger and watched Rhun very closely, seeing a glaze of tears in the sorcerer's eyes. Rhun was terrified. Apollonius seemed to scent his comrade's fear, and tried to make his corpulent body as small as possible.

"Very well then, Rhun. I'll play this game of yours, but you have but three short weeks."

Peremptorily, Vortigern signaled to the captain of the guard to step forward.

"Send your men out. Search the north for the son of a demon and, if you hear of him, bring him to me, regardless of who he is. We will meet again at Dinas Emrys in three weeks, and if I have no demon child, then I'll use the blood of Apollonius and Rhun to cement my tower together. Now, go with the gods."

And, although his sorcerers were near to fainting with terror, they fled from the presence of the king.

"You CANNOT IMAGINE how frustrating it is to learn Greek from the alphabet," Myrddion complained as he sat cross-legged before his mistress's fire and filled clay pots with dried herbs and fungi. Myrddion was particularly skilled in drying, chopping, and preserving the raw materials of Annwynn's art. Even as he complained to his mistress, his nimble fingers sorted and packed the herbs and then sealed the jars with rag and soft wax plugs.

Annwynn had rendered sheep's fat over a fire outside her cottage, and once she had reduced the thick, yellow clots to a rather turgid liquid, she proceeded to beat and stir herbs and the mysterious substance into a smelly mix that fired Myrddion's imagination as well as his olfactory senses. The unguent that was the end product of the healer's labors served many purposes. One version was an exceptional drawing ointment that could force inflamed flesh to thrust out thorns, slivers of metal, and any other sharp invaders with a small rush of healing pus. Another ointment, with one or two added ingredients, soothed burns, scalds, and some infections. With her armory of opium, henbane, mandrake root, speedwell, juniper, tansy, figwort, and other plants, Annwynn fought her constant battle against injury, disease, and accident.

But Annwynn had been trained by a master who provided her with instruction based upon the teachings of Galen, the ancient healer who had revolutionized physicians' knowledge of anatomy. An oilskin on her wall, kept rolled up for protection, showed the hidden interior of the body and ascribed purposes to each organ according to Galen's wisdom. Annwynn whispered to her apprentice that Galen had dissected a human corpse, an action that was frowned upon as blasphemy by all sensible Celts.

"All battlefield surgeons have seen those same organs ripped apart by sword, axe, and spear, so there's no mystery in the human body to those who work elbow-deep in the blood of the wounded, except for where the soul lives," Annwynn explained as Myrddion continued to fill the pots with dried herbs and simples. "I've always believed it to reside within the brain."

"From my readings, I don't believe that any man can live when the brain is breached, mistress, although one of the Egyptian scrolls has a drawing of a physician opening a hole through the skull."

"Aye, Myrddion, it's called trepanning," Annwynn answered idly as she mixed tinctures of opium. "I've never seen it, although my master told me that the procedure relieves pressure on a wound by letting out excess blood. He said that some men have been known to live through the operation."

"Well then, mistress, since all other organs die when the heart is stilled, perhaps the heart might be the dwelling place of the soul?"

Annwynn grinned at her apprentice as her hands followed their accustomed patterns.

"The scrolls speak the words of the Greek, Hippocrates, who bound his apprentices to the principle that no healer should use harmful poisons or do anything to hurt the body of the patient. Hippocrates makes sense to me, Annwynn. He also speaks against bleeding out bad humors in the blood, which Galen proclaims to be a healthful cure. I know that you don't bleed your patients, mistress, even though you admire and practice many of Galen's ideas."

Myrddion looked so serious as he confronted his teacher that she laughed with delight.

"Oh, Myrddion, how serious you are. Aye, I don't approve of bleeding generally because the patient becomes very weak during the treatment. And sometimes that feebleness causes their illness to advance. But I saw my master achieve miracles with one man who suffered from choler. His face was bright red, and he had peculiar lapses wherein he was desperately short of breath. While my master treated him, he was well." Annwynn could almost see the workings of Myrddion's mind. "See, boy? You've already helped me by offering the words and thoughts of another healer. I will dwell on your words, Myrddion."

"I will also dwell on the practice of bleeding, mistress."

She smiled at him affectionately. "The sun is still warm, Myrddion, so today's a good time for you to spend the afternoon at play. It's not healthy for a lad of your age to spend all your free hours with an old woman."

"Aye, mistress. I've finished the dried herbs anyway," Myrddion replied as he uncoiled his long body and climbed to his feet. As she watched, Annwynn envied her apprentice his youthful flexibility and ease of movement.

"We'll look at the tools of the physician and the surgeon tomorrow. You'll need to have your own set made by the blacksmith, so bring all your attention when you arrive in the morning. Shite, boy, they're only tools of iron, you know," she added as Myrddion's face glowed with pleasure at the promise of such a treat. "They aren't made of gold or silver."

"I'll be early, Annwynn, I promise."

Then, with a skip to his step, the boy was gone. He left an empty space in her afternoon, and even the warmth of the sun seemed weaker for his absence.

Myrddion's buoyant spirits lasted all the way along the track and the Roman road that led from Annwynn's cottage towards Segontium. With eyes blinded by pleasurable anticipation, Myrddion scarcely felt the nip of late autumn in the wind, for his thoughts were wholly occupied by the excitement of finally learning to use scalpels, bone drills, and nasal probes. He saw the golden gorse and hawthorn hedges, the green hills with sheep grazing on their flanks like little puffballs of cloud, and, in the town itself, the wheeling, crying gulls. Even weak sunshine was sufficient to give the mean streets a glister of gold on rough cobbles where a light shower had marooned little puddles of water. All was well in Myrddion's world and he believed that nothing could dim his happiness.

A gang of small boys was chasing each other through the marketplace as Myrddion strode past. One of the larger boys was throwing stones at a skeletal dog that yelped piteously when a rock struck its thin flanks. Without thinking, Myrddion scooped up the trembling animal and turned toward its tormenters.

"Pick on someone your own size," Myrddion yelled as the dog stuck its head pathetically into his tunic. "This poor hound is nearly dead from starvation."

"Who are you to tell me what to do, Demon Seed?" the bully yelled back, while his friends shouted encouragement in the way of all packs of dangerous animals. "Come over here and make me. Perhaps I'll bloody your nose for you."

"Yeah!" his friends chanted. "Demon Seed! Demon Seed! Demon Seed!"

Myrddion flushed so that two spots of color stood out on his pale face. "Next time my mistress asks me to lance a boil on your arse, perhaps my probe will slip and you'll sing castrato," he snapped back, for this bully was prone to suffer from painful swellings on embarrassing parts of his body.

His friends now shrieked with laughter at the bully's expense. "Castrato! Castrato! Castrato!" they howled, and the large boy turned beet red with fury.

"I'll catch you and turn *you* into a girl," he screamed as he rushed towards Myrddion, who skipped agilely away.

"You won't catch anyone with those fat legs of yours," Myrddion replied with a reckless grin and, with the dog still cradled in his arms, he ran lightly and gracefully away from the boys and their raucous catcalls.

From the arbor of a nearby inn, Democritus watched the exchange. Under the meager shadow of a gnarled, bare vine, the Greek's eyes snapped with sudden interest. Until the boys had started to shout their insults, Democritus had forgotten the talk that had swirled around Myrddion's birth some eleven years before, but now he began to wonder whether the story might be turned to good account. Perhaps he could still gain possession of the boy's scrolls.

The scholar was beyond any considerations of right or wrong. The existence of the scrolls ate at him, awake or sleeping, and he knew he was prepared to dare almost anything to hold those precious rolls and absorb their ancient wisdom. He had even stayed in Segontium when his master had ridden back to his palace, pleading illness, so he could find a way to steal them.

After all, what did the boy matter?

Democritus admitted to himself that Myrddion, his family, and every soul in Segontium was less important to him than even one of the scrolls that languished in the child's possession.

Within twenty-four hours, Democritus was presented with his chance for intervention when three armed men, king's guards by their torcs and arm rings, rode into Segontium. Their task was to find the child of a demon who was reputed to live in the north, and Democritus hurried to meet them as soon as he became aware of their mission. Not only were there three new gold coins in his purse, with the promise of more to come if his information proved correct, but the boy would be separated immediately from his most treasured possessions.

Myrddion's ultimate fate didn't worry the avaricious old man in the slightest, even when the troop captain explained that the boy would be sacrificed. Democritus shrugged. The knowledge of the ancients was more important than his duty to his lord or the Deceangli nobility. Melvig was a noisy cock strutting about his malodorous dung heap, as if Canovium were Rome or Athens and he the emperor.

As the warriors rode towards Annwynn's cottage, Democritus rubbed his palms together as if he could already feel the stiff papyrus between his fingers. He scuttled away towards the sea path.

Above his head, the gulls still squabbled as they waited for food scraps dumped into the open gutters. What did they care for right or wrong, theft or murder? Only the need for a full belly drove them as they swooped to snatch up rotting bread in their cruel, sharp beaks.

Chapter IX

TAKEN

For late in autumn, the day was clear and sunny once the mists had burned away and the light cloud had dissipated over the strait off Mona. A sea breeze hurried any rain clouds onto the mountains and sunlight turned the sea into a pattern of dark blue and pale washes of green and turquoise. The citizens of Segontium enjoyed the good weather, while even the animals in the pastures frisked and rolled through the dying grasses as if spring had come again.

Myrddion had reached Annwynn's cottage not long after dawn, just as the sun began to stain the grey sea. In fact, Annwynn was still plaiting her long grey hair by lamplight when the boy knocked on her door.

"You *are* eager, little apprentice. Are the tools of my trade so fascinating that you must haunt my footsteps before I have even broken my fast?"

Myrddion began to mumble embarrassed apologies until his mistress took pity on him.

"I joke, Myrddion. You must be hungry, lad, being up and out so early. I swear you've not eaten this morning—unless your gran begins her day in the dark."

"I didn't want to be late," Myrddion said. "I suppose I could eat a little something."

"A little something? Aye, my young prince. You'll eat me out of house and home given half a chance. I've porridge, new bread, honey, and fresh milk for you, so take what you need."

With a quick glance at her face to ensure that she wasn't angry with him, Myrddion sought out an early meal with the appetite of a healthy young animal. While he ate, he told his mistress that he now had a mongrel dog, and recounted his adventures of the previous afternoon.

"You must be careful, young man. Spite is a terrible spur for some people, driving them to almost any lengths to have their revenge. Other people aren't necessarily as honest or as well motivated as you are."

"Yes, Annwynn, I'll remember. Now, when can we begin working on the tools?"

The boy was like a sea sponge that wholly absorbed his mistress's words.

Mistress and apprentice were sitting companionably under her hazel tree, Myrddion practicing with a scalpel on the skin of an apple, when Annwynn observed three warriors riding up the path leading to the cottage.

They brought their horses to a halt, the three large, grim-faced men, fully armed, looking at the boy as if he were some dangerous beast. Annwynn struggled to her feet, her face creased with concern and a dawning fear that Myrddion was in danger. She positioned herself to stand between the boy and the three bearded, hulking warriors.

"How may I help you? I presume from your presence here that you need a healer."

"Stand aside, woman," one warrior ordered, as he unsheathed his long, barbarian sword. "We mean you no harm. We want the boy to accompany us to the fortress of King Vortigern. He is the son of a demon, and the king has urgent need of him and his special talents. We don't wish to hurt either of you, but the boy goes with us."

"But he is Myrddion, great-grandson of Melvig ap Melwy, king of the Deceangli clan. It's not fitting to drag a young prince of both the

Ordovice and the Deceangli tribes away from his home as if he were some common felon. Nor is it wise to draw a naked blade under a hazel tree. The gods will bring trouble to you and yours, for the hazel is sacred even to your barbarian peoples."

"King Vortigern decides what is fitting, woman. Enough! Tell the boy to put down the knife and come with us, or else we'll tie him down, muzzle him so he can't enchant us, and beat him senseless anyway, before we take him to Vortigern."

Myrddion shakily stood his ground and handed the scalpel to Annwynn.

"Tell Gran what has happened," he whispered. "And ask her to guard my scrolls with her life." He held his hands out to the waiting warriors, who looked a little shamefaced before the courage of such a young boy. "And take care of my dog, sweet Annwynn. I haven't named him yet, but he's nearly dead of starvation. I'll return, I swear to you!"

One of the warriors, the youngest, who had yet to grow a full, manly beard, coughed with embarrassment. He hadn't yet learned how to tell lies with his face as well as his mouth, and Annwynn felt the firm earth shudder under her feet as if it were dropping away from her. Although Myrddion's capture made no sense, she knew that the boy was in deadly peril, but she also recognized that she lacked the power to protect him. As the warriors bound his hands, she embraced him from behind.

"Your ancestor, Ceridwen, will protect you. Be bold, speak truthfully, and the Mother will protect you too. Here!" She reached up and thrust his satchel into Myrddion's hands. "Take it. My master swore that a healer always needs his kit when he hasn't got it."

As the warriors swept him onto the back of a horse where he was held tightly in front of the youngest warrior, Myrddion smiled warmly down at Annwynn as if she were the person needing comfort. Then, in a clatter of hooves and flying stones, the warriors galloped away to the east, bearing the apprentice with them.

Annwynn paused to tie up her trailing skirts, and then she ran as if all the demons of chaos were pursuing her. By the time she reached Segontium, her breath came gasping into her lungs and her heart was thudding painfully in her breast. Ignoring her exhaustion, she shuffled onwards, oblivious of the stares and superstitious mutterings of those citizens who took one look at her livid face and staring eyes and stepped aside. On the cliff path, the ocean breeze cooled her flushed skin and she knew that Olwyn's villa was close.

When she reached the forecourt at the double doors of the villa, she leaned on the doorjamb as she tried to catch her breath.

"Myrddion's room!" she gasped when Olwyn and her steward appeared, their eyes round and staring at Annwynn's disheveled appearance. Then, following Olwyn's pointing finger, she staggered to the indicated door. As she pushed it open, another guest of the house leapt back from Myrddion's sleeping pallet, which had been torn to pieces.

"You! What do you want, Democritus? Have you come to pick over Myrddion's bones before he's even dead?"

Annwynn's voice shook with so powerful a rage that she trembled visibly as she confronted the scribe. Fearfully, he stepped away from her shaking, accusatory finger.

"What are you talking about, mistress healer?" Olwyn whispered. Her dark eyes were suddenly very large in her ageing face. "Why should my grandson be near to death?"

"He's been taken by King Vortigern's warriors. He was abducted by force, but before they carried him off I swore to him that I would tell you of his fate. I also vowed to protect his scrolls and his dog from this scum."

As understanding dawned on Olwyn's face, Annwynn rounded on Democritus, who shrank back against the wall when the healer raised her long nails towards his eyes.

"You know why the warriors came to my door, scholar, don't you? Myrddion told me that you lusted after my master's old scrolls."

"He's here because he asked to see them," Olwyn interrupted. "I couldn't see any harm in it, so I allowed him to enter Myrddion's room. However, I refused permission for him to search through my grandson's possessions without my being present myself. It seems that Democritus hasn't respected my wishes."

"Anyone could have told Vortigern's men about Myrddion's birth," Democritus whined, every line of his face screaming his guilt. "Why do you judge me?"

"Myrddion's birth?" Olwyn whispered. Then, rigid with anger, she turned on the scribe with all the venom of a mother protecting her infant.

"Get out, Democritus! Leave this house before I set the field servants after you. My father will be informed of what you have done in spite of his warnings, so go now before I lose control."

Olwyn's face was parchment white, and her hands shook as if she had the palsy. Democritus ran as if the demons of chaos were after him.

"This land is not wide enough to protect you or hide you from me and mine if Myrddion should be harmed," Olwyn yelled at the scribe as he fled. "I swear you will beg me to cut the memory of those accursed scrolls out of your living brain before you meet your death." She turned. "Someone find Eddius in the south field. Run!" Her voice was hoarse with panic. "Please sit, Annwynn, for I swear you're about to collapse. That worm! That cowardly, lustful worm! Plautenes, find Crusus and some wine for our visitor. She needs sustenance, and our cook will soon restore her to strength. Hurry! I swear I'll murder Democritus if our boy has suffered harm. Hurry, Plautenes! Myrddion is in terrible danger."

But Plautenes had already departed and the villa seethed with scurrying servants.

Eddius came running, his face smeared along the jaw with a line of soil from where he had been supervising the plowing-in of the last of the crops before the winter winds froze the earth to iron. As he clattered into the atrium, Plautenes returned with a tray bearing beakers, a dusty flagon, and a platter of small oaten cakes. Eddius saw at a glance that Olwyn was terrified and that Annwynn was exhausted from her frenzied dash from her home to the villa.

"What's amiss? Are the children ill?" he began, but Olwyn cut off his questions and explained, with remarkable clarity, the terrible danger in which Myrddion had been placed by Democritus.

"We must do something, husband, for Vortigern will kill my boy, thinking he is a child of evil."

Olwyn was beside herself with dread, and Eddius longed to lift the fear from her shoulders, but only one solution presented itself.

"I'll send a message to your father. He'll not easily permit one of his great-grandsons to be carried off so arrogantly. I'll find Democritus as well, for I've a notion that Melvig will require an accounting from that creature."

"Aye, husband, but Vortigern won't care. I must go to him and petition him to spare our boy. Gods, let me arrive in time."

She hurried to the door, but turned back on the threshold to fix her husband with angry eyes. The gentle Olwyn was hidden now, and the Mother stared out at Eddius with an inflexible fury.

"If any harm should come to my boy because of the Greek, I want you to petition Melvig to have him choked by being forced to eat the scrolls that he lusts after. The man was prepared to sacrifice my boy's life for his own ambition and the contents of a sandalwood box."

Beg as they might, neither Eddius nor Annwynn could shake Olwyn's resolve to pursue the Saxon warriors. The stable boys were set to work preparing two horses for a long journey, while Plautenes and Olwyn's maidservants were sent running to pack a small leather bag with clothing and prepare another containing provisions for the journey. With some difficulty, Eddius convinced Olwyn to take a manservant as a guard, and Plautenes offered his services immediately. Within three hours, against the wishes of the household and with the wailing of her children following her into the long dusk, Olwyn was on her way.

HAD MYRDDION BEEN free, he would have enjoyed the journey from Segontium to Dinas Emrys. He had received few opportunities to examine fighting men and Saxons had been described to him much as monsters are used to frighten small children at bedtime. Even bound and uncomfortable, the boy listened intently to the warriors' conversations, examined their dress, and tried to work out the nuances of the Saxon tongue.

His personal guard, the young warrior called Horsa, was still child enough to while away the tedious journey by describing points of interest along their path. Sometimes he spoke in his own language and he would have been amazed had he realized how quickly Myrddion absorbed its common words, and how the boy's retentive memory allowed him to catch at the meaning of the Saxon's private conversations with his fellow warriors.

"I would not have thought that Saxons were so kind to demon children," Myrddion told him as they rode through the gorse-covered hills. "The old people of Segontium have told me that Saxons *eat* children, but you seem civilized to me."

"I am Frisian—which is not exactly Saxon—and I spent years with my brother in the court of the Jute king, Hnaef, in Denemark, which your people call Jutland. Yes, I'm civilized, but I wouldn't say such things to my brother if I were you, Demon Seed. He takes his ancestry more seriously than I do. I just follow him, even to this particular *Udgaad*."

Myrddion looked puzzled at the unfamiliar word and asked what *Udgaad* was. Fortunately, Horsa was an even-tempered young man.

"*Udgaad* is the Underworld, through which the world tree grows. Don't you Celts know anything?" He laughed delightedly at the look of consternation on Myrddion's face. "See how it feels to be spoken to as if you're feeble-witted?"

Myrddion drew his brows together and thought hard, then his brilliant smile washed over Horsa with genuine appreciation. "I do understand, and I'm sorry if I was insulting, but I wanted to know the truth. Saxons aren't all fair-haired people, nor are all fair-haired people Saxons. Only a child, or a fool, would make silly comparisons. Is that right, Horsa?"

The young Frisian laughed and nodded, then kicked his horse into a canter for the sheer joy of feeling the breeze through his hair. Seated in front of him, Myrddion laughed with the shared pleasure of being young and alive.

In the future, many of the Saxons of Dyfed would present as lice-ridden, cruel barbarians, but these later remnants of a once-proud people were parodies of Horsa and his companions. Horsa was tall, over six feet in height, and his body was already ropy with heavy muscle at the shoulder, forearms, thighs, and belly. Under his fur cape, Horsa's dress was unremarkable and Myrddion chided himself for believing that all Saxons were primitive brutes who were only washed on the day of their birth. Horsa's skin was mostly clean and his teeth were white and healthy. He had obviously chewed mint to cleanse his mouth, for his breath smelled sweet. With an engaging, quick smile, a pair of frank, pale-blue eyes, and a sprinkling of freckles across his nose, Horsa appeared to be a wholesome, amiable young man.

Nor were the other Saxon warriors so very different from their young companion. Their hair was pale, shaded from honey blond to auburn brown, and their beards were usually a little darker, luxuriant, and often curled. Of course, compared with Eddius, Horsa's companions were hairy and rather wild in appearance, but the boy recognized that they were the same as warriors everywhere, being primarily concerned with the weather, when they would next be paid, and how to keep their kit shining and clean. Willing women also figured prominently in their thoughts and their conversation.

Other riders joined the three successful members of the king's guard after the first day, and Myrddion was prodded and poked as if he were an exotic and dangerous animal. By Saxon standards, Myrddion was an unusual-looking boy with his long, blue-black hair, his forelock of white, and his odd, narrow hands and feet. They even forced his mouth open and examined his teeth. Myrddion suffered his humiliation equably, including the stripping of his entire body to the skin while the warriors searched for signs of his demon ancestry on his torso and limbs. Finding no obvious signs of abnormality, Vortigern's Saxons were disappointed, so they left Myrddion to dress as best he could with bound hands.

Myrddion was forced to beg for water on the second day because his captors seemed convinced that a demon's seed neither ate nor drank. The warriors weren't deliberately cruel, or even stupid in their misconceptions, Myrddion decided, merely superstitious and curious. But their fears and precautions caused him hunger, thirst, and acute embarrassment.

On the evening of the second day, Myrddion was given the opportunity to prove his worth to his captors. Horsa was an adequate horseman, as were all his fellow warriors, but he was nervous around his huge, hairy-footed mount and only prevailed by brute force and the beast's own passive nature. However, the most placid horse will still rear and fight his rider if fear applies sufficient spur. Under its hooves, the stallion saw a serpent coiled in the grass and, like all of its kind, was immediately maddened with terror.

The snake was small and brilliant in the autumn light, but cold, irritable, and frightened too, with a great creature blotting out the light of the sun. Fangs exposed and coiled tightly to strike, the viper aimed its head at the muscular legs that reared over it.

Down came the huge hooves. Myrddion gripped the mane with both hands and prayed to the lord of light that he'd not be thrown. Horsa wasn't so fortunate, and tumbled back over the rump of his terrified horse as it reared once more, before its hooves snapped the back of the reptile like a twig. With Myrddion clinging like a limpet to its mane, the huge beast reared again and again, until the snake was a dull, mashed mess of skin and bone smeared on the hard sod.

With admirable discipline, the Saxons threw themselves from their mounts. One warrior dragged Horsa to safety from under the dangerous hooves of his horse, while another lifted Myrddion off the broad back of the stallion and dumped him unceremoniously out of harm's way. When the animal finally quietened, Myrddion scuttled back to it and used the reins to draw it away from the battered remains of the snake before carefully checking its legs. He paid particular attention to its knees and hocks, especially where the coarse hair grew in whorls and spirals, as he searched for signs of a puncture wound.

"Hoi! What're you at, Demon Seed?" one of the Saxons bellowed.

"I'm checking to see if the snake bit Horsa's mount, because he'd hate to walk," Myrddion said quietly.

"Horsa's done for," the man replied laconically. "His leg's broke."

"He's broken his leg? That won't kill him. I'll have a look at it."

The warrior snorted at Myrddion with derision, as if any boy, demon or otherwise, could be of any help. "We all know bad breaks don't heal, and what use is a warrior who doesn't walk on two good legs? If he ever walks again, that is."

"I've been apprenticed to a healer, and I've mended dozens of broken bones. A clean break isn't always dangerous, so I'll try to help Horsa if you'll allow me to do so. He's been nice to me since we left Segontium."

"You're just a boy," the captain of Vortigern's troop muttered, although his pale eyes were speculative under his auburn-brown brows. Myrddion decided that blue eyes were expressive, contrary to popular wisdom that described them as cold and blank. This warrior was examining the boy with a careful, analytical interest that belied all the rumors of Saxon stupidity.

"I'm supposed to be a demon's seed, remember?" Myrddion retorted.

The Saxon spat with disgust and led Myrddion to Horsa, who lay prone on a soft swath of grass. One leg was turned at an odd angle and Myrddion found himself praying that the bone hadn't breached the skin. He knew he had insufficient skill to deal with such a complex wound.

Horsa was moaning and cursing in his own language, but Myrddion turned to the Saxon captain. "May I have a sharp knife, please?" he asked. "And I need my satchel. Would someone fetch it from the horse?"

The Saxon captain looked suspicious and lowered his red brows aggressively. "What purpose requires you to use a knife?"

"Horsa's wearing laced leggings that need to be removed if we are to fix the break in his leg. I want to cut the leather thongs that tie them together along the outer leg. It would be far too painful to take the leggings off otherwise."

The captain took a thin blade out of its narrow leather scabbard and proceeded to cut the lacings down the side of Horsa's right leg. The two pieces of leather fell apart, and Horsa stopped moaning long enough to try to cover his genitals with his hands. Realizing how foolish he looked, he pulled the leathers across to cover his embarrassment.

Myrddion and the red-haired captain both peered down at the affected leg. The apprentice sighed with relief, for although the lower leg was very swollen, the skin was unbroken. The captain reached out one large, freckled hand as if to touch the shiny, reddened flesh.

"Don't touch him! You can do serious harm if you don't know exactly what you're doing," Myrddion yelped, and the captain quickly withdrew his hand as if Horsa's flesh was about to burst into flames.

"Here's your satchel," another Saxon muttered as he handed over Myrddion's bag with the straps untied and the opening gaping wide. "I think everything's still in it."

Myrddion scrabbled through the contents. A small bottle of henbane seeds lay at the bottom, along with some clean rags, his notes, which he kept in a roughly cased scroll, a small jar of drawing ointment, and his quill and ink. As he drew out the scroll case, the Saxons eyed him as if he were mad.

"I need two stones, one as flat as possible, a beaker, and clean water. Boil the water! Then I'll need at least two large trimmed branches. They must be as straight as possible, and the length of Horsa's leg from the knee to the ankle. Can you do that for me?"

"What's to stop you taking off while we're playing healer?"

Myrddion rolled his eyes derisively. "How far would I get? I'm only half-grown and I don't know how to ride."

With much grunting and complaining, the Saxons set to work, using their wicked, two-edged axes to chop down several young saplings and beginning the task of trimming off the excess branches and foliage. The red-haired captain personally sought out a stone that seemed flat enough for Myrddion's purpose, while the boy hunted for a round piece of granite to use as a pestle. Before the splints were prepared, Myrddion had already begun to grind the henbane seeds into a fine dust, which he tipped into a small beaker of water.

As Myrddion worked, the Saxon captain lowered himself down on his haunches next to him and placed one large and surprisingly well-shaped hand over Myrddion's as he ground.

"Horsa is my brother, Demon Seed, and I have been both father and mother to him since we fled Frisia for Jutland when Horsa was nine years old. If you do anything to harm him, you won't have to worry about Vortigern. Do you understand me?"

"I understand, sir, but the duty of any healer is to do no harm. I will try to push his broken bone into its proper position and then bind it against a splint to immobilize the limb and keep it straight. This henbane will put your brother to sleep and take away the pain while we work on him."

The boy was so young and was proposing such a complex process that the captain was dumbfounded. He used his hand to turn up Myrddion's chin so he could examine the boy's face.

"You're like no boy I've ever met, Demon Seed or not," the captain murmured after he had peered into Myrddion's eyes.

"I've never met a Frisian except for Horsa," Myrddion replied. "So I don't know if you're like others of your race. But I know you're not a proper Saxon."

"You've a bold tongue about you, boy, I'll say that for you. Let's hope you're as good at your trade as you talk."

Myrddion nodded and lifted the beaker to Horsa's lips. Despite his pain, the patient looked doubtfully at the cup.

"Drink this, Horsa," Myrddion said softly. "It's grainy and hasn't suspended well, but try to get it all down. I know the taste is horrid, but it will put you to sleep so I can set the bone in your leg. You'll dream and you won't feel my probing and tugging."

Horsa stared up at the boy with dumb hope. He had seen the twist in his leg and knew that, untreated, he would always be forced to hobble around on a useless limb. Bravely, he took the beaker and gulped down its contents, then forced himself to scrape out the residue with the side of one finger and swallow the paste that remained on his nail.

"Good," Myrddion encouraged him. "Now we'll wait for the drug to take effect."

The Saxons brought samples of splints for Myrddion's approval. By now, the tall, muscular warriors were treating the boy as another man in response to his aura of knowledge. One of the warriors had shaped the sapling's trunk by splitting the bark and young wood away from one side to create a snug fit along Horsa's leg. Myrddion nodded with approval and the other Saxons sent wood chips flying as they copied the general shape of the accepted splint.

As soon as Horsa's head began to nod, the pace of the treatment escalated. Myrddion ordered two of the Saxon's friends to hold down his shoulders and arms while two others pressed their full weight onto his thighs and good leg. Once Horsa was securely pinioned, Myrddion knelt at the side of his patient and used his sensitive fingers to find the break.

"He's broken the large bone in the lower leg, and the two ends are overlapping each other. I'll have to pull on his ankle to draw them apart, and then reposition them so the bone can knit together. But I won't have the strength to do it by myself." Turning, he examined his scroll that was unrolled on the ground, then pointed to the captain of the guard. "As Horsa's brother, you must do exactly what I say. Please? I know I'm just a boy, but Horsa needs you to listen to me. I want you to sit at his feet, grip his broken leg by the ankle, and pull back steadily towards your chest. I'll guide the two broken ends together once we have pulled them apart and separated them. You'll hurt him and he'll be in some pain, but better a little hurt now than a lifetime as a cripple."

Rather pale, the captain did as he was told, and Horsa began to thrash his limbs and scream thinly, even through the soporific effects of the henbane.

"Ram a stick between his teeth if you can do so without losing a finger," Myrddion instructed a watching Saxon as calmly as he could. "But don't let him move."

Amazingly, the Saxon warrior obeyed the boy's commanding voice.

Myrddion acted quickly, his fingers beginning to probe the site of the break. Exerting all the pressure that his growing fingers could muster, he maneuvered the bones, praying that his strength was sufficient to complete the task.

Just when he thought they had failed, he felt the two edges of the bone slide together, the ragged edges grinding sickeningly against each other until they locked in position. Horsa had lapsed into unconsciousness at the most painful part of the operation, and Myrddion sighed with relief as one of the men placed the finished splints close to his hand.

Myrddion bound the leg at the site of the break, hoping to brace and protect the skin. Then, as quickly as possible, with the assistance of the Saxon captain, the splints were bound around the leg to immobilize it. Only when his task was finished did Myrddion allow himself the luxury of taking a deep, shuddering breath.

"Can Horsa ride when he wakes?" the captain asked.

"No, definitely not. Any untoward movement can dislodge the bones again. Next time, we might not be so lucky," Myrddion replied tersely, although he could see the captain reverting to his position as uncontested, autocratic leader of the troop now that the emergency had passed.

"Alric, ride to the nearest village and order a cart to collect Horsa. Once he can travel, take him back to Forden. We'll ride on with the Demon Seed to King Vortigern."

As far as the boy could see, the only advantage he had gained was a horse to call his own.

As Myrddion held out his hands to be bound once more, his packed satchel carefully placed over his shoulder, Horsa woke and saw his bound and splinted leg, although he was still groggy and his eyes were heavy-lidded.

"Boy! Come here!" he called, and the captain permitted Myrddion to kneel beside his patient. "Will I walk properly again? Will I remain a warrior?"

Myrddion gazed into Horsa's pale eyes and saw the terror hiding like a huge shadow behind the young man's flimsy façade of courage. The boy understood, for a cripple lived off the pity and charity of more fortunate men.

"As long as you are prepared to stay off your leg for at least six weeks, the bone will knit together and you will be strong again."

The young Saxon winced and his eyes clouded.

"I swear to you, Horsa. Your leg will heal if you follow my instructions and take care. The skin was not breached, although your leggings might never be the same again."

Horsa laughed, then quickly sobered. "May the gods bless you, Demon Seed, if such you be. And when I stand on my two good legs again, I will bless the boy who saved me. I will pray to Loki that you might undo King Vortigern's sorcerers, for only the trickster god can save you from Vortigern's intent."

The red-haired captain tossed Myrddion onto the broad back of Horsa's stallion, while a warrior held the huge beast by its reins. Myrddion looked down at Horsa and the warrior who was remaining with him, and the young healer's face was stern and serious.

"I doubt that we'll ever meet again, Horsa. But if we do, we will always be on opposing sides. That is a pity, because I admire you and I hope that you'll recover—even if time decrees that one of us may kill the other. I see you're smiling at my words, for we both know that King Vortigern intends to kill me." He shrugged like the child he was. "You must think I'm talking nonsense."

"I hope all goes well for you, Demon Seed."

"My name is Myrddion, named for the sun, the lord of light."

"Then I hope that you are right, Lord of Light."

Myrddion broke the serious tone of the farewell by giggling at Horsa's address and waving childishly as the warrior at the stallion's head arranged the boy's bound hands in its white mane. The Frisian captain kicked his mount's ribs and the small cavalcade moved out onto the path leading into the barren hills.

"We've lost hours of time and Vortigern expects us to arrive at

Dinas Emrys by noon tomorrow," the captain muttered, as he lashed his horse's flanks and the beast leapt forward. "We'll be forced to ride through the night."

As the afternoon descended into evening, Myrddion was seduced by the beauty of a moon that rose like a large, perfect pearl out of a grey-edged nest of cloud. Its soft, luminous glow touched the mountains, the helmets of the Saxons, and the bronze plates on their leather cuirasses with a gentle, opalescent sheen. Myrddion recognized the beauty that existed in their armor, even in their wild beards, stern profiles, and heavily muscled arms. These men were fashioned for war, but they weren't animals. Like the warriors who came from Dyfed or Gwynedd, they were also capable of love, honor, and gratitude, as are all men who fight for their coin.

Ignorant of their captive's thrall in the light of the moon, the Saxons pressed on, maintaining a steady pace to spare their horses from becoming overly distressed. When they paused in the early hours of the morning to rest their mounts for an hour or two, Myrddion was almost asleep and his legs and hands were numb from disuse. When he was lifted off Horsa's stallion, the Saxon captain was gentle as he laid him on a soft swath of heavy grass that had dried in the colder weather of late autumn. Hengist draped his own woolen cloak over the boy, remembering his own sons, far away in a sturdy hut on the island of Thanet.

A small kindness, but a nothing, really, in the fate of a promising lad who had been cursed from birth. Or so the captain told himself as the boy turned onto his side and lay with both hands curled childishly under his cheek. But Horsa was the captain's young brother, and Hengist had feared the prospect of losing him to suicide if the younger man had been doomed to spend the remainder of his life as a cripple. Hengist kept his own counsel, but he was sure that Vortigern was more truly a demon than this child of light. Then Hengist, mercenary and king's man, closed his eyes and surrendered to a brief hour or two of sleep. What would come on the morrow was beyond his power to change.

Dreams chased Hengist into the darkness. He relived the murder of his father, Uictgils, in one of the bloody power struggles that occurred after the death of King Uitta of Frisia. He remembered the loneliness of being an outlander in the court of the Jute king, Hnaef. And then the face of Myrddion loomed out of his dream like a memory of guilt. He owed the boy a bloodguilt that he would never have the opportunity to repay.

Above the boy, the oak tree shivered in the breezes that come before the dawning. Only a passing fox, returning to its den with a partridge between its teeth, scented danger and watched from the deep shadows. Myrddion awoke and saw its yellow eyes across the clearing, but he made no sound and allowed another wild thing to pass out of the sight and scent of man.

Not for the first time, the boy wished that he could live away from the prying questions and the untrusting eyes of his own kind. As he closed his eyes again, he knew that the day would bring a threat that would be far more dangerous than anything he had faced before. He would run in the wild with the fox, if he could, but he was the Demon Seed—and he had a destiny to fulfill.

FAMILY TREE OF VORTIGERN
(High King of the Northern Britons)

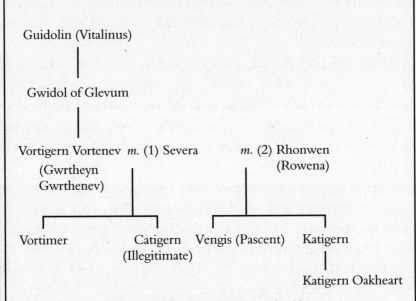

Guidolin (Vitalinus)

Gwidol of Glevum

Vortigern Vortenev *m.* (1) Severa   *m.* (2) Rhonwen
  (Gwrtheyn   (Rowena)
  Gwrthenev)

Vortimer   Catigern   Vengis (Pascent)   Katigern
             (Illegitimate)

                                             Katigern Oakheart

Versions of the legend vary considerably.

Vortigern's first wife is believed to be Severa, the daughter of Magnis Maximus and sister of Constantine III, a union that justified Vortigern's seizing the throne from Constans.

Vortimer is the legitimate heir of Vortigern and Severa.

Catigern is generally believed to be illegitimate, and was born to a servant girl.

The names of Rowena's children to Vortigern vary significantly throughout the sources.

Vengis (sometimes called Pascent) turned against his father after the death of Rowena. He is also reputed to have poisoned Ambrosius in revenge for the death of his mother.

The second son, when mentioned, is usually unnamed. I have called him Katigern and his imaginary son, Katigern Oakheart.

Chapter X

DINAS EMRYS

Their first leaders were two brothers Hengist and Horsa . . . They were the sons of Uictgils, his father Uitta, his father Uecta, his father Uoden, from his stock is drawn the royal race of many provinces.

—BEDE, *ECCLESIASTICAL HISTORY*
OF THE ENGLISH PEOPLE

T he sun had risen above them when Hengist finally ordered that the horses should be forced into a gallop. Every bone in Myrddion's body ached and he vowed to master the skills of riding if he should survive this ordeal. As the sun rose ever higher towards noon, the Saxon troop thundered through small hamlets, their conical mud huts surprisingly well tended, and the vegetable plots neat and weeded. Here was prosperity rooted in a narrow river valley of rich soil and plentiful water.

But the good earth was soon left behind the massive horses and their equally hulking riders. Now the landscape was the familiar, bitter pattern of bare earth, flint, basalt, and beetling mountain peaks.

"There, boy!" Hengist called, and pointed his free hand towards the heights. "Dinas Emrys awaits you. Behold the ruined tower!"

Myrddion looked upward as his horse bunched its muscles to attack the steep path. The fortress gaped, ripped away on one side so the rooms of the main structure were partially exposed where the tower had collapsed. Huge misshapen stones lay at random beside the pathway where they had rolled from the heights. Even now, slaves and masons labored to drag the heavier boulders back up to the plateau that was the greatest strength of the fortress.

Just when Myrddion thought his exhausted mount would founder, the captain forced the troop into a last, desperate effort to climb the slope and then, in a forecourt alive with workers and marred by fallen masonry, he ordered the Saxons to draw rein.

He threw himself from his horse's back and lifted Myrddion from the saddle, supporting him while he struggled to restore feeling to his numbed feet. "I'd untie you, young Myrddion, but my master would be angered by my impertinence," he apologized, his face drawn at his loss of honor.

"It's no matter, my lord. I understand."

"It matters to me!" the captain snapped as he engaged the boy's eyes. "Horsa is my brother, and you healed him when another enemy would have left him to his fate. My father was Uictgils, son of Uitta Finn, king of Frisia, and we are both honor-bound to repay a debt to you. If you survive the test of the sorcerers, you may call on me and I will give you whatever help I may."

"Truly, Lord Hengist, you are like no Saxon that I have heard of."

Hengist laughed. "Watch out, little man, and try to avoid speaking your mind quite so bluntly. King Vortigern approaches from behind you and he is a man of sudden passions, no humor, and no trust in anyone or anything." Before Myrddion could turn, he went down on one knee in a gesture of respect to the approaching man. Oddly, he lost no dignity in this obeisance. "Master, I have brought the Demon Seed to you by noon today, as you commanded."

Myrddion spun round and his upturned face felt Vortigern's shadow blot out the sun.

Vortigern looked down and saw a child gazing up at him with eyes that were cool and appraising. Those eyes! Something in those black pools was familiar and Vortigern felt cold fingers slide sharply down his spine.

"Demon Seed indeed!" he muttered in response.

The boy opened those traitorous eyes very wide. Vortigern saw surprise there, and intelligence, and a fierce curiosity that the child made no effort to disguise. "My name is Myrddion ap Myrddion, my lord," he said.

"I will call you whatever I choose." Vortigern flushed angrily. "Who are you to assume the title of the son of the lord of light?"

Myrddion looked down at his tied hands. "You are a king, my lord, and you can address me in any way you wish, although I would prefer my given name. I was presented to the lord of light at my birth and he accepted me as his son."

He grinned impishly, and Vortigern felt the devastating force of his charm. Behind his back, the king made the warding sign that would protect him from evil.

"Do you blame a nameless boy for choosing a father when he has none?"

"Say no more, Demon Seed. Your parentage is unimportant to me—except that your father is a demon. You are unimportant. At sunset this evening, you will be given to the gods in sacrifice to bind the walls of my tower together. My magicians assure me that only the blood of a demon's seed can prevent my tower from falling—again and again! What you feel or think won't matter in the slightest once darkness comes." Vortigern turned his attention back to Hengist. "Take him away and give him water. But shackle his feet. He'll run, if given half a chance."

Myrddion was affronted by the accusation of cowardice, and his eyes snapped briefly in anger. Once again, Vortigern felt an odd stab of familiarity, coupled with an irrational fear.

I've never seen this boy before, so why does he make me afraid? Where have I seen those eyes? Strange memories scurried through the High King's mind like black rats. He shuddered, for he almost felt their scaly, prehensile tails grate against the inside of his skull.

"Take him away, Hengist, and keep him within your sight at all times." He grimaced. "Find Rowena. I want my wife."

HENGIST INTENDED TO honor his promise to care for Myrddion, so the burly captain found a patch of shade that would grow as the afternoon advanced. Reluctantly, he obeyed his master and tied the boy's ankles together. When Myrddion complained of thirst, Hengist held his own leather bag of water to the boy's lips and was thanked with a brilliant, direct smile.

"Where did you come from, Hengist? Why would you leave your home to live in these hills? Dinas Emrys is not a pleasant place."

Disconcerted, Hengist stared at Myrddion and wondered why a child in such peril would be interested in the past life of a mortal enemy. Still, the afternoon was warm and Hengist had nothing better to do.

"My grandfather was Uitta, the King of Frisia, but my branch of the family was very poor. The present king, who is my cousin, was suspicious of two possible claimants to the throne who were so close in blood to him, so when I was eighteen and Horsa was nine we fled northward to seek sanctuary in the halls of Hnaef, the Jute king. As an exiled mercenary, I won some renown until Hnaef died and my cousin went to war against the Jutes."

"Life as an exile must be almost as unpleasant as living as a demon's seed," Myrddion murmured sympathetically. "We are both outcasts."

Hengist laughed ironically. How strange to be pitied by a child who was about to be executed. "I'm still an exile, so nothing but my location has changed. We came here with other peoples from Germania to find a homeland. Yes, most are Saxons, but we are all homeless, and all landless. We are all hated for one reason or another."

The boy said nothing. The silence drew out until Hengist felt a need to fill the aching void.

"King Vortigern was warned by his sorcerers that his sons were unhappy with his new marriage and sought to hasten his death. I had won the respect of my men through years of bloodletting, while I accepted the coin of desperate kings. When Vortigern called for mercenaries, I saw the opportunity to have land of my own and a secure future for my sons. Cymru—or Britain—is surely big enough for all of us."

Hengist appeared to be pleading for understanding, so Myrddion nodded. He could empathize with Hengist's need for space of his own, but the boy knew that Britain wasn't big enough for what Hengist represented.

"The king called for willing warriors to come to Dyfed to serve as his bodyguard, promising us wealth and land as incentives. But I've nearly despaired of Vortigern, for no land has been forthcoming, and the pay is irregular—at best! We would have been better off taking what we wanted like the Saxons of Caer Fyrddin, who have made alliances with Vortigern and then settled where they chose. But I have been bound by my oath to the king." He paused. "This whole business turns my stomach. It's superstitious nonsense. You may believe that Saxons are barbarians, but I can't see how your blood will hold up Vortigern's tower. Whether you are a demon or not, my honor has been besmirched by the whole search and the circumstances of your capture. But I gave my word to my master and my word is my bond. Do you understand, Myrddion? I don't wish your shade to reproach me after you are killed."

The boy placed his tied, long-fingered hands on Hengist's arm in a gesture of sympathy. Hengist was shocked to see tears gathering in Myrddion's eyes and he felt so guilty that he was lost for words.

"I sometimes see things, Hengist," Myrddion whispered. "I try not to, because people might believe that I really am the child of a demon. But I know Vortigern can't kill me, so you may be at peace on that score, my lord."

Hengist grunted in disbelief. Then the boy's expression suddenly stiffened, and he stared fixedly ahead.

"I am sure, Hengist, that you will own great lands one day, and not too far in the future. You will rule a kingdom in the south and Horsa will die in the process of winning that land, but his sons and your sons will dig deep roots into these lands, even though I will fight my whole life to drive you out. You and I are brothers, Hengist, under the skin."

"What are you gabbling about, boy? By dawn, you'll be dead and I'll still be a landless warrior."

"Remember my words, Hengist, for we'll not meet again once my work here is complete, although we'll hear of each other many times in the years to come."

The eyes of the boy seemed so large that Hengist feared he would drown in their black, lightless depths. Then Myrddion shook his head, removed his hands from Hengist's arm, and blinked rapidly as his visions faded. "What happened? What did I say? Was I in a fit of some kind?"

He doesn't know what he said! Hengist thought furiously. Could the Demon Seed be a true prophet? Could he be a genuine master of the serpent gods? "By Baldur's belt!" he breathed. "Do you often have these lapses, Myrddion?"

"I remember telling you that I sometimes see things, but then I felt as if I were enveloped in a thick, black fluid. I see shapes in the black water . . . armed warriors, a fortress by a great sea, and a strange stone with a white horse standing beside it." The boy shook his head again as if to clear away the disjointed images. "But I swear I don't know if the images I see are real or simply a sign of brain fever. They frighten me, because I don't believe in such things."

Hengist started, bit the nail of his thumb, and then came to a decision. "Whatever happens, Myrddion of Segontium, I vow to help you to leave Dinas Emrys alive. My honor demands it but, more important, you offer me hope for the future because you might have true far-sight. My people are more used to women with the sight . . . but you've proved to me that your gift is true. You could not have known."

"Known what?" Myrddion asked, his voice small and frightened.

"That my name means stallion, and Horsa's name means horse. My war shield is red for blood, with a white stallion on it. As you may have noticed, I ride well for a Saxon."

"Frisian," Myrddion replied, his eyes wide.

Hengist chuckled with real amusement. It was now his turn to offer a fillip of sympathy. "Fighting men have little time for soothsayers although, by and large, we're a superstitious lot. Blind chance rules many battlefields, so our inclinations are natural. But I've only met one genuine magician, and that person was terrifying because he had no idea of the words he uttered. He was a small, twisted man who lived on the charity of my grandfather and was a constant source of amusement and scorn in the court. But when his eyes turned up in his head . . . well, brave men felt their knees turn to water."

"I don't want to be an object of pity or fear," Myrddion whispered. "I want to be a healer. I believe in what is real!"

"That crippled object of derision told me that I would become the ruler of a far-off land, and that my name would live on throughout the uncountable ages." He paused, and then stared fixedly at Myrddion's face. "He also warned me to beware of a lad with black eyes whose blood would poison anyone who threatened his person."

"I couldn't be such a child," Myrddion protested.

"I was told my future many years ago when I was but a boy myself. You weren't even born then. I am glad that I have been kind to you, young master, for I suspect that you are a true seer. Apollonius is a mountebank, a man who lives on his wits, but Rhun is something else. His runes speak the truth, perhaps, but he prostitutes any gift he has by telling fortunes for coin. Vortigern will be very sorry if he tries to kill you on their account."

Then, with a warrior's embarrassment, Hengist bowed low and knelt in the dust before the boy. "Remember that I mean you no harm, Myrddion. Remember, too, that I vowed to repay my debt to you before I knew that you had the gift of the sight."

"Please don't bow to me, Hengist," Myrddion begged, almost in tears with distress. "Please? I'm just an ordinary boy, truly I am."

But Hengist smiled a knowing, satisfied grin and held his tongue.

· · ·

THE AFTERNOON PASSED slowly, which allowed Myrddion an opportunity to examine the site of Vortigern's ruined tower before the light began to fade. Although the ground was flinty, bare, and dry, a patch of soil at the base of the tower flaunted long, lush grass, even though the tender shoots had been trodden flat by the feet of the stoneworkers.

If grass grows in abundance like that, there's usually a good water supply, Myrddion thought to himself. But why is it only in that spot? There doesn't seem to be any other growth here. Perhaps there's water under the foundations.

A worm of curiosity gnawed away in Myrddion's mind for the rest of the afternoon.

Darkness had fallen and a persistent breeze rose up the valley slopes from the faraway sea, stirring the boy's black hair as he waited in the ruins of the tower to learn his fate. The wind had a chill to it as it whined through the ruined tower with a thin keening.

"They're coming, lad!" Hengist whispered. "It's time to be courageous and trust that the gods are with you."

The warrior pointed to a line of torches that lit the way for Vortigern, his wife, his two sorcerers, and other notables and warriors. In the wake of the solemn procession, two peasants labored to carry a large tub made of tin. Hengist grunted a short exclamation of disgust as he realized the purpose of this prosaic object.

"Don't be afraid, lad," he whispered as he lifted Myrddion to his feet.

The king picked his way over the rubble to stand before man and boy. Hengist bowed low but Myrddion remained standing, his face raised towards Vortigern's frowning visage.

"My physician will open your veins, boy, for I am not unduly cruel. Once your blood has been mixed with mortar, my tower will stand tall and strong, giving purpose to your life."

A bent, white-clad ancient flustered his way forward, followed by a servant carrying a tray of sharp scalpels. Although Myrddion's stomach churned to see the instruments of death, he noticed that the healer was more frightened than he was and the old man's knees were visibly shaking. Despite his fears, Myrddion began to laugh.

Vortigern's head snapped back like a striking snake.

"Why such mirth? Don't you realize that you're about to die? Or do you expect your demonic father to save you?"

"No, my lord, since I doubt a demon is my sire. At any rate, even if my blood seals your stones, your tower will fall down again as soon as it is rebuilt."

Now it was Vortigern's turn to laugh. "But you won't be here to see it, Demon Seed! Still, I'll satisfy my curiosity. Why will my tower topple once again?"

"If you dig into the foundations, my lord, you will discover that your tower is built upon a deep pool of water, so the structure has no foundation on which to stand. If your sorcerers tell you otherwise, then they are liars."

Apollonius and Rhun protested loudly and gathered their robes about their bodies in derision. "Do not listen, sire. The boy is trying to save his worthless, evil hide."

As Vortigern opened his mouth to reply, Hengist shot a questioning glance towards Myrddion and saw the boy's eyes were fixed and ruddy in the torchlight. His face seemed set and pure, filled with shadows and insensible to thought. Hengist felt his heart leap into his mouth.

"Within the pond, if you care to drain it, you will find two dragons that are locked in battle." Myrddion was speaking in a voice that was older, deeper, and more threatening than any that should have proceeded from his childish lips. Hengist heard a superstitious muttering issue from the warriors who clustered just out of the torchlight and he resisted an urge to step away from the child and that unearthly voice. Mindful of his oath, he stood his ground.

"One dragon is white, like the banner of the Saxons, and its breath is freezing sleet and snow. Its claws are sharp scythes of cold iron and its scales are blue-white plates of ice. Whatever its claws or breath touches is killed instantly by the unnatural cold of eternal winter."

167

The silence was absolute. Listeners scarcely dared to breathe as Myrddion's shadow lengthened and flickered in the torchlight.

"The other dragon is red, like the banner that you bear as your personal totem, King Vortigern. It is a creature of fire and elemental heat, and where its red claws and steaming plates move, the water sizzles and smokes. Its breath is fire, brimstone, and steam and wondrous are the ruby jewels of its bloody eyes."

Vortigern stared at the boy as if a monster inhabited his flesh.

"These dragons fight until the end of time, the dragon of ice and the dragon of fire, as if Germania and Britain are locked in mortal combat forever. You will see them if you dig into the foundations, as the ice dragon melts under the lash of the red dragon's deadly breath. Dig, my king, and you will see that I speak the truth. The blood of a child will never trap the monsters of chaos."

Vortigern rocked back on his heels and would have struck Myrddion had Hengist not stepped between them.

"No, my lord. Look! The boy is in a trance. The father speaks through the son's lips. Instruct the workmen to dig, for I fear for your life if you kill this boy."

Still, Vortigern would have ordered his healer to cut the great veins in the boy's throat, but Rowena rushed forward and gripped her husband's arm in a passionate and terrified grasp.

"Look at him, husband! This is no boy for all that he's small and slight. Even now, his eyes don't blink, for his senses are fled. Dig into the foundations of your tower, my lord, lest great misfortune befall us."

Apollonius and Rhun darted frightened glances around the gathered warriors and would have slipped away from the circle of light. Vortigern saw their movement and waved his hand, and they found themselves surrounded.

"Please, husband? This boy frightens me. Do not call down the wrath of the immortals on us needlessly."

Vortigern began to pace back and forth as he struggled to maintain his reputation for decisiveness without any loss of personal dignity. His warriors were rapt and in the thrall of the Demon Seed's impassive eyes, so the magicians slid out of the light and vanished into the gloom. Only the sound of Vortigern's pacing feet could be heard over the thunderous beat of each man's heart.

Finally, he threw up his hands in surrender.

"Hengist, since you believe the boy is speaking truly, organize some stout peasants to dig at the base of the broken tower. If no water is found, I will hold you personally responsible for the time we have wasted."

Hengist paled a little, but he nodded his head bravely in acquiescence and trotted out of the torchlight to arrange for workmen and tools to carry out his allotted task.

Shortly afterwards, twelve peasants returned at a run with Hengist at their head. Using their digging implements, the laborers began to hack furiously at the site where the grass grew so prolifically. Under the basilisk eyes of the king, dirt flew and the hole grew larger and larger.

"Lord, water is beginning to seep into the hole," Hengist called, his voice cracking with excitement.

"Keep digging!" Vortigern ordered, his face stiff and implacable.

The peasants worked on dourly in ankle-deep mud, although the work went more slowly as they tried to move the sticky layers of wet clay. Then one of the workmen swung a pick deep into the soil and a small jet of water forced its way through the hole made by the implement. Within moments, under the pressure of the underground stream, the hole began to cave in, widening so quickly that the peasants were forced to flee from the pit for their safety. The water soon filled the excavation, overflowed, and then began to pour down the slope of the hill in a red trail of muddy, rust-colored slush.

"There is a deep pool under the tower," Hengist called. "Do you wish to see the dragons, my lord?"

Vortigern gave a little shudder of disgust and apprehension. "No. When the water slows, fill the hole with rubble. The new tower of Dinas Emrys will be built on the other side of the fortress, once a suitable site has been determined." Vortigern turned back to the blank face of the slender boy who had neither moved nor spoken in all the time that had been spent in digging the excavation.

"Are you happy, Demon Seed? Your prediction was correct. Answer me, sod you!"

Although the last demand was shouted, Myrddion made no sign that he had heard the king's question. Then, just when the silence seemed to stretch out painfully and insultingly, the boy launched into a long, unemotional speech.

"Hear, Vortigern, king of the lands of Cymru. Long have you lived, but now your days are numbered. No hired mercenaries or charlatan magicians can change the shape of your destiny. Long will your name endure, but your courage, wisdom, and battlecraft will be forgotten. In ages to come, men and women will speak of this moment in time, and marvel that you could believe so easily in foolish lies."

Vortigern raised his fists as if to strike the boy down, but the inexorable voice went on, robbing the king's muscles of their strength.

"The barbarians you have welcomed into your realm will steal the whole land, until your people will be forced to hide in the far, high places, just as the Pictish peoples were driven out so many generations ago. In turn, warriors will come from Gaul, and the Saxons will know the taste of bitter defeat. Beware of the king who looks skywards, for he will surely die. The lion will do battle with the unicorn, the crescent moon, and the dragon, but the lion will prevail. Even the leopard of the north will bow before its might when the sacred stone is stolen. A rose will rule in blood, disease, and fire and the crucified god will be cast down in his churches. A queen will preach sweet reason for a time, but then the roses will be crushed under the leopard's claws and a triple throne will rise to make the Holy Roman Empire shudder. Beware, O king, for in the centuries to come those who remain of your race will hate you as the harbinger of chaos."

Rowena paled and her hands gripped Vortigern's arm as if she feared he would kill the boy to still that calm, insistent voice.

"Men who eschew beauty will kill a king and the land will bleed as brother slays brother. Rods will spit fire and weapons of war will blow

170

men into bloody slabs of meat. From afar, warriors will kill, until the crown is filled again by children from across the grey sea, so strangers will rule while Cymru fades away into a memory.

"In the ages to come, men will live in castles of glass and fly through the air on weapons of iron that spit death across many miles. Men will kill and never see the faces of the enemies they slay. Monstrous rulers under crooked crosses will murder millions whilst the world is silent and afraid, until new monsters come to drag them from their thrones.

"The city of the Romans will melt and Londinium will burn to ash. Men will walk among the stars, and turn whole nations into glowing, burning coals while skeletons dance in sheets of iridescent flame. Yet, though the very earth is poisoned and the sky is grey with dust, men will still open strange scrolls and read your name."

Myrddion paused and the relieved listeners thought that he had finished, but the boy convulsed from head to toe as if an inner demon shook his slight frame from within.

"Hear me, those of you who will live through the wars of Vortigern that will come. All is not lost, for a child will be born of the dragon of fire, a child who is noble and pitiless, gentle and murderous, true and false by turn. For a little time, so brief that it will be sung of as a golden age in aeons of chaos, this child will pluck a sword from a stone and halt the children of Hengist in their march from sea to sea. You will know him when he comes, although many men will turn their faces away from his glory. The Trine, three men great in the powers of the west, will bring him to you, and everything that Vortigern has wrought out of superstition and ambition will be cast out of the land. You will curse this day, because Vortigern will not learn from my words. The regicide will perish, as will every trace of his treasonous blood, and only his crimes will stain this land and his memory."

"Enough!" Vortigern screamed. "Speak no more to me of burning towns and weapons that pierce the sky. I'll not listen! Take him out of my sight. Gag him if he tries to speak. Take him away!"

Prudently, Hengist clapped one hand over Myrddion's mouth as he lifted the boy bodily off his feet and carried him out of the circle of light.

Foaming at the mouth, spittle flying and staining his beard, Vortigern raged as he sought to control his anger and his terror. Rowena found herself cowering away from his purple, congested face.

Dumping the boy behind a ruined wall, Hengist checked to see if Myrddion was still breathing. The boy's limbs jerked as if he was convulsing, as perhaps he was, so Hengist found a short length of wood to ram between his teeth to protect his tongue.

An hysterical roar carried through the still air. "Hengist! Where are you? Where is the captain of my guard?"

"Here, sire," Hengist responded, panting a little from the exertion of leaping over the broken wall to answer the frenzied summons of his master. "How may I serve you?"

"Bring me those tricksters, Apollonius and Rhun. They're missing, of course, now that they've proved they desire my death. Only a traitor would require me to kill a seer. Better that they had never lived than that I should hear such words . . . such horrors. Find them, Hengist, and bring them back to me in chains."

"That duty will give me pleasure, my king." Hengist grinned wolfishly through his beard as he led the guard in a thorough and rapid search of the ruins, the fortress, and the road leading down to the valley. They found the magicians within the hour, for the two fools had lacked the wit or the courage to force their horses to leave the steep road and flee through the forests. Although they wept and begged for mercy, Apollonius and Rhun were dragged back to Vortigern in chains.

The king had scorned to leave the semicircular ruin of his tower. The same torches burned low, rammed into the earth by their long wooden hafts, while Rowena and the assembled notables were refused permission to leave the grim circular space where the pool had been excavated. Even the physician, his servant, and the peasants with the tin tub were forced to remain within the hellish, fitful light.

"Apollonius, Rhun, you deserted me without permission," Vortigern began, even before the two sorcerers had an opportunity to rise from the ground where Hengist's warriors had thrown them. "Your manners are nearly as poor as your predictions."

"Lord, we were ensorcelled by a demon who desires our death. He has blinded our eyes and tricked us, just as he has duped you," Apollonius began, his double chins quivering and his fat cheeks whitening with fear.

"I wasn't duped! Nor was I ensorcelled, unless it was by you, Apollonius. The Demon Seed told me exactly what was to be found under my tower. I should feed you to the dragons that live there—but such an end brings me nothing. I will use you as you would have used him. Bring fresh torches!"

An expression of relief slid across Rhun's face, although Apollonius began to blubber like an overlarge infant in his terror. Hengist could smell the sharp reek of ammonia as the sorcerer's bladder emptied in his panic.

"Oh, so you think you might avoid my justice in the Dragons' Pool, Rhun? No, my brain is not so soft that I'll give you a chance of life, or even a speedy and merciful death. Since all the tools are ready, you shall provide the blood. When I raise my tower on new ground, the blood of my sorcerers will cement the stones together and your corpses will be buried under the flagging to drive away all evil spirits."

"I warned you, master," Rhun began, and his narrow, skeletal face was a study in terror and pride. "The runes threatened death. I warned you, so I don't deserve your punishment."

"Someone does, and as you professed to understand so much of the spirit world, your blood will be nearly as good as that of a Demon Seed, wouldn't you say? I'm actually paying you honor, Rhun. Aren't you grateful?"

Apollonius fainted, so he proved easy to tie hand and foot, but Rhun chose to fight and was soon bleeding from a number of minor wounds and grazes.

"In punishment for making your king look foolish, you will both be castrated and allowed to bleed to death slowly. I offered the boy mercy, but you attempted to dupe me."

"Curse you, Vortigern, and all your works," Rhun began before Hengist thrust a dirty cloth into the spitting, broken mouth.

Vortigern began to laugh. "You can't curse me in any way that I would fear now. The Demon Seed has already cursed me for eternity—because of you. Now, physician, begin. And don't feel that you need to use a sharp blade."

THROWN ONTO THE back of a huge carthorse used to drag stone up the mountainside, Myrddion was spirited out of Dinas Emrys on the orders of Hengist. The peasant who led the horse down the mountain to an isolated hut a little off the roadway counted the coins in his pocket that the captain of the guard had slipped to him before he disappeared into the darkness.

Behind them, screams rose in the still night like the spiral flight of crows that followed Vortigern's war parties by day. In crescendos of pure agony, the horrific sounds drove the peasant on and confirmed his view that he would never speak of the strange young master who lay over the neck of his plow horse. He had stood in the muddy waters of the excavated pit, and felt the fear of an ice dragon that could reach out its wicked claws and widen the hole in the foundations. Then, trapped, it would freeze him and his pick into a statue of ice.

No! If he had his way, the peasant would hand the boy over to the woodcutter and his wife and forget that he had ever set eyes on the Demon Seed.

From a great distance, Myrddion heard the peasant muttering to himself over the shrill keening of men in an extremity of pain. Most of his mind and spirit still danced among the stars and was entranced by the sweet music that the planets made as they glided in their immutable patterns through time and space. No earthly pain or fear could touch the boy with its cold fingers, for he beheld the face of God.

Chapter XI

WALKING WITH KINGS

Time is a traitor. It trips men up, makes them late, and deceives their minds. Sometimes it runs fast, sometimes it crawls, but through all its tricks and travails it hustles all living things inexorably towards the great nothingness.

And so time deceived Olwyn and Plautenes as they drove their exhausted horses along the crumbling path that led to Dinas Emrys. Twenty heartbeats earlier and they would have seen the patient plow horse turn off the road and head up a half-concealed track leading into the forest. Twenty heartbeats earlier, they would have spurred their tired horses into a gallop, met the trudging peasant, and, in gratitude and laughter, taken Myrddion back to the villa beside the sea.

But time is a traitor—as Myrddion would learn.

The pair of exhausted riders could have seen the flickering outline of a plodding horse through the deep forest—had they known to turn their heads and peer into the darkness. Myrddion was so close to his beloved Olwyn that he would have heard her voice, had he chosen to listen. But Myrddion was far away in his mind, and when the peasant heard raised voices on the roadway he thanked all the gods that the strangers had failed to see him in the oppressive darkness of the forest.

So grandmother and grandson passed each other, and remained ignorant of the ironies of chance.

Olwyn and Plautenes rode upwards on a track scoured into dangerous ruts by every downpour, until the sounds of the suffering magicians wove around them like a cruel rope of sound. Terrified by the implications, Olwyn panicked, for she was unable to recognize the begging, gibbering voices. Her blood froze with horror.

"We should beware, mistress," Plautenes hissed. "Something terrible is happening at the fortress. Perhaps we should turn back, at least until the morning."

"Perhaps Myrddion is the one who is suffering," Olwyn hiccuped in distress as a long, ululating scream sent icy shivers down her spine. "Dear protector of all mothers, let the noise come from another throat than that of my sweet boy."

Instead of pausing, as any sensible person would have done, Olwyn was driven on by her love, so that she rode her horse heedlessly over the lip of the plateau to see the hellish work that still continued in the rotted teeth of Dinas Emrys.

Hengist was the first to notice the intruders. Olwyn's hood had fallen off in that last desperate effort of her horse to mount the crown of the hill, so the Saxon warrior saw a dark female form with red torchlight crawling over her face. He clutched his amulet for protection and shouted a warning to his king.

Vortigern turned from his contemplation of Apollonius's pallid, cheesy flesh as it quivered in the final extremity caused by his gross injuries. The king saw a woman with long grey hair spurring her horse towards him, her hazel eyes burning scarlet in the fitful light of the torches. Just as Hengist began to draw his huge sword to intercept an attack, the rider dragged up her horse's head by the reins and the beast skidded to a halt. She threw herself from its back, and ran towards the tableau of pain in the center of the flickering torchlight.

"Myrddion! Myrddion! Where are you?" the woman screamed, so that her thin cries joined with Rhun's disjointed, crazed wails.

"You disturb King Vortigern's administration of justice, woman,"

Hengist roared. "Stand to and be questioned by the High King of all the tribes of Cymru and the north."

The warrior's voice cut through the entwined noises of grief and agony and, for a brief moment, a shroud-like silence settled over the dying men and the crazed woman. Plautenes came running to grip her hand, and lead her away from the blood, the gasping last breaths of Apollonius in all his gross nakedness, and the suffering of Rhun, whose baleful eyes had been put out lest he should curse the king with them.

Olwyn's huge eyes wept tears, but Rhun wept blood.

"Come away, mistress," Plautenes whispered to her, and wrapped her cloak around the shivering woman's shoulders. "Myrddion isn't here."

"I must find out where he is. I must, Plautenes. If he's dead, I want to return his body to his family. Which among you is Vortigern?" She peered around the circle of faces, some sympathetic, some sickened, while others remained blank with the seriousness of the night.

"I am Vortigern," the king said. "Who are you to flout my judgment with your impious screams and demands?"

Vortigern was a dark, bulky shadow with his back to the torches. She could see the thickness of his form and the power that radiated from his raised head and rigid body. He was dressed to officiate at the execution, with all the regalia of gold, bronze, and scarlet wool of a High King, and he thrust his face, chin first, towards her in obvious contempt.

"My name is Olwyn, daughter of King Melvig ap Melwyof the Deceangli, whom you know. I am the priestess of Ceridwen in Segontium. I claim the goddess as my ancestor and I worship the Mother whose name must not be spoken by men. You have no right to steal my grandson. Were it not for his mistress the healer, we would have been desperate to learn of his fate." She gazed directly into Vortigern's face, so he was unable to tell if she was cowed by his status or half-demented with worry. "Now you know who I am, where is my grandson?" Olwyn's voice rose hysterically, until Vortigern's brows drew down with irritation.

"He is no longer here. Be gone, woman, unless you wish to earn my wrath. My sorcerers demand my attention."

Olwyn muttered something under her breath that Vortigern couldn't hear distinctly, but he understood the sentiments. His face clouded and Hengist readied himself for trouble.

"What did you say, woman? Perhaps you are reluctant to speak your thoughts aloud in case I call you to account—regardless of your sex."

"I called you a traitor," Olwyn answered simply, oblivious of the indrawn breath of the warriors that ringed her. "You have betrayed your own people by welcoming mercenaries and Saxons into our lands. You trampled on the honor of the Deceangli tribe when you stole a prince of our house. You have blasphemed against the Mother by stealing her favored child, and you have insulted Ceridwen, whose priestess is kin to Prince Myrddion. The goddess will punish you for it when she is ready to make you suffer."

Vortigern acted impulsively and so quickly that even Hengist had no time to intervene. With his gauntleted right fist, he struck Olwyn full in the face, driving her slender body back until she fell like a rag doll on the wet, bloody soil.

"Mistress," Plautenes wailed, aghast.

"Get her out of here, Hengist. Put her on her horse and pack her off to her family. Hopefully, they'll teach her to keep her mouth shut."

Plautenes threw himself down beside his mistress. Her eyes were open and her nose was obviously smashed inwards. She neither moved nor blinked and her hands were flaccid and lifeless. A dreadful thought assailed the faithful servant and he bent his ear to his mistress's mouth. He felt and heard nothing, for no breath stirred her slightly opened lips.

"Mistress Olwyn!" Plautenes wailed again, his voice cracking with horror.

"Get her up, servant," Hengist ordered, shoving the kneeling man with his sandaled foot. Plautenes turned a tearstained face up to stare at the Saxon. Against his will, Hengist felt a touch of cold run up his spine, as if the night had not been terrible enough.

"She's dead! The king has driven her nose back into her skull. The bones have breached her brain and Princess Olwyn is dead. Now the goddess will destroy us all."

Hengist stepped backwards, muttering prayers under his breath. Everyone knew that women's magic was terrible and couldn't be deflected by threats, prayers, or sacrifice. The Mother, and Ceridwen, her servant, would require a blood price for the murder of this priestess and kinswoman. Hengist whispered the news to Vortigern, who looked shocked for a short moment, but then his face was transformed with irritation and sulkiness.

"Prepare the corpse, then, and send it back to her family. I can't be held responsible for the ravings of a silly woman. I only hit her the once, so her bones must have been weak. Her goddess obviously decided she should die, otherwise the accident would never have happened."

Vortigern must have known that his explanation was callous and ill-considered, because his face began to flush unbecomingly.

"Husband, you cannot send a dead princess back to her family slung over the back of a horse," Rowena begged, one hand on his shoulder. "I know you never meant to kill her, but a blood price will stand between you and the Deceangli king. Please be sensible about this matter. She must be returned by wagon under escort, at the very least."

Plautenes was still rocking and weeping over his mistress's still form, clutching her warm hands in his. Except for her unnatural stillness and the blood that had trickled from one nostril, Olwyn could easily have been asleep. Her flesh made Plautenes feel sick with its memory of once-rushing blood and fierce life.

"She died without knowing what happened to her grandson. Dear heavens, she loved Myrddion more than life, so if you've killed him my lady would have chosen to be dead." The tearstained face of the servant lifted to fix on Vortigern with huge, wet eyes. For all his protestations, even the stern, selfish Vortigern felt a moment of guilt.

"Very well. As a mark of respect to the goddess and the Deceangli king, my guard will see to your mistress. Lady Olwyn will be securely wrapped for the journey and Hengist, as captain of my guard, will personally escort the cart that returns her to her kin. As for the Demon Seed, I have no idea where he is, but he lives. These two magicians are dying in his place."

"They are already dead, my lord," Hengist interrupted. "Rhun stopped breathing a moment ago, while Apollonius has been dead for five minutes. What do you want done with the bodies and the blood?"

"Didn't I speak clearly enough? I thought every person present understood my edict that the corpses would be buried under the flagging of my new tower, while their blood will be used to mortar the stones. The death of a woman, no matter how well born, is no reason for my orders to be changed. I trust you, Hengist, to set all to rights with the Deceangli king."

"Melvig will kill me and send my corpse back to you in payment for the death of his daughter at our hands," Hengist said quietly. He realized that a stranger in Gwynedd, on such an errand, had as much chance of survival as a rooster in a fox's den.

"Then you must think of some way to save your neck." Vortigern shrugged casually. "I've done everything I can do to provide reparation." He turned his back on his captain. "Rowena?"

His wife rose from a small stool that had been provided for her comfort during the long hours since darkness had fallen. She had retreated back into the shadows once Vortigern had been convinced to see sense, tousled, frightened, and disconcerted by her husband's random cruelty and casual lack of humanity.

"How may I help, my husband?" she asked in a rather stilted voice.

"The bangle with the pearl," Vortigern growled, without even looking at her. He held out one hand while still facing Hengist. "The gold band with the large river pearl that came from the north. I gave it to you three years ago at Olicana. It was with the treasure in the Pict war chest we captured when we routed the blue barbarians in the north. I want it back . . . now!"

Rowena looked down at the many bangles and bracelets that

adorned her arms. They clattered and rang as she struggled to isolate a thick, solid band of pure orange gold. Her face was furrowed in concentration, as well as an almost invisible disgust, as her fingers wrestled with the huge, pearl-studded clasp. Finally, the hinge snapped open and the bangle slid into her hand. Without looking at Vortigern, she placed the jewel in his waiting palm. Anticlimactically, Vortigern tossed the bangle at Hengist, who barely had time to react and catch it.

"For the woman's family. The price of her spilled blood is paid."

Vortigern is no king, Hengist should have snarled, before dropping the bangle in the mud and walking away. He could taste the rebuff building in his mouth, but self-preservation and the knowledge that the trinket now belonged to Olwyn's kin held his temper in check. This man is a brute, for all that it is we northerners who are supposed to be barbarians. I am ashamed that I must be the one to carry such a gift to Myrddion, but it shall be the last task I carry out for this king of straw. He has acted dishonorably, thrown away my loyalty, and freed me from his service.

Hengist nodded and bowed to Vortigern, who scarcely bothered to acknowledge the warrior's respectful gesture. The captain looked up into Rowena's eyes over Vortigern's shoulder and saw in her face a certain rigidity that spoke of dislike and forbearance.

As the Frisian assisted Plautenes to lift Olwyn's flaccid body and carry it to a rough cart in the stables, he lacked the words to express his shame at the lady's death. While Plautenes straightened his mistress's body, Hengist excused himself and jogged back towards the queen's small apartments in the fortress. He expected to be forced to steal a shroud for Olwyn, but he discovered that the queen had already excused herself from the aftermath of the executions and was pacing through her small room, driving her maids to set the already tidy chests in order.

The captain skidded to a halt on the threshold and bowed low, cursing inwardly. Then, with a wry grin, he decided that honesty might work better than theft.

"My queen, I seek a shroud to deck the Ordovice priestess. I confess that I'd have stolen it from you, for I am ignorant of any other source of a suitable length of cloth. You may order me to be flogged, if you wish, and I'll deserve it."

"You do not need to steal from me, Thane Hengist. If I had acted sooner to save the boy, the poor woman would still be alive. You rescued him, didn't you? Wait but a moment."

She threw back the lid of a long, carved chest that always traveled with her, regardless of where Vortigern rode. Inside were precious robes, lengths of fine wool, and valuable linens that were embroidered with fine, spidery stitches to suggest vines and flowers. One of these precious lengths of linen was lifted out of the chest with scant respect for the design of olive trees that edged the top and bottom of the old and slightly yellowed cloth.

"Take this trifle to wrap the priestess. Perhaps her shade will forgive me for her murder. The trees, I've been told, are olives, not the sacred oaks, but they will serve. According to the Pict who owned it, the cloth came from Rome itself and was looted from the legions. Whether he spoke the truth or not, I cannot say." She paused. "When you see the Demon Seed, beg him to intercede for me with the Mother and the goddess, for I meant them no harm. I made vows to our own gods when I was taken as Vortigern's second wife. I have borne him two sons whom I love dearly and will protect until my death, but my master has grown in arrogance until he cares for nothing but the power that he has gathered around him. He eats it from his enemy's flesh, he sucks it in from the blood of his dead, and he grows bloated with it. He will do anything to gain ever more power, and even countenances the murder of his elder sons. Understand me, Hengist, for we are kin through your grandmother's line. I regret the monstrosities that the king espouses, but he is my husband and the lives of my own sons depend upon my compliance with his wishes."

"I understand, my queen." Hengist took the cloth from her hands, and then kissed the cabochon garnet on her thumb. "You will see me no more, my lady, for your husband has broken our mutual oath by ordering me to certain death. Instead, I will return to Thanet Island, where my family awaits me. Many of the guard will follow, so beware of Vortigern's wrath and wait in silence. I think we will not meet again on this side of the Shadows, but I wish you well. Pray for our people, for the winds gather against us and the emperor stirs in the south. May Freya guard you and yours."

Rowena straightened and Hengist recognized at last that she was something more than long, golden legs and plaited, glorious hair that could snare a man's senses in its glittering waves. Like Mother Sea, her eyes were shadowed with storms under their peaceful blue sheen.

"Go quickly, Thane Hengist. Vortigern will return soon, for the shedding of blood inflames him and he will surely seek me out. Be safe on your journey in the certainty that I'll not betray your plans."

As Hengist turned to go, Rowena's robe slipped away from one golden shoulder and the Saxon saw a handprint bruise clearly marked on her fair flesh. Rather than shame his queen with pity, he straightened his spine and stared straight ahead. But he wished, with all a strong man's contempt, that the High King of the north would learn that his vassals and his kin were not mindless slaves but creatures of flesh, blood, and ill will as real and as immediate as his own.

"Ah, well," he confided to Plautenes as they wrapped Olwyn in her fabulous shroud. "The High King will learn soon enough that a strong right hand does not make a ruler."

Plautenes stared at the bearded warrior as he set Olwyn's horse between the shafts of the wagon. Then the servant tied his own mount to the rear of the cart and climbed into the driver's seat to take up the reins.

"Surely, Thane, you are like no other Saxon I have ever met."

"I'm a Frisian!" Hengist joked, as he recalled Myrddion's comments a day earlier. "Let us leave this place of blood and death before Vortigern changes his mind. The king's more than half-mad with the power of life and death that is his to use as he chooses. But we minnows plan to escape the pike, don't we, my Greek friend? We are both strangers in a very strange land."

In a burst of ironic laughter, the pair left the glowering fortress of Dinas Emrys as the last of the torches in the ruined tower guttered into darkness.

WHEN THE CART reached the point in the roadway where the narrow, overgrown track branched off into the forest towards the woodcutter's isolated cottage, Hengist instructed Plautenes to wait while he fetched the young healer. Ducking to avoid overhanging branches, the captain grimaced as he considered the difficult task ahead of him, but he squared his shoulders and set his mount's head along the almost invisible path that led through the dense trees. Plautenes watched the northerner go with impatience. Less than a week had passed since Myrddion had been stolen. How would his strange young master respond to the loss of the person he loved best?

Hengist was thinking along similar lines as his horse thrust its way through long grass, gorse, and saplings, one arm protecting his face from low-hanging thickets. When a faint light flickered in the distance, the Saxon felt a wrench of dismay at the coming confrontation.

A simple conical hut and an equally ramshackle outhouse had been erected in a small clearing where a weed-choked vegetable plot bore witness to the slatternly natures of its occupants. When Hengist thumped on the flimsy door with his mailed fist, the wood shuddered and rattled and he heard scurrying sounds inside that sounded like rats stirring in straw. The door was opened a crack and a seamed, weathered face squinted out at him.

"Yes?"

The woodcutter held a worn knife close to his belly and Hengist took a step backwards and spread his arms wide to show that he held no weapons. "I've come for the boy," he explained in tones as curt as the greeting of the woodcutter. The door slammed shut and the captain heard a sharp slap followed by the sound of feet shuffling over bare sod. The door was pulled fully open to allow him to see into the hut.

"Here he is, so where's my pay? My wife's tried to feed him but he's wanting . . . you understand?" The peasant whirled a finger beside his ear in the universal symbol that signifies madness.

"You'll get your coin. Just send him forth!"

Myrddion was pushed out of the door and stood blinking in the waning light of the moon. He seemed dazed and sick, as if his fit in Vortigern's ruined tower had drained his body and his mind, so that he was only now beginning to recover.

"Hengist!" the boy murmured, as his eyes gradually began to focus.

"By Baldur's belt!" Hengist swore bluffly with a shamefaced grin. "You look as sick as an old cat. What ails you, boy?"

"I've been wandering in my wits, but I think I'm just hungry," Myrddion muttered. His face was even paler than usual, so the streak of white hair at his right brow was very pronounced. With a pang of guilt, Hengist realized that the boy hadn't been fed for at least four days, largely because of the ignorance and superstition of the Saxon troop.

"Never you mind, boy. We'll get some food inside you and you'll feel better quickly. Boys your age can eat more than an old man like me."

Myrddion examined Hengist's face and felt a presentiment of trouble at the captain's hearty, unnatural manner.

"Lordship?" the woodcutter interrupted, exposing a mouthful of brown, broken teeth when he grinned. "My pay?"

Mildly revolted, Hengist tossed him a handful of Roman copper coins as he mounted his large horse and offered his other hand to Myrddion. While the woodcutter scrambled on the threshold for his spoils, Hengist swung the boy up in front of him.

"Where's the gold you promised?" the woodcutter howled, using some uncouth words about Hengist's female relatives.

"Where's the food you were supposed to give the boy? But, if you wish, you might ask King Vortigern for your due. We won't care, but he might be interested in your concerns."

With the curses of the woodcutter ringing in their ears, man and boy rode back into the brooding forest.

With his spine pressed against Hengist's torso, Myrddion could feel the rigidity of the Frisian's body through bronze-studded leather and coarse wool. Without the need for words, the young healer knew that some calamity had befallen and that, even now, Hengist was attempting to frame the words of explanation in his head. Myrddion didn't need the curse of prophecy to warn him of approaching tragedy. The thane was transparent because, despite their birth roles as sworn enemies, Hengist respected the lad and agonized over imparting the unwelcome news to him. Myrddion's heart grew heavier with each step of the horse towards the roadway.

The two companions came out into the full light of a dying moon almost on top of the cart, and Myrddion saw Plautenes gripping the reins loosely in one hand and wiping his watering eyes with the other.

"Plautenes? What . . ." His voice trailed away as the steward lifted his face and the young healer saw the glistening snail tracks of tears running down his gaunt cheeks. He threw himself off the horse and climbed the wheel of the cart to look down at the wrapped shape that lay within it. With hands that were as tender and as deft as those of any young girl, he unwrapped the fine linen and exposed Olwyn's sleeping face, with the lines of care smoothed away by the loss of all her personality and vividness of spirit.

"Oh, Gran! Gran! How did you come to this pass? Why did you follow me?"

"She couldn't rest until she knew that you were safe, young master. My lord Eddius and I tried to dissuade her, but she wouldn't listen. She was determined to bring you back, regardless of the cost. Well, it has cost her life. And I don't know what we'll do without her."

"How? What happened? How did she die?" Myrddion's voice was rising towards the edge of hysteria, although no tears had fallen. He climbed over the edge of the cart, laid himself down alongside his grandmother's body, and pressed his face against her still shrouded breast.

"Get up, Myrddion," Hengist ordered brusquely. "It's not seemly. I will tell you everything that happened, if you must know about your grandmother's death. But, first, you must rise and be seated beside Plautenes. Lady Olwyn showed great courage and we must honor her, not shame her with our weaknesses."

"You don't understand, Hengist, the hole that her death leaves in my heart. I'm sure you've lost near kin in the past, but unless you are responsible for the death of the one person who has always protected you from the ills of the world . . . then you can't know how I'd give everything to be a child in her arms again."

The boy was weeping soundlessly and Hengist felt a little ashamed at the harsh words he had uttered, whether they were true or not.

"I do know how you feel, Myrddion, but I don't have the time to help you to understand how we Saxons and Frisians deal with our grief. Let me explain simply that we exact guilt in blood, gold, or suffering to the full measure of our tears. I know you believe Saxon customs to be barbaric, and perhaps they are, but a man of our race who kills another, even by accident, is expected to care for his victim's family or face the same punishment himself. A harsh land breeds a harsh, seemingly un-feeling response that eases our pain. But weep if you must, for I was wrong to try to chide you."

"Then tell me how Olwyn died. I'll not stir a step until I know. And don't spare me, for the guilt is already mine."

Hengist mounted his horse and nodded to Plautenes to set the cart in motion. "We must be gone before full light and the sun will be ris-ing soon. Vortigern will regret his magnanimity in letting you go free, Plautenes, and will wish that both you and Olwyn should disappear. He will not willingly antagonize the northern kings."

The sky in the east was already lightening and a stain not unlike thinned blood touched the bottom of a thick bank of cloud. Rain threatened, and Myrddion almost welcomed it so that its wetness could hide the tears that he believed would never stop. As they moved in unison with the creaking and groaning of the old wagon and its huge wooden wheels, Hengist told Myrddion everything that had taken place at Dinas Emrys. No detail was too small or too painful to be overlooked, for Hengist understood that Myrddion must be made aware that it was Vortigern, and not the boy, who was responsible for what had occurred at the ruined fortress.

"Saxons, Frisians, and Jutes are stern peoples, but we aren't complete barbarians, as you may believe. Queen Rowena provided your grandmother's shroud because she couldn't save the priestess. And I have Vortigern's bribe, his foolish idea of a blood price, which was designed to separate my head from my shoulders when I gave it to the king of the Deceangli tribe. I give it to you, for it is Pictish and has no shadow of Vortigern upon it. Wear it, and remember her."

At first, Myrddion would have thrown the circlet away, so great was his revulsion, but he almost heard Olwyn's whisper in his ears urging common sense, so he changed his mind. It barely fitted his wrist, but he managed to snap it into place.

Hengist rode with them until the broad Roman track leading to the south came into view. Then, reluctantly, he explained that he would be leaving them.

Myrddion looked up at him, seeing him as a dark shape against the brilliance of the rising sun. The red in his tawny hair created a coronet around his head and touched his hands and fingers with golden flakes.

"You'll be a king before too long, Hengist," the boy murmured to his savior. "But I doubt you'll think it's worth it."

"Is that a prophecy, Demon Seed?" Hengist retorted with a grin that was a little uncertain at the edges.

"No, thane, it's an observation. Good-bye, noble Hengist. Were all of your countrymen like you, we'd have no quarrel between us."

"Ah, but they're not, are they? Nor are all your countrymen like you and your steadfast grandmother, so it seems that we shall always remain enemies. Farewell, Demon Seed. I expect to hear great things of you in the years to come."

Then Hengist was gone on his huge horse as if the earth had swallowed him, leaving Myrddion to grieve and rage in peace.

The journey to Segontium was long and hard, and with every turn of the ironclad wheels Myrddion heard Olwyn's voice whisper to him: "Wait, beloved! Wait, beloved! Wait, beloved!"

Chapter XII

WHEN EAGLES FLY WITH
NIGHTINGALES

The mournful journey to the villa by the sea at Segontium took a long and wearying time, unbroken by the solace of speech. Myrddion's eyes were red and puffy but dry, for his tears had ceased over the two long days of the journey. The small cavalcade paused rarely, to water the two horses, to rotate them in the traces of the wagon, and to search for fodder. Plautenes and Myrddion had only a heel of hard cheese and some moldy bread that remained in the steward's pack, strung over the withers of his horse. They shared the meager rations on the dawn of the second day in virtual silence.

Myrddion excluded Plautenes, not out of resentment or anger, but because the boy was deeply engrossed in thought. He understood the train of events that had led inexorably to Olwyn's death, so he realized that many minds and hands had contributed to her murder, for so he believed her death to be. The boys who had stoned the dog, trivial as the incident had seemed at the time, had reminded Democritus that a way existed to lay his hands upon Annwynn's scrolls by stealth. Horsa, Hengist, and the Saxon troop had obeyed their king and searched for an elusive demon's seed that had been predicted by charlatans who sought to cement their power with an autocratic ruler. The Saxons had meant no harm to Myrddion personally, but they followed orders as mercenaries invariably do, while the magicians understood their master's ruthlessness and sought to avoid punishment. Myrddion had avoided death by chance and fear, while Hengist had organized his escape out of gratitude for his brother's medical treatment. But, in this case, benevolent motives had meant that Myrddion had not been at Dinas Emrys to be found by his grandmother. Even Olwyn's grief and anger had contributed to Vortigern's intemperate actions.

"Greed, fear, chance, gratitude, anger, and grief killed her," Myrddion whispered, as he broke his self-imposed regimen of silence. "She was a white dove flying far from her dovecote and prey to eagles who cannot help what they are. She was a nightingale, bred for beauty."

"I don't understand, young master," Plautenes whispered. "Vortigern sent us away without the slightest common decency or regret. To me, he's a shrike rather than an eagle. At least the eagle possesses some nobility."

Myrddion rested his head on his palm and moved easily with the shuddering motion of the death cart. His eyes were stoic and sad.

"The Saxons are wild eagles, unused to training or the civilizing effects of man. They are noble, as you say, but theirs is a fierce honor and a savage pride. They don't think as we do. If we are ever to drive them from our shores, then we must study them. Between Vortigern's hunger, Saxon fierceness, and the scribe's greed, my grandmother was doomed weeks ago. Taken to its most extreme limit, my embittered mother sowed the seeds of Olwyn's death when she named me a demon's child. How strange are the tangled skeins of fate."

Plautenes sighed wearily. In the steward's tired, despairing mind, Vortigern was an egotistical murderer who had no redeeming features. The goddess Fortuna had no part in the death of his mistress, although Myrddion seemed to be one of the favored few who was fated to rise on the goddess's great golden wheel. But the boy thought too much, seeking to find patterns where none could exist.

In time, the cart creaked up the road to Olwyn's villa, where the initial joy at seeing Myrddion perched up on the high seat changed to wailing when the body of the mistress was lifted out of the nest of dried grass in the bottom of the cart. Eddius was inconsolable, and because the children were still too young to give orders, Myrddion coached two servants to take horse to Canovium and Tomen-y-mur with the memorized tale of Olwyn's death. As it turned out, Melvig ap Melwy had already begun the journey to Segontium, which he was taking in slow stages, for he was now very old and his strength was failing. His curmudgeonly nature hadn't improved with time, for the pain of arthritis made him unpredictable.

Between them, Plautenes, Crusus, and Myrddion assuaged the grief of the bereft servants, for Olwyn had been truly loved during the twenty years that she had been mistress of the villa. Crusus drove the kitchen girls to begin preparing those funerary foods that could be made in advance, while Plautenes searched the markets for the very best game, fish, and delicacies to honor his mistress. Every inch of the villa was scoured clean lest sand, dust, or spiders' webs should speak of poor housekeeping. Mistress Olwyn's reputation must shine like purest gold.

Myrddion would have ordered fine woods to burn his beloved grandmother, but he knew that Melvig would never permit a mere woman to go to the flames. With Eddius's distracted permission, he sought out a fine carpenter to build a box of great beauty that would house Olwyn's perishable flesh while she lay in state in the villa. By the time Melvig arrived, with rheumy, red-rimmed eyes a little moist with regret, Myrddion had found a stoneworker to build a bench tomb upon the cliff tops where the wildflowers grew in the spring, a site that was visible from the villa. Eddius's only comfort was the knowledge that he could visit his love where sun, sea, and sky met the earth, raising her frail flesh and bones towards the light.

Guests came slowly while Olwyn waited in her wooden box, which had been sweetened with herbs and tinctures of flowers distilled by Annwynn's skilled hands. King Bryn ap Synnel came with his son, Llanwith, and laid several golden coins and a necklace of amber on the shroud of the princess.

King Bryn was one of Melvig's most valued friends, as the two men shared uncompromising views on Celtic honor, Saxon settlers, and Pict warriors. The Ordovice tribe ruled the largest part of Cymru, and had made useful treaties with the Cornovii tribe of the mountain spine, as well as the Deceangli. These two old kings could marshal a significant army of warriors between them that would be sufficient to rival the forces of Vortigern himself, but they were cautious men who never risked their alliance or their warriors capriciously. Bryn's presence at Segontium, accompanied by his son and heir, was a powerful demonstration of the north's disapproval of Vortigern's part in Olwyn's death.

Branwyn arrived with her new husband, Maelgwr, the brother of her late husband, and insisted on commandeering her old room, forcing Olwyn's children to sleep on one pallet. She had brought apples, hazelnuts, and oaten cakes for her mother's journey to the shades, but Melvig snorted quietly at such miserly fare. Crusus had already made the tiny honey cakes that Olwyn had loved, while Plautenes had given a large piece of uncarved jet that he had cherished for many years. Jet was for death, and its precious, shining surface reflected the steward's homely, lugubrious face. As the patriarch, Melvig had pressed gold coins into each of Olwyn's palms and hadn't begrudged the rope of river pearls that he laid across his daughter's marbled throat.

Yes, Branwyn showed her lack of respect in the grave gifts she gave to her mother, but what did she feel? Myrddion wondered.

Like many unstable women who have been forced to live their days at the beck and call of an unloved husband and his kin, Branwyn was treating the death of her mother as something of a holiday, and was enjoying the comforts of her old home rather too enthusiastically. In the darkness of night she might look out of her window and over to Mona and weep for her innocent youth, but during the day her heart burned with anger and her eyes were almost blinded with her hate. Her mother had lost her life trying to save the cursed Demon Seed. Jealousy and curdled love that could never be put right poisoned Branwyn's every waking thought. As usual, she was thinking only of herself.

Myrddion was scarcely twelve, a little younger than Llanwith pen Bryn, but the boys were the same height, although Myrddion was far more slender than the Ordovice prince. Melvig examined the bastard through eyes that held a grudging regard.

"Damn all demons, but he is surely a beautiful boy," the king muttered, as he watched Myrddion offer honey and oatcakes to a visitor with heart-stopping grace. The boy's face, hands, and feet were so like those of Olwyn that the old man wanted to weep with latent sentimentality, but Olwyn had never possessed such confidence and elegance, as far as her father could remember. The Deceangli king watched several noblewomen, who were all old enough to know better, as their eyes followed Myrddion's slender form with a quite unmaternal longing. Melvig snorted. His own great-nephew, Mark, although still very young, was also staring at Myrddion with slightly lustful, worshipping eyes.

"At least he'll not lack for lovers," Bryn whispered at his side. "He's clever, graceful, and tactful, but if you've set your heart on another warrior to guard your back, then you're out of luck, my friend. Those shoulders of his will never lift anything heavier than a knife, and as for his hands? . . . hmf!"

"He intends to become a healer, and I've heard reports that his aptitude is considerable," Melvig muttered, his eyes following Myrddion as the boy served Eddius the only way he knew how, by lifting the crushing weight of courtesy from his stepfather's shoulders and donning it himself.

"Excellent!" Bryn exclaimed, clapping Melvig on the back as if he was solely responsible for Myrddion's apprenticeship. "Well, as a bastard and a demon seed, he could hardly inherit anything, could he?"

"Hm!" Melvig replied noncommittally. "Sometimes, I long for the old days. I wonder if Olwyn's soul will be reborn as her great-grandfather believed, now that we have given up the holy rites of be-heading. As her eldest kin, I confess to you that I would have found it damned difficult to separate my Olwyn's head from her body to allow her soul to escape. But Myrddion assures me that many different races now believe that the soul goes on a journey from the moment that breath ceases and life ends. He says, quite believably, that separating the neck bones serves no purpose for, if it were so, we Celts would be the only race who would find ourselves in the Otherworld. He has a way of explaining things that makes me wonder if perhaps he's going to become the most brilliant and the best of my progeny."

Melvig laughed, and Bryn joined him in a raucous, ironic state-ment on heredity and its pitfalls. Soft-footed as any cat, Myrddion appeared at Melvig's elbow.

"May I serve you, my lord? Wine, perhaps? I remember the one that Gran Olwyn always served you. It will take but a moment."

"I'll have water, Myrddion, and a promise."

"My lord?" Myrddion's head was cocked sideways like a listening faun from one of the lifelike Roman statues that Melvig had once seen at Aquae Sulis.

"I'm long past sixty, Myrddion, too old to wish to live. I've lost most of my teeth, my hands can scarcely grip the reins, and I ache night and day. But we live long in my family, so I pray that the goddess Don comes for me soon, as a good mother should."

Myrddion paled a little at Melvig's impiety in speaking the god-dess's name aloud, but he nodded his understanding of the pangs of old age.

"I'd like to go to the pyre in the old way, boy, and without my head. Just to be certain!"

Both Myrddion and Bryn opened their eyes very wide with an un-spoken question, causing Melvig to chuckle like the fractious, wicked old man that he was.

"Well, I'd hate to be burned alive, and beheading rather solves the difficulty of any mistakes in diagnosis. Don't look at me that way, Bryn. Don't say that you haven't wondered. All ageing men do! Besides, I want to be sure that my spirit isn't stuck in my throat so I fail to reach the Otherworld. I've not always been a good person, not like my Olwyn!"

Myrddion swallowed convulsively and Melvig wondered if the boy would weep, but his clean, strong jaw hardened and those ebony-black eyes, so lustrous and long-lashed, raised themselves to impale Melvig's with a fierce intelligence and understanding.

"Aye, my lord! Few of us can claim the goodness of my gran Olwyn."

"So it is agreed that you are to behead me when the time comes? I'd like it done properly, if you take my meaning. And neatly, too, so I don't frighten my kin. Don't fear that my sons will take this last request amiss. They've all been quite unhappy to think that they may have to separate my head from my body, so if you do it with the expertise of a healer, I know they'll be relieved. I've endured in this world by looking back to the old ways, not forward to the new, because I've a feeling that our people's dominance is coming to an end."

"You're wrong, Great-grandfather. I can promise you that our people will stay on your soil for many thousands and thousands of years. Our race will suffer and will be driven into the high places, but we will always rule Dyfed, Gwynedd, Powys, and the smaller states of the south until the end of time."

Melvig's jaw dropped. "How would you know the future, young sprig? Did you dream such pleasant nonsense?"

"No, Great-grandfather, but I am the Demon Seed, remember? We monsters know things that other men cannot possibly guess." Myrddion grinned as he spoke, but Bryn recognized a thread of bitterness beneath the humor underlying the boy's words. "I promise that I will do as you ask, provided your sons and grandsons don't forbid me."

When all the gathered mourners had paid their respects, Myrddion presented Olwyn's children, three of them, aged nine to six. Each gave their mother their most precious objects, a fine leather belt with a silver buckle shaped like a fish, a small bow with three iron-tipped arrows, and a boat carved with such realism that Eddius kissed his youngest child as he watched him relinquish his most precious toy to his mother.

Then Eddius came forward with a crown of twisted hazel twigs given by the sacred tree and plaited to form a coronet. Within the network of wood, Eddius had woven what flowers the late autumn had to offer, with mistletoe, holly berries, and wild gorse entwined around them. He had finished the rare and fragile offering with narrow chains of gold that had come to his house as part of Olwyn's dowry. With tears pouring unchecked down his face, he lifted her head and placed the crown upon her hair. Then, in company with Melvig's sons, he would have raised her coffin, but Myrddion stepped forward and looked earnestly into the eyes of the older man.

"I ask that you allow me to speak and to present a gift to my grandmother, who is my mother by love."

"How dare you offer anything to my mother!" Branwyn exclaimed in a flat, bitter voice. "You caused her death and it would be more appropriate if you were lying there instead of her. Any grave gift that comes from you will spoil and rot, desecrating my mother's holy corpse."

Taken aback, Myrddion responded by speaking directly to King Melvig. "Queen Rowena and Hengist, the Saxon captain of Vortigern's guard, were appalled at the death of Princess Olwyn and counseled Vortigern to avoid bloodguilt by making reparation for his lapse of temper and honor. The High King was arrogant and cruel, and would have thrown my grandmother over her horse and sent her back to us in ignominy, but Queen Rowena begged him to reconsider his decision. So Vortigern offered an ornament of gold and pearls to the Mother and to Gran Ceridwen. Here it is, cleansed from his murderous hands." He held up the bangle with its large, grey pearl on the clasp. "Hengist gave this jewel to me, because he thought I'd know what to do with it. We think of the Saxons as cruel barbarians, but Princess Olwyn's shroud is a gift from Queen Rowena herself and Hengist sent her back to us in a cart, an offering that was far more fitting than King Vortigern's choice. What am I to do with the Pictish bangle, my lord? Would Ceridwen accept it, or would the Mother, whose name should not be spoken, accept it in her stead?"

"Impious! Tainted!" Branwyn hissed, and Melvig, who had been about to reject the insulting grave gift, paused. In the face of such spite and envy, he determined to support his great-grandson.

"Olwyn would not care for a blood price, and would have insisted that her death was a stroke of bad fortune. But I say that it was no accident. Nor was Myrddion at fault, for my daughter *chose* to beg Vortigern for the life of her grandson. She would accept the bangle from his hands, but from no other. I declare the gift is outland, but not tainted, and Myrddion may place it among my daughter's grave gifts. I also aver that King Vortigern is to blame for my daughter's death and, in recognition of his sin, I'll no longer give him men or red gold as tribute."

"And the Ordovice tribe will follow your lead, King Melvig," Bryn murmured harshly. "Vortigern's arrogance grows daily. He is a traitor, as fair Olwyn named him, because he invited the Saxons onto our soil."

Myrddion bent over the coffin and slipped the bangle into the shroud near his grandmother's hand. Then the coffin lid was pegged shut, sealing her away from the light.

Long were the songs sung in Olwyn's honor, while wine and food flowed freely as if a great warrior had passed beyond the shades. Myrddion assisted Melvig and Eddius to their beds when their grief and the potent Spanish wine robbed them of their legs, but for himself he drank only water, in the full knowledge that there was nobody left to protect him from the inescapable realities of life without his grand-mother.

So Olwyn was placed in the earth, and the stoneworkers raised a basalt cairn over her grave, with a smooth slab of marble pilfered from a Roman building pressed into new service as a base. Olwyn was rocked to sleep by the sound of the waves, and the sea grasses whispered to her gently as the wind stirred their sharp, dry fronds.

The day after the cairn was finished, Myrddion took his misery to the sea cliff and leaned his back against the basalt stones, which were pleasantly warm in the unseasonal sunshine. Lulled by his surroundings, he began to talk to his grandmother, telling her his thoughts about random chance, the small acts of spite that had led to her death, and his feelings of impotence in the face of the vast sea of human error. He wept a little and explained his relationship with the brothers, Hengist and Horsa, and how he had come to see the northerners as something more than simple barbarians. He told her his dreams and his terrors but, most pressingly, he told her about his strange fits and the prophecies that froze the blood of his listeners.

Silently, like the predator that dwelled in her heart, Branwyn had crept up on her son, so she had heard his one-sided conversation with his grandmother. Her lips curled with contempt. How like the demon's brat to try to avert attention from his part in Olwyn's death with irrelevancies!

She interrupted his reverie. "You have poisoned blood, Demon Seed. Can you be surprised that you spew out fearful predictions to harry the minds and hearts of clean-blooded people? You should be dead, while my mother should be alive."

Branwyn moved to stand between Myrddion and the sea. Her brown hair whipped around her face like serpents and the gloating in her expression made her son feel dizzy and sick. Her irises were an odd shade of yellowish green in the sunlight, as if something foul lived behind her almond-shaped eyes. Her nose was pinched and narrow, while her mouth had lost its shapeliness as if her hatreds were about to spew out. As Myrddion's gaze roved down her face, he recoiled. Then, as the sunlight struck his mother's throat, he made a sickening discovery.

"Why do you wear Olwyn's priestess necklace? You don't worship the Mother, nor set any store by Ceridwen's knowledge. That gem should have gone into the ground with her, but all you gave her was oaten cakes."

Myrddion spoke intemperately, for he could feel his temper rising dangerously until it almost choked him. Branwyn grimaced, but there was no humor in her smile.

"Well, it's certainly not for you, Demon Seed. Mother never loved me as much as she loved you. Her necklace simply redresses the imbalance of the scales. She owed it to me."

"Beware, woman!" Myrddion's voice was hoarse and deep, totally unlike his usual tenor. Had Branwyn truly believed in her heart of hearts that her son was a demon, she would have been more cautious when she heard that baritone voice and beheld his wildly staring eyes. "You must drink no milk, trust no hands from family, and watch the eyes of a girl with red hair. If you fail in your caution, woman of grass, you will die."

Branwyn laughed, but her outburst died away as she registered that her son was oblivious of the land and sea around them. "He came from the sea, the proud Roman with his black eyes and his hyacinth beauty. Did you think to trap him and make him yours? He was an eagle of the Eagles, a raptor born to kill, so be grateful that he only fathered a child upon you. He would have killed you, had you not amused him with your body."

Branwyn moaned and bent at the waist as if she had been struck by a dreadful spasm of pain. Her clawing fingers gripped a fist-sized rock left over from the cairn, and she struck out at the boy—once, and then twice—until blood flew from the side of his head. She would have struck him again, but Eddius's strong hand twisted her arms backward until the bloodied rock fell from her fingers.

"What are you doing, woman? Are you crazed, or drunk? Do you court the executioner's cord?"

Eddius had come to visit his wife and, by sheerest chance, had saved Myrddion's life. Branwyn flew at him with her claws extended towards the older man's eyes.

"To me!" Eddius roared at the top of his voice, and distant servants heard the cry that warned of attack, picked up their hoes, pitchforks, and axes, and came at the run. When they arrived at the sea cliff, they found their master binding the hands of a spitting, cursing Branwyn with part of her own long skirts. On the coarse grass beside Lady Olwyn's cairn, the Demon Seed lay pale, unconscious and bloodied.

"Oh, shite!" one sturdy peasant muttered under his breath. The ways of the nobility were very strange, but a mother trying to murder her son with a rock was a new sin to him.

"Save your cursing, man, and run for the healer. I'll expect your legs to move faster than your tongue. And you." Eddius pointed at two sturdy men armed with pitchforks. "Tie the lady's cloak around your forks to make a stretcher so you can move my boy back to the villa. Hurry, for the Lady Olwyn will place a curse upon us all if her grand-son should die."

The servants scurried to obey, and Eddius ordered two large servants to carry Lady Branwyn back to her room and lock her in. "Warn her husband, Maelgwr, that he will face Melvig's justice if he frees her."

As the men moved Myrddion, his limbs were so flaccid and his face was so unnaturally pale that Eddius was fearful for the boy's life. His scalp bled freely, his white forelock was scarlet, and his tunic was wet with blood. Eddius loved Myrddion only slightly less than his own strong sons, and in ten years he had never seen any serious flaws in Myrddion's nature that suggested to him that the child deserved his reputation as a demon's seed. Privately, Eddius believed that Branwyn had lied about her son's conception. Many other women had used deception in the same circumstances, eager to save their reputations. Branwyn had proved to be neither likeable nor kind, and underlying his fear for Myrddion's safety Eddius felt a savage desire to see justice meted out to the daughter who had made Olwyn bitterly unhappy for so many years.

Once Branwyn was locked in her room, spitting, scratching, and biting like the coarsest camp follower or trull, Myrddion became the focus of the villa's attention. A serving woman bathed his face and pressed a clean part of the lad's ruined tunic against the two jagged wounds that cut through his long hair. Another woman warmed a brick and thrust it in a blanket that was pressed against his feet. He was wrapped in thick wool, for his flesh was very cold, but his eyes remained closed and unresponsive.

Melvig came roaring into the sickroom and took in the situation at a glance. "We've just survived one death in this family. What's amiss this time?"

"I found your granddaughter trying to murder Myrddion with a rock, but I managed to stop her."

Eddius's response would have been laughable in its laconic brevity but for his furrowed brow and the glint of disgust in his eyes.

"Hmf! That evil witch has always been slightly mad, not to mention spiteful and self-centered, something that neither her mother nor anyone else in my family ever was."

Eddius repressed an instinctive hoot of laughter, for Melvig had always been entirely self-centered and vain, characteristics that his granddaughter had inherited from him. But then Eddius considered Melvig's intrinsic sense of justice and his benevolent, almost loving despotism, and felt ashamed of his initial reaction. As king, father, and man, Melvig had no real streak of malice in him.

Then the chaos in the villa was stilled, for Annwynn arrived with her satchel, her needles, her herbs, and her plump, warm common sense. No spite or viciousness had time to take root around Annwynn, for she tore it out with a look, a wave of her fingers, and the turning of her sturdy, unresponsive back.

She muttered to herself as she examined her apprentice, and her face grew grave as she noted the deep gashes on his skull.

"Let us pray that Myrddion has a hard head or he'll die of brain fever. I can't feel a breach of the skull, but these blows were very heavy and meant to kill. Who could hate Myrddion so much? The boy is sweet and good, as I have cause to know. I've been so worried for him, especially since I became aware that Lady Olwyn had been murdered. This boy loved his gran more than his own self."

"Can you cure him?" Eddius interrupted. "We can deal with all else that is amiss, but the boy hasn't wakened and I fear for his life."

"I swear that I'll try. But I'll not promise, for blows to the head can kill."

Annwynn's face was bleak and sad, but she called for hot water, a beaker, clean rags, and a goodly supply of warm bricks to keep the boy warm. As she cleansed the wounds, she shook her head at the torn flesh, but she set to work at once, thoroughly cleaning each gash and shaving around them with a sharp knife. Carefully, she caught up the cut locks, wound them into a long curl and put them into her satchel.

"For I'll leave nothing in this house that can be used to harm or curse my boy, especially his hair," Annwynn said softly. As a healer, Annwynn knew that charms to kill could be spun out of the hair of the intended victim. Her thoughts were bleak as she threaded a fine needle with gut and prepared to mend what she could.

Eddius stayed throughout the stitching of Myrddion's wounds and watched with interest as the healer smeared each gash with a vile green salve and covered them with clean rag pads that she bound firmly into place. A tisane of something dark was prepared with hot water and Myrddion was forced to swallow a little of the hot mixture. Then, once she had swaddled his slender body in warm wool, she settled down to watch and wait.

"There is nothing else that a human being can do for Myrddion now, and there's no panacea for a broken head other than time. Even if he wakes and heals, he may be wanting in his wits."

Both Eddius and Melvig winced at such a prognosis, for Myrddion's sharp intelligence had been the wonder of the villa. Neither man cared to consider the lad as a drooling idiot. When they had left Myrddion's small room, they paused in what passed for an atrium, both frowning and disconcerted by the turn of events.

"What will you do with Branwyn, my lord?" Eddius asked quietly.

"Nothing. At least till I know whether she's guilty of murder or not!" The old man's red-rimmed eyes were very hard, as flinty as the mountains above Segontium. Eddius was grateful that he had never been the object of that cold, unflinching gaze.

"I'll see to my boys. They're already deeply disturbed by the death of their mother, so these injuries to Myrddion will be more than they can bear. They love him, you see."

"Aye," Melvig agreed. "I wish I knew the lad better, for he seems to attract loyalty and affection, but the oaths his mother uttered about his birth forced me to keep my distance. Oh, I didn't believe a word she said. Some man got her with child, and not a demon, but her lies touched on my honor. It was my fault that the boy was labeled for life, so now we can but wait."

Eddius recalled the words he had overheard when he was approaching the cairn. He had seen Branwyn's reaction to them, and stored that knowledge in his heart until he could use it wisely.

As in days gone by, happy days before she had discovered the truth about the world, Branwyn stared out of her narrow window towards Mona. The afternoon was grey and wintry, and the sun was dying in the ocean in bands of bloody cloud. Mona stood out blackly against the sanguine red of the sunset, menacing and unforgiving, and Branwyn felt the malice and hatred that seemed to ooze out from the rocks and sand of the island. She felt feverish and hot, as if the shades of the dead druids had pressed their skeletal hands against her, layer by bony, fleshless layer, until their weight had generated a cold heat that inflamed her blood.

"Please, Ceridwen . . . Mother . . . whoever will aid me," Branwyn prayed, as the light slowly faded in a bloody sea. "Let the Demon Seed die so I can be whole again. Please, let him be gone so I can think without pain. Let me live free of the memory of what was done so long ago. Let Myrddion be dead, so I never have to see his eyes again."

But the sea, the sky, and the air of the freshening night denied her any solace. Through her weary resentment, she wondered if her son was the incubus who had stolen away her soul.

"Perhaps I never had one to be stolen," Branwyn whispered softly. "How did he know who his father was? How did he know?"

But not even the gulls cared to answer her as they slept on the breast of the sea.

Chapter XIII

THE RETRIBUTION
OF TIME

Two long days passed while Myrddion continued to lie unmoving like one who was already dead. Annwynn slept fitfully on a pallet beside him and she was able to report to King Melvig that the lad's brain was still working, for below his closed, bluish lids the eyes still moved rapidly.

"His mind wanders," she told Eddius. "I worry that sorrow over the loss of his grandmother keeps him hiding in dreams. He chases the illusion of happiness."

"You guess, healer," Melvig growled irritably. "How can you know all this, simply by the movement of his eyes? He could be dying of brain fever." The old king was worried, for as each day passed Myrddion's death seemed more likely.

Annwynn refused to take offense at Melvig's irascibility and his slurs on her capabilities. She understood that his temper merely covered concern for his kinfolk and the decision she might be forced to make in the future. If Myrddion died, Melvig would have to punish his granddaughter, who had committed her murderous attack on her son during the very public days of mourning. The people of Segontium, the servants of the villa, and the Ordovice contingent all knew the circumstances of Branwyn's crime, so Melvig would have to pass some kind of judgment.

"I don't know anything for certain, your highness, but I have seen other patients in the sleep that feigns death, and their eyes rolled and moved rapidly just as Myrddion's are doing now. When they eventually awakened, they spoke of how they dreamed and believed that this sleep was life itself. Forgive me if I cannot reassure you further, King Melvig, but I can only offer you what hope I have."

"You're being unkind, Father." Eddius added his reproof softly, for he could see the palsy in Melvig's liver-spotted hands and he knew how the old man reproached himself for what had happened. "Annwynn is doing her best and I can think of nothing else that she could do."

The old king dragged a low stool alongside Myrddion's pallet so he could stroke the lad's face. "I'm sorry, healer. I regret my harsh words, so put my discourtesy down to my worry. Would it help if I spoke to the boy? Can he hear me?"

"I cannot say, my lord, but how can it hurt? If Myrddion is truly wandering in dreams, then perhaps he might hear you and return to consciousness."

Over the next hour, Melvig ordered and then pleaded with his great-grandson to open his eyes, but Myrddion remained unresponsive. Much to Eddius's surprise, the old king began to beg his great-grandson's pardon for years of neglect. He spoke slowly and hesitantly, revealing more of himself in a few moments than Eddius had learned in a decade. As if he were disturbed, Myrddion turned his head restlessly, but his eyes stayed stubbornly closed.

Annwynn was excited by her apprentice's response. "We must speak to him constantly, especially those people who hold his affection. Perhaps the children can help?"

"What should we talk about?" Eddius asked quietly. His sad eyes reflected the first glimmers of hope since Myrddion had returned with Olwyn's body.

"Anything at all. My lord king touched Myrddion and interrupted his dreaming by the natural honesty of the words he spoke. We may be able to lead our boy out of the darkness simply by the sounds of our voices."

Melvig was embarrassed and angry by turns. He had exposed his hidden sentimentality and now he was beginning to feel foolish. "If you gabble about what you've heard me say, healer, you'll be sorry," he warned.

Annwynn pressed his old hand in response. Her smile was warm and understanding, which only made King Melvig feel more awkward. "There is no sin or foolishness in honest words, your highness."

So Eddius spoke to Myrddion for several hours, followed by Annwynn, Plautenes, Crusus, and each of Eddius's sons, one by one. With each speaker, Myrddion seemed to respond more clearly. His hands moved, or he turned his head away, and on one occasion he moaned Olwyn's name. After another day, Annwynn finally began to feel real hope and stubbornly refused to submit to Myrddion's illness. With great difficulty, she forced her patient to drink water and warm soup regularly, lest his body should fail through lack of sustenance.

Eventually, fear gave her voice an edge. Myrddion had been lost in dreams for five days, and soon his body would begin to weaken. If he was ever to waken and feel the sunshine on his face again, then she must shake him out of his lethargy and grief.

"For the sake of all the gods, apprentice, I need you. No one knows where you hid the sandalwood box, and who will teach me the contents of the scrolls if you persist with this nonsense? Wake up, damn you! I'm tired and I'm fed up with keeping your body alive while you hide your mind away from us. The children suffer, Eddius suffers; even King Melvig suffers. Only your mother Branwyn is happy, for she prays for your death. Wake up, my Myrddion!"

This last command was shouted out and brought Eddius running to Myrddion's room, so he was present when the lad suddenly sat bolt upright. His eyes snapped open, but Annwynn could tell that he was disoriented and dazed. She knelt beside him as quickly as her bulk would allow.

"Under the winter hay in the stables," Myrddion gasped with a voice that was rusty from disuse. "It's under the hay to the right as you enter the door."

"Yes, sweetling! Now lie back on the pillows and rest, my darling. Eddius is going to organize a bowl of chicken broth that Crusus has made just for you. All you have to do is open your mouth and let old Annwynn do all the work. Now, let me raise you just a trifle so you can drink this water. Crusus has fresh milk from the icehouse, so it will be lovely and cool."

While Annwynn coaxed her patient to sip a little water, Eddius disappeared quietly out of the room, then raced across the atrium to the kitchens, which were separated from the main building in case of fire.

"The young master is awake and the healer wants chicken broth and cooled milk . . . immediately!" Eddius ordered, and, as Crusus set the kitchen maids running to heat the one and cool the other, word spread through the villa like Greek fire.

Melvig hobbled into the sickroom and attempted to appear stern. "Well, young man, you've frightened us all a great deal by lying abed these many days like a sluggard. I never took you for a lazy lad, so I expect you to become well very quickly, now that you've decided to rejoin us."

"I dreamed I heard your voice calling to me, your highness," Myrddion whispered, and the old man shuffled his feet with embarrassment. "You called my name from a great distance, and you begged my pardon for your neglect. Did I hear you truly, my lord?"

"Aye, boy. Since you've been injured, I've regretted my coldness towards you. Many people hold you in high regard, and if you had died I'd never have learned what special qualities you have that I've ignored in the past. Besides, who else will agree to cut off my head when I'm dead?"

Eddius and Annwynn stared at the king with dropped jaws, for this was the first time they had heard of Melvig's plan to undergo the beheading rites after his death. On the other hand, Myrddion's disused vocal cords caused him to cackle like an old man at the expressions of revulsion on their faces.

"I live to serve you, Great-grandfather."

"Aye, you'd better," Melvig retorted grumpily, but affection lurked under his growl. "Now, how were you injured?"

Myrddion tried to maintain his silence, and Eddius understood that betrayal of his mother would be a shameful act for the boy, regardless of her lifelong treatment of him. Eddius attempted to reason with Myrddion, reminding him that Olwyn had saved him from suffocation when he was still a babe. He invoked Olwyn's own wishes in an attempt to sway the young man's stubbornness, but finally he resorted to the argument that justice demanded that the truth should be told, no matter how brutal the repercussions might be to the persons involved.

"Like it or not, Myrddion, your grandmother's grave was desecrated with your blood. Olwyn, my dear wife, chose your part over her own daughter's, so how can you be silent when your mother tried to undo all that Olwyn died for?"

Myrddion hung his head, considered what Eddius had said and the inescapable logic of his reasoning, and then determined to wring a promise from King Melvig.

"I will say nothing against my mother, my lord, unless you swear to me that she'll not be harmed on my account. Regardless of what Branwyn has done, I cannot deliberately raise my hand against her. Provocation is not enough, for I believe she has undergone much suffering."

"Your sentiments do you honor, Myrddion, but I'd not kill my own granddaughter without very good reasons. I resent your attempt to bargain with me, young man, so don't be an ingrate and explain what happened—immediately—before I lose my temper."

Slowly and apologetically, Myrddion told his story, or at least what he remembered of it.

"I lost my temper, your highness, when I saw Lady Branwyn wearing my grandmother's fish necklace, the one she always wore in her role as priestess. My mother has never officiated at the festivals, nor expressed any interest in the ancient rites of the priestess. I told my mother that the necklace should have gone with Lady Olwyn into the grave."

Melvig nodded. "True enough."

Myrddion recognized the slow anger in Melvig's eyes and suddenly felt ill and dislocated. "Doesn't my mother have the right to face her accuser, my lord, and explain her reasons for her actions? Besides, I'm very tired."

"Is he likely to die overnight, healer?" Melvig asked, only half in jest. "Because if I can be sure that he need not give a dying declaration, he is correct. The lady Branwyn has the right to face her accuser, even if it is her own son. If his health is improving, we shall continue this questioning in the morning."

"Thank you, my lord. I believe a postponement would be the best solution for Myrddion's recovery," Annwynn agreed. "Besides, Crusus has arrived with my patient's broth."

"After we break our fast in the morning, I intend to get to the bottom of this distasteful mess. Be warned, young man, that if I discover that you taunted your mother and contributed to your injury, then I will be forced to punish you as well, regardless of your scruples."

Eddius flinched. He made an immediate decision to keep silent about the discussion he had heard on the sea cliffs.

"Sleep well, boy." The king gave a smile that touched his eyes. "But remember to wake up this time."

After Eddius and Melvig had left Myrddion with Annwynn and his broth, the confused young man grimaced at his teacher through the beginnings of a painful headache.

"I don't understand, Annwynn. I thought that Great-grandfather was fond of me. Yet he'll happily punish me for almost being brained by my mother. What did I do wrong?"

Lamplight flickered gently on Annwynn's plain, motherly face and softened the wrinkles and pouches that aged her so cruelly in pitiless sunlight. As Myrddion gazed up at her loving, gentle smile, he knew he was seeing an aspect of the Mother in Annwynn's homely softness.

"Melvig is an old man who is developing a sentimental fondness for you, which makes him feel both foolish and weak. To add to his guilt, he dislikes his granddaughter. I suspect he has always loathed her, so he will do everything he can to present an appearance of fairness, even to overlooking many of her faults. You do understand the contradictions of love, don't you, sweetling?"

"No," Myrddion whispered. "But I'll think about them if my head ever stops aching."

"Finish your broth and drink all your milk. Then the lamp goes out and we'll both drift off to sleep. If you feel unwell during the night, wake me. I'm only an arm's length away."

Once the lamp had been extinguished, and despite his determination to cure his headache, Myrddion found that the rest he craved escaped him. He knew he had only to call and Annwynn would give him a few small drops of poppy tincture to make him sleep. But to flee from pain seemed paltry after the days of dreaming that he had endured.

So he struggled to understand love and her twisted brother, hate. But life was new to Myrddion, and despite his sensitive nature he remained an immature boy whose life had scarcely begun. As he puzzled away at the passions that had led to his losses, he fell asleep without recognizing the transition from wakefulness. He did not dream.

THE DAY WAS well advanced when Melvig called his granddaughter to account for her actions in the old triclinium of her mother's house. The dining couches had been torn out of the room decades earlier and replaced with a long table with bench seats. For today's inquisition, the room was stripped bare, except for Melvig's chair and a stool for Myrddion, who was still very weak and pale. All other witnesses and guests stood, including Branwyn, whose hands were now free, although Melvig had taken the precaution of placing two large warriors at her back. Bryn ap Synnel and his son had been persuaded to remain at the villa until after Melvig's judgment was complete, for the Deceangli king valued Bryn's opinion and experience.

Cold weather had finally arrived at Segontium, accompanied by sleet and rain that buffeted the villa walls and intruded chilly fingers through every aperture to penetrate the inner rooms. The hypocaust no longer functioned, so the tiled floors were cold, obliging servants and nobility alike to wear warm footwear and their thickest wools and furs. Melvig looked like a plump and bad-tempered badger whose pointed nose and crest of salt-and-pepper hair was just visible over a thick wolf pelt. The wind rattled the shutters and whined through any opening with a sound like the moaning of a lost child.

"Your son insisted that you should have the opportunity to answer any accusations, granddaughter. You owe him a debt of gratitude for his sense of justice."

Branwyn pressed her lips together defiantly and lifted her chin accusingly at her son.

"Myrddion, last night when you awoke, you told me you were angry with Lady Branwyn because she was wearing the priestess's necklace that my daughter wore when she officiated at religious ceremonies. Is that correct?"

"Aye, lord. I was very angry that my mother hadn't permitted Gran Olwyn to wear her chain into the Otherworld."

Myrddion's lips were pale and Melvig prayed the boy wouldn't faint during the questioning. He swiveled his head towards his granddaughter and noted her clenched fists and wire-taut body, and the electrum necklace that still hung round her neck.

"I await your response, Lady Branwyn. Myrddion was right: you have no right to touch the Mother's necklace. If it didn't go into the ground with Lady Olwyn, then it legitimately belongs to her sons rather than to you. You are guilty of theft."

Branwyn clutched the central medallion with its leaping fish as if she dared the king to strip her of her birthright. "This necklace is part of women's magic, and I protest that I am its rightful owner. I don't accept the right of any man to claim it."

"I will overlook your impertinence just this once. You do not officiate at the festivals, nor do you show any sign of your mother's piety. The necklace is not yours."

"Mother owed it to me for her years of neglect when she chose the Demon Seed over me."

"Stop whining and tell me how you stole it," Melvig demanded angrily. The old man detested excuses and had never known his granddaughter to take responsibility for her own actions.

"I didn't steal it. Mother kept her necklace in her clothes chest with her priestess robes. I took it because the necklace can only pass to a woman, and Mother had only sons. Except for me!"

The last sentence was pronounced triumphantly, as if her sex justified her sneaking into her dead mother's room and ransacking her possessions. Her eyes were muddy with resentment and something peculiar that was repulsive to any right-thinking man. With a grimace of dislike, Eddius pushed aside several warriors who stood behind Myrddion and insisted that he should be permitted to speak.

"Lord King, I had forgotten Olwyn's electrum necklace, but she often told me that it had belonged to her mother's family and had been passed down through the generations to devout priests or priestesses. In this case, the necklace was stolen, my lord. Olwyn would never have given the necklace to her daughter."

His face flushed with distress, Eddius tried to explain the tangled and poisonous relationship that existed between mother and daughter.

"Olwyn regretted the loss of her daughter, whom she had loved and protected from birth. Branwyn rejected both her son and her mother, choosing to hate her mother for an implied slight when she refused to kill the newly born boy. My wife explained to me how frightened she had been for both Branwyn and Myrddion, especially when her daughter tried to smother her baby at Caer Fyrddin not long after the birth. Olwyn would have cherished her daughter forever, but Lady Branwyn chose to cut her mother out of her life. Olwyn regretted the fact that she never met her other grandchildren, for Branwyn kept them from us for selfish reasons that she has never explained."

Branwyn shot a narrow glance at him that froze his blood. Steeling himself, he addressed her.

"Don't try to silence my tongue, woman. My wife owed you nothing, for she neither neglected nor rejected you. She loved you, but you rejected her as you rejected your son."

"Remove the necklace," Melvig ordered one of his warriors. "I will decide what to do with it shortly. But you may be very sure, granddaughter, that you will never possess it."

Branwyn refused to assist in the removal of the wide electrum chain, and the warrior caught a lock of her hair in the mesh, giving her an opportunity to shriek and cry as if she had been deliberately harmed.

"Hold your tongue, woman, except to explain yourself. I will decide the fate of the necklace." Melvig paused. "Now, we shall discuss more serious matters. Why did you try to kill your son?" Branwyn remained sullenly silent. Only her eyes seemed alive, albeit trapped. "Myrddion, why did your mother try to kill you?"

Myrddion's bandaged head drooped and he appeared to be ashamed. "Forgive me, my lord, if I seem confused, for I only remember fragments of speech and disjointed pictures. In the past few weeks, I have experienced waking dreams that I often can't recall afterwards. Hengist, Vortigern's captain, told me that I gave a prophecy after I told Vortigern that his tower was built on a pond filled with water and therefore would continue to fall. I prophesied to my mother—I know I did—something to do with a girl with red hair. And I remember seeing a long sweep of beach, a very young girl with dark hair and a man speaking Latin who was alien, cruel, and beautiful. I can't remember anything else."

A collective shiver ran through the room as if cold fingers had toyed with the necks of the onlookers. Several warriors looked at Myrddion with startled, superstitious eyes, as if the boy they had known for years had suddenly sprouted two heads.

"I told you he's a demon's seed," Branwyn moaned, and her eyes filled with hot tears. "He couldn't possibly know, unless he's a creature of the darkness. I tell you that he couldn't know! Myrddion didn't exist when the monster found me, so how could he see the beast so clearly? How could be know? He couldn't possibly know! *Hyacinth beauty,* he said to me. *Eagle of Eagles!* What does he mean? How could my son know his father, if I don't?"

Myrddion turned his lustrous black eyes, now filled with pity, towards his mother's pallid face and quivering lips. She bit down on her lower lip until blood came, and began to shake her head as if she would remove it from her body. To the many pitying eyes in the triclinium, Branwyn was like a child's wooden doll, stiff and unresponsive, except for the violent movements of her head.

"Don't look at me with those eyes—his eyes! I hate black eyes. They speak of nothing but hatred. His eyes . . . his eyes . . ."

Then, to the horror of everyone present, Branwyn began to tear at her skin with her nails. The nauseated onlookers saw her arms for the first time, and the white ridges of scar tissue that covered them, layer upon layer.

"Restrain her," Melvig ordered, his voice hollow with shock. "What have you done to yourself, child? Tie her arms, for the goddess's sake! Dear gods, she's carved herself to ribbons!"

As soon as the warriors laid their hands on Branwyn, she screamed shrilly like a child. She begged them not to hurt her, while tears poured unchecked down her face. Maelgwr looked away from his wife, his face set like stone, and Myrddion realized that the man knew his wife mutilated herself but didn't care. Only now, when her family was finally learning her secret, did Maelgwr make a pretense of husbandly love.

Melvig was a sharp thinker for all that he was nearing the end of his life. Many old warriors failed in their heads, forgot the simplest actions, and died because they no longer remembered to eat and drink. But Melvig was more acute than in his youth, having learned to think before he reacted. Branwyn's shocking behavior had rocked the old king, but hadn't deflected him. No matter how pathetic his granddaughter now seemed, she had tried to murder her son.

"The boy spoke about his father, didn't he? And the man who raped you was no demon, was he?" Melvig's voice was as hard as iron and just as inflexible. "Come, girl, the time for deception is over. Let justice be done, for you as well as for your son. Bring your old terrors out of the shadows of memory and face them squarely. They have harmed you long enough."

Branwyn's lips quivered at the sympathy in her grandfather's voice. Somehow, her manic outburst had wiped away much of the bitterness in her face and she seemed younger, softer, and more vulnerable.

"I was twelve, Grandfather—and foolish! I thought that the man thrown up on the beach by the storm was a gift to me from the gods. But he was cruel and would have killed me if I hadn't told him how to escape. Oh, but I hated him, and I'll hate him for ever. I hate his black eyes, and his fair face. *Hyacinth beauty*—how did Myrddion know? I can hardly bear to look at my son, who looks so like his father with his lying eyes. I would kill the monster and put out those eyes if I could. I thought I had, but here he is, and he's still alive. He probably can't ever be killed. The storm over Mona didn't kill him and the ocean didn't kill him. He is sitting here, as naturally as can be."

"I'm Myrddion, Mother! I'm no Roman!"

His eyes were wounded but alert, as if he had discovered something valuable by accident—as he had.

Branwyn continued to rave, to remember, and to protest her need to destroy the lying black eyes that had terrified her for twelve years. Even Maelgwr, who had little love for his difficult, frigid wife, felt a moment's pity, for Branwyn was crazed and would never be whole. She had survived her rape and the threat of murder because even as a child she was prepared to do anything to live. Poor Branwyn! She had been as wild and as feckless as a young hawk, heedless of any constraint, arrogant and imperious in her selfishness, and, at bottom, an unlikeable, egocentric child. But no little girl deserved the ordeal she had suffered, its aftermath, and the long unhappy years that followed. Her madness and her viciousness had grown out of her flaws of character, but her rapist had made that growth possible.

When he arrived at a decision, Melvig acted speedily.

"Take your wife, Maelgwr, and return to your home," he instructed Branwyn's husband. "I'll not punish a woman who makes herself suffer both by day and by night. You should care for her as best you can, for her wits are damaged. Nor should you punish her. Be warned. If you should harm her for the sake of her dowry, I will exact punishment from you as if she were whole."

Myrddion rose slowly from his stool, his face pinched with pain. As all eyes followed him, he walked across the room to Maelgwr and spoke softly, but loud enough for those watchers who were closest to hear him clearly.

"I will demand justice for any harm done to my mother. Aye, and I'll take it for myself," he said. "I will be watching you, Stepfather. I don't truly understand my mother, but I know she is not responsible for what she thinks and what she does. You are. And you should beware the temptations offered by a red-haired girl, for that way lies death and your own destruction—especially if you give poisoned milk to my mother. I'll find you, Stepfather, though Hades should stand between us."

With narrowed, angry eyes, Maelgwr assisted Branwyn to her feet. She made no effort to resist him. Myrddion felt a sob begin to form in his throat when he saw her staring eyes and the long ribbon of spittle that trailed from her mouth. He had the strange, sad presentiment that he might never see her again.

"She's quite mad!" he whispered softly, for he knew that this farcical trial had tipped her over into a world tilted crazily out of alignment. "I should have remained silent when the opportunity was there."

Suddenly, Melvig decided to dismiss the witnesses, and instructed a strong warrior to assist Myrddion back to his bed. There, free from prying eyes, the boy began to weep quietly for the opportunities that had been lost in the choking sands of the past, going back to a time before he was even born.

GRADUALLY, SADLY, THE villa by the sea returned to a semblance of normality and, for the sake of Eddius, whom they loved, there was no slacking or laziness in the servants' eagerness to do their various tasks. As always, winter was a time for mending, sharpening, and cleaning, so the villa smith was always busy working on tools and remaking what could not be repaired. The maidservants aired bedding, mended precious cloth, wove the wool that Olwyn had spun with her industrious hands, and shed tears for the happy days that had been.

Eddius struggled to keep himself busy around the villa, but his passion for the fields and growing things had become blunted. His bed was cold, now that Olwyn's warm, patient presence had fled, and no river of tears or promises to the gods would bring her back. Because he was a man, a master, and, most important, a father, he couldn't wallow in the sharp immediacy of his loss, but must comfort his children. Numbing grief made the smallest action very difficult, so Eddius was grateful to Myrddion, who had put aside his own crushing pain to take the young boys to visit their mother's grave. Myrddion encouraged them to open their hearts to her, knowing that voicing their misery to their mother's memorial stone helped to ease their loneliness.

"Feel the sun on your faces, boys. It's winter, and the snow will soon be here, but your mother has sent the lord of light to kiss you with his warmth because she can't do it herself."

The eldest boy, Erikk, had shaken his head with the cynicism of a nine-year-old.

"Mama is dead, so she can't do anything. She's like our pet rabbit that died. She's nothing!"

His voice had been shrill with the beginnings of hysteria, for the children had seen the torn and bloody corpse of their pet after the wild dogs had killed it. Myrddion had knelt down on the cold earth and dead grass. He had pulled the youngest, Melwy, to his side and placed his other hand on eight-year-old Camwy's shoulder.

"Inside you, Erikk, where it can't be seen, there is a little spark. It's so tiny and so strong that it can't be put out. That spark is your soul, and it's what you really are. I've seen inside our bodies, just as you saw what hides under the pelt of a rabbit, a chicken, or a deer. But I could hunt forever for that tiny spark and not find it, for it comes from the lord of light and it cannot be trapped or killed."

The three boys watched Myrddion's eyes intently. They wanted to believe him so much that their small bodies leaned towards him as if they could fold themselves into his flesh.

"That spark, our soul, lives forever. We Celts believe that the soul goes on to live again in the body of a newly born baby, although the child will never remember the life that was lived before. All over this huge world, other races believe the same thing, because it is true—and we all know the truth when we hear it, don't we?"

All three boys, including Erikk, nodded seriously. Their eyes were wide and hazel gold, as clear and as pure as Olwyn's had been. The poignant memory made Myrddion's voice tremble.

"As long as the sun rises and sets, that spark cannot be killed and Olwyn, your darling mother, lives on. When you wish to talk to her, she is here and listening, but she is everywhere the sun shines, so she is with you always. Feel her warm touch—I can!" Myrddion raised his face to the weak sunshine. "Feel it? Your mama is telling us that she loves us."

"But the sun isn't always there, so Mama must go away too," Melwy whispered, and Myrddion could tell that the boy wanted to suck his thumb for comfort, despite trying desperately hard to be a man.

"The sun only sleeps, just as you do when you're very tired. Even when the clouds cover it, the lord of light is still there. Because we can't see him doesn't mean that he's deserted us. It's the same with your mama. She will never leave you as long as the spark that is her soul lives on, and when you are very old, and your body begins to wear out, she will come to take you up to the light."

So, with stories and love, Myrddion gave Olwyn's sons a reason to believe that they had not been abandoned. Melvig and Eddius watched his efforts and blessed him.

"He's a good lad, Lord Melvig. My wife loved him very much, and I finally understand why. He's gentle inside, which is rare."

Melvig snorted, for he had seen Myrddion's eyes when the lad spoke of Vortigern, and had come to the decision that his great-grandson had a large heart, a clever mind, and a sharp, unrelenting sense of justice.

"I must return to Canovium, but I'd feel easier in my mind if I knew that the boy remained here and resumed his apprenticeship when he's well enough. I have had news from the south that suggests we'll soon be embroiled in Vortigern's schemes, so I have some hard decisions to make."

"You needn't fret on Myrddion's account, my lord, for I'll take good care of the boy."

Melvig bit one gnarled thumb. "You must keep him out of politics, if you can. He hates Vortigern and we'll all be required to make choices soon. Before Olwyn's death, I received a messenger from Vortigern's son Vortimer. It appears that the High King has upset Ambrosius Imperator, the king of the south, who has ambitions to take back the lands that Vortigern stole from him so long ago. I expect him to send men and siege machines to aid Vortimer to usurp Vortigern's throne. No word of this must pass your lips to anyone else, Eddius, and I mean *anyone*. Vortigern would treat our involvement in these plots as treason, especially if any communication is intercepted. Personally, I don't believe in writing messages, even if I could. I have no desire to have my head separated from my neck before I'm dead."

Both men laughed, although Eddius's eyes narrowed. Night and day, he dreamed hot murderous thoughts as he discarded one means of Vortigern's death after another as being unworthy and painless compared with the loss of his Olwyn. Melvig must have caught some trace of his murderous thoughts, because he placed his age-spotted, arthritic hand on Eddius's arm. That old hand still possessed surprising strength, although it shook a little with infirmity.

"Do not consider it, Eddius. What would happen to your sons if you should try to kill Vortigern? What would happen to Myrddion? What retribution would be wreaked on the people of Segontium if you raised your hand against the High King? Think of Olwyn and her wishes, and hold your instincts at bay."

"That Vortigern lives while Olwyn sleeps in the cold earth is a travesty, Melvig, a hateful jest of the gods. He should pay for what he did."

Eddius's eyes burned hot, then cold, and Melvig was afraid, because such a depth of anger and grief was almost too great to be contained. Then, just when Melvig had decided that he would have to protect Eddius from himself, the younger man ran his hands through his hair and shook himself, as if to cast off the thoughts that threatened to consume him.

"You're right, Lord Melvig. Olwyn would demand that I protect all our boys, Myrddion included, rather than demand my revenge. I'll not touch Vortigern while you live, nor while my boys are too young to protect themselves."

"Fair enough," Melvig replied slowly, his face still creased with worry. "Still, my old father lived by the adage that revenge is a dish that is best served cold. I'll not hold you to this promise for life. If I were younger, and my kingdom were stronger, I'd raise my sword against Vortigern myself."

Eddius tried to maintain a calm face, although he lusted to see Vortigern brought low, preferably at his own hands. "What will you do, my lord? Will you aid Vortimer?"

"I will do nothing, Eddius. I meant it when I said that Vortigern will receive no tribute or troops from me. But a sensible man will sit on the wall and act only when the wind shows on which side the outcome will fall. No, I'll send no help to either of them, for there's bad blood in that family and Olwyn's death lies heavily on my heart."

"May change come quickly," Eddius agreed, as the two men strode back to the scriptorium to sample the last of Olwyn's special wine. Both knew that their safe, quiet world was at risk and their frail strength would be insufficient to save either the Deceangli clan or the quiet villa by the sea from the power struggles that would soon come to the north.

"Who wants a quiet life anyway?" Melvig demanded with a snaggle-toothed grin.

"I do," Eddius replied with perfect truth, as he watched his boys returning from the sea cliff with Myrddion. The boys were cavorting like young lambs, as if a heavy load had been lifted from their childish shoulders, and Melvig prayed that war wouldn't come to the villa to rob them of their childhood.

As they played, the weak sun disappeared behind banks of grey cloud and Eddius shivered in the sudden cold wind. "Snow's coming," he murmured. "Time to put the shutters up on the villa and prepare for a long, bitter winter."

"And spring is likely to bring swords to our doors. Never fear, lad, Myrddion has a demon's own luck, although now we know that he's no demon's seed. He'll protect you and yours with his life."

"Aye!" Eddius replied, and heard Olwyn whisper agreement in his ear. He hugged his arms to his body and remembered the sweet smell of his dead wife's hair.

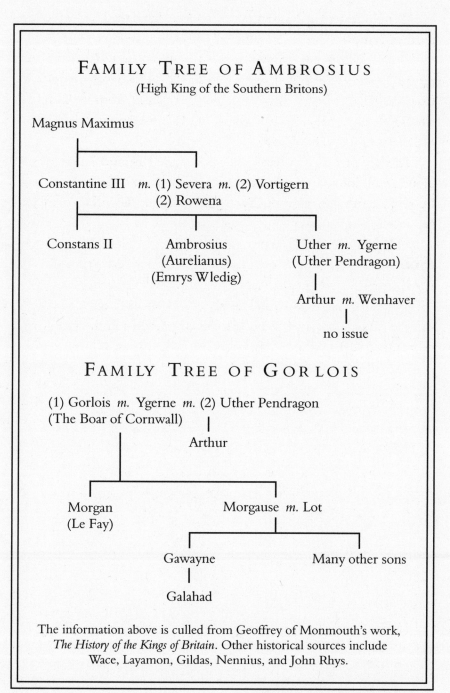

FAMILY TREE OF AMBROSIUS
(High King of the Southern Britons)

Magnus Maximus

Constantine III   *m.* (1) Severa *m.* (2) Vortigern
                         (2) Rowena

Constans II   Ambrosius   Uther *m.* Ygerne
                     (Aurelianus)   (Uther Pendragon)
                     (Emrys Wledig)

                                        Arthur *m.* Wenhaver

                                             no issue

FAMILY TREE OF GORLOIS

(1) Gorlois *m.* Ygerne *m.* (2) Uther Pendragon
(The Boar of Cornwall)

                              Arthur

Morgan   Morgause *m.* Lot
(Le Fay)

          Gawayne   Many other sons

          Galahad

The information above is culled from Geoffrey of Monmouth's work, *The History of the Kings of Britain*. Other historical sources include Wace, Layamon, Gildas, Nennius, and John Rhys.

Chapter XIV

HEALER

Spring had come to Cornwall and the fields outside the city, already called Hengistdun, although King Gorlois flinched to hear a Saxon name given to his southern stronghold. Hengist had taken the town while carving a route through to the sea with his massive sword and the might of his Saxon followers. Gorlois had arrived too late to crush the interloper. Saxon feet had tainted this place, and the king's rage knew no bounds when he was unable to call the invaders to account.

But Ygerne loved the place, the long sweeps of low hills crowned with oaks, beech trees, and hazel, and would not willingly leave the pleasant fields in the winter and the spring.

Now, pregnant and dreamy, she wandered out into the morning, bored with the enforced captivity caused by her condition. Daisies, both white and yellow, bloomed in the long grasses, and spikes of bluebells and the shy buttercups of spring entranced her as she filled baskets with the wild flowers to sweeten her rooms. Her maids carried her bounty, and her flower face was wreathed in pleasure as the sun kissed her wonderful hair with streaks of gold.

When Gorlois rode out to find her, he felt his heart stop with love, just for a moment, in the perfect joy of a happy husband and father.

Little Morgan saw him first and she cried out to her papa in her childish treble, throwing herself almost under the hooves of his destrier before Gorlois lifted her up into his strong brown arms.

"Ah, my little piglet," he murmured, and kissed the toddler's rosy cheeks. His daughter was as brave as any son and Gorlois glowed in her adoration and her fierce, childish joy in his company. Putting the child before him on his horse and holding her securely, he drank in the sight of his wife, her arms full of flowers and her face wreathed in smiles that spoke her love more clearly than words.

He kneed his horse into movement. "Wife, the day is brighter for your laughter. The child goes well?"

"Aye, husband, it moves and kicks lustily." She blushed to speak of such intimate matters in front of her tiny daughter, but embraced in his muscular arms, Morgan had no eyes or ears for anyone but her father.

"Should you risk yourself out here in the open? Any brigand could take you unawares." Although Gorlois's words were admonishing, his fondness shone through his dark eyes and made his plain face beautiful with his love.

"I am well protected, my lord. See? The guard watches me, so I am very safe. I had a sudden desire to fill our room with flowers when I heard of your imminent return. Are they not beautiful, Gorlois, love of my heart?"

"Aye, but not so beautiful as you."

Morgan pulled on his strong, calloused fingers to gain his attention and, as Gorlois could deny his two ladies nothing, he pulled his eyes away from the radiance of Ygerne's face to look down into Morgan's soft dark eyes that were so like his own.

"Yes, little queen! How may I serve my small sweetheart?"

"Mama wishes to visit Brigid's Fountain to bring luck to the new baby. Can we go, Papa? I have heard of the waters. I really want to go with you to Tintagel. I'm old enough, because I'm four now."

"Brigid's Fountain? The waterfall? Aye, it's a sacred place for women, but dare I risk my dear ladies on such a journey? We'll discuss this matter with your mother."

"But Papa . . ." Morgan began, but Ygerne reached up to place two fingers gently over her daughter's protesting mouth.

"Hush, darling, we will speak of this matter later. Papa will decide."

Gorlois laughed, knowing he could deny nothing to the two females who owned him so completely. So Gorlois, his wife, his daughter, and a cavalcade of ladies-in-waiting made their joyous way back to his summer palace. Those they passed gloried in the happiness of their king, and thought themselves citizens of the finest land in Ambrosius Imperator's whole kingdom.

THE INTERVENING THREE years had been kind to Myrddion. Although Eddius and King Melvig worried about the unsettling news from the south, little turmoil or death touched the far north of Cymru where Mona remained an eternal reminder of the winds of invasion. Isolated, lacking in wealth, and far from the courts of hostile kings, Segontium, Canovium, and Tomen-y-mur were sheltered by their distance from the courts of power.

Meanwhile, Myrddion healed. The scars on his head were hidden by new hair growth and, much to Annwynn's relief, he bore no physical, outward reminders of the dangerous blows to the head that had almost killed him. Only Myrddion knew that he had suffered a real loss, the sudden decline of the gift of prophecy that had been gaining strength as he entered puberty and adulthood. While he still dreamed with puzzling but vivid imagery, no waking fits came to disturb his daily routines or to terrify the servants.

Did Myrddion regret the loss of his prophetic episodes? Not for a moment. He would gladly have relinquished the dreams as well, for his rational mind preferred a more scientific explanation for the world and its workings. Yet, because he valued the mechanisms of body and mind, he regretted that he neither understood the prophetic fits that had once come upon him, nor had any further opportunity to examine them.

But Myrddion had more pressing problems of the heart. The unnecessary death of Olwyn had been a blow that he couldn't rise above, for it filled his thoughts with the desire for revenge. He had seen this poison at work on his own mother, so he understood all too well how bitterness soured the person infected with it more terribly than the object of that revenge. But, for all his logic, he couldn't escape his burning desire to crush Vortigern's skull with his bare hands if the opportunity ever presented itself. Even worse, he had learned enough about his conception to feel thoroughly lost, and no Olwyn remained with whom he could discuss those feelings of dislocation.

For his entire life, Myrddion had been a bastard, an oddity, and a demon seed, but at least he had had an identity, no matter how alien or fearsome that legacy might be. Now, he was the bastard son of a Roman rapist who had been washed up on the shore during a violent storm. Again and again, Myrddion wondered how the man had come to this pass. Had he been shipwrecked? Had he been cast overboard? The only facts he knew about his father were that he claimed to have murdered his own mother and that he was ruthless, cruel, and violent. When Myrddion stared in his silver mirror, his own beauty was a blow, for his father had been fair in face and body—a hyacinth beauty, as his fit had told him. In his tangled, confused thoughts, Myrddion discovered that it was easier to be a demon seed than the by-blow of a brutal stranger from another land.

"I am nothing and I come from nowhere," he often told Annwynn once he had returned to his apprenticeship. The wise woman read the misery in the lad's voice and was afraid for him. Myrddion was unsettled and the center of his identity had been so shaken that he couldn't find a way out of the maze of lies and half-truths that bewildered him.

Three years followed in this fashion, and Myrddion left the villa by the sea where memories flayed him day and night, for the children had grown sufficiently to develop without his support. Every room of the villa was infused with Olwyn's spirit, and although he clutched at his memories of her love as a drowning man holds on to any means of flotation to keep his head above water, so each day in Olwyn's home was a sweet agony. He saw her shade stand by the great doors, arms folded and eyes thoughtful as she looked out over Mona. When he wandered through the bare atrium, there she was with her spindle, turning raw washed wool into yarn. When he went to his lonely bed, she came to him in the night to kiss his forehead and stroke the cheeks that were already growing soft with down. Myrddion had hoped to find peace through his mastery of the healer's craft, but the acquisition of knowledge couldn't quite fill the gap in his heart. With some little regret, he left the villa by the sea and moved into Annwynn's humble cottage, where he could seek comfort in its dearth of memories. The quiet patterns of life in the cottage, and the lean-to he built with his own hands as a sleeping chamber, gave him some balance, but unanswered questions remained to torture him, even in dreams.

As Myrddion struggled to master Greek and decipher his scrolls, he could not escape the twisted face of Democritus and what had occurred as a result of that elderly man's viciousness. Melvig had taken vengeance on the old scribe, for the Greek was a convenient scapegoat for the death of Melvig's daughter. The king could be as cruel as Vortigern, especially when one of his kin was the victim, and he had responded with speedy and predictable justice. The scribe had been found and dragged to Canovium to face Melvig's righteous anger.

Democritus had pleaded, but Melvig was immovable.

"How could I know that Mistress Olwyn would die?" Democritus had begged.

"How much were you paid by the Saxons for your information?" Melvig had countered, his face becoming red with choler. Had Myrddion been present, he would have warned the terrified scribe to deny everything.

"A trifle! A pittance! I didn't ask for payment—the Saxons pressed it on me, saying that I was ensuring the safety of Cymru."

Melvig had grinned like a wily old goat that sees a tasty nettle within the reach of its sharp, yellow teeth.

"I will let your punishment fit the crime. I'll not kill you, because you never intended to harm my daughter. But you lusted to read the scrolls, to possess them, and your attempt to steal them caused the tragic events that led to my daughter's death. Therefore, like your Homer, I will let you go sightless through the world and beg for your bread."

Myrddion shuddered at the thought of Democritus, a scribe, blinded on the orders of Melvig ap Melwy, a king who dispensed justice with a careful, callous nicety. Were the scrolls worth such a penance? Myrddion couldn't tell, for Olwyn had been worth more than the lives of ten men to him, although his grandmother would have been horrified at her father's retribution. But deep in his heart, in the atavistic part of him that had no shame, he was glad that Democritus had suffered.

From Annwynn's perspective, she had an apprentice who broadened her skills and provided her with knowledge that she could never have gained alone. Despite the trouble and strife caused by the scrolls, she should have been content, but her apprentice was taking such terrible risks as he attempted to master herb lore that her heart was troubled in case he courted suicide. Sometimes, when they found unfamiliar plants about which they had little knowledge, her apprentice carried out his own experiments using himself as the patient. In several cases, he became very ill, so that only significant intervention by Annwynn saved his life.

Late one afternoon, as the healers were eating a frugal meal of cold venison, flatbread, and radishes, Annwynn broached her greatest fear.

"I believe you are becoming reckless with your life, Myrddion. Whether or not you are consciously punishing yourself, you are taking risks that are too dangerous for one so young. If you continue with these experiments, you will die."

"I have no desire to harm myself, Annwynn," Myrddion protested. "Honestly I don't. I'm seeking knowledge in the only way I know."

"Your grandmother's shade reproaches me for allowing you to place yourself in jeopardy. Besides, a war is coming, and your skills will be needed to help the wounded. An experimental treatment might be used on the dying as a last resort—not on yourself. The world has need of you, Myrddion. Besides, I love you like a son, and my heart would break if you harmed yourself unnecessarily."

This final, rather sentimental plea was robbed of any trace of mawkishness by Annwynn's obvious sincerity. Childless and husband-less, Annwynn had poured all her warm, passionate nature upon the boy-man who had enriched her craft and her life.

Shamefaced, Myrddion had nodded, and no more was said on the subject. But when his beard finally began to grow, he determined to shave and pluck the hairs away so that the face he saw daily was the same countenance that Olwyn had last seen. If his odd behavior seemed bizarre in a world of bearded warriors, Annwynn accepted his eccentricity as the least of several evils.

Spring had come again, with all the promise of budding trees, wildflowers in brilliant drifts under the trees and in the fields, and births that reflected the fecund richness of the soil, the sea, and the sky. Even Myrddion's frozen heart melted a little when he took the time to notice the wild beauty of the land around Segontium.

The only sign of trouble was the arrival of a mounted warrior whose horse stumbled down the main road leading into the quiet town. The warrior was delirious and bore an infected spear wound on his thigh, so he was carried to Annwynn's cottage. The leaders of the community of Segontium were desperate to learn the courier's message, but the young man was raving with fever.

The two healers set to work. Annwynn prepared a concoction to fight the fever and promote cleansing sleep while Myrddion addressed the ugly, suppurating wound. Because of the fever and the probable pain to be inflicted during Myrddion's treatment, the young man was given a little poppy juice in Annwynn's draft and then tied down on the healer's scrubbed table for good measure. Myrddion smelled the wound carefully and easily detected the faint, sweet odor of rot. The wound was swollen, dark, and marbled, causing Myrddion's face to turn grave.

"I'll need to cut away the dead and poisoned flesh," he explained to Annwynn as he cleansed a series of probes and knives in hot water and then held the blades over a flame to sterilize them. A translation of one of the papyrus pages had spoken of evil humors in the air and in the human touch that led to death after the flesh became corrupted, so Myrddion took pains to use water and fire to burn all taint away.

The two officials who had accompanied the warrior from Segontium winced when Myrddion cut into the wound. Green and black pus poured forth while he worked, and he cleaned up the mess with small tongs and strips of rag designed specifically for this treatment. The rags were thrown onto the fire to be burned to ash at the earliest opportunity.

Once he had opened the wound Myrddion could see the extent of the damage, and with a sinking heart he began to slice away the suppurating flesh until fresh blood came to the surface, indicating that healthy tissue had been reached. The wound grew larger and larger until an ugly pink furrow, two fingers wide, extended down the patient's thigh. Myrddion sighed with some satisfaction.

"Stay back!" he ordered abruptly as one of the town fathers moved forward to examine the procedure. "I think I've removed most of the rotting flesh, but I have to be sure or this warrior will either lose his leg or die. If you come too close, any open cuts on your body could also become poisoned."

"But will he regain consciousness?" the citizen asked, as he prudently backed away towards the door.

"Aye, if the poison has been removed. As you can see, the wound is now oozing fresh, cleansing blood." He turned to Annwynn. "I think a seaweed poultice might promote healing. Do we have any already prepared?"

"No, but I'll make one in a trice," Annwynn replied briskly, and set to work at once to prepare a vile, green-black substance that still smelled of seawater in a clean, glazed bowl. Then she used a small paddle of carved wood to fill the gaping wound with the resulting paste.

In the meantime, Myrddion had stripped the warrior and washed his limbs efficiently and without embarrassment. All the clothing was set aside for boiling or burning, in case the patient became a source of infection. Myrddion spread pads with one of Annwynn's drawing salves, placed them carefully over the wound, and bound them firmly into place. During the operation, he blessed the ancient physicians of Egypt who had passed down so much knowledge of wounds, body poisons, and infections, for much that he did was drawn directly from the papyrus scrolls.

"Now we wait! The dressings must be changed regularly to be effective and the wound must be cleansed every time. I may need to cut away more flesh, but we must be grateful that the bone has not been exposed. If that had occurred, and the poison had reached the bone, this young man couldn't be saved."

For three days, the warrior slept fitfully, assisted by the use of poppy juice to prevent any excessive movement that would hamper the healing process. Gradually, after several more applications of the knife, the deep furrow along the thigh began to develop the pink growth of scabbing flesh, and although the scarring would be terrible Myrddion felt a moment of pride in the certainty that the young warrior would keep his leg.

After informing the town council that the patient would now rouse out of his artificial sleep, Annwynn bound the young man's legs to prevent excessive movement and waited for him to regain consciousness.

Anticlimactically, the young man emerged from his deep sleep and appeared to be unconcerned with either his wound or his message. After his initial disorientation, his first thoughts were for his wife and his horse.

"I'm trying to get home to my wife in Deva. I need to go now if old Rhiannon is fit to ride. The poor old girl was nearly blown when I arrived at Segontium. I don't remember much about the journey, so I'm not sure where you are—or where I am, for that matter. I've got to get home, healer, before I'm caught on the road. Deva's been declared neutral to protect the port, so I have to keep riding."

Myrddion grinned at the young man's ready, well-exercised tongue.

"Has anyone ever told you that you're a talkative bastard? No? Don't take offense—I really am a bastard, so you can call me the same whenever you want. At any rate, the town fathers are eager for any news you might have. But don't you want to know the condition of your wound? If I seem to be laughing at you, it's because you're one of those very rare patients who seem uninterested in what I've done to them after I've carved them up."

The young warrior flushed, then laughed at his situation. Myrddion felt an immediate rush of affection for him, and was glad that he had managed to save his leg.

"I knew I had a wound in my thigh, but I had no time to treat it for I had a task to complete. When I developed a fever, I believed that I would die. If I talk too much, it's because I come from a family of women, as well as my wife, so I rarely get a word in when all my darlings are talking at once."

"It's a good thing, then, that I worked so hard on your leg. It's not pretty, but you'll walk again and, if you're sensible, you won't need a stick."

The warrior sighed and extended his hand. "My name is Ceolfrith. Yes, I know it's an outland name, but apparently there's Saxon blood somewhere in my ancestry, although it's well hidden." He brushed one hand through a bush of curly red hair too unruly to be braided. Myrddion snorted with sudden humor. "As you can see, I'm neither fair, tall, nor blue-eyed."

As Ceolfrith's eyes were brown and he stood barely five feet six inches in height, his name was indeed misleading. His shoulders were very broad and he had a disarming smatter of freckles over his nose and cheekbones, giving him the appearance of a cheeky, muscular boy. But Myrddion wasn't deceived. Ceolfrith's hands were scarred from years on horseback and countless sessions of sword practice. His eyes were surrounded by a network of wrinkles that spoke of years in the sun, so the warrior's boyishness could only be a happy trick of heredity.

Before Myrddion could explain the nature of his treatment, Annwynn ushered in the two chief councillors of Segontium and suddenly the cottage became cramped and overcrowded. The town's leaders were badly starved for news from the south.

"We hear so little of the struggles of the great ones," Selwyn the grain merchant explained with some urgency. "And wise men need to know the way the wind is blowing, if you take my meaning."

Ceolfrith nodded gravely. A township that chose the wrong side in a civil war was likely to be sacked and put to the sword without mercy.

"I serve Vortigern, as do all the men of the Deva levy. We have good cause to fear the Picts, who still come over the Roman wall when they believe us to be weak, although Vortigern has crushed them on so many occasions that they think twice before they invade in the spring. Yes, the High King has used Saxons to defeat the blue warriors and I can understand how foolish it is to invite foxes into the henhouse, but we northerners know what a scourge the Picts can be."

Selwyn nodded his understanding. As a businessman, he understood that compromise was sometimes necessary in political situations, but Myrddion felt his lips thin with disapproval at the hated name.

Ceolfrith had caught that twist of the lips.

"Healer, I understand that Vortigern's ways are cruel and capricious. Why, I have even heard that he killed a priestess from these parts some years ago, and what sensible man alienates the goddess? But Ambrosius has little interest in the north, so the Brigante, the Coritani, and the Cornovii would be left to fall to the Pictish brutes if it were not for Vortigern. We northerners make treaties for our protection, not because we like the sword hand that keeps us safe."

"Sensible!" Myrddion agreed brusquely.

"Ambrosius Imperator has promised the throne of the north to Vortimer, Vortigern's son, if he will guarantee to drive Vortigern's Saxons out of the south. Vortimer has sworn to serve the emperor and so a huge army has marched into Venta Silurum, seeking to crush the High King."

235

Selwyn and the wool trader exchanged nervous glances. Venta Silurum was far away, but war can spread very quickly.

"Vortigern has been the victor of a score of battles and his skills are legendary, so he was not so foolish as to meet his son in equal combat on level ground. We met the southerners at Y Gaer where the ground is high, uneven, and barren, and provided little opportunity to deploy the cavalry which Ambrosius had given to Vortimer in generous numbers. Nor were siege machines useful, as the terrain prevented their transportation into the mountains."

"And what happened?" Selwyn asked breathlessly, his eyes very large and nervous.

"Neither side gained any advantage, but the loss of life was terrible. Unfortunately for Vortigern, Vortimer received fresh men from Ambrosius to swell his ranks. Like any sensible commander, Vortigern abandoned the field.

"As we retreated into the north, the southern army followed us past Forden and along a river valley leading to the mountains above Caer Gai. They caught us there, and we fought to a standstill. The loss of life was even worse than at Y Gaer, so Vortigern surrendered."

"Sweet Mother!" Myrddion breathed, his heart filled with savage joy, although he took pains to ensure that his face remained impassive. "Is Vortigern dead?"

"No," Ceolfrith replied, rather affronted to discover that the healer believed that Vortigern was so stupid as to place himself in the hands of his son. "Vortigern brokered a peace by unconditionally handing over the throne to Vortimer. That should have solved the conflict, but as we moved into the hills we fell into a treacherous ambush. Vortimer had decided to rid himself of his father permanently. We managed to fight our way out of the trap and eventually reached the mountains past Tomen-y-mur. Those of us who were mounted were sent to obtain assistance, while the bulk of our men, including many hundreds who are wounded, are dug into the high ground overlooking the peninsula. They are dying like flies, for Vortimer is determined to have his way. Vortigern cannot leave the field without abandoning half of his army."

"Is Segontium under any threat from the fighting?" Selwyn asked, his face a little pale to think of the young men from the town who were unlikely to return to their homes.

"No, sir. There is no possible way that Vortigern's troops have the will to attack Segontium, nor any reason for them to do so. Vortimer has turned southwards in triumph, ready to attack the Saxon enclaves of Hengist and Horsa in the Cantii tribal lands to the east, for he must repay his debt to Ambrosius. The north is safe from this war—for the moment!"

Selwyn sighed with relief, and both businessmen gave coin to Ceolfrith out of gratitude. Like any sensible man with an eye to the future, Ceolfrith bit the coins to gauge their purity and kept them, for a provident man takes what bounty he can when an opportunity arises.

Once the senior citizens of Segontium had left the cottage, Myrddion unwrapped Ceolfrith's wound so the warrior could see the deep furrow that was now beginning to grow scar tissue to protect the flesh around the wound. Ceolfrith paled until his freckles stood out like an old man's liver spots.

"You promised that I'd walk again," he whispered. "How?"

"I had to cut away the rotting flesh or you would have lost your leg. However, I saved most of the muscle and the bone isn't compromised. The wound looks worse than it is."

"Take no notice of him, young man," said Annwynn. "He achieved miracles, but he's far too modest to say so. I could smell the stink of corruption when you reached us, and I thought you would soon be a dead man. You are very fortunate that Myrddion was the one who treated you."

"The Demon Seed!" Ceolfrith whispered and grinned shakily. "Have I been healed by the Demon Seed who defied Vortigern at Dinas Emrys? The goddess must protect me and I never knew it. I am very grateful, my lord, and my family will say prayers for your continued health and well-being." Thoughtfully, he gazed into Myrddion's face. "Healers such as you are needed at the peninsula, for those we have there are worse than useless. Initially, I was sent by my com-

237

mander to find medical aid for our suffering wounded, but all I could focus on was returning to my home and my family."

Annwynn glanced briefly at Myrddion and then began gathering together her whole supply of herbs, tinctures, and unguents, including the raw materials that had yet to be prepared. Soon she had filled a wooden chest that did double duty as a bench seat with a plentiful supply of rags, oils, herbs, and the tools of her trade.

Myrddion watched her with a hint of scorn. He knew that Annwynn could not see the suffering of anyone without offering succor, regardless of their beliefs or their vices. Annwynn had the pure soul of a healer, a virtue that Myrddion despaired of ever possessing. He knew that his hatred of Vortigern should not translate into a refusal to help the men of the north, but hatred is a vile, selfish sin and he couldn't stop himself from snapping, "You aren't going to assist Vortigern, are you? The man is a monster!"

Annwynn stared him down until his eyes dropped away from her accusing stare.

"Yes, Myrddion, hang your head in shame! We are healers, and we have no right to choose who should live or who should die. How many decent men are suffering at this moment because no one will help them? But you needn't travel with me if you do not wish to do so, for I'm prepared to go alone if necessary. Besides, Ceolfrith needs nursing, so it's best if you stay in Segontium, if your sensibilities are so delicate that you can't bring yourself to treat those men who are sworn to assist Vortigern in his battles. I'll be on my way by first light tomorrow morning, if Ceolfrith will draw me a map and give me directions on the best route to follow."

Faced with his own bitterness, Myrddion wondered if he was no better than Branwyn in his hoarded anger and malice. With a wrench, he acknowledged that Annwynn was correct in her assessment of his prejudices. He thought of that old Greek healer, Hippocrates, who told his students that they should never harm their patients. Wasn't it worse to withhold treatment than to hurt a patient through honest error?

"I'm sorry, Annwynn. We must both make an attempt to save those warriors who can be helped. As for Ceolfrith, I'm sure that Selwyn can find a family to care for him. All he needs now is rest and regular changes of his dressings."

Like Melvig, Myrddion was able to move like lightning when he became convinced of the necessity to take immediate action. Arrangements were made for Ceolfrith to be cared for by an elderly widow whose sons were at the war. In her comfortable home, the warrior would be treated like a minor king and the widow would follow Myrddion's instructions on his treatment to the letter. Then Myrddion went to the villa on the cliff top to ask for the loan of a wagon to carry Annwynn's chest and his own tools, which had been made in the style of the Roman military surgeons' implements. Eddius agreed to lend him a cart, but was not happy.

"Vortigern is a murderer, Myrddion. He doesn't deserve any medical assistance. Have you forgotten your grandmother? Have you forgotten what the misbegotten bastard did to her?"

Eddius's face was white with anger, and Myrddion felt a pang that this beloved man, who was his father in all but name, was still suffering so acutely. He tried to explain.

"I'm not going there to assist Vortigern. He can rot in Hades for all I care. But Celtic warriors are suffering, and dying, and I cannot sit back when perhaps I could save their lives. To do so would be to damn men who have been impressed by their lords to serve the king. Can't you see, Eddius, that these men have no choice as to whom they serve? If I pick and choose whom I heal, then I'm as much a murderer, by omission, as Vortigern is through his actions."

Eddius sighed. "I understand, Myrddion. I'm sorry for taking my frustration out on you. Men such as Vortigern cause so much damage to other people, yet their own suffering is minimal."

"I'm glad you understand, Eddius. But if you're angry, I shudder to think what Melvig will say. He'll blister my skin with his fury, even from a long distance." He smiled wryly. "I don't blame either of you for your reactions. I dread having to face the regicide, and I pray I'm not forced to speak to him."

"Take care, Myrddion. Vortigern has no reason to love you, and I'm sure he'd be happier if you vanished permanently."

Myrddion could only nod, for every word that Eddius spoke was ominously true.

WHEN THE SUN rose over the mountains in the early morning, the two healers were dressed and ready to depart. Until they returned, the cottage livestock would be fed by a local woodcutter who had been paid good coin to care for them. Everything had been considered, so they were free to leave for Vortigern's encampment. With the first rays of the morning sun behind them, they set forth towards the southwest.

Any journey by cart is slow, tedious, and painful, for every muscle and bone seems to be jolted out of place by the slow-moving wooden wheels. The farm cart that Eddius lent to Myrddion was even more cumbersome than usual, for it lacked even a flat bed, having been built in a large V shape to store grain or hay for transport. The two healers wrapped their fragile tools of trade in blankets of wool for protection, but nothing could shield their bodies from the jouncing, cruel ruts in the country tracks that led them towards Vortigern's encampment.

Three days of painful travel brought them to a low rise overlooking the ordered chaos of an army in the field. It was an easily defended site with excellent water and fodder, protected from the worst of the weather by a low cup of hillocks.

"Vortigern's a brilliant tactician," Annwynn murmured, as she gazed down at the defensive positions laid out in concentric circles like the layers of an onion, designed to protect the core, which was the area occupied by Vortigern's tents.

An unnatural stillness seemed to hang over the bivouac. There was scarcely any movement, and the most noticeable signs of life were the birds of prey that hovered over the camp in dense clouds. On the edge of the encampment, where the midden was situated, gulls fought and screamed over the scraps left by the men. Scavengers of a more ominous type flapped and stalked through ash and mounds of turned earth a little way removed from the main encampment, and Myrddion guessed at the grim purpose of this sheltered area. The long lines of privies were situated downwind from the lines of accommodation tents, well away from the sources of drinking water, and Myrddion accepted that Vortigern had set out his bivouac with intelligence and experience.

Nevertheless, ravens, rooks, and crows waited in every tree, hungry for carrion. Myrddion shuddered and slapped the long reins against the horse's withers. A miasma seemed to hang in the air and a faint, sweet scent came drifting into the healer's nostrils as the cart moved slowly forward.

"We'll have our work cut out for us in this place," Annwynn murmured. "I hope that Aesculapius and the gods of healing stand with us today."

But the birds knew better than to cease their long and patient wait. Death had come to the vale, and no puny healers had the power to put aside his dreadful sword.

Chapter XV

IN THE VALE OF PAIN

F ar away, in a place of hazel trees and sweet running water, Gorlois held his wife's arm firmly as they stepped carefully down a natural staircase of mossy rock towards the rushing stream below. One huge tree had fallen and blocked their path halfway down the long, spiral descent, and someone had carved a trough out of a piece of sandstone that collected a steady trickle from the springs in the hillside. Delightedly, Ygerne had drunk a little of the sweet water from her husband's cupped hands. The air was full of the sounds of busy insects and the rustling of leaves in the light breeze.

"How beautiful it is here," Ygerne murmured, gazing upward at the golden, dappled light. "We are so close to Tintagel, but the fierce winds don't reach this gentle valley. Thank you for bringing me here, for I feel a weight has been lifted from my heart."

Gorlois kissed her palm and Ygerne could feel all his love in this simple act of affection.

"Ah! Here we are at the bottom of the stairs," he said softly, but his voice still seemed too loud in this holy place.

The stream ran quickly but shallowly over glistening pebbles. Ygerne sat on a mossy log near the water's edge and removed her sandals. The texture of the wood beneath her thighs was rough, ancient,

243

and comforting, and she saw a narrow ray of sunlight pierce the trees to glimmer in the clean, living stream.

"Where are the falls, husband? My heart aches to see them and feel the goddess touch my feet through the waters."

"Take my hand and I'll lead you to them."

Ygerne lifted her skirts, placed one hand in Gorlois's warm, rough clasp, and waded into the shallows. Around a bend in the stream, husband and wife hugged the bank until they reached a deeper pool that was fed by a low waterfall backed by huge hazel trees.

Ygerne gasped and even Gorlois, who had seen Brigid's Fountain before, was struck anew by the presence of the goddess in this sacred, secret world. Over untold aeons, the water had eaten a circular hole through a great round boulder through which it gushed with a sweet, powerful sound. Below that stone was another, also pierced by the water, so the symbols of the fertility goddess were there for any eyes to see.

"The air is charged with Brigid's presence," Ygerne murmured. "This place belongs to women, and the touch of the goddess pierces my heart. My children will be great, for so she promises me."

Once again, Gorlois kissed her palm and the blue veins of her wrist, fearing to break the music of flowing water with a masculine voice. He shivered slightly, ankle-deep in the waters that seemed to purify even his bloodied soul, and he prayed that Brigid would not find him wanting in piety.

Time slowed. Whether they stood below the falls for ten minutes, or half a day, neither husband nor wife could later decide, but when they turned to leave the sacred place, its beauty had settled into their souls. The waters had given them the briefest glimpse of the huge, immutable passivity of nature that blesses the good and curses the wicked, with neither malice nor regret. For the goddess simply is—and no rational person will question the gifts of the gods when they stoop to bless us.

• • •

As THE HEALER's wagon lurched down from the hill, a cavalry officer and a dozen foot soldiers appeared out of nowhere, encircling the healers with drawn swords that threatened exposed throats. Calmly, and without obvious fear, Myrddion lifted his open hands to show that he was unarmed, while Annwynn untied the loose scarf that protected her plaited hair from the dusty roadways.

"Who are you and what is your purpose in coming to this vale?" the tall leader snapped, his eyes searching constantly for concealed weapons or any other signs of possible treachery.

"I am Annwynn, healer of Segontium, and this young man is Myrddion, my apprentice. One of your cavalrymen, Ceolfrith of Deva, reached Segontium with a putrid wound. When we returned him to health, he begged our assistance for the injured and dying among Vortigern's army. We came to assist your men, as our vows demand."

Annwynn's simple explanation had the ring of truth, but these dour, stark-eyed men trusted no one and nothing. The healers were ordered to unpack every item from the wagon, and the warriors would have pawed their way through the boxes and caused damage to their supplies had Myrddion not intervened.

"Can you see any weapons? Have you the eyes to recognize aught but herbs, scrolls filled with medical knowledge, bandages, and these surgical knives? Do you seriously believe that I could pit myself against your sword with this scalpel?"

The warrior examined the small, shining blade with interest. The haft of the scalpel was also made of iron, but the metal was scored to prevent the grip of the surgeon from slipping in bloodied hands. The burly warrior gave a small shudder, more than half convinced by Myrddion's indignation.

"Still, King Vortigern must decide. It is not so long since we were foully ambushed after a truce had been agreed, so you can surely understand our caution when strangers come into our bivouac."

"I understand, but are you so overblessed with healers that you can afford to turn us away? We journeyed three days from Segontium to offer our skills to your suffering comrades."

One of the foot soldiers, a man with a nasty burn extending from his cheekbone down into the collar of his bull-hide cuirass, squinted up at Myrddion and offered the obvious solution.

"King Vortigern will know what to do," he said. "Let him decide. There are too many good lads dying to ignore help because of a fear of betrayal."

Myrddion winced as the foot soldier grimaced painfully with the movement of his facial muscles as he spoke. "If Vortigern permits us to stay, come to see me immediately. Your burns need treatment, and quickly. What is your name?"

"I am Cadoc, from the Forest of Dean. Aye, master. If the king permits you to go to the place of healing, I will come to you."

The man's face was saturnine where the flesh was not angry, split, and swollen, but Myrddion had been attracted to a pair of warm brown eyes that sparked with intelligence. He was glad, now, that he had chosen to join Annwynn in their mission of mercy.

"Don't fear to leave your kit unprotected," Cadoc added with more cheerfulness than Myrddion could have summoned with such a burn. "I will stay and guard it, personal-like, having an interest in seeing it kept safe."

"Thanks, friend Cadoc," Annwynn answered, a warm smile enlivening her plain face. "I hope we will be brief."

"My lady," Cadoc responded and bowed, much to Annwynn's blushing confusion.

The cavalry officer led the healers on foot through the bivouac, where they saw at first hand that few men were completely unmarked. Myrddion wondered aloud why soldiers such as Cadoc, and innumerable others who struggled to clean kit, and man the cooking fires, should avoid the tents of the healers.

A strange calm hung over the encampment. Small groups of men shared simple tents of leather or waxed cloth, and these companions kept themselves occupied by cleaning their area, polishing and honing their kit and cooking what foodstuffs they collected or could scavenge. King Vortigern's provisioner issued barley, oats, and wheat each week, but the warriors found their own nettles, wild turnips, or small beasts that were trapped or brought down in the hunt.

Normally, an army is a hive of activity, but Vortigern's men were unnaturally quiet and a number were lying in their tents under the care of their compatriots. Despair and pain were almost tangible figures, sitting at campfires or stalking in the wake of the healers.

"It doesn't bode well, lad. It doesn't bode well at all. The quiet and the stink tell me that the situation here is far worse than Ceolfrith suggested," Annwynn hissed quietly through her teeth. "You must hold your temper when you confront Vortigern, for both our sakes. He will be very angry and frustrated after his experiences with Vortimer so he's likely to want to separate our heads from our necks. Keep your mouth shut, if possible, and remember our purpose here is to heal the wounded, not argue with the king."

Unwillingly, Myrddion acknowledged the wisdom of Annwynn's warning, but he still doubted his ability to look Vortigern in the eye without showing his hatred. He prayed to the Mother to give him the compassion to treat Vortigern as a man who was suffering from the betrayal of his sons.

Vortigern's tent was large and gaudily painted, and sited at the very center of the bivouac. Huge timber poles, gilded and decorated to add to the beauty of the structure, held up the hides, which were decorated with mythical beasts and strange mystical shapes that Myrddion recognized as runes from his experiences at Dinas Emrys. Inside the tent, woolen mats had been placed over the sod to provide a softer, drier surface for the king's feet, while the furnishings included a raised pallet with fine fabrics that served as Vortigern's sleeping arrangements, folding tables, and simple stools, which all pointed to a practical but luxurious environment. In the very center of the tent, Vortigern sat with his feet resting on a stool, brooding over a fine leather map.

The king raised his head like a striking snake. How odd, Myrddion thought. The old man's smallest, most innocent actions always seem to be infused with a deadly intent.

"Who are these odd people?" he muttered. "Why do you interrupt me to bring them here?"

Vortigern's temper was uneven, so the cavalryman took an involuntary step backward. Annwynn moved forward with as much grace as she possessed, and bowed low to the erstwhile High King.

"Your highness, we are healers from Segontium, and we have come to your bivouac to offer our skills and to assist your physicians. We were told by a patient, a cavalryman called Ceolfrith, that your healers were stretched to breaking point and needed assistance to treat the wounded who survived an ambush inflicted on your army."

Vortigern absorbed Annwynn's words, but his attention was focused on Myrddion's downturned face. "I know you. Who are you and where have you come from?"

Anger bubbled up into the young man's throat. He closed his eyes as he tried to compose himself, but he found the discipline very difficult. Then he raised his head, and Vortigern gripped the beaker in his hand so hard that his knuckles gleamed white in the dim light. Irrelevantly, Annwynn feared that the precious horn beaker would smash under the strain.

"I know those eyes! Who are you?"

"I am Myrddion, my lord. I am the Demon Seed!"

"Shite!" The crudity hung coarsely on the still air and the king's guard suppressed automatic shock at their master's response. "I thought you were dead, but I suppose it's difficult to kill the son of a demon. You've grown taller."

"Aye, lord." Myrddion's response was brief. The less he said, the more likely he was to keep his temper and avoid alienating Vortigern. "I have studied hard to master the healer's craft since we last met. Annwynn is my teacher, and she is a famed and a highly skilled practitioner of herbal lore. I have been her apprentice since I was nine years of age."

Smiling, Annwynn interrupted her young charge.

"Lord, my apprentice is too modest. He reads Latin and Greek and has studied the skills of the battle surgeons who served in the Roman legions. I have taught him everything I know, but his abilities surpass all my skills. Our most earnest desire is to save the lives of our countrymen. We can sense their suffering in the corruptive stink that fills the air, and have seen the birds that wait to feed on the flesh of dead and dying men."

"Very well. I'd be a poor commander if I turned away those who might save the lives of my men—but I will be watching you, Myrddion. Your eyes tell me that you still wish me harm. You have heard, no doubt, that my son has stolen my beloved wife, Rowena, and hopes to use my love for her to force me to capitulate. I am grateful that her sons were safely at Caer Fyrddin when she was taken, since Vortimer and Catigern undoubtedly see them as a threat. The boys have since been moved for their own protection, but I remain constantly on my guard against treachery."

Vortigern's eyes softened as he thought of Rowena and his sons, and seeing it Myrddion felt his deep-seated enmity towards Vortigern weaken . . . just a little.

"We appreciate your offer of help, and Cadoc will show you to the tents of the healers," the king continued. "Anything you can do to assist those fools will earn my gratitude, for our men die like flies. At least dysentery and other diseases have yet to scour my ranks further. I will demonstrate my gratitude to you at the appropriate time."

Vortigern spoke almost exclusively to Annwynn, and Myrddion was under no illusion about how far Vortigern trusted him. But at least they had been accepted into the camp, and could set to work immediately for the good of the common soldiery. Perhaps Myrddion could forget Vortigern's cruel, smiling lips and the hand that killed Olwyn.

When they returned to the wagon, now surrounded by curious warriors, they discovered that Cadoc had supervised the repacking of its contents, as well as watering their ever-patient horse. He greeted them with a lopsided grin as they trudged up the incline.

"You've still got your heads, so it seems that we have more healers than before. At least you almost seem to know what you're doing. Don't forget your promise, young sir."

"There's no chance of that, Cadoc, after all your efforts to help us," Myrddion replied seriously, while Annwynn rummaged through her box and pulled out a jar of salve. "The king has ordered you to show us to the tents of the healers, so perhaps we can see for ourselves why sensible young men like you avoid having your injuries treated."

Annwynn smiled at the young warrior, her medication in her hands. "Stand still, young man. That burn on your face must hurt excruciatingly, especially in sunlight. Smear a little of this preparation on it—it will last until we can check you out thoroughly." Then she noticed his grimy hands and black-rimmed nails, and changed her mind. "On second thoughts, my young friend, stand still and let me do it."

She worked quickly, knowing how much even her gentle touch must be hurting the warrior.

"There! The salve cools the skin and gives it some protection from the sun."

"My thanks, healer. It feels better for your touch," he murmured. "Now, see the two big tents near the very edge of the encampment? That's where the healers treat the sick and the wounded."

"Those tents are right next to the midden!" Myrddion's voice was incredulous.

"Aye," Cadoc agreed with a scornful half smile.

"Tell me what you know about these healers," Annwynn said as she helped the foot soldier onto the narrow seat above the traces of the wagon.

"There's three of them, and they have six or seven servants. The chief healer calls himself a surgeon and claims to have served with the legions in Gaul. He says his name is Balbas, but he looks like no Roman I've ever met. The other two are more like fortune-tellers than healers and spend most of their time praying to their gods and selling the wounded charms that they claim will save the lives of their patients." He noticed Annwynn's expression. "Aye, dying men will trade their last copper, or even their swords, to give themselves a chance of survival. The healers call themselves Crispus and Lupus, and we know nothing of their origins. They've certainly amassed modest wealth out of the injured during this campaign. I can't stand them, because prayers don't cure sword cuts or burns like I've got. Besides, everyone within their tents seems to die."

Annwynn and Myrddion exchanged worried glances, and the journey continued in silence.

An area of empty ground separated the hospitals from the soldiers' campsites, and as soon as the wagon entered this no-man's-land the two healers understood the reason. Their horse shied in the traces and the smell struck them at the same time. A reek of ammonia from urine, feces, old blood, rot, and vomit assailed their nostrils and prepared them for what they would soon face. Reluctantly, they descended from the cart.

"Stay here, Cadoc," Myrddion ordered, his nose wrinkling with distaste. "I don't want you exposed to the evil humors in these cesspits."

"They'll take no notice of you, sir. They're arrogant and greedy, and they'll think you've come to rob them of their profits."

"Why does Vortigern allow this?" Annwynn asked as she stared, aghast, at a dying man who had been dumped on a stretcher in the sun. A deep wound on his shoulder was black with flies.

"He has no choice. There are few healers since the druids were killed, and even fewer wise women are accepted in an army. These three drones were the best that Vortigern could find."

"Guard the wagon, Cadoc. I've a feeling we'll need tents of our own to treat our wounded."

Annwynn was bending over the warrior on the stretcher, her face grave as she felt the faint beat of his heart in the great vein of the throat. No attempt had been made to treat his wound, or to alleviate his pain. With a gentle touch, she stroked his matted hair and the sick man called for his mother.

Sickened, Myrddion shouldered his way into the hot semidarkness of the first tent and entered into something worse than Hades.

Fifty men were laid out like cordwood on dirty straw pallets in three long rows that stretched from one end of the tent to the other, with barely a foot or two between each row. Servants fed, watered, or bandaged wounds while the air was thick with groans, prayers, and weeping. Dressings were filthy and Annwynn watched, appalled, as a dirty roll of cloth that was obviously stained with old blood was reused on a gaping sore on a feverish man's foot.

Before their eyes had absorbed the full ugliness of the conditions, a coarse, condescending voice addressed them rudely.

"You there! You! Who do you think you are, disturbing my patients? And a woman at that! Your poisonous woman's blood will kill everyone unless you get out of my tent—now!"

Annwynn and Myrddion swiveled their heads in unison to better examine the man who swaggered between his charges with the arrogance of a king.

Balbas was of middle height and soft in the belly, with flabby arms and thick, womanish thighs. He was dressed in a tunic and toga that had once been clean, but were now liberally stained with blood and food. Annwynn noticed that his face was florid, with the wide-pored nose of a man who was overfond of wine. His fingers were thick and stubby, and each joint had a spatter of long black hair that matched the thick growth in his ears and nostrils and on his forearms, chest and legs. He looked like a fat monkey that Annwynn had once seen at Portus Lemanis on a Spanish galley. But that poor creature had been shivering with cold and its very human eyes had been glistening brown and bewildered. Balbas looked too smug and well fed to be afraid of anything.

"At last report, this tent belongs to King Vortigern," Annwynn relied mildly. "And he has sent my apprentice and me to assist you and your colleagues in the treatment of the injured."

"What use are a woman and an apprentice in the treatment of battle wounds? Perhaps you could treat the odd scratch and leave the practice of surgery to someone who knows what he's doing."

Balbas was so patronizing that Myrddion felt his temper begin to rise. He had been struggling with his emotions all day, and this insult to his teacher was the last straw.

"I may only be an apprentice, but I'm at a loss to recognize the school of medicine you follow, Master Balbas." Myrddion's words were honey sweet and barbed with poison. "Galen relegated prayers, sacrifice, and payment to the same level of expertise as fortune-telling. I'm told your colleagues favor the mythic approach, and reject Galen's careful observations of the internal workings of the human body."

"And he hasn't even examined the Alexandrine sources yet," Annwynn added with a grin. Truth to tell, she enjoyed baiting this bloated bag of wind, and delighted in airing names and techniques that she had only heard during discussions with her apprentice. "You really should read the observations of Herophilus, who charted the differences between veins and arteries. His work on the nervous system is a little gruesome, for he experimented on criminals while they were still alive, but where would we be without Herophilus and Erasistratus? Don't you agree, Master Balbas?"

Balbas's jaw had dropped, and he was looking both angry and baffled. Myrddion could not resist continuing the game.

"I can tell you don't follow Galen's principles, for you aren't bleeding your patients. But the values of Hippocrates don't seem to be present here either, for the reuse of dirty dressings must fall into the category of doing harm to your patients. The dictums of Erasistratus on the human brain, perhaps? But no, I think not, for there's no evidence of trepanning here. Tell me, Master Balbas, which principles do you follow?"

"Get out! How dare you question the methods of a surgeon who has twenty years' experience with the legions of Rome? Shysters! Common Celtic charlatans! Remove yourselves from my tent before I have you thrown out."

"I am impressed with you, Master Balbas, for you still don't feel a need to wash your hands, even after twenty years with the legions. This, in itself, is a remarkable achievement."

"Out! Out!" Balbas screamed, his face growing dangerously engorged with blood.

"We are leaving. I'd hate to cause your pulse rate to rise dangerously, for Herophilus warns us that stresses on our consciousness can cause brain or heart problems. We will be setting up our own poor tents very shortly, and should any of your patients care for a second opinion, we shall be happy to oblige."

"A man of your learning and experience will hardly be threatened by either a woman who dabbles in herbs or a mere apprentice," Annwynn added, turning to follow Myrddion as he hurried out of the small hell of human suffering.

If anything, the second tent was worse.

Balbas had some pretense of knowledge, but Crispus and Lupus were charlatans of the lowest and vilest order. Conditions in the second tent were even worse, for medical treatment consisted of the burning of holy oil, largely based on rancid fat and fish, the reciting of prayers, and the use of holy tokens and water from sacred wells, which was suspiciously cloudy. These ancient remedies, which invoked a host of Roman, Celtic, or even Christian gods and saints, all came at a price, and Myrddion found that he couldn't summon up even the ghost of sarcasm when he saw the waxen faces of dying men staring up hopefully as the two charlatans intoned sonorous prayers to cure gangrene, depressed skull fractures, and pierced intestines.

Crispus and Lupus were clean, well dressed, and fastidious. Despite a tendency to vanity in dress, the two men were both interchangeable and forgettable in appearance. The two healers felt their scornful words die in their throats. Such wickedness couldn't be shamed or ridiculed, only soundly crushed and uprooted.

With steely determination, Myrddion and Annwynn strode out of the second tent and returned to their wagon.

"Cadoc," Annwynn asked, "do you know of any healthy foot soldiers who would help us to set up a field station for treatment of all the sick and dying troops, regardless of the coin they possess? We treat our patients without charge, but we will need any camp followers who are prepared to volunteer and as many whole warriors as we can find. I know we promised to treat you first, but we need your help for those men who are dying."

"Of course. I'll find the men and women you need. No one who's seen those pits of evil can fail to offer assistance to real healers. Besides, Lady Annwynn, that salve has helped me already, so it will hold me until I gather up a few fellows to help us. The women will be easy, because many of their men are in those shitty tents. They've been banned, because they're women and they might be bleeding or some such nonsense. They'll come, and some of them will steal their men by force to get them away from those monsters in there."

"Thank you, Cadoc! Your help has been invaluable. We'll set up near those far trees where the air is clean and we're close to the stream." Annwynn patted Cadoc's shoulder and he blushed beet red.

"Is there anything else you need? If I can't get it honestly, I can surely steal it."

"I don't suppose there might be a few larger tents? Small ones just won't serve our purposes, unless some stout lads can build us a large cover by lashing them together between the trees. We need clean pallets, and someone to man a fire, day and night."

Cadoc grinned painfully and winked. "Can do, never fear! Just don't tell anyone where it all came from."

The tents of the healers used paid servants to do all the manual labor that Balbas and the charlatans required, but Myrddion and Annwynn preferred to use volunteers to carry out the chores needed to run a hospital. But Annwyn's judgment was correct, and a number of women, including both wives and prostitutes, traveled at the rear of the force. These women and their children were often a nuisance, but they kept the men happy with sex, hot meals, and an illusion of family, and now provided a natural supply of eager hands that would labor mightily to save the lives of the men who provided the food they ate and the protection they craved.

Now the work really began. Annwynn had brought her large iron pot and its tripod, so Myrddion set to work with a small hatchet stripping down small branches and dead wood to prepare a fireplace within a circle of stones. The two healers worked so well together that the fire was soon blazing cheerfully, while water was already coming to the boil in the pot. The wagon was quickly unloaded and the two healers cast their tools of trade into the hot water for cleansing.

A dozen men soon arrived at the small clearing in the coppice, loaded down with coarse rope and a number of leather tents, all small, that two of their number immediately began to lash together with twine, taking care to overlap the edges once they had used augers to make holes in the hides. Still others carried scythes and knives and set to work cutting the long grass that hadn't been cropped by the horse lines, stuffing crude woolen blankets with their booty to fashion makeshift sleeping pallets.

The men were followed by a ragtag group of women whom Annwynn sent to bathe in the stream, clothes and all, knowing that they would dry quickly in the warm sun. With amazement, Myrddion watched the discipline of warriors in action as the hides were strung between four sturdy trees, creating a low, mostly weatherproof roof, and the pallets were placed in position. The man suffering outside Balbas's tent was collected, stretcher and all, and Myrddion supervised the removal of his clothes. A woman with chattering teeth was set to work washing him with warm water and other fires were started to meet the needs of the patients who were soon to arrive.

Cadoc was still issuing orders to volunteers to beg, borrow, or steal woolen blankets when Annwynn instructed him to strip to the waist so she could make an assessment of his own burns. His undershirt had stuck to the burned tissue, so with the gentleness of a mother she soaked his garments to ease them away from his ruined flesh as painlessly as possible.

The burns, while not overlarge, were over a week old, and lack of treatment, other than application of cold water in the stream, had resulted in infection, especially on the shoulder and on the shoulder blade where movement of his arm had caused the charred flesh to split, tear, and ulcerate. The burns that stretched from his cheekbone to his jaw and parts of his throat were cleaner and, although angry and red, were already showing signs of healing.

"You are a strong young man, Cadoc, to still be on your feet with these injuries."

"It's that bad, is it, Lady Annwynn? I'm not going to croak, am I?"

Despite his wry grin, Annwynn could tell that Cadoc was frightened, and that he was in considerable pain.

"Not if we can help it, lad, but I'm afraid we will hurt you. I'll prepare you a small drink, and you'll become drowsy. But then I'll need to remove some of the dead flesh. I'll not lie to you, Cadoc, and I must tell you that you'll not be very pretty when I finish with you. I will say, however, that you are lucky that your arm is mostly untouched."

"Hey ho! I wasn't too pretty to start with, Lady Annwynn, so do your best."

"One more thing before I forget, Cadoc. Myrddion and I are healers, and I am not a lady. You should call me Annwynn."

"Yes, Lady Annwynn!"

Cadoc's treatment was messy, but relatively minor compared with that of many of the wounded warriors who were beginning to make their slow way to the makeshift healing tents. He was soon lying on his stomach on a clean pallet, his wounds thickly smeared with salve and the seaweed preparation in those places where Annwynn had been forced to dig deeply into the flesh and muscle. Henbane had put him to sleep, for she intended to have him return to his feet relatively quickly, for pallets would soon be in short supply as the number of wounded presenting for treatment increased. Leaving the warrior with one of the women with instructions to keep away the flies and to ensure he kept drinking clean water and broth once he wakened, Annwynn moved on to the next patient.

Myrddion had been unable to save the warrior who had been left to die by Balbas. A little poppy juice had assisted him to dream his way into death, before his body had been carried away for burial.

Volunteers were sent to find rags that were taken from anywhere and everywhere. These scraps were then placed in sand-scrubbed cooking pots and boiled over a fire. At first, the warriors found the emphasis on cleanliness very odd, but even a blind man could tell that these healers knew what they were doing, so the volunteers set to work at seemingly crazy tasks with good will. Within a few hours, several chickens and cleansing root vegetables were boiling over a fire to make a healthy broth; body waste and ruined clothing were burned some distance from the tent, and even women with babies in slings round their necks were working constantly to cleanse the probes, bone saws, drills, scalpels, and forceps that the healers used to remove arrowheads deeply buried in flesh, clean suppurating sword cuts, and even amputate limbs allowed to rot from neglect.

Myrddion worked like a butcher, his long hair plaited around his head and his tunic protected by a makeshift apron of leather that covered most of his body. Annwynn would have willingly assisted her apprentice, but she lacked the requisite strength to saw through bone speedily, retain a flap of skin to cover the stump, and stitch with quick, sharp eyes. The whole weight of removing infected legs, feet, and arms fell on the still-narrow shoulders of her apprentice, assisted by several very large cavalrymen who immobilized the flailing limbs of his patients.

At first, Myrddion's assistants had been appalled by his actions, but the young healer had taken the time to point out the greenish flesh, the red streaks that extended up towards the groin or the underarm, and the reek of rotting flesh that no amount of incense could disguise. Without realizing their new skills, these soldiers quickly became expert assistants, often able to offer their own observations to the healers and save valuable diagnostic time.

Balbas, Crispus, and Lupus, or the Three Shitheads, as the soldier-nurses called them, came once to observe the treatments that were cutting into their prestige and their profits. Lupus had discovered Myrddion's background and trumpeted his findings to the patients, as if the young man's past was a curse on everyone who met him.

"He's the Demon Seed, the son of an inhuman creature of chaos that lives in the cracks between this world and the next," he shrieked. "Every touch of his fingers can kill."

Cadoc was now well enough for light duties at the fireplaces, and he rounded on Lupus with a sneer of withering contempt.

"Yes, the Demon Seed brought death to King Vortigern's magicians, didn't he? But you're forgetting, Lupus, that they were liars, greedy charlatans who attempted to cheat the High King and blame innocents for the fall of the tower at Dinas Emrys. We've all heard the tale, haven't we, lads?"

Those nurses and patients who were listening gave murmurs of agreement, although they still watched Myrddion out of narrowed eyes.

"The magicians had good reason to try to kill our healer. Vortigern discovered how they cheated and robbed him, and snickety-snick— they lost their equipment. Are you afraid of the same fate, Lupus? How many of your patients die? How much gold and valuables are stored in your strongbox? Snickety-snick!"

Lupus paled visibly, and as he fled from the tents it was to the cries of "snickety-snick" that followed him like a portent of the future. By dawn, he had taken his strongbox, his goods, and his wagon and gone.

Annwynn and Myrddion slept in shifts. In the first week, many men died horribly, for their wounds had been neglected for too long. The healers used their precious stores of poppy tincture to ease the passage of suffering men who were doomed to undertake the journey to the Otherworld. Annwynn instructed her team of women how to comfort the dying in their last delirium, insisting that comfort, as well as relief from pain, eased the minds of the helpless.

Crispus was the next to depart, hot on the heels of Lupus, after he was threatened by the common-law wife of a man who had been left untreated when he ran out of coin. With a face streaked with tears, the woman had attacked Crispus with murderous intent and only the intervention of his bodyguard had saved his life. Like the scavenger he was, he took everything in the large tent that was of any use or value, and left his patients to their own devices.

Annwynn ordered Crispus's tent to be struck and raised close to her own makeshift hospice. She decided that the larger tent should house the seriously ill patients, while those bearing minor wounds could manage within the open shelter that had a tendency to leak in the late spring showers. Even then, Annwynn insisted that the door flaps of Crispus's tent be pinned open to allow for the free, cleansing passage of air.

As for Crispus's patients, Myrddion wished ardently that he possessed in truth the powers that were accorded to him. Skeletal men, the flesh melting from their bodies with fever, had been starved once they had spent their coin on useless charms and prayers.

"How we've avoided a serious outbreak of plague is a small miracle," Annwynn murmured as she moved between the seriously ill, cleaning wounds, changing bandages, and preparing her salves for treatment of a slew of injuries. Myrddion had sent the women to find radishes from nearby farmers and used the pounded paste on the most infected wounds with some success, as the Egyptian scrolls had promised, so Annwynn had added this ancient remedy to her armory of treatments. To every woman, foul-mouthed and coarse or not, she gave unstinting praise for their tireless efforts as, inch by inch, the healers began to win the long battle to save as many of Vortigern's warriors as possible.

One woman in particular earned unreserved commendation from Annwynn and Myrddion. Annwynn had discovered her as she wailed over the body of her man in Lupus's tent, manic with grief. All Annwynn could see of the fierce-looking creature, when she had been lifted bodily off the corpse, was a bush of red hair that curled in a bird's nest of disorder. The healer had held the angry, cursing vixen and then had rocked her like a heartbroken child when she had dissolved into a storm of weeping. Her name was Tegwen, but Myrddion doubted this bedraggled creature could ever match her name, which meant *beautiful* in the Celtic tongue.

Once Tegwen had recovered sufficiently to speak, Annwynn had promised her that her man, Gartnait, would be buried properly and not tossed unceremoniously into a communal grave. Tegwen hadn't trusted the healers, so she had insisted on digging the grave for herself.

Then, with a fierce determination, she had sought out a failed Christian priest who now served as a foot soldier in Vortigern's army.

The poor man had protested that he wasn't fit to bury anyone, but nothing stopped Tegwen when she had made up her mind. Unlike most of Vortigern's warriors, Gartnait had been a Christian, and he would be buried as a Christian.

"But I cannot do this thing, woman. I cannot! I forsook the church of Jesus years ago, and these lips aren't clean enough to pronounce the holy words or speed your man's journey to heaven."

Tegwen was obdurate. Her green eyes flashed with purpose and the lapsed priest was certain that she would use the knife in her leather belt to force his compliance, if he persisted in his refusal.

"If not you, then who? Where will I find a priest in these heathen lands? God will forgive us both, as long as my Gartnait has the holy words spoken over his grave. Will you deny my husband the solace of heaven?"

In the face of such determination, the soldier had relented and Myrddion heard the Christian intonation of the prayers for the dead for the first time. Perhaps the ceremony lacked the dignity of cremation, but the sonorous repetition of "ashes to ashes, dust to dust" fitted the mournful occasion so well, and yet contained such a hopeful message of rebirth, that Myrddion was deeply moved.

Once Gartnait was buried and Tegwen had filled in his grave and stamped the earth down over him, she seemed to collapse from within like a pricked bladder. Her determination to ensure that her man was given a Christian burial had consumed and sustained her, and now she was empty and lost.

"Tegwen, get up and go to the river," Annwynn demanded in a voice that would not be denied. "Now, Tegwen, for there are other men who need your help. I need you, but only if you are clean and willing. Here is some sheep's fat, so hurry to the river to scrub yourself clean with it. All your body must be cleansed, and your clothes. Then, when you are dry and dressed, join me in the large tent. On your feet, woman. The time for tears is over."

Annwynn had slapped a hard lump of fat into Tegwen's grimy paw and the woman had looked at the healer with a blank expression that registered her shock. Then, slowly, like someone who sleepwalks, she had obeyed. Later, the creature who trudged back from the river looked a little like a half-drowned mop of orange wool, but she was undeniably clean. Her skin was raw where she had abused her flesh with sand to remove layers of grime, while her hair was desperate for the services of a strong wooden comb.

"Tegwen," Myrddion demanded roughly, so that the woman was forced to meet his eyes. "How tough and strong are you? Over the past few days I have learned that you are determined, but will you faint at the sight of blood? Can you hold flaps of flesh where once legs used to be, without flinching? Can you help me to save the lives of dying men? If you cannot carry out these tasks, tell me now, else you'll be of no use to me."

Tegwen blanched, for Myrddion had been deliberately blunt. Better she should know the truth about her duties now, and therefore not cause added problems by vomiting during an amputation. Myrddion needed an extra pair of hands—deft, woman's hands—that could help him during bloody and urgent surgery.

Tegwen pulled herself together visibly, then raised her newly cleansed face so that she could assess the young healer. Her voice was rusty and scratched from the tears she had shed.

"You weren't here to save Gartnait's life, but perhaps you will heal other men whose women weep as I did. Yes, I can do whatever you ask of me. I won't faint or vomit, but you'll need to explain what you want very carefully, because I've got no learning. Gartnait said I was stupid."

Tegwen's voice was a deep contralto that had the consistency of warmed honey. Surprisingly, Myrddion discovered that the voice charmed him, and he said as much to the young woman. She laughed ironically.

"My old da used to swear I could call the birds down out of the trees, which was useful, as I'm a long, awkward sort of woman."

As Tegwen was nearly as tall as Myrddion, she towered over most of the warriors who made up Vortigern's army. Myrddion spared a moment of sympathy for a girl whose only beauty was in the promise of seduction in her voice.

Within a surprisingly short period of time, Tegwen proved that she possessed a nimble pair of hands, matched with a strong stomach and an earnest desire to serve with her whole heart. With her calm presence across the table from Myrddion, surgeries were completed faster and seemed less traumatic for the patients. When the early hours of morning came creeping, and Death took more than his share of sufferers for his own, Tegwen sang tunefully of the countryside, of young love or the lambing, so that more than one man survived the dreadful darkness. Her voice had the power to rekindle hope, a skill as potent as her agile fingers and her unflinching stubbornness in the face of terrible wounds.

Ten days of endless toil had passed in a nightmare of death, little sleep, and the maintenance of discipline among their volunteer staff. The healers also spent many hours treating the small injuries that occur in any large group of soldiers, such as burned hands from cooking fires and broken limbs from falls, as well as the colds and dysentery that are a warrior's lot in life. When Vortigern sent for Annwynn and Myrddion, the healers had no reason to fear that any complaint had been leveled against them.

They were wrong.

Jealous of his damaged reputation, Balbas had asked for an audience with Vortigern and had accused the Segontium healers of consorting with demons to save the lives of the wounded warriors from Vortigern's army while stealing their souls and their allegiances. Although the charges appeared entirely crazed, Vortigern was so suspicious of treachery within the ranks that he was eager to question the healers in case he was nurturing threats from within his own camp.

When Balbas repeated his accusations with an oily, confident smile on his greasy face, Myrddion felt the hot blood of fury rush to his cheekbones. Recognizing the signs of anger exacerbated by the boy's exhaustion, Annwynn placed one hand on her apprentice's arm and took a step forward towards the king, making a full obeisance.

"My lord king, I ask that you send your most trusted servants to our hospices to observe what we have done. Let them question the patients and ask if any prayers have been made over them to any god, let alone the agents of chaos. Balbas lies, because his patients die from his ministrations while others demand to be treated by us. He loses those fees that he considers to be his due because we charge our patients nothing and bear all costs ourselves. Lord king, malice has come close to you in this fine tent, because Balbas's spite will keep your army weak and unable to defend itself if you accept his tainted words."

Vortigern was shrewd, so he sent his trusted horse captain to check the truth of Annwynn's explanations. Then while Balbas began to sweat profusely, Vortigern bared his lower leg to expose a bandage that covered the fleshy part of his calf from knee to ankle.

"If you speak the truth, Annwynn, you should be able to explain why this scratch refuses to heal. Balbas maintains that the weapon that nicked me was poisoned and that I risk serious illness unless I find a priest of Mithras to cleanse the wound with water from the secret underground temple where the god presides. What is your opinion?"

While Annwynn carefully unwrapped the dressings, Myrddion asked the king if he had any pain or swelling in his groin. Vortigern nodded, rather nervously.

"Then you have a deep-seated infection in your leg, lord king. I don't need to see the wound to assure you that it cannot heal without skilful intervention."

Vortigern shot a malevolent glance at Balbas, who tried to look skeptical and superior. Meanwhile, Annwynn had removed the stained bandages, and asked if she could wash her hands in hot water.

"Why?" Vortigern's head reared back in the action that the healers realized was habitual with him.

"If I touch clean bandages with these fouled hands, I'll only reinfect your wound. We try to remain as clean as possible and always use tongs rather than our hands if we come into contact with infections. We always boil our wrappings."

"Balbas?" Vortigern snapped. His dark eyes had become hard and suspicious.

"These healers follow the Egyptian and Alexandrine methods which have no standing with either the legions or the recognized philosophers. I ascribe to Galen and his methods."

"Then we shall see!" Vortigern warned darkly. "The Demon Seed hates me, so it's possible that he could try to kill me while I am ill. But if his words are true, Balbas, then you are a proven liar."

"Lord," Myrddion interrupted, "may we collect our tools of trade to treat this wound? It's already corrupted by the humors in the air and will soon become gangrenous if we don't lance it immediately."

"Get on with it, Demon Seed. Collect what you need, but the herb teacher will treat me herself. I'll not trust you anywhere near me with a naked blade in your hand."

A servant was instructed to bring a bowl of very hot water and some clean cloth. When it arrived, Annwynn allowed some of the liquid to drizzle over the wound. What she saw gave her no pleasure.

"I'm afraid that you'll need to trust my young colleague, my lord, for this wound must be reopened by a healer with great skills. See the red swelling? There's no green flesh as yet, nor is there a red line heading towards the groin, gods be praised, or we'd have to remove your leg. But the damaged and dead flesh must be removed from this injury."

"Don't listen to them, lord." Balbas whined. "See? New flesh already seals the wound."

"Then why is it shiny, red, and swollen to twice its normal size?" Annwynn countered.

Vortigern peered at his calf, which was indeed red and angry in appearance and swollen to almost twice the size of his other leg. Annwynn could imagine the thoughts that were chasing each other behind the king's slate-green eyes, and she was glad she wasn't standing in Balbas's place.

As a silence charged with menace began to develop, Myrddion arrived back at the king's quarters at a run, followed almost immediately by Vortigern's cavalry captain, who was looking a little green and appeared to be on the point of vomiting. The king stared at him.

"Caradoc, what did you find in the tents of the healers?"

Balbas gave every impression of a man eager to cut and run, but Vortigern lifted a finger and Caradoc blocked the entrance to the tent.

"What did you find in the tents, Caradoc?" the king snapped again. "Be brief, because my leg pains me greatly."

"Both sets of tents contain seriously wounded men, but the stink in Balbas's tent would make a sound stomach empty. It was disgusting. There were only six men in the Roman's tent to care for the many dozens of wounded—who all seemed close to death. However, there were a large number of workers in the tents of the Segontium healers. In fact, there seemed to be at least one volunteer caring for every seriously wounded patient, while the air and surroundings seemed congenial. The patients were eating and seemed to be mostly free of pain."

Vortigern grinned like a wolf. "If I were to stab you in the shoulder this very second, Caradoc, and you were forced to choose your healer, whose tent would you attend for your treatment? I can easily organize the wound if you have any difficulty in making up your mind."

Caradoc looked slightly apprehensive, knowing his master as he did, and decided that truth was the best policy.

"I would go to Annwynn's tent without hesitation, my lord."

"Good enough!" Vortigern muttered, before turning his attention back to Balbas. "You will remain here, my friend, for I have plans for you." Balbas paled.

"My lord," Annwynn interrupted bravely, for she had no wish to see Balbas killed, despise him as she might. "Myrddion is the surgeon, so he must be the healer to open your wound."

"I'm bound by my oath, lord," Myrddion added, although every fiber of his being shouted that he should use his scalpel on the great vein in Vortigern's thigh and watch him bleed to death in front of him. Character and the dictates of his craft pushed down the urge for revenge, but left his mouth dry and cottony with distaste. "Besides, I know you would take revenge on Annwynn if I moved against you by even the flicker of an eyelash. I'll not risk my mistress, even if I hate you forever."

Vortigern nodded and ordered a bench seat to be placed under his foot. "I'll be watching every move, Demon Seed. Don't let that pretty knife slip."

"There's no chance of that, King Vortigern."

The young man stood over the swollen flesh where the two edges of the wound met, partly joined by tissue and partly gaping, and slashed the injury open with speed and accuracy. Except for a sigh of surprise, Vortigern didn't react until he saw a viscous ooze of yellow pus pour out of the cut. He paled a little, and his fingers clenched with fury. As a warrior of many years, he understood the significance of this putrid flow of corruption.

"I must cut deeply into your wound until I reach the healthy flesh and clean red blood comes to the surface," Myrddion told him. "Then I'll thoroughly cleanse the wound before treating it with a salve and herbs. Later, when I'm satisfied with your progress, I'll stitch it together again."

"Get on with it," Vortigern demanded, and Myrddion obeyed cheerfully, hoping that every necessary action caused some pain to the king. When the wound had been thoroughly cleansed, smeared with radish paste and seaweed, and then bandaged by Annwynn's gentle hands, the king's face was a little pinched around the mouth, but he was visibly impressed with the competence of the healers. He was also angry with Balbas.

"You might have killed me with your incompetence, Balbas. I have paid you well for your services in the past, but now I discover that you're a fraud. Therefore, for the fate I might have suffered if I had relied on your tender mercies, your right hand will be severed at the wrist so that you aren't tempted to harm any more of my loyal warriors. Heal yourself, surgeon! You have made enough red gold out of your position here to be able to pay for your own treatment. Then you will take your tent and depart this place quickly, before I decide that you should lose your other hand. For the sake of their lives, your patients will be cared for by the Segontium healers."

A silence followed, until the Roman, recovering a little from the shock that had held him speechless, tearfully begged for mercy. Normally Myrddion would have remonstrated with the king, but Annwynn unobtrusively kicked his ankle to ensure he remained silent. Besides, Myrddion was sure that the loss of a hand was a trivial punishment for the sins Balbas had committed out of love for money.

Justice was done, and the Roman was packed off in his wagon after Annwynn had used fire and salve to seal the bleeding stump. Weeping, and only half-conscious, Balbas had to endure the curses and thrown rubbish of Vortigern's warriors. He was fortunate to leave the camp alive.

But the ravens and crows still waited in the forest, although they had been cheated of their prey. And Myrddion had passed an enormous test for any healer. Finally, he had come to accept that all suffering must be alleviated, regardless of the character of the patient. The healer has no right to choose, for every saint, hero, sinner, and criminal has the right to be treated. Now, at last, Myrddion had won the right to claim that he was a true healer.

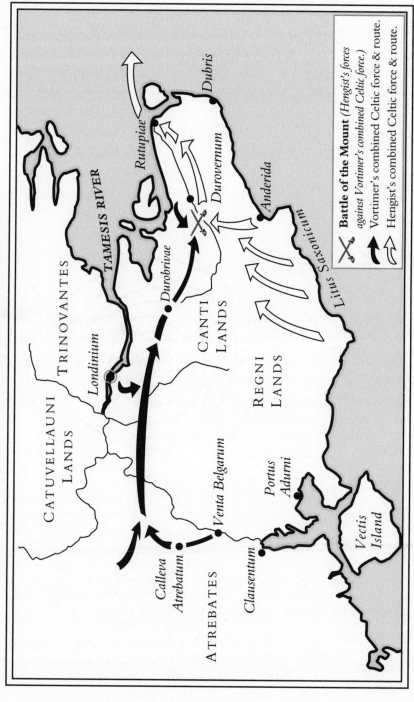

Hengist's War in Southeast Britain

CATUVELLAUNI LANDS

TRINOVANTES

TAMESIS RIVER

Londinium

Durobrivae

Rutupiae

Dubris

Durovernum

Anderida

Litus Saxonicum

CANTI LANDS

REGNI LANDS

ATREBATES

Calleva Atrebatum

Venta Belgarum

Clausentum

Portus Adurni

Vectis Island

Battle of the Mount *(Hengist's forces against Vortimer's combined Celtic force.)*

Vortimer's combined Celtic force & route.

Hengist's combined Celtic force & route.

The Battle between Vortimer/Catigern and Hengist/Horsa

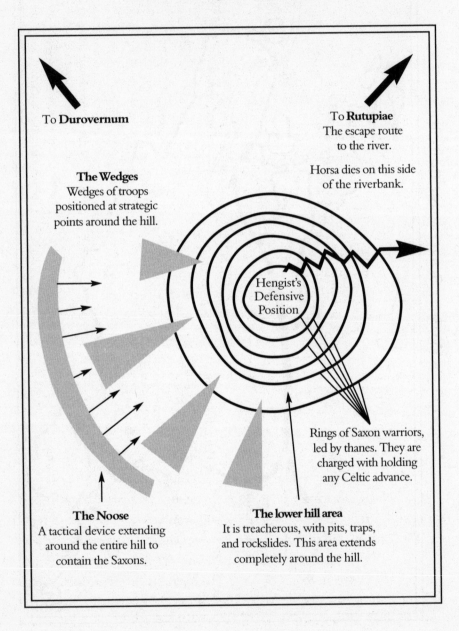

To **Durovernum**

To **Rutupiae**
The escape route
to the river.

Horsa dies on this side
of the riverbank.

The Wedges
Wedges of troops
positioned at strategic
points around the hill.

Hengist's
Defensive
Position

Rings of Saxon warriors,
led by thanes. They are
charged with holding
any Celtic advance.

The Noose
A tactical device extending
around the entire hill to
contain the Saxons.

The lower hill area
It is treacherous, with pits, traps,
and rockslides. This area extends
completely around the hill.

Chapter XVI

A GOOD DAY TO DIE

Then all the councillors, together with that proud tyrant Gurthrigern [Vortigern], the British king, were so blinded that as a protection to their country they sealed its doom by inviting in among them (like wolves into the sheepfold) the fierce and impious Saxons, a race hateful both to God and men, to repel the invasions of the northern nations.

—GILDAS, *ON THE DESTRUCTION AND CONQUEST OF BRITAIN*

Three years earlier, Hengist and Horsa had made their separate ways to Thanet Island, accompanied by a small army of the disaffected Saxons from Dyfed and Glywising. Horsa had been forced to travel slowly because of his healing leg, but Hengist's warriors had raged through Cornwall to remind the young, newly returned Ambrosius that his lands would never be safe while Hengist drew breath.

The isle of Thanet crouched at the mouth of the Tamesis. To the south lay the green, tempting lands of Durovernum, Durobrivae, Rutupiae, and Portus Dubris. With his wolflike brain, Hengist compared the distance between these places and the lands of Gaul, Belgica, and

Lugdunensis. Smelling the tang of the salty Litus Saxonicum and its plentiful shoals of fish, he determined to thrust his warrior's hands deep into the black soil of the south.

"We wander no more, brother," he told Horsa, who grinned his boy's smile in a man's face. "Here we make our stand, and tempt the goddess of fate."

Accustomed to existing cheek by jowl with the great Roman cities of Londinium and Durobrivae, the Cantii warriors were unprepared to stand against barbarian warriors who made lightning-fast, destructive raids deep into their homeland. The Cantii had greeted the arrival of Ambrosius, grandson of the legendary Magnus Maximus, with renewed hope, but Vortigern still held the entire north of the isle in his mailed fist, so Ambrosius's benevolent reign seemed doomed to be transitory, making the Cantii elders cautious in their dealings with both kings. Fast couriers brought the news that Vortigern had been defeated in battle by his sons, but as the old tyrant still lived, the Cantii dreaded that a civil war would shake the fragile peace. They had never expected an invasion so close to home—a barbarian attack designed to steal everything they possessed. Now the unthinkable had come to destroy the peace of generations.

Hengist's fighting ships, the ceols, made the brief journey out of Thanet to the lands of the Cantii tribe. As Myrddion had recognized immediately, Hengist was an unusual barbarian, a man with a considered, almost cold nature who would never unleash either violence or forgiveness unless he had something to gain. Therefore, Hengist and Horsa brought fire, destruction, and death to the south not for the pleasure of smashing the glorious past, but to dishearten the Cantii and to force them to run.

And run the Cantii did, straight to young Ambrosius, the last of the Roman kings, who had his own demons and the fear of failure dogging his heels.

Hengist controlled the seaports of Rutupiae and Portus Dubris, understanding that a good commander always maintained a line of retreat, not to mention a funnel through which allies and supplicant thanes could arrive from Germania to swell his forces. Besides, the Celts had no ships and the Roman galleys had long departed. Hengist was well aware of the great advantage that he held in this regard.

His rear secure, Hengist turned his attention towards Durovernum, with its wealth and strategic importance. Alarmed by the sudden emergence of sea wolves on his doorstep, Ambrosius stirred at Venta Belgarum. Durovernum fell, and refugees began the long trek to Londinium with every stick of furniture and personal item that could be carried, as Hengist successfully carved a huge swath out of Ambrosius's kingdom.

This dangerous situation could not be permitted to endure. Ambrosius looked to the north and placed the blame for the Saxon presence in his domain squarely where it belonged, on the greying head of Vortigern, who had long been accused of treachery. Ambrosius already loathed Vortigern with a hatred that could not be assuaged by land or power. Following the death of their father, Constantine, Ambrosius's older brother, Constans, had briefly been High King of the Britons. Vortigern had been his chief adviser but, hungry for what he saw as his right, a Celt as king of the Celts, he had slain Constans with his own bloodstained hands. The years of Ambrosius's childhood, spent wandering with his infant brother as homeless refugees from the isles of Briton and living on the charity of the Romans in Byzantium and Brittany, had carved a scar of bitterness through Ambrosius's soul. Should Vortigern ever dare to come within range of Ambrosius's sword, the ageing megalomaniac would die.

And so, during the last three years, Ambrosius had played a careful waiting game in which, out of a desire for revenge, he courted Vortimer and Catigern and attempted to destabilize Vortigern's kingdom and force the old king into making intemperate decisions.

Now, in Venta Belgarum, Ambrosius stared down at the bowed heads of Vortimer and his bastard brother Catigern. The young warriors were little like their father in either appearance or manner, which was fortunate for their continued health. Raised in a land rendered secure by powerful kings, the sons of Vortigern had a soft, deceptive courtliness that sat awkwardly with their traitorous desire for their father's bloody throne. Despite their usefulness to his ambitions, Ambrosius felt his lip curl with disgust at their easy treasons. For all his viciousness and treachery, Vortigern was a man. The qualities of his half brother, Vortimer, and the bastard, Catigern, were open to debate.

They've never had to struggle, or to eat the bread of charity, Ambrosius thought contemptuously as he schooled his face to smile. As the bastard son, Catigern resents his brother. He looks me straight in the eyes, and lies without hesitation. I can understand the barbarian Hengist far more easily.

As always, Catigern rose first, for, although younger than his half brother by some three years, he was impulsive and often reacted before he had taken the time to reflect. Catigern was the prototype of his people in appearance, with dark brown hair, freckles, a snub nose, and a pair of dark brown eyes that had no softness in them. His face was long and far more saturnine than his nose suggested, and he possessed a pair of dark, mobile eyebrows that drew the eye and created an impression of extreme animation. Ambrosius didn't trust him an inch.

Vortimer seemed to have little of Ambrosius's mother, Severa, in him, although they were kin. While his thinning hair had traces of red in it, the overall effect, out of the sun, was of a rather rusty brown. His eyes were blue with yellow lights. To this unfortunate coloring was added a long nose inherited from his father, and eyes that sat too closely together above a mouthful of crooked teeth. However, this unprepossessing face was set atop a warrior's body that was hard, compact, and disciplined. A traitor to his father he might be, but Vortimer was a thinker with the physique that could put ideas into action whenever he chose to do so.

Ambrosius was not so foolish as to judge Vortigern's son on his appearance. What he saw before him was a man who had always stood in the shadow of his ruthless father. Their shared mother, Severa, had been a Roman with patrician blood, but as Rowena's sons grew tall he envisaged a future where he was rejected in favor of his younger half brothers, regardless of his impeccable lineage.

Never, never, never!

Raised with the same harsh necessities for survival, Ambrosius recognized in Vortimer his own capacity for great patience and dark anger. When he examined him closely, Ambrosius understood Vortimer all too well.

The brothers were dressed in Roman battle harness of plated ox hide, greaves, arm rings, and wrist guards, but they had been forced to relinquish their weapons at the doors of Ambrosius's official residence at Venta Belgarum. Because he recognized the necessity, Vortimer's sangfroid remained intact, but Catigern was sulking at the lack of trust exhibited by the Roman king and the loss of his ostentatious weaponry, for the younger man lusted after outward display. Like many bastards, he was always quick to take offense.

"Your presence, unharmed, suggests that you have won the field, Vortimer. Or should I now address you as the supreme warlord of the north?"

"Aye, Lord Ambrosius." Vortimer was obviously a man of few words.

"Why dissemble, King Ambrosius?" Catigern boasted unpleasantly. "No doubt your spies have already informed you that we soundly drubbed Vortigern's warriors. My ambush was especially effective."

The sneer on Catigern's face was repulsive to the Roman king, who recognized an immediate similarity to the man who had assassinated Constans. Nauseated and angered by the flail of memory, Ambrosius decided that the younger prince was an obnoxious, snide young man who, jealous of his less demonstrative brother, would attempt to steal the throne without a qualm. He appeared to be proud of the fact that he had driven his harried father into a trap, forcing Vortigern to fight his way to safety without striking a blow against his sons.

Ambrosius smiled ambiguously. Better and better! In Hades, Constans would be fed the rich blood of his murderer and his sons should Catigern be left to his own devices.

The younger brother's irritating, feckless grin flashed again, revealing his perfect teeth, so unlike the crooked fangs of his more responsible brother. At that moment, as an honest man, Ambrosius felt a twinge of shame at his use of such an unworthy tool as Catigern. But necessity makes monsters of all kings.

He stared across the flagged floor of the great hall of Venta Belgarum. A grey building, all told, that would look the better for paint and gilding. It was a dim and dreary countryside, too, after the golden sunshine of Byzantium or the soft fields of Brittany. Gilded domes and walls of shimmering white, cobalt blue, or brick red swam for an instant in Ambrosius's blue eyes. He saw the tessellated floors, rich with gold, silver, precious glass, and mica so that imaginative fish appeared to swim in a jeweled sea of dolphins, gods, and brilliant anemones. Memory was a trap, a curse that he tried to lock away so that those brilliant days were lost with his grandfather in the glittering illusions of memory.

"I intend to hold you to your oath, Vortimer. As High King of the north, you are sworn to destroy the Saxon enclave that has taken the lands to the south of the Tamesis. From Thanet Island, Thane Hengist, his brother, his house carls, and his slaves have sunk their shallow roots into *my* earth. He must be destroyed before he is joined by other landless Saxons who seek to steal our land. Believe me, Vortimer, in case you harbor any hopes that the legions will return one day, all that was Rome is finished, and all that stands between the Celtic people and slavery is our mailed fists. If you wish to live in freedom, then you must be prepared to shed your blood with the southern tribes."

"I remember my oath, my lord," Vortimer replied, a little tersely. "I will drive the Saxons out and I will dance on their bones. Then I will pursue my father into the land of the Picts, north of the wall, from where he will never return. So have I sworn, Lord Ambrosius."

"And will you swear allegiance to me, to Ambrosius, as the High King of all the Britons? You will rule all the tribes north of Sabrina Aest, but you must ultimately bend your knee to me."

Vortimer and his brother looked up at the man seated on the dais. He was older than either of them, almost thirty and his eyes were very blue, while his artfully curled hair was fair, short, and thick. He dressed in the Roman style, in a tunic and toga edged with the imperial purple; he was clean shaven and his skin had a deep golden tan, even in the watery sunshine of Venta Belgarum, as if hotter suns had seared him in his youth. His face was beautiful in a cold, patrician fashion, but no man would have dared to call him effeminate. Deep lines scored his face between his golden eyebrows and dragged down his well-shaped mouth. Vortimer shivered, knowing that this man had experienced places, people, and abominations that he hoped he would never see for himself.

Then, with good grace, Vortimer and Catigern vowed to serve Ambrosius to the death.

"I have watched the ruination of Rome, Vortimer, and the decay of order in Gaul. I have seen the barbarians burn, loot, and rape everything that was ordered, beautiful, and pure. I have watched the fall of the gods and, unless we succeed, we will oversee the destruction of these isles and all that has been constructed out of mud and struggle. You must win this battle, Vortimer. You must kill Hengist and his brother, or else they will go elsewhere in this land and take chaos with them. They have nowhere else to run to, you see. In fact, they are rather like us."

Then Ambrosius laughed with such bitter humor that Catigern looked at his brother with raised, questioning eyebrows, as if their ruler was a man wanting in his wits. But Vortimer had caught a glimpse of a possible future in Ambrosius's pale-blue eyes, and remembered the tall, chill power of Hengist when he was a member of his father's guard. Although he had tried to convince himself then that such a brute had neither the intelligence nor the character to pose a threat to his ambitions, Vortimer had suspected that Hengist could read the treason that already lived, full grown, within his mind.

"Hengist is a clever man and he's been tested by years as a mercenary to the Jute king and anyone else who would pay in coin," Vortimer said. "He's a mercenary by necessity, for he is the grandson of a king who was forced to flee to the far north where the winters freeze the body while the blood of the warriors runs hot. Homeless and bitter, Hengist and his brother Horsa seek a homeland for their people—at any price."

Although Catigern snorted with contempt, Ambrosius smiled in regretful agreement with Vortimer's assessment of Hengist's character. The Saxon brothers had known the same brutal childhood as Ambrosius and his younger brother, Uther.

"Very good, Vortimer; you begin to understand the enemy." He paused. "Gentlemen, our way of life is changing. For years beyond counting, the Romans maintained the rule of law across most of the civilized world. But the caesars have deserted their cities and their citizens, and have run to the old capital of my ancestors in the far east, leaving the wild tribes to march out of the north. Bring me Hengist's head, for nothing else will convince his brethren to stay within the lands of Frisia, Bernica, and the Anglii."

Then Ambrosius dropped his head and stared at the grey flagging, his thoughts far away in space and time, as if this short audience had sapped his spirit. When the brothers backed away and left his presence, Ambrosius scarcely noticed.

CATIGERN HAD HIS uses, Vortimer decided, as his brother began the onerous task of provisioning Vortimer's wholly inadequate army for a prolonged campaign. For his part, Vortimer pored over maps of the terrain, exploring the probable outlines of Hengist's strategies. As an irregular, the Frisian was a man who always had an exit strategy, but Vortimer was certain that only a dire emergency—like a huge, conventional army in direct attack—would convince Hengist that he must withdraw his forces from the field.

But Hengist on the loose with small bands of independent warriors meant that a strategic genius would be at large, and the worst fears of Ambrosius would come to fruition. No! Vortimer knew that a strong army would be vital if they were to crush the Saxons, once and for all.

As soon as Catigern had secured sufficient provisions for his army, Vortimer sent him to the great cities of Londinium and Durobrivae. Built on flat land, these ancient centers had no defenses against a determined invading force and, therefore, were eager to halt any Saxon attackers in their tracks. Acknowledging Vortimer's only possible strategy, Ambrosius sent a scroll demanding that the city fathers of these two wealthy centers place a levy on their young men and provide well-armed and experienced troops for the coming conflict.

Catigern was amazed at the enthusiasm of the city fathers of Londinium, who quickly provided supply wains loaded with food, a large number of experienced foot soldiers and archers, all of whom were Roman-trained, and a war chest of gold pieces donated specifically to fund the campaign.

"They'd have given me anything I asked for, brother," he enthused on his return. "Shite, but they fell over themselves to be helpful. Why were they so eager?"

"Just look around you, Catigern," Vortimer replied evenly, having ridden to the outskirts of the city. "It's flat, transport is easy, and it's the hub of many major roads, so how would you keep out determined invaders?"

"There are walls," Catigern retorted. He had no respect for his brother's caution.

"Yes, but the city has grown beyond those walls and they are now totally inadequate. Any clever, well-organized commander can simply row up the river, just as the Romans did. Londinium is a huge prize and it is very, very vulnerable. I also heard that Durobrivae is sending troops. Apparently, Ambrosius explained to its city fathers the need for a large army to send the Saxons back across the Litus Saxonicum where they belong. The masters of Londinium are aware of the seafaring skills of the Saxons and Jutes, whose ships are capable of sacking the very heart of their city. Nor does Ambrosius care if Hengist learns of our plans, because he realizes that the Frisian is no fool. He will guess anyway that we are on the move and attacking in strength, and Ambrosius wants the Saxons to experience the taste of fear."

Vortimer looked out over the growing camp of warriors, most of them still trained and disciplined in the old Roman way. Londinium had been a great fortress of the legions, so the warriors still set out their camp in the squares that the legions had demanded. For a moment, Vortimer felt tears leap into his eyes. He had been a very small child when the Dracos Legion had sailed out of Glevum for the last time. He remembered the Red Dragon insignia blazing in the sun before the pennon was furled and the galleys set their huge sails. He had felt a similar sensation when his grandfather had deserted him in death.

"Why so glum, brother? We'll have over a thousand men while Hengist will take to the field with four hundred if he's very lucky. We can't lose." Catigern managed to sneer and smile at the same time, suggesting wordlessly that his brother was an old woman who was weighted down with the fear of failure.

Vortimer held his temper, although sometimes he longed to smash his brother's sardonic face and perfect teeth. As a bastard, Catigern had never been expected to succeed in everything he touched, unlike Vortimer, and he existed in a world where snide, unkind whispers were used to denigrate those you detested. If too much had been loaded on Vortimer's shoulders, then Catigern had been trusted with too little. Even now, Vortimer displayed an empathy that his brother derided, while still being aware that it was his greatest strength. That he managed to resist the temptation to strike Catigern showed the patience and self-control that had contributed so much to the defeat of his father in the recent pitched battle. Sometimes, Vortimer felt very alone, for he knew that Catigern would kill him without a second thought if he sensed a weakness, or believed that he could capture the loyalty of the tribes. Vortimer often forgot that Ambrosius was his half brother and he was an implied threat to the Roman. Would Ambrosius kill both of Vortigern's older children, even his mother's son?

"You're an idiot at times, Catigern."

"And you're an overcautious old woman, shithead!" Catigern responded cheerfully. "We can't lose, brother, so stop looking for problems that don't exist."

"Hengist will. That bastard frightens me. He always managed to make the hairs rise on my arms, even when he stood behind Father's chair looking meek and subservient. Horsa is a good-natured ox who was born to follow a stronger mind and a more controlled sword arm, but Hengist is different. Right now he's thinking very hard."

Catigern gave an exclamation of disgust and stalked away, and Vortimer turned to his personal guard, suddenly energized the way his brother never was, for all his furious activity. "Call out the captains. We leave for Durobrivae in five hours by forced march. Now, bring me my armor."

HENGIST ISSUED ORDERS in a flurry of activity and urgency. "Send the women, children, and old men to Rutupiae. The ceols must be ready to run if we should fail in the field. Accept no excuses. Not a woman or a child can be risked, for they are our future. They are both Britons and Saxons, and they will avenge us if we should fall in this battle. Move it, Horsa!"

Hengist had a remarkable mind, in that he forgot almost nothing. Unlike the other thanes and warriors, he had taken easily to horseback and checked every mile of his land. He could remember every hill, every fold in the ground, and every stream and river between his army and the sea. His people had no maps, a lack he regretted, and he decided to put this matter to rights at some time in the future if he survived the coming conflict. For now, he must find land of his own choosing as the site of the imminent battle. His captives had regrettably died under torture, but all men soon volunteer information when in extremities of pain, no matter how brave or patriotic they might be. Even hatred cannot defeat unremitting agony. Hengist had been told the size of the horde he faced under the command of Vortimer and Catigern.

"Praise to Odin," he whispered aloud as Horsa reentered Hengist's small room in the Saxon stockade.

"For what?" Horsa responded, his face alive with excitement. Horsa was still a boy, although he had bedded a wife and fathered two children in three years. Hengist grinned with affection for a brother who never failed him in thought or deed.

"We will face Vortimer and his brother in battle, rather than Ambrosius, or even Vortigern who is a bear when he is cornered. From all reports, Ambrosius fights like an intelligent Roman and therefore is less predictable than the sons of Vortigern. The brothers will try to swamp us by sheer numbers while Ambrosius risks very little—either in men or in prestige."

"Our men are taller and stronger than the Celts, and they are the best fighters in this whole land," Horsa muttered as he bit into a crisp apple with noisy appreciation. "Damn me, but this earth grows wonderful fruit."

"Our men fight as individuals and, like individuals, they can be cut down by inferior warriors with better leadership. Numbers, Horsa. It's numbers and organization that win battles, not skill or talent."

"You're saying that we're defeated before we begin, brother." Horsa struck the timbers of the log wall with his open hand. "I can't believe that you'd just cut and run. I'll never believe it."

Hengist slammed both his leather boots onto the sod floor with a dull thud. When he rose to his feet, his back uncurled until he stood like a tree, his feet wide apart, and faced Horsa down until the younger man's eyes dropped in respect.

"Listen, brother. Just shut your mouth and try to follow my reasoning. We cannot win if we fight as individuals. They'll chop us off at the knees in the same way that Caesar defeated our brethren in Gaul and all the way up to Germania. Hear me, Horsa. They will attack us in squares so we can run at them like demons, but we'll only impale ourselves on their spears. No, we must use a new technique. We must make them come to us."

Taking his brother literally, Horsa kept his mouth shut.

"To the south of Durobrivae and Durovernum, and a little to the east, there is a hill that I believe could make the perfect defensive position. We will occupy the crown of that hill. Vortimer's army will be forced to run up the slopes to engage us. On such terrain, his fighting square then becomes a useless tactic, because we will use a shield ring as part of our defensive strategy. If we can hold the high ground, I believe we can kill two of them for every man that we lose."

Horsa's mouth split into a wide grin. Hengist saw complete acceptance of his risky plan reflected in his brother's admiring eyes. Gods! To fail! To risk everything on a hill, and on the inexperience of Vortimer who had only fought one battle as a commander, and that against his own father as foe. Hengist understood how terrible the coming war would be, and how vulnerable the Saxons would become if they were cut off from an effective retreat. Holding the hill might cost his army everything.

"I have no other choice," he told Horsa roughly as a cover for the sudden lump that had formed in his throat. Beyond the stockade, he could see the rich, deep lands of the Cantii, backed by low hills and deep forests. If he craned his neck and looked eastward, he could see the ocean, miles away over land that was so fair and so flat that, in time, his warriors could learn to become farmers and tillers of the soil.

He hungered for land that he could call his own. These isles were Hengist's last hope and he would risk a great deal to secure his dream for his people. The thane had always known that every slight, slur, setback, and bitter disappointment had only been preludes to the achievement of his heart's desire. All he had to do to win his dream was to hold one sodding little hill.

Loki laughed as he crouched at the feet of the world tree, Yggdrasil. The trickster god of Hengist's forefathers smelled the man's desire and was amused.

SOMEHOW, HENGIST HAD cajoled and convinced the thanes that running directly at Vortimer's force at breakneck pace would be stupid,

wasteful suicide, without any trace of honor in it. Like many northerners, the Saxons prized courage above all other virtues. Saxon men
and women could not stand heads high in the sunshine without brave
hearts. But to endure, Saxons also needed the qualities of duty and
self-sacrifice. In the harsh winters of the northern countries, the snow
trapped the younger hunters within their huts and the cold became
a living monster. When food supplies ran low, the old ones walked
outside into the darkness, naked, to ensure that the children and grandchildren were fed. Hengist now called upon these deep instincts in his
men.

"This miserable hill is the key to our strategy. We must hold the
crown until we are threatened with overwhelming defeat, or we secure
a great victory. Then, and only then, will we use a wedge like an arrowhead to drive into the Celtic forces, either to escape or to advance
to victory."

"Do you fear that we might lose the coming battle, Thane Hengist?" one tall, red-bearded warrior challenged him, his hairy jaw jut-
ting forward aggressively.

"I fear to lose this land . . . not necessarily these particular acres,
Otha, but these soft lands whose tribes have grown fat and complacent
under Roman rule. Even if we lose this battle, I swear to you that we
will ultimately win the war."

"If we lose, my thane, I vow that I'll not leave the battlefield alive,"
Otha swore, his blue-green eyes glittering with a kind of madness.
Hengist would have torn great tufts out of his own beard in frustration
had he not needed to sway these stubborn men, who mistrusted anything that their fathers had not known. He had learned through painful
experience that old ways are not necessarily the best ways.

"I honor your courage, Otha, but who will father sons on your wife
if you die needlessly here? Who will sing of your deeds at the feastings
a hundred years from now, when we have sunk our roots so deeply
into this soil that nothing and no one will ever root us out? You must
live, if you can, to father children who belong in these lands by the
right of birth."

284

Otha was mollified, but unconvinced. Like many of the thanes, he couldn't think beyond the immediate problem. Sometimes Hengist despaired of his people.

"Each thane will command a defensive ring at the top of the hill. Use your shields to repel arrows and to fight in tandem with your fellow thanes. When the first ring is weary, the next ring can take their place, and so on. Each of you must hold your ring and prevent your warriors from allowing the chain to break. Are you equal to this task?"

Faced with such a challenge, what thane would deny his ability to maintain discipline among his warriors? To a man, they roared their approval.

"Most important of all, if we are in danger of being swamped by what will be a huge Celtic force, we must change our defensive position into the shape of an arrowhead. Then our warriors must charge at the attackers and cut a swath through the enemy so that our survivors can reach the ceols at Rutupiae. Our families will be waiting there, and we'll live to fight another day. I am determined that we will hold a kingdom in this land, one way or another. The Celts are idle from years of protection by the Romans, and their resolve has been weakened. This is our time!" He smiled encouragement at his audience. "And this is our land! I have served Vortigern, and his will is not as strong as ours. I have watched the young Vortimer and he has never felt the pangs of hunger, nor feared the agony of watching his children die. I have not met Ambrosius, but he is a Roman and a man raised in plenty. We are the new way! We are the new kings!"

As the thanes saluted Hengist's speech, which had been delivered with such strength and certainty, Horsa experienced a moment of surprise. His brother had always been a leader, had always planned and thought ahead, but never before had he shown a capacity to change the destiny of his people. In the wake of his brother's optimism, Horsa now harbored no doubts. These isles would belong to the Saxons till the end of time.

• • •

Vortimer had marched into the field with a combined army of legion-trained troops, a number of archers, the dour Celtic warriors of Dyfed and Glywising, and a very small contingent of cavalry consisting largely of officers and the sons of kings. Because of the flat terrain, he believed that horses would be less than useless in this battle, where force of numbers and disciplined strategies would bring an easy victory. As the horde approached Durobrivae, Vortimer made camp and sent out mounted scouts to determine the location of the Saxon forces. When they returned and recounted their discoveries, he was perplexed.

"The Saxon stockade is deserted, my lord. The smallholdings, the huts, and the wooden forts with their rings of sharpened tree trunks are all empty," one young lord of Dyfed reported, his eyes expressing his disappointment.

"I don't believe that Hengist would retreat without striking a blow," Vortimer snapped, his temper stretched uncharacteristically by nerves. "He's waiting for us—somewhere."

In the long, frightening hours of anticipation that followed, the young warrior lordlings expressed their disappointment that the Saxons had run like mongrel dogs. Vortimer knew better, and his bowels clenched with nervousness. Once again, he remembered Hengist's sharp, proud eyes, and determined to wait for the last of his scouts to return before he took precipitate action.

Near nightfall, the last two scouts from the Dyfed levy returned to camp on spent horses, and were ushered into Vortimer's command tent, where the king, his brother, and the chieftains waited.

"We found the Saxons," one of the young warriors gasped out, as a mug of ale was thrust into his hand. "What they have done is barely credible, but I swear it to be true. They have fortified a low hill southeast of Durovernum, close to here as the crow flies. They've actually dug trenches and pits into the forward slopes. We could see them working from a nearby copse of trees. I was surprised, because I've never seen Saxons prepare this way, so I assume that Hengist learned the rudiments of modern warfare while he was part of your father's guard."

"No," Vortimer stated baldly. "Hengist is very clever, so we'll have to fight for our victory, every inch of the way up that damned hill. Use that charcoal to draw me a plan of what you saw. You can use my table top."

The young men argued and wrangled like children about the details, but the overall plan of the hill was soon scratched in black soot on the raw wood of the folding table.

"Our squares aren't likely to be of much use to us," Vortimer decided. "And we'll be attacking uphill, because they'll make us come to them."

"We can wait them out," Catigern suggested. "If we set up camp around the base of the hill, we'll soon starve them out. They'll crack before we will, because these barbarians have no strategies."

"Hengist is a strategist, so stop thinking of this thane as if he is like all the other Saxons we've known over the years. He's different. He'll force his war chiefs to break their old rules of engagement and he'll stiffen their spines if we try to besiege them. The longer we wait to strike, the more probable that disease will spread through our ranks. A thousand men shit and piss a river of foulness, and they're none too particular about how close to their tents they do it. By all means, Catigern, if you can guarantee that the troops will travel a mile or so each time they want to relieve themselves, we'll sit at the base of that hill and starve them out for a year or two."

Catigern shook his head sullenly. Every experienced war chief knew the dangers of tainted water, unsanitary conditions, and the common soldier's casual attitude to cleanliness and disease. In war, more men died of disease than sword cuts.

"So we attack them from all sides, but in wedges. We'll pierce their lines at a run and fan out to engage the Saxon warriors. We'll force them into individual combat, and tie them down, because I'll send half the army in bands of men as deep as we can manage up to the crown of the hill and trap them in a noose. Once our wedges have softened and broken through their lines, the noose will choke the Saxon bastards until there're none of them left alive."

Perhaps, at that moment, in the absence of Ambrosius, only Vortimer could have devised an attack strategy that had any hope of matching Hengist's defensive plan. The war chiefs looked at the drawing of the hill, now embellished with shapes that represented groups of men, many men, for Vortimer had decided to throw the dice and trust to the weight of numbers to bludgeon Hengist into either submission or death. Saxons never ran and rarely surrendered.

Rested and eager, Vortimer's army marched at dawn.

Those broken citizens of Durovernum who had been too ill, too poor, or too stubborn to flee from the empty city appeared like grey wraiths out of the rubble of the old Roman wall, their eyes empty of hope until the sheer size of the advancing army became obvious. Then, as if freed from a heavy burden of fear, old men, women, and children ran to kiss the cloaks of the warriors, or press scarves, hairpins of base metal, or field flowers into embarrassed Celtic hands and to cry words of welcome and joy.

Buoyed by the elation of being hailed as both liberators and saviors, the horde marched at speed to the low hill that was the only elevated geographical feature in a land that was otherwise flat for as far as the eye could see. Vortimer immediately recognized that Hengist had planned the battle to gain the maximum advantage for the Saxon defenders.

Pits full of wicked wooden spikes encircled the hill. While some were open, others were cunningly disguised. Above the earthworks, the Saxon warriors stood with their huge rounded wood and bull-hide shields in overlapping rings that were at least three men deep, all the way to the summit. Iron spikes in the center of each shield made close combat a deadly proposition.

Vortimer's war chiefs had already assigned their warriors to positions in either the wedges or the noose. As soon as they reached the rise, Vortimer's army split into three parts to encircle the base. Those warriors selected to put into action the highly dangerous wedge attacks moved purposefully up the hill in squares to disguise their eventual strategy.

An occasional scream indicated that a man, or a group of men, had stumbled on a concealed trap. The perilous climb was rendered even more dangerous by sudden, lightning-fast tactical moves within the Saxon lines that revealed large, precariously balanced piles of rocks which, with a neat levering, were sent tumbling down the sides of the hill to crush the unwary or less nimble men. Inevitably, the Celts were only tricked a few times before they began to anticipate and avoid the rock falls, but however minor the pits and rockslides were, they caused Vortimer to lose a steady number of men and hindered the forward movement of the fighting squares.

When the Celts had reached a point some ten paces from the outer Saxon defensive ring, brazen horns sounded from within Vortimer's lines. The sound grated along Saxon nerves while Hengist screamed to his men to hold on to their courage.

"Hold position! Hold to your circles whatever they do and however much noise they make. We are Saxons and they are only Celts!"

He understood the purpose of the wedge of men with its narrow head and broader rearguard as soon as he saw the Celts move into their formations.

"Run to the chiefs, Horsa, and tell them that the Britons will try to force their way into the circles by sheer impetus. Our thanes are to allow them entry, and then attack them from the sides and the rear. Kill them all, and show no mercy!"

Horsa ran through the circles, spreading the message around the hill, but the wedges were already running, bare feet clutching the scoured grass with their toes to gain a solid grip while muscular thighs thrust upwards. Where Horsa's message had been received, the Saxon warriors stepped aside as the Britons charged up the hill, then encircled the whole wedge and settled down to fierce individual fighting. Where Horsa did not reach the defenders, the effect was much as Vortimer had anticipated.

Our communications are hopeless, Hengist thought bitterly as he watched the wedges carve into three more rings of his defenders. The loss of life among the attackers was dreadful, but always as one man died another moved in to take his place.

He looked down at the chaos below him. The result of the battle was poised on a knife edge, but the Saxons had finished off the men of the wedges. Their rings were closer, but thinner, and Vortimer had sacrificed nearly half his men. Vortimer still has about the same number of warriors available to him as I had at my command when this battle started, Hengist thought. But I've lost far too many of my own men.

Battlefields are rarely what the tyro expects. There is little honor, glory, or beauty in muck, spilled brains, and body parts, for it is the gory, rank trade of sudden and grotesque death. The earth was churned by struggling feet, and rendered dangerous by heaped corpses.

Below him, Hengist watched as men were hacked to pieces with axes and swords. The Saxons had a particular advantage in this gruesome dance of death for, although the ground was uneven and slippery with mud and blood, they could rain axe blows down on only partially defended heads and shoulders. Saxon axes were fearsome weapons—double-sided, razor sharp, and sweetly curved—and they could be used to slice a throat as neatly as a razor, or as a brutal, heavy bone breaker and decapitator. The best Saxon warriors fought two-handed, wielding swords and axes with almost inhuman strength, and in individual combat the Celts had little chance against their ferocity. But, like ants on a pile of fresh meat, the Celts had come to feed and run. Under the raised arms of the Saxons, the attackers thrust with their spears, short swords, or daggers, and for each Celt who died, another struck upward into unprotected Saxon bellies, genitals, and throats.

"We don't have enough men to replace those who fall," Hengist whispered.

"But we are winning, brother," Horsa protested, cleaning his axe, which had been fouled with blood and brain matter as he obeyed the last of Hengist's instructions.

"You're wrong, Horsa. Look at the melee below us. The weight of numbers in the main body pushes us back further and further. Vortimer plans to block our means of escape, leaving us nowhere to go so that we will be annihilated on this hilltop. I must make my decision soon."

Horsa looked puzzled. From his perspective, the battle was being won by the Saxons.

"Our families will be enslaved and this good land will become our grave rather than our gift to our children's children if we are overwhelmed in this battle. But if we retreat and sail north to a more uninhabited shore, we can dig into the land, fortify our towns and homesteads, and then spread southward as more of our brothers come to join us from across the Litus Saxonicum."

"I understand your thoughts, brother, but I don't agree with you," Horsa protested.

"Of course, we could become mercenaries once again."

"Never again, Hengist," Horsa swore with simple honesty. "I would prefer death to being another man's paid assassin."

"If you feel so strongly, Horsa, you will set the beacon fire before our losses become too great—and while we have space to form the arrowhead which will fight our way to freedom. As befits our bloodline, you and I will be the last to leave the hill. Order the thanes to leave no wounded to the enemy. Where a warrior cannot be carried, release his soul to the Valkyries. The remnants of our army will escape to Rutupiae."

Horsa's face reflected his dissatisfaction. "I cannot bear to be defeated by these dogs. The Celts have treated us like animals from the day we swore our oaths of loyalty to Vortigern. I'll not bow my head to another arrogant farmer or shopkeeper ever again, as if a Roman bastard or the children of a defeated race are superior to us. We are free men who answer to nobody, except for our gods and our thanes."

"You speak truth, Horsa, but I don't have time to debate the issue. Obey me, and I'll explain myself later. This is only one battle, but I will eventually win the war."

The order went out that when the ram's horns trumpeted their alarm the Saxon forces would divide into two large arrowhead formations, one on the eastern flank of the hill and the other on the west. Then, at speed, the Saxon army would charge through the ring of attacking Celts. The losses would be great, but the rewards would be worth the bloodletting.

The ram's horn sounded with a deep, raucous roar and Saxon muscles leapt to obey their call. The Celts were unused to the concept of barbarians retreating, so even Vortimer was caught off guard. The Saxon impetus had almost cut through the noose before the Celts settled down to the task of penning them in.

Freed from the constriction of unnatural orders and the frustration of permitting an enemy to attack them without taking preemptive action, the Saxons screamed defiance and plowed into the massed Celtic troops. On foot, the Saxons were almost unstoppable, especially with the assistance of a downhill slope, but the Celts were also proud and they settled into spiteful, vicious combat. The Saxon charge was blunted, but the warriors gradually broke through and headed towards a river slightly to the northeast. Fortunately, Saxons could swim, unlike many of their enemies.

Hengist and Horsa were now on the move as well, protected by their guard and choosing the western route, by far the hardest and most brutal path of all. As they ran, Horsa sang with the glory of combat and Hengist's spirits lifted as he watched his brother fight with the grace and beauty of a trained killer, hands moving in a glittering parabola of death as he strode through the packed Celtic enemy.

When they broke through the Celtic ranks, Hengist ordered the Saxon warriors to head towards the river at a mind-numbing run. As the rearguard, Hengist and Horsa held the muddy, churned bank. The brothers were extraordinary warriors and wreaked havoc on the enemies swarming at their heels, until Vortimer was forced to dispatch Catigern to stiffen the spines of the Celts. The Saxons were now playing the game of combat on their own terms.

"They run, Vortimer, that's all that matters," Catigern protested, for he saw little chance for glory in harrying retreating men.

"Don't be so naive, brother. If Hengist and Horsa survive, then we've wasted near four hundred men for nothing. They'll regroup and reappear somewhere else, like ticks or lice, and we'll have to crack their skulls again."

Catigern raised his hands in angry submission before running to join the Celtic pursuit. In his heart of hearts, he lusted to achieve what his brother had failed to do, to kill the Saxon leader.

Hengist and Horsa had almost broken free with the remnants of their personal guard when Catigern reached the defensive line. Hengist was using a wicked axe in his left hand as both a bludgeon and a cleaver, breaking bones and severing limbs, using shoulders and forearms strengthened by twenty years of killing while his sword with its fish-skin pommel dispatched any warrior so unwise as to be mesmerized by the shining murder of his axe. Horsa had already broken free and was looking back to watch protectively over his brother's final escape.

On horseback, Catigern saw his opportunity. Horsa's back was turned, but no compunction or honor stayed the Celtic prince's sword. He charged at Horsa from behind and decapitated the huge grinning warrior with a single, sweeping blow of his heavy sword.

Hengist screamed like a wounded animal as he saw Horsa's head separate from his body and roll onto the bloodied earth. Instead of losing his self-control in the fountain of rich blood that poured from his beloved brother's arteries, he changed into a machine of death and destruction.

"To ruin!" he screamed. "To death! Send Horsa's shade to Valhalla in blood! Blood! Blood!"

In a crazed skein of shining and blood-flecked iron, he swung both weapons at the enemy, fighting to reach Catigern and bring that laughing face down into the dust. He howled when Otha slashed Catigern's steed across the belly, bringing the beast to its knees in a sickening spray of entrails and hot blood. Hengist would have pursued Catigern himself if one of his guard hadn't firmly gripped his master's shoulder just as the thane used his axe to block a wicked underhand blow aimed at his genitals.

293

"Later, Lord Hengist! We must live, if we are to avenge Lord Horsa."

Hengist's brain cleared and he led the last of the Saxons out of the melee into an all-consuming run through the river shallows. As he glanced back, he saw Catigern hacking at his brother's body and hate flooded his brain with a deadly, icy fury. His mind repeated a single refrain as he struggled into the deeper water to begin the swim to the far side. As he drove himself through the shallows on the far bank, he could see that a mere one hundred Saxon warriors remained unwounded.

Across the river, the Celts jeered, swore, and shouted insults but Hengist turned his back, gathered his last war chiefs together and ordered the men to continue the run to safety.

"To Rutupiae," he ordered with a voice that had no tremor in it. "But first, I require twenty volunteers amongst the thanes who will stay with me in that copse of trees over there. My brother has been killed shamefully and I will have blood price, or I'll tear the Britons down to Udgaad to have my way. You, Otha, will lead the other warriors to the ceols and make ready to depart for our new home. But wait for us! I will come, or call for you, even if the Fenris Wolf and the dragon that guards Yggdrasil stands between me and Rutupiae. Now, run, you sons of whores. Run!"

A bloody day! Horsa would have laughed and called it a good day to die, but Horsa was dead and his body had been desecrated near the river among the carnage of the retreat. As a sullen night darkened a bloody western sun, Hengist swore that he would make the sky burn with Celtic blood.

But first, he must think. The Celts would come to him because they believed that he was helpless. He must lay his pride and his honor in the dust, and he would do it gladly, for only the blood of Catigern would permit him to stand in the sunshine, as a Saxon should.

Behind him, on the small and nameless hill, dark animal shadows flittered from one prone corpse to another. Foxes, wild dogs, wolves, and other scavengers feasted on the exposed parts of Saxon flesh, for Vortimer left his enemies to rot. The corpse of Horsa was the only

Saxon body retrieved, and the desecrated parts were displayed like grisly trophies of Celtic superiority for the mirth of the Cantii peasantry.

Hengist's mind flickered with the beginnings of an idea, but only the arrogance of his enemies could bring it to his chosen, bloody conclusion. If he was forced to act like a mongrel dog to obtain his revenge, then so be it. Honor was for the living—and Horsa was dead.

The Night of the Long Knives

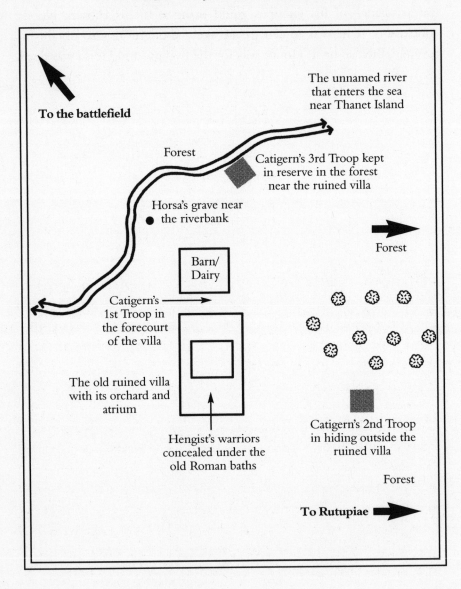

To the battlefield

The unnamed river that enters the sea near Thanet Island

Forest

Catigern's 3rd Troop kept in reserve in the forest near the ruined villa

Horsa's grave near the riverbank

Forest

Barn/Dairy

Catigern's 1st Troop in the forecourt of the villa

The old ruined villa with its orchard and atrium

Catigern's 2nd Troop in hiding outside the ruined villa

Hengist's warriors concealed under the old Roman baths

Forest

To Rutupiae

Chapter XVII

THE NIGHT OF THE
LONG KNIVES

A moonless night was followed by a slate-colored, chilly day, as a cold wind brought rain in grey sheets from the sea. Careless of personal comfort, the Saxon thanes had commandeered a ruined Roman villa where they slept on the tiled floors, wrapped in their thick homespun woolen cloaks. All were sunk in gloom, and only Hengist had possessed the curiosity to explore the traces of luxury that were still evident in the chipped paint, the marble columns, and the remnants of gardens in the atrium. Old seed heads hung from withered stems in sad, ghostly clumps and nettles grew thickly around a dead linden tree. But the fountain still trickled clean water, indicating that the pipes were still intact, so Hengist had braved the darkness to venture through a trapdoor in the empty baths to find strange workings below the floors. Huge containers of water had once been heated by furnaces and then pumped throughout the house. Hengist immediately saw possibilities in the vast echoing spaces into which he had wandered.

Cobwebbed and dusty, he stared at the twenty volunteers who accompanied him. Their shoulders were bowed and they had the worn look of men who felt the multiple stings of failure and defeat.

"Horsa's blood shouts out to me from the earth," Hengist began. "The Valkyries have carried him to Asgaad, but his shade demands blood price. It will be paid."

He paused, while his warriors slowly raised their weary eyes as they gained confidence from his stern, unbending form.

"The enemy has left our dead to rot on the hill where they will be devoured by wild things, while they parade the remains of Horsa's body for the amusement of their farmers. Such desecration is deliberate and denigrating. Do we let this insult pass? Do we retreat once more and try to forget the blood of our brethren?"

The Saxons who remained with Hengist listened to the words of their thane, their brows furrowed with the implications of their defeat. The men were angry and their slow, growing resentment showed in their tired eyes.

"Our honor has been stamped into the dust and I, Hengist Horselord, contributed to it. I retreated to save the remnants of our people so we might sail north to a new homeland, far from Ambrosius's Roman-trained troops. I had thought that I could live with the shame, but I was wrong. Look around you, my brothers in arms. This place was a Roman house, a rich man's abode and a plaything for his family. These floors were heated and the family washed daily, something that wouldn't hurt a few of you mongrels."

Some Saxon warriors raised their heads in anger, but Hengist smiled a slow, lazy grin that convinced the men that he meant no offense.

"In fact, these empty baths have given me an idea. And it's more than just a notion, it's a plan whereby we can strike the bastards in their naked hearts when they have been fooled into believing us to be barely worth watching."

"You're right there, Hengist." A tall, gangling scout offered his opinion. "A troop of their cavalry passed close by the villa two hours ago. They knew full well that some of our warriors were hiding here, but they decided we mattered so little that they left us alone as they headed towards Rutupiae. They just didn't consider us to be worth the trouble. No doubt they'll be back later, when they've run out of prey."

Hengist curled his lips in contempt for enemies so confident that they failed to remove even a small number of combatants from the field.

"Aye, Gunter! In their place, I'd show no mercy and clean out the whole nest of us, as neatly and as bloodlessly as possible. However, if they choose to leave us to dig in, who are we to stop them?"

"Who indeed!" Gunter grinned like a grey wolf, his lupine eyes glinting in the lamplight. "But we'll need more men than we've got if we're to defeat them, even if their numbers are few."

"Aye, and our warriors wait for us in Rutupiae. They most probably think that I've run mad with grief for the loss of Horsa."

"Mad?" one wit in the back corner of the atrium piped up. "Mad like a fox!"

It was a snaggle-toothed old man of thirty-five, the survivor of dozens of raids into the lands of the Britons. At his age he possessed little hope, but a dark, savage pride remained which told Hengist that when this warrior perished the enemy would pay dearly for his life.

"Baldur!" Hengist smiled. "Your courage deserves an opportunity for revenge, while your grey hairs have earned you a place in my plan. Your loyalty will be rewarded." As Baldur nodded slowly, Hengist swung back to impale Gunter with his bright, piercing eyes. "Gunter, I need you to run to Rutupiae, in company with Baldur, who will carry out a special task for which he is admirably suited. You will order Otha to return to me with all our able-bodied warriors, but only the strongest and the fiercest of those who are left alive."

The younger warrior was shaking his head in refusal before Hengist had finished speaking. His scarred and weathered face was aged beyond his years by a lifetime of staring into far skies, pulling on wildly gyrating oars, and searching for physical weaknesses in the attacks of opponents. That he still lounged against a wall in a darkened Roman atrium stated volumes about his flexibility, his intelligence, and his resilience.

"No, lord! I'll not run away, even for you!"

Hengist continued to speak as if Gunter had remained silent, although every warrior in the room felt the temperature drop. Their eyes swiveled between the two men, and most decided that they would rather be elsewhere when their thane decided what to do with a disobedient warrior.

"Baldur, I must ask you to sail with the women to Belgica. Not in retreat, but to escort them to safety. I will not leave this land, which is stained with Horsa's blood and enriched by our noble dead, until I've extracted my blood price, so on your shoulders rests the task of convincing landless men that there are acres of fertile land for the taking in these isles. On your shoulders rests the responsibility for the success of my whole plan. We will meet again when I follow you into the north."

"Don't ask me to do this thing, thane," Baldur begged, knowing in his heart that he could deny Hengist nothing, yet unable to contemplate a world where he had run away from an enemy.

"Otha's men must return under the cover of darkness. They will sleep by day, and in trees if necessary. The Celts are aware that we are using this villa as a resting place, so we will hide our warriors in the hypocaust during the daylight hours."

Annoyed by Hengist's refusal to acknowledge him, Gunter lowered his eyebrows in irritation. "What is your plan, my lord?"

Gunter's tone wasn't defiant, but Hengist read the same resistance in the faces of the other warriors. The thane began to pace. How far dared he take his warriors into his confidence? Would they understand the necessity for the brutality and the cruelty of his plan, or the lack of honor entailed in its execution? Probably not. But what choice did he have, when all was said and done? Regretfully, Hengist decided to explain some of his reasoning to his warriors. Better a half-truth than total denial. And Gunter's stubborn resistance might be turned to advantage.

"Vortimer believes we are finished as a fighting force. He pursues the main pack of Saxons and leaves our stragglers to be mopped up later. As far as he is concerned, we are negligible, an insult in itself, but one that serves my purposes perfectly. When Otha returns with my warriors, they will secrete themselves in the hypocaust and we will wait for as long as it takes to entice a large number of our enemies into our ambush." He paused. "Meanwhile, I need a volunteer. The role will be very dangerous and, should Catigern have his way, the chosen warrior will not live for very long. This warrior will go to the Celts and beg for the body of Horsa, my brother. He will go down on his knees and tempt the Celtic lords with the gold that is to be sent to Belgica with the ceols. My volunteer will trample his honor in the dust to carry out my wishes, for he will implore the Celts to bury or burn our dead. Will you face the fury of Catigern, Gunter, or do you prefer to go to Rutupiae? I have told you my plan, and now I await your choice."

Hengist's eyes had taken on a dangerous red glow. The warriors saw the promise of bloody murder in those eyes and their own gazes lowered. Even their shoulders bowed in submission, except for the warrior who had defied Hengist in the first place.

"Well, Gunter? I'm waiting."

Gunter wished fervently that he had kept his mouth shut, no matter that all men had permission to stand before their thane and question his rulings. Hengist had proved his superiority again and again, through feats of arms and in his clinical ability to judge men and lead his people. Nevertheless, Gunter would not go to Rutupiae.

"I beg your pardon, my lord Hengist. Your decisions are always wise, and I was wrong to question your judgment . . . I beg your pardon, my lord . . ."

"Enough, Gunter. Since you appear to have the ability to think ahead, you may have your way and not go with Baldur. Instead, you will volunteer to seek out Vortimer's lair while Baldur will go to Rutupiae with a trusted warrior of his choice. He will send Otha back with the warriors I require. Is that agreed, Baldur?" The ageing Saxon nodded. "Then you will sail to Belgica to the old Roman port of Gesoriacum. There you will discover Saxons, Frisians, and Angles by the score. You will also meet Jutes aplenty in the waterfront taverns, all seeking a master who will lead them to good lands and the spoils of war. Many of them will be the sweepings of the northern climes—thieves, murderers, and boasters—but take them all. You may use half the Saxon gold to buy ceols, but be ready to sail as soon as you receive word that you are required to reenter my service."

Baldur stood taller under the heavy burdens laid on him by his thane. Like many men, he lacked the ability to decide on his own path in life and had sought a brilliant comet to follow, and he was grateful that he now rode in Hengist's powerful wake. His age wouldn't deter him, for he could still run as far as the younger men, and he would obey his thane to the death if need be.

"Where will we meet again, my lord?" he asked.

"You will sail down the Abus Flood to a flea-bitten port that the Romans called Petuaria. It is swamp and light forest, a land more sea than soil, but it will suffice. If we cannot have the rich lands of the south, then we will take the wide, green lands in the north. But I swear to you, Baldur, that we will have land, and this time no one will drive us out."

On a wave of enthusiasm, Baldur and another grizzled veteran of dozens of battles took their leave at dusk. As they set off, with only the bare essentials for the grueling journey, Hengist felt a weight lift from his mind. He watched the steady, loping run of the two warriors as they disappeared into the deepening blue shadows of the tree line.

"Baldur has survived a long time because he is clever in sea, wood, and war craft. He will succeed. Now, Gunter, let's consider your conundrum."

"Con . . ." Gunter repeated, his weathered face screwing into wrinkles of confusion.

"A problem, Gunter! Don't ever—ever—question my decisions again. Since you will not go to Rutupiae, then you shall find Vortimer at Durovernum. But be very sure that I'm not sending you to Vortimer so you can be murdered, or Ambrosius can be the one who punishes you. I'd do that myself, if you really annoyed me."

"I understand, lord."

"In fact, your argument against my plans tells me that you are a man who is prepared to speak his mind. I am hoping that you have the wit, the courage, and the ability to lie with the bland face that is needed to convince those fools that I really would surrender. Baldur's warriors won't return for another three nights. During this time, you will return to the Celtic encampment outside Durovernum."

Gunter nodded, relieved that Hengist was permitting him to redress his lack of loyalty.

"I have prepared this gift to tempt them." Hengist threw back the lid on a simple wooden box that he always carried as a part of his traveling kit. The warriors sighed as they glimpsed heavy rings set with cabochon gems, a lump of gold, coins, and an arm ring of particular beauty.

"This box contains all the wealth that Horsa and I have collected in fifteen long years of wandering. The arm ring is all that is left to me of my father, so I consider it precious, while the rings came from the Jute king who bought our swords when Horsa was little more than a boy. Coin by coin, we set aside wealth for our house and our children. Take the large nugget of gold as a surety of my good faith, and promise Vortimer the entire Saxon hoard if he is prepared to comply with my wishes. Horsa is gone now, but his sons deserve his share, so I am gambling everything I own and hold dear on your ability to convince the Celts that we are sniveling barbarians without honor."

Cowed by the weight of his responsibilities, Gunter nodded, wide green eyes round with the complexity of Hengist's plot. "I will do all that a man can to achieve your ends, Thane Hengist. All!"

"Even unto death, Gunter? Even if they torture you to try to discover my plans?"

"Even this, lord. I will kill myself before I say a word."

Hengist clapped the warrior on the back. "Then you may have to sacrifice your own life, Gunter, for all men will speak when they undergo determined torture. It is my hope that you will deal with Catigern rather than his brother, for Vortimer scents danger under every bush. But Catigern would give his birthright for treasure, so if the gods are with us you'll bring Horsa's body back to me in company with a large contingent of Celts. They'll believe that this trifle is part of a larger treasure, so they'll search for it. Catigern will expect treachery, but he will intend to betray me anyway. We might all die here in this villa." Hengist paused to allow the dangers of his orders to settle into Gunter's mind. "You will offer Vortimer the whole of our treasure in return for Horsa's body, the burial of the Saxon dead, and safe passage for our warriors to proceed to Rutupiae. He'll agree to your demands, but he'll lie. Your life will hang on Celtic greed."

"As Horsa often said, my lord, we live only to perish," one warrior put in. "I, for one, will gladly die to wipe the smiles off those smug red faces."

"And I," Gunter agreed. He knelt and kissed Hengist's booted foot.

"Then eat and rest, for tomorrow we go into the hypocaust and make it habitable for a hundred men. In two days, our plans will begin to unfold."

Hengist looked out into the darkness. His eyes and heart were icy, colder by far than the glaciers he had seen in the cold north in shades of blue and white that resonated with beauty and terror. Once, as they stood at the foot of a great wave of ice that towered above them, Horsa had joked about the cold, but Hengist hadn't truly recognized the truth behind the laughter. Until now.

"Those little men in the south think that Hades is hot, brother, but we know that Hell is cold, cold, cold. Wait for me, Horsa, and watch from the Abode of Heroes, for the day of reckoning is coming and it will surely be bloody."

VORTIMER RODE OUT of Durovernum after dismissing the levies from Londinium and Durobrivae and completing the dispersal of the city's gold to the various troops, while keeping a measure of the Saxon spoils for Ambrosius. Although Hengist had left little of value behind him during the retreat, Vortimer had ordered the looting of the dead, who had given up a fortune in golden torcs, arm rings, and weaponry. Most of the troops from Dyfed and Glywising rode with the king, and only a token force of two hundred men were left with Catigern, who had been instructed to drive every surviving Saxon into the sea.

Vortimer's decision was sound, for Catigern had a boundless capacity for hatred and he would enjoy the destruction of the Saxon stragglers. Besides, Vortimer was discovering why his father had always been distrustful of those closest to him, preferring hired mercenaries to good, patriotic Celts. In recent times, Vortimer had become engrossed with watching Catigern out of the corner of his eye, in the full knowledge of his brother's growing ambition.

Nor was Catigern without his own cadre of supporters. Capable of easy, superficial charm and blessed with an open, handsome face, Catigern had no difficulty in winning the affections of those men and women who were easily seduced by surface values. Vortimer was all too aware that he cut a grim, cheerless figure beside his younger, illegitimate brother.

Vortimer rode away from Durovernum with relief. He had won the battle, and he would ensure that Ambrosius knew all the details of his victory. A shiver of mingled distaste and premonition stirred the hairs on his arms as he remembered Catigern's desecration of Horsa's body. Hengist would desire blood price beyond doubt, and if Catigern were to be killed because of his foolish bravado, Vortimer would shed no tears.

Within the folds of his woolen cloak, Vortimer shivered once again. Brushing aside the concerned hand of his nearest guardsman, he tried to banish Hengist's face from his memory. Vortimer would forever remember the expression of those wolflike features when the Saxon had seen Horsa's head leap from his shoulders during the melee on the riverbank. Vortimer knew that he would be unable to sleep soundly until both Hengist and Catigern were dead.

Let the gods be kind for once! Let them kill each other!

So Vortimer set his face towards the southern hills and Venta Belgarum, carefully choosing the words of flattery that would make him an integral part of the kingdom of Ambrosius Aurelianus.

FAR AWAY, AMONG hills whose steep escarpments rose like broken teeth in serried ranks towards a grey sky, Myrddion and Annwynn labored in the healer's tent in Vortigern's encampment. The tribes who had sworn to deny troops to the old king now found themselves embroiled on the fringes of an ugly civil war. The ancient Melvig ap Melwy of the Deceangli and the Ordovice king both sent food, fresh men, and words of conciliation to Vortigern, choosing to be offended by the treasonous actions of his sons. Nor did they love Ambrosius, a stranger and an outlander, who had swept into the soft lands of the south and now lorded his Roman ways over the southern kings. Neither the Deceangli nor the Ordovice knew the High King of the south, because he had made no overtures to them when he forced them to live under the thumb of Vortimer and his bastard brother Catigern.

"Faugh! It's a filthy business all round, and my dear Olwyn would be sickened by the carnage that Celt has brought to Celt," Melvig commented. "Still, strange as it is, my daughter's killer is the best man to lead us through these troubled times."

By and large, the people of the north agreed with Melvig, but they counted the days until Vortigern and his whole army marched away to some other place. Any other place!

By now, the healers' tents were almost empty of patients, for their charges had mostly recovered from their wounds and returned to their homes. Between them, the healers had saved large numbers of the wounded and only a few gravely ill warriors still needed Annwynn's medication and Myrddion's surgical skills. Even Vortigern had survived Balbas's incompetence, although he would walk with a limp for the rest of his days.

Myrddion had grown very fond of Tegwen, who had gradually relaxed in his company until the healer had been able to discover something of her past. She had been born at Gelligaer in the south, on the fringes of the grey mountain chain, where her parents had scratched out a precarious living shepherding the small, woolly mountain sheep. The family cottage had been built of stones, piled one on top of the other with the cracks smeared with clay to keep out the winds that blew cold off the mountains. The roof, with its primitive rafters, was covered with thatch and the single room within the house had a hard-packed sod floor. Life was hard, and Tegwen and her brothers were rarely warm or free from hunger.

When Tegwen was twelve, disease had struck Gelligaer, and when the contagion had passed she was the only survivor from her family. For the first time in her life, Tegwen had been forced to dig graves out of the iron-hard shale of their land. She would have perished of starvation, but she was a grown woman and she sold her body for food. Then, at a time when she was desperate through abuse, rape, and violence, Gartnait had appeared and offered his protection.

"Gartnait was an ugly, misshapen little man who never truly believed that I loved him, but I did. At a time when I needed someone to take care of me, Gartnait was there—gentle and sad. He had beautiful eyes with long, curling lashes, just like a girl. His irises were golden and tawny, like a wild cat's, and most men thought he had a bad temper. But he only shouted to cover how sweet he was inside, like a juicy apple that has grown irregularly and small, but still tastes wonderful anyway. I miss him every day."

Myrddion was moved by Tegwen's candor, and he realized that when her spiral curls were combed and her face was clean she had a piquancy and charm that few women possessed. Perhaps it was the lines of suffering around her fine eyes, or the delicate line of her neck as she bent over a patient, but Myrddion found himself becoming more and more conscious of her presence as she moved through the healer's tent.

Quick-eyed, empathic Annwynn noticed Myrddion's interest and grinned behind her hand. The boy was almost a man and she had nearly despaired that he would ever take a man's interest in the other sex. His curious, far-ranging mind was so in control of his emotions that it left little space for the desires of the flesh, but at last, it seemed, Myrddion was experiencing the first stirrings of lust.

Tegwen understood his interest as well. Women are quick to recognize the sideways glances of a man and the way his eyes linger on breasts, lips, and the sweet curve of female hips. Tegwen knew that Myrddion was beginning to see her as something more than an ageing camp follower who labored with him to tend to the injured and dying. Privately, she sought out Annwynn, the wise woman who ruled the leather tents of the hospice.

"What shall I do, mistress? Master Myrddion looks at me with the eyes of a man, but he lacks the experience to put his desires into action. He's so young and beautiful, Mistress Annwynn, that he makes me afraid. What do I do? What do I say? I'm too old and far too tired to be of any use to him. I've . . ." Her voice faded, and her head dropped with shame. "I've been a common whore since I was twelve years old—not out of choice, but because everyone has to eat. But I'm not for someone as kind or as nice as the master."

Sluggish tears slid from her eyes, and with a sharp pain in her breast Annwynn recognized the lost child who existed in Tegwen's body. Life had not been kind to the shepherd girl from Gelligaer. She had lost everything and every person she had loved, and now circumstances were tearing away the friendship and comforts of the battlefield hospital as well.

"Myrddion has never known the touch of a woman," Annwynn murmured. "Until now, he has never felt the lack, but I can see his mind working when his eyes follow you. Whatever you do now, Tegwen, your friendship with my boy will never be the same again."

Tegwen wept bitter tears of loss for the brief period of security she had known. "Where will I go? What will I do with the rest of my life?"

Annwynn enfolded the woebegone young woman in her arms. "Oh, darling, did you think I would set you adrift in the world? When my dear boy has such true affection for you? Never! After . . . afterwards, you shall go to Segontium, to the villa of Eddius where you will be given work and a bed. Eddius has served as Myrddion's stepfather in all but name, so he will happily welcome you."

Tegwen hid her face and wept in earnest. Years of despair had made her old. A decade of shame had soured her disposition as she had loitered in the lee of Gelligaer's shabby inn and accepted any man with coin in the putrid alleyway where she plied her trade. Crude sex that assailed her body with bruises, contusions, small broken bones, and, on one occasion, a knife slash over the abdomen, had taught her to distrust and loathe men almost as much as she hated herself. For five years Gartnait had filled the hollows in her heart, and, out of gratitude rather than passion, she had followed him all over Cymru as he carried out the dangerous trade of soldiering. Now she stood on the brink of a new life, one that could resurrect the child who had been murdered by circumstance.

"What should I do, Annwynn?" she asked, her eyes beginning to smile in the way of women who are desired. "Should I seduce the young master?"

"No, child! He'd see your advances as a mark of pity or gratitude and so reject your gift. He has pride, does my wild young lordling, so you must wait for the time when he seeks you out. Perhaps it will never come. But Fortuna and our Mother have plans for my boy, so I believe he will come to you when they have decided that he should."

Annwynn saw no inconsistency in melding Don, the Mother, and the Roman Fortuna together as one deity. All sensible Celts accepted the goddess in any form she chose to take.

Tegwen nodded her acceptance, and smiled a lazy, wholly feminine smile that spoke of many things that even Annwynn couldn't understand. But in that transformed, numinous face, Annwynn beheld the features of the Mother transformed into the Maiden.

She was content.

A MONTH HAD passed since the healers had arrived, during which time Vortigern's camp had developed an almost festive air, despite the brutal sting of winter. Good rations, a daily mug of ale for each man, and the time to rest and become whole in mind and body all contributed to the morale of the Celtic warriors.

Myrddion was changing a small dressing over the last of Vortigen's ugly wounds. Satisfied with his handiwork, he examined the fresh pink tissue that had formed spectacular scars along the old king's leg.

"You've survived this injury, and you'll have little more pain from the wound," the young healer informed the king as he bound a fresh poultice into position. Even after weeks of tending Vortigern's cursed flesh, he felt his stomach clench and unclench at the sharp smell the man carried with him, which was composed equally of sweat, old blood, and the faint tang of rotted teeth. The healer had learned not to gag on the hatred and disgust he felt, but still the loathing never left him.

Myrddion would never forgive.

"I'll allot you your due, healer. You could have killed me easily and no one here would be any the wiser for your treachery. Perhaps my luck was in when I chose to let you live."

Myrddion struggled to maintain his usual impassive face as Vortigern filled a mug with fresh beer.

"Will you join me in a drink, healer?"

"Any man of medicine who drinks would soon prove to be a worse danger to his patients than a fully armed warrior," Myrddion retorted, using a smile to deflect Vortigern's mercurial temper.

Vortigern snickered then, just as an armed warrior burst into his tent, knocking over a map case in his haste to gain entry. With a vicious oath, the king leapt to his feet with a curse and a wince of pain.

"By all the dead druids on Mona! What do you think you're doing, you oaf, by charging into my presence without warning or apology?"

"I beg your pardon, my lord, but a warrior has ridden all the way from Durovernum to bring news to you. Your son Catigern is dead."

"Dead?" Vortigern's face was quite blank for an instant. "Catigern is dead?"

Then Vortigern began to roar with long peals of coarse, ribald laughter that were shocking given the nature of the message that he was receiving.

"Send the courier to me, then, you dolt. I welcome the news that my treasonous, turncoat son is dead. If the messenger is telling the truth, I'd like to hear all the grisly details at first hand."

As the warrior bowed and slipped out of the tent, Myrddion and Annwynn packed their satchels and prepared to make their escape, but Vortigern's sudden good mood prompted him to insist that they share his enjoyment of his son's untimely death.

"Stay, healers, and eat a little stew. My slave will see to it."

As wine was pressed into their hands in finely carved horn cups, the healers seated themselves in the farthest corner of the tent. Their faces were creased with a disgust that they hid as well as they were able. Vortigern was unnatural in every way that mattered, for even a traitorous son was part of the father's blood. Who could forget that an infant had once lain in Vortigern's arms and now the king was glorying in its destruction?

The messenger who entered and knelt respectfully at Vortigern's feet wore a cloak pin and arm rings marked with Vortimer's hawk insignia. Vortigern rose to his feet and dashed his mug of ale into the warrior's upturned face. The warrior accepted the insult with a bowed head, and the beer ran through his long black curls.

"Your markings tell me that you are from Dyfed and that you slew my warriors in battle. You risk death to come to my encampment. Do you or your cursed master expect to trick me into trusting you again? I'll kill you myself with my bare hands if you play me false."

"Please, my lord. Since Prince Vortimer raised his hand against you, many of us have been sickened by the slaughter of our brothers in cowardly traps and treasonous battles. I was sent to my Lord Vortimer to deliver the news of Prince Catigern's death, but I chose to bring the information to you instead. Should my disobedience become known to Vortimer, he will surely execute me."

"And so he should, if he's got any sense," Vortigern retorted, his face twisted with the internal fires of fury that seemed to keep the blood running through his ageing veins. "Why should I trust another turncoat?"

"This land will suffer, my lord. King Ambrosius is no friend to our people, because he sets his sights on all the lands throughout Britain. Prince Vortimer doesn't see the dangers in the Roman's larger plan, but many of us are afraid that we'll be betrayed by Ambrosius and his brother Uther."

The warrior flinched as Vortigern's face darkened, but although he gulped visibly he managed to keep his eyes riveted on the face of his liege lord. The old king must be forced to recognize that the message he carried was true.

"Who can our warriors turn to, other than a wise king who kept our land free of war for twenty years?"

Mollified, Vortigern seated himself, snapped his fingers for more ale and ordered that the messenger should be given a stool, dried meat, and a mug of foaming ale to recover his composure. The courier's face was pale with fatigue, and deep, purple shadows surrounded hazel eyes that were sunk deeply into their sockets. Even his cheekbones were overly prominent, as if he had starved himself on the long ride from the east.

"Now, tell me!" Vortigern ordered after the messenger had finished his ale with one convulsive swallow. "I'm starved of information of my sons."

May the Mother protect us, Myrddion thought with contempt. The death of this man's child is trivialized into a desire for good intelligence. This king is a monster!

"What is your name, cur? I demand to know the history of the traitor who tells me of my son's murder."

"My name is Finn, your majesty, and I am a warrior born into a prominent farming family in the south whose name I am no longer comfortable even voicing. When so many better men than I are dead, I have shamed my ancestors because I am still alive. I served at the Battle of the Mount where Prince Vortimer destroyed the Saxon invaders, so I was selected to be part of Prince Catigern's force that hunted the last of the Saxon stragglers. I had thought myself to be a man of honor, but now my name is soiled in the dust."

"I don't give a shite about your honor, so just recount the events that you saw," Vortigern snapped irritably. "Get on with it, or I'll order my men to encourage you."

The messenger swallowed as he prepared to tell his story. As a man of sense, he realized that he could not permit himself one careless word, or this volatile king would order his execution. His life was over anyway, for harbingers of bad news invariably suffered for the truths that they told.

"A man, a Saxon warrior, came to our camp at Durovernum ten days ago," he began. "We were aware that a small group of Saxons had been hiding in a ruined villa some miles from the battlefield, but our spies told us that only a dozen or so men were taking refuge there, so Lord Catigern chose to leave them be until he had rooted out the larger nest at Rutupiae. He called them a last, tasty morsel." The courier's face flushed. "In retrospect, it was a serious error of judgment. When we reached Rutupiae, the port was empty of Saxons and the ceols had sailed for the shores of Belgica before we arrived. We returned to Durovernum, and that was when this particular Saxon came into Catigern's camp. He was unarmed and was carrying a simple wooden box containing a huge nugget of gold."

"Obviously a brave man," Vortigern murmured. "But suicidal, unless he had a specific mission to perform."

"So Lord Catigern thought," Finn agreed, more relaxed now that he was recounting events. "He toyed with this Gunter, as he called himself, and gave him to the guards to soften up before commencing his interrogation. The Saxon took beatings and burnings with stoicism, as if he knew we weren't going to kill him until we obtained what we wanted to know."

"Don't ever underestimate Saxons," Vortigern told the occupants of the room. "They are hard men, turned into barbarians by the loss of their lands and family. They are clever, in an uneducated fashion, and almost insanely obsessed with personal honor and courage."

313

"Aye, lord king, so we learned," Finn agreed respectfully. The courier's fingers were dirty and the nails were stained with old blood and grime. They twisted and flexed with minds of their own, separate from the calm, reasonable voice that he used to impart his news.

"Your full name, messenger," Vortigern demanded. "I like to know the history of the men I talk to. Don't put me off with maunderings about shame or dishonor. Answer like a man . . . unless you lack respect for your forebears."

"He treats everyone as things until he discerns a useful purpose for them," Annwynn whispered to her apprentice, almost as if she could read his mind. "Then they become real."

"My name is Finn, lord, son of Finnbarr of Caer Fyrddin. My family has dwelt in that town since the days when the Romans called it Moridunum. We have always been true to our Celtic ancestors, even when the Romans were our masters."

"Well, Finn, get on with your message," Vortigern drawled, and smiled his secretive, almost triangular smile. "I am agog!"

"Gunter was dragged into Prince Catigern's presence and forced to stand upright while he gave our lord a message from Hengist. The Saxon thane begged for the body of his brother, Horsa, which Catigern had nailed on the gates of Durovernum for the amusement of the citizens. Through this Gunter, Hengist offered a treasure of gold chests, similar to the gift in the small box, if the body of his brother was brought to the ruined villa of which I spoke. As well, he asked that the bodies of the Saxons who died during our victory at Durovernum should be buried or burned. The offer was made willingly and Hengist guaranteed that he would sail far from Rutupiae if the exchange was made."

"Did Vortimer kill Horsa?" Vortigern asked incredulously.

"No, my lord. Catigern slew the Saxon from behind, and then desecrated his body."

Vortigern laughed again, with the grating note of contempt in his voice. "Don't my sons understand the first thing about those men who stood behind them and guarded their backs for so many years?"

Finn shook his head and his hands became very busy as he tore the hem of his shirt to shreds. "I saw Horsa's body. The common folk of Durovernum had thrown dung, mud, and refuse of the filthiest kind at the corpse. Gunter also saw Horsa's body when he was brought into the town. He growled deep in his throat, just like a wild dog, when he saw what the people had done to the remains."

"From what you are telling me, my son deserved everything he appears to have received," Vortigern snapped. "For stupidity, if for nothing else."

"After Catigern discovered the hour and the place of the intended exchange, he took pleasure in describing to this Gunter how he would now be given to the children of Durovernum for their blooding. I hated such disrespect, my king, for I knew no good could come of our dishonor."

"What happened to Gunter?" Myrddion asked from his corner, his eyes already sad with foreknowledge.

"He was dead before the children had the opportunity to touch him. We failed to check on him throughout the night, for we believed that no man would die by his own hand if even a small chance of life existed. He gnawed into the veins on his own wrists and bled to death."

"*Ave*, Gunter!" Myrddion murmured. "He had much courage. Such a suicide wouldn't be easy or painless."

Vortigern stared across at Myrddion, but could read nothing in the young man's chill, marble features. "Aye, he surely had courage and purpose. Knowing Hengist as I do, every detail would have been planned in advance by the Saxons. They knew how my son would react, so Gunter was more than Hengist's pawn. He was Hengist's justification."

"That's true, my lord. Many of your son's warriors were offended that a fighting man of any race could be given to small children who needed to practice their knife work and archery skills."

"So Catigern reacted by going to the ruined villa," Vortigern went on, dismissing Gunter's death from his mind. "I assume he had treachery in mind?"

"Yes, my lord. We were told that we were to attack and kill each and every Saxon present once the exchange was made and the killing signal was given. Catigern took twenty men with him for the initial meeting with Hengist and kept eighty of us in reserve either in the old orchard or across the river. Primed to await the signal from our prince to commence the attack, we arrived in our positions shortly after dusk. The villa seemed secure and quiet."

Finn had feared the squat, still-sound building because fighting in tight, enclosed spaces was never a good proposition for seasoned warriors, but Catigern was unconcerned. A single light had burned in the atrium where a dead tree had been set aflame, but otherwise the Roman villa was too quiet, too brooding, as if something primal waited inside.

Catigern had felt no such qualms and had dismounted and swaggered into the courtyard, surrounded by his fully armed guard. The body of Horsa had been wrapped in oilcloth in all its filth and was dumped before the doorway to the house. The stench was terrible. Finn had been the forward scout of the second force and he had moved stealthily into the shelter of an old dairy to watch the initial confrontation between Hengist and Catigern.

"So what happened, man?" Vortigern demanded, his hoarse voice even more sardonic as he saw the tension in the messenger's manner.

Finn raised his eyes and Myrddion could smell his fear and horror from across the tent. The healer realized that this man had witnessed violence that would travel with him to the grave, regardless of his life span.

For a moment, Myrddion's old sight reasserted itself and he smelled the stench of voided bowels, the hot stink of urine, and the sweat of fear. Over the nauseating smells, the healer saw a dead tree, blazing and being consumed, with a warrior in black waiting behind the collapsing limbs. Something old and dead hovered over the scene, and then Myrddion could see no more.

"Continue, Finn!" Vortigern growled. "What happened next?"

"They killed us all, King Vortigern. Every one of us—except for me! I was spared by Hengist to tell you of the revenge he took during the Night of the Long Knives. He allowed me to live, my king. Why?"

Chapter XVIII

FATHERS AND SONS

Painfully, in excoriating detail, Finn dredged up his recollection of the slaughter that occurred on the Night of the Long Knives, a few brief hours that would shape the relationship between Saxons and Celts for generations. As Finn spoke, every person in the tent saw what he saw and felt his terrible pangs of fear and shame. The listeners were transformed as profoundly as Finn had been, and would repeat the blood-soaked tales of that night to their companions and their families for years to come. From his first words, Finn held Vortigern, the healers, and the king's guard in thrall as he told how Hengist enacted his terrible revenge on Catigern.

Hengist waited impassively in the atrium of the ruined villa with the remains of the burning tree blazing at his back and his twelve warriors in a semicircle behind him. Perhaps it was his imagination, but he sensed his brother's presence just beyond his peripheral vision, watching and waiting for the inevitable bloodshed that would be unleashed by Catigern's arrival. A large chest with the lid thrown back revealed treasures looted from the Christian churches and a huge quantity of gold and silver that the Saxons had stripped from the Cantii towns.

Silence fell. The Saxons were content to wait, as they had done for days while Hengist had planned his revenge and Otha had infiltrated the countryside with small groups of warriors who regrouped at the villa.

The Saxons smelled the Celts before they saw them. Perfumed hair, nard, sword oil, and the sickly sweetness of death teased Saxon nostrils as Catigern and his warriors dismounted in the forecourt of the villa. The Celts made no attempt to muffle the sound of their horses' hooves and Hengist grinned appreciatively at Catigern's predictable arrogance.

The wooden doors, unlatched, were pulled open with a noisy crash and Catigern entered the ruined colonnade at the head of twenty armed warriors. So great was his confidence that the concept of defeat had never occurred to the prince, a man who considered Saxons hairy servants who were only slightly superior to his horses in usefulness. That they could embrace honor, anger, or a desire for revenge was never a consideration.

"Hengist?" he called silkily. "Where are you hiding? I bring news from Gunter, your messenger. He'd have come in person, but he's indisposed."

Catigern's voice echoed through the empty room with a hollow, eerie sound. The long shadows of his warriors crawled up the walls and a disturbed owl spread barred wings and flew at the prince's head, causing him to flinch momentarily. He recovered quickly, although his warriors whitened, clutching their amulets and sword pommels in superstitious dread.

"She's out and she's hungry," one man whispered, before his companion stood painfully on his foot to ensure that no further words were spoken.

"I thought you wanted your brother's body, Saxon," Catigern shouted. "We have it with us, although it's a bit ripe." He negotiated the colonnade and entered the atrium with its blazing tree, now collapsing into ash.

Hengist stepped forward so that his form was outlined with a rim of fire.

"The gold is here. It's yours, Catigern. I've given my word, so take it and leave Horsa's body for us to bury. Then I'll retreat to Belgica."

Catigern advanced into the barren, confined space that was, paradoxically, wide open to the skies. His booted feet crunched through the dried flowers and dead grasses until he stood over the chest with its piles of looted gold.

"You did well during your years in the south, Hengist. I'm surprised that you stayed to be trounced by our army, for any sensible man would have taken what you have and run."

The sneer in Catigern's voice caused the Saxons to stiffen a little, but Hengist had ordered them to remain silent and to keep their hands away from their weapons.

"Take the treasure and go, Catigern. I gave my terms to Gunter, so there could be no misunderstanding in any agreement between us."

"None whatsoever," Catigern replied casually. "I'm surprised you haven't asked about Gunter. Don't you care where your courier might be?"

Hengist allowed the silence to stretch out almost unbearably. His face was impassive, as heavy and as dark as seasoned oak above his beard.

"Cat got your tongue, Hengist?" Catigern probed.

"Gunter knew you would order his death. We realized that you would act dishonorably and he was prepared to die for his people. Whether you killed him or whether he killed himself is immaterial. I don't need to know how Gunter chose to go to meet his gods."

Silence fell again, pregnant with foreboding and the promise of sudden death. Catigern was compelled to break the unnatural stillness as the largest limb of the burning tree broke away from the trunk with a nerve-stretching snap.

"Your brother's corpse is outside, if you'd care to see it. I presume that two of your men will carry the chest out to our horses."

"I'd prefer the exchange to take place inside. I don't trust you an inch."

"Hengist, my friend, I don't believe you're in a position to demand anything, do you?"

"Otha?" the thane called. "Did the prince come alone?"

Otha climbed back into the atrium through broken shutters from a side room off the opposite colonnade. Stepping carefully to the ground, he avoided a sagging door and dusted off his rough homespun shirt with an epicure's expression of distaste.

"The Celt came with a large number of warriors. Most of them are hiding in the orchard." Otha snickered with contempt as he stroked his axe with his forefinger. "But there's another large group down by the riverbank." The warrior smiled at Catigern. The effect of that curving, delicate mouth below a pair of hard green eyes was unnerving. "I haven't used my lady here since I sliced through the belly of your horse during the battle at the river. My aim was right off that day!"

"You're an uncouth lout," Catigern snapped. "Why do you query the size of my guard?"

He pointed to a pair of his warriors, whose eyes became round with apprehension.

"You two! Pick up the box and let's get out of this shite hole. The smell of unwashed Saxons is making me sick."

Hengist turned to Otha. "Send half your warriors out to the orchards by the rear of the villa to circle behind Catigern's men," he ordered quietly, one eye on Catigern to check that the Celt's attention was elsewhere. "The others will attack the warriors on the riverbank. Ensure that the men are as quiet as they can be, for our advantage will be lost soon enough."

Suddenly alert to danger, Catigern and his warriors began to back away, including the two who had been instructed to bring the treasure chest with them. The narrow colonnade seemed even longer and more claustrophobic now, while the wicked hiss of iron and steel sliding out of scabbards was very loud in the confined, shadowy space. The Celts retreated cautiously, until the villa door slammed open behind them with a sudden, dislocating crash.

The men in the rear whirled round to find themselves confronted by half a dozen huge Saxons, grinning through their beards with obvious pleasure. With neither warning nor mercy, the Saxons attacked Catigern's men while Hengist waited, his sword still sheathed as Catigern looked around the colonnade and atrium in an attempt to remain calm.

"Use the rear door!" the prince ordered. "Cut them down!" He pointed his sword at Hengist and the twelve warriors at his back. He was still confident that he could break through the Saxons before him to escape into the open, rejoin his concealed force in the woods, and then destroy the last of the Saxon enclave.

"I'll make you beg for death," he promised. "You'll wish you'd died like your hulking brother before I'm through with you."

"You talk too much," Hengist grunted, drawing sword and axe, and rejecting the use of a shield in such an enclosed space.

Catigern charged at him with a banshee scream of rage, but Hengist avoided the shoulder-high swipe of the prince's sword by a simple, graceful sideways movement of his hips. His answering stroke was so elegant that any gladiator, used to performing for the admiration of the crowds, would have been proud to execute it. He twisted, with a straight back, bent his knees and sliced through Catigern's hamstrings with a single, delicate swing of his axe. As Catigern dropped to his knees, screaming, on the mosaic floor, Hengist moved on to the next warrior—and the next—bringing death with both hands in a grim dance. The skills of a lifetime that had been developed in the service of many masters brought a beautiful economy to the thane's movements.

From outside, peering through the spaces in the walls of the old dairy, Finn heard the screams and was torn between shame that

Catigern would attack men during a truce and his own superstitious horrors. He had seen the six muffled shapes enter the villa and, mistakenly, had cursed the captain of the reserves in the orchard for acting before his orders had been given. Now, with his heart thudding painfully in his breast, Finn watched Saxons pour out of the side entry of the villa where, unknown to the Celts, the baths were situated. There were so many of them—fifty, sixty, perhaps as many as a hundred. At once, Finn instinctively understood that no Celt who had ridden into this trap with Catigern would survive the night.

Half the group set out in the characteristic, effortless lope of Saxon warriors as they sprinted towards the nearby river, while the other group moved stealthily towards the orchard on the other side of the villa.

Finn's thoughts raced. *She has come! The goddess Blodeuwedd is abroad and the reckoning will be terrible. My comrades in the orchard can hear that the attack has begun, but they're waiting for a signal to join Catigern's forces. The Saxons will be upon them before they know it.*

Finn's mind scrambled for his next move, for he had to try to warn the warriors in the orchard, regardless of the risk to himself. Reaching into his pouch, he found his tinderbox with fingers that shook with urgency and a superstitious undercurrent of fear. As he struck the flints to set old straw ablaze, his mind couldn't escape an image of the goddess of flowers, angry because the sons of Vortigern had raised their hands against the sanctified king. *She* would have blood on her soil in reparation, no matter what he did in an attempt to thwart her. Even now, the empty building seemed filled with the large, swiveling eyes of owls, Blodeuwedd's other self, and he heard the stirring of great wings as the moldy straw finally caught alight.

"Forgive me, Blodeuwedd, but I am oath-bound to Vortimer and Catigern," he prayed aloud, as flames threatened to cut him off from the barn entrance and safety. "I must fulfill my vows. Forgive me and mine, for I have no choice."

Scrambling out of danger, he began to run towards the orchard screaming a warning, but he heard wings close behind him. He stumbled and fell, and something hard seemed to rise out of the earth and strike him with a mind-numbing blow.

His senses fled.

With the exception of Catigern, every Celt inside the villa was dead for the loss of only three Saxon warriors. The thane kicked Catigern's sword away as he stepped over the prince's twisting body, pausing long enough to proffer advice to his fallen enemy.

"If I were you, Catigern, I'd kill myself while I had the chance. I'll be back to deal with you when I have more time."

Then Hengist and his remaining warriors ran unhurriedly through the villa doors to join the battle in the orchard.

Alone, and unable to do more than crawl on his belly, Catigern checked the slaughtered bodies of his men. He found a long, curved knife and attempted to cut his wrists, but the life force remained strong in his veins and each time he tried to sever his wrists he only succeeded in leaving superficial cuts. Crying with frustration, he rammed the knife into his belt and dragged himself along the colonnade by his elbows, leaving a snail's trail of blood behind his body, all the way to the open villa doors.

The night seemed full of fire as outbuildings blazed and created shadows that seemed even darker and more threatening because of the scarlet light that outlined every detail of the villa's forecourt with a wash of flame. Catigern found himself beside a crudely wrapped, stinking bundle and recoiled with an oath. The corpse of Horsa seemed to move in the flickering light, as if the Saxon was trying to tear away the untanned hides that concealed his mutilations so that Catigern's handiwork could be exposed for his enemy to see.

Just as Catigern mustered the strength to crawl towards the picketed horses, which were screaming and struggling in their fear, two coarsely booted feet filled his vision. A hand holding a rock swung at his head and Catigern collapsed beside the body of his victim.

The confrontation in the overgrown orchard was quick, bloody, and inevitable. For all Finn's attempts to warn his fellows of their danger, the Saxons fell on Catigern's confused troops like a wave of death. Frustrated by their defeat in the Battle of the Mount, the Saxons enjoyed their revenge in dozens of vicious, individual combats, and regained some of their lost honor in personal acts of valor and savagery. Although Catigern's men were taller than average, few stood higher than five feet eight inches, while the Saxons were at least three inches taller and possessed significantly longer arms than their enemies. The men of Dyfed and Glywising died like flowers that withered during early, unseasonal snow.

The second group of Saxons had set out to circle behind the warriors who had been held in reserve near the river, but the Celts had been alerted by a blood-red sky over the burning villa, the sound of distant screams, and the eventual silence that all men of war recognize—the chill quiet that comes with death. They were already preparing to head for the villa when a pack of Saxons appeared over a fold in the ground, running towards the Celtic position near the stream.

Moonlight glinted on the drawn swords and axe blades of the approaching Saxons. They ran in a rough arrowhead formation, with the warrior in charge of the troop at the front, which was unusual for Saxons, who tended to fight and generally conduct themselves as individuals rather than as a cohesive group. But these huge fighters were Hengist's men, so they were disciplined from years of fighting as mercenaries with him. Catigern's men saw the troop approaching at a swift, easy lope and felt the presentiment of disaster.

Without the firm hand of their prince to stiffen their backbones, some of the Celts broke ranks and took to their heels. Later, the Saxons would report the tale of this cowardice to Hengist with much scornful laughter, while Finn would feel such shame over the actions of his frightened comrades that he yearned to die of the loss of honor. Meanwhile, on the river flats, the Saxon leader simply pointed his axe with one hand, without breaking stride, and the warriors running to his right changed direction, increased their pace to a lung-bursting charge and took off after the deserters. The Celts who remained formed a rough square, and readied themselves to repel the charging Saxons as best they could.

Those warriors who had fled soon began to slow, even though the Saxons had covered far more ground than they had. Panic had initially given the Celts wings on their heels, but fear is a mindless spur and, as terrified individuals, they were pursued until they were exhausted, or the futility of their positions forced them to turn and fight. They were cut down like withered grass in the wind.

One fleeing man had climbed a tree, so the Saxons placed dead branches around the trunk, set the wood alight, and waited until the rising smoke choked the Celt's breathing and set his eyes watering. He was forced to drop to the ground and the Saxon response was summary and merciless.

The Celtic warriors who held their ground didn't die easily, or without cost to the Saxons. Cornered, and with no possible means of escape, they made the Saxons pay in blood for every friend who fell. The Saxons prized courage above all else, so the braver of the warriors were given fast, merciful deaths when the square inevitably broke and hand-to-hand fighting became the last Celtic defense. With half their number dead, the Saxons returned to the villa with their spoils.

Finn regained consciousness slowly in the half-lit hell of the villa forecourt, where he was confronted with the realization of his impending death. As he levered himself up onto his elbows and knees, with stifled groans of pain that he tried to suppress, he saw cheerful Saxons dressing each other's wounds and cleaning their weapons, while more of the heavily bearded men collected Celtic bodies and dragged them into the villa like so much dead wood.

Hengist sat at his ease on fallen masonry from the gutted dairy, wrapped in his woolen cloak to keep out the early morning chill, and reflectively cleaning blood from his massive axe. Finn remembered the pale eyes and impassive stance of the Saxon thane when he had served as the captain of King Vortigern's guard. Finn had been present at Dinas Emrys when the whole shape of his world had changed. Regardless of his position, then and now, Finn cursed the long-dead Apollonius and Rhun who had brought this night to its inevitable conclusion.

Hengist heard the Celtic oath, and raised his head in surprise. A charge of energy seemed to pass from Hengist to Finn, but the captured Celt was beyond caring if he earned the enmity of the Saxon thane. He was a dead man and he knew it.

"Were you at Dinas Emrys, Celt? I don't remember you."

"I was little more than a boy at that time, newly come to manhood and sent to serve the High King as a standard bearer. Why would you remember someone so young and unblooded?"

Hengist grinned at Finn with a friendliness that was wholly superficial. "So you blame the sorcerers for your plight? But you chose your masters long after that precious pair lost their balls."

"True, Hengist. As a Dyfed man, my fealty was given to Vortimer, son of Severa, who came from Caer Fyrddin. I served as my father had, and his father, under Celtic and Roman rule. I make no excuses, but the attempted sacrifice of the Demon Seed was dishonorable and stained us all on that day. The shame had to be washed away with blood, so perhaps the Mother will forgive us for the wrong we did to the boy. Perhaps Ceridwen will also pardon us for the death of her priestess, Princess Olwyn."

Hengist smiled reflectively as he remembered those almost forgotten days, over three years earlier, when he had broken his vows to Vortigern and begun the long struggle to earn a Saxon homeland. The face of Myrddion, that remarkable boy, swam through his mind, and he remembered Myrddion's promise of an eventual victory in some future time.

"I wonder where the Demon Seed is now. Aye, Celt, you are right. The roots of today first sprouted at Dinas Emrys. Civil war, the death of countless warriors, and the games of kings have all stemmed from the ruined tower and the Demon Seed's visions of the fighting dragons. Perhaps the Red Dragon is the sigil of your people, while the white dragon is the emblem of mine. If so, we will be at war for a very long time."

Finn understood little of Hengist's philosophy and cared even less for what would come in the long decades ahead. More imminent and more frightful was the nature of his impending death and whether he would be able to comport himself as a man.

"If you are going to kill me, Thane Hengist, I ask that you order it done now. I never saw you as a cruel man, but as a warrior like myself. I am ashamed at tonight's carnage and the oath broken by Prince Catigern. I was soiled by the desecration of your brother's body, as were many of my fellow warriors, but we were oath-bound, so you must understand our position. I say these things, not to earn an easy death, but because they are true. Please, Thane Hengist, order my execution so I may join my friends."

The Saxon thane smoothed his stained mustaches as he thought over Finn's demands. He was neither offended nor deceived by Finn's explanations. Truth has a compelling nature and a wise man recognizes it when he hears it.

"I have decided that you will live, Celt. You warned your fellows of our presence in the ruined apple orchard, you set fire to that building behind me, and it's not your fault that you aren't one of those heaped bodies in the villa atrium. Unlike Catigern, we will not leave your dead to be devoured by the beasts. We'll burn the villa around them before we take our leave of this place."

"Then do not torture me, thane. To remain alive when so many better men are dead is agony enough for me—and a stain on my honor."

Hengist shook his head slowly and drew his whetstone along the edge of his axe with a teeth-grating growl of metal.

"No, Celt. I have decided that my justice and my revenge will be known to all your people so that Horsa, who was a better man than either of us, will be remembered with truth down through the ages. You are charged to ensure that the story of what you have seen will not be changed by political necessity or perverted by the personal ambitions of other men. I realize I will be demonized by your comrades, and that I'll be hunted by the Celtic kings from one end of this land to the other, but hear me and remember. I will return, for this land will belong to the Germanic peoples sooner or later. We have the need, the will, and the heart to take it, for ourselves and for our descendants." Hengist paused and contemplated his decision. "What is your name, Celt?"

"I am Finn ap Finnbarr, Thane Hengist," the Celt replied, his face whitening until it looked like a living skull in the flickering light.

"From now on, son of Finnbarr, you shall be known as Finn Truthteller, so I burden you with the punishment of life. You must watch, learn your stories, and report what you see."

Aghast, Finn realized the full scope of Hengist's wisdom and cruelty. As an honest man, Finn would be forced to perpetuate Catigern's treachery and viciousness.

The Saxon thane ordered torches to be brought to light the villa forecourt so that the dim night was transformed by a ruddy, sanguine glow. As if they could read their master's mind, some sixty Saxon survivors gathered to encircle the tableau that turned the shabby forecourt into a judgment hall or a field of single combat, roofed by the black, starless night and walled by the villa and the burned ruins of the dairy. The heap of broken masonry was invested with the dignity of a throne, simply because Hengist sat upon it, while the watching warriors became the witnesses who legitimized his final delivery of justice for the death of his brother.

Laid out, malodorous, but impressive in the power that seemed to radiate from it, was the wrapped corpse of Horsa. Finn could scarcely bear to look at it, for the decaying body was the reason for tonight's loss of life. Love and ambition had brought them all to this lonely place.

"Bring in Catigern, the Prince of Glywising," Hengist ordered, his voice somber. He put aside his axe and whetstone to sit with his elbows resting on his knees. The thane had no need for panoply or golden robes. He wore his authority like a cloak, regardless of his casual stance or his rough clothing.

Catigern was dragged into the lit circle. Blood had trickled through his dark hair and was smeared across one side of his handsome face.

His hands were bound behind him with a broken spear shaft rammed between his elbows in order to draw back his shoulders painfully. Disheveled and begrimed, he stood as upright as he was able on legs that no longer answered to his bidding. Two large warriors supported his weight, but Catigern lost none of his presence because he could not stand unaided. His face was twisted into a grotesque mask of hatred.

"I could have ordered you killed out of hand, Catigern ap Vortigern, but as a prince of these isles I pay you the courtesy of permitting you to give an explanation for your actions. Men die in battle, for that is the chance we all take when we live by the sword. Horsa, my brother, knew the risks he faced when he followed me into exile, so I do not accuse you of murder."

Catigern spat on the crazy slate paving of the forecourt.

"I should make you clean that mess up with your tongue, but perhaps I might react in the same fashion if I were in your shoes. Hear me, then, Catigern ap Vortigern. I do not accuse you even of killing my brother, Horsa, from behind. Such actions, dishonorable as they might be, occur in battle too many times to count."

The ring of Saxons growled their disapproval, as was their right under Saxon law, but Hengist silenced them with a single, icy stare. Man by man, his eyes roved the faces of the assembled warriors and, one by one, their eyes fell.

"But these eyes saw you desecrate the body of an enemy. Such is not the action of a warrior, least of all a prince of these lands." Hengist turned to face Finn. "Stand forth, Finn ap Finnbarr, and be questioned."

Rough hands gripped Finn's shoulders and thrust him forward into the firelit ring. Bemused and confused, he stared round the circle and saw no sympathy or respect in the gazes that raked him from head to foot.

"Keep your mouth shut, Finn," Catigern howled, twisting in the grip of the Saxons holding him upright. "You are Vortimer's man, so give these dogs nothing!"

Finn trembled from head to foot, torn between loyalty and truth.

"Finn Truthteller! What was done to Horsa's body on the orders of your master?"

Perceiving an honorable way to answer the question, Finn drew himself up to his full height.

"My master is Vortimer ap Vortigern, legitimate son of Vortigern who was High King of the north until he relinquished that title to his eldest son. My master gave no orders regarding the disposition of Horsa's body."

Hengist's face seemed to flush, but perhaps it was simply a trick of the light.

"Do not play semantics with me, Celt. I am no shambling oaf who has neither wit nor reasoning. What did *this* man, Catigern, order done with the body of my brother? You are a warrior and I believe you to be a man of honor. Speak out, Finn Truthteller, and be just in your answer, for your gods will hear you."

Finn bit his lip until blood came. He thought of the bodies heaped untidily in the atrium of the ruined villa, he thought of the death of Gunter, alone and betrayed, and then he spoke out, softly and truthfully, describing what he had seen.

"Lord Catigern ordered Horsa's body to be nailed to the walls of the gates at Durovernum, for the amusement of the citizens."

"And?" Hengist prompted inexorably.

"The crowd were encouraged to throw dung and foul rubbish at the corpse. I was ashamed, as were many of my brothers in arms, men who now lie dead in this villa."

"And what of my courier, Gunter, who brought my message to this man?"

"Your courier chewed through his own wrists until he bled to death."

A silence followed this answer. Every man present, even Catigern, was able to visualize Gunter's desperate way of taking his own life. After a moment, Finn explained the reason for Gunter's suicide and, oddly, he felt the weight of the messenger's death lift from his soul in the telling. Then, over the outraged exclamations of the Saxon warriors, Hengist elaborated on the justice he was about to impose.

"I lived in Vortigern's court for years. I may have stood mutely behind the king's chair, but I had ample opportunity to judge the customs of your people, Catigern. Actions such as yours are not the norm in Celtic codes of behavior. Such disrespect towards an enemy is not enshrined in your legends, your tales of heroism, or even your father's twisted heart. Only a man who pays mere lip service to honor could besmirch the helpless in such an ugly fashion. Such a person does not warrant a warrior's death. So hear my justice, bastard son of Vortigern, prince who defiles all that is good in his own people. You will go to the grave with the man you killed, but, unlike him, you will still be alive when you are buried."

The warriors roared their approval, while Finn felt his shoulders sag with shame. His words had condemned Catigern to a terrible punishment, however just the decision might be, and he knew the responsibility for the fate of the bastard prince would weigh on his shoulders forever.

As his eyes darted from one Saxon face to another, Catigern screamed thinly and struggled with his bonds until his wrists and elbows bled as freely as the wounds behind his knees.

Hengist ordered five warriors to bring Finn into the ruins of the villa. There, in the abandoned triclinium where the Roman family had dined with their guests, a slab of white marble still remained. Broken along one edge, it was probably too heavy to have been looted over the years. Finn recognized it as a part of the low table used by Roman families to display the delicate feasts prepared for wealthy epicures. In one corner of the slab, like a cartouche or a family symbol, was carved the worn image of a galloping horse.

"Use whatever manpower is needed to carry this slab outside, then harness two of the Celt horses to drag it to the burial site near the riverbank. Don't break it, for I will be very angry if you do. Horsa must have a marker for his grave and this stone is sent by Baldur to honor him."

Finn was forced to travel the mile or so to the burial site, a slight rise overlooking the river, while Catigern was carried, struggling all the way, behind him. Other warriors set to work with a will, chopping into the cold, early-winter earth to form a deep trench for the grave. Once they had broken the cold crust of soil, the work was much easier, although Finn was prepared to swear that there would be some blunted axes in Saxon hands before the task was completed.

Once Hengist was satisfied with the depth of the hole, Catigern was thrust into it, still struggling. Two warriors leapt in after him and lashed his thighs together, telling him he should be grateful that he had a grave at all, when so many of their brother Saxons had been given none. They climbed out, and respectful hands lowered Horsa's tightly bound corpse down into the trench, directly over the writhing, screaming figure of Catigern.

"Open your eyes, Finn Truthteller, for you will watch this execution through to the end," Hengist ordered and, because the thane had judged Catigern with wisdom, Finn obeyed. The Saxon warriors used their shields as shovels to fill the trench with earth until, eventually, Catigern's screams were muffled by the weight of soil that covered him.

The end of the headstone was lowered into position before the grave was completely filled, allowing earth to be packed around the monument as it was held upright by Saxon muscle. Sickened by what he had seen, Finn could still hear Catigern's cries in his head, although logic told him that the screams now existed only in his imagination.

Or so he hoped.

"Take a horse and go," Hengist ordered. Gagging and dizzy, Finn obeyed, riding until he could no longer see the white stone rising out of the earth, its carved horse angled to gallop into the first flush of dawn.

WHEN FINN TRUTHTELLER ran out of words and sat, dejected and lost, at the feet of the old king, even Vortigern could find no humor in his son's death. As a healer, Myrddion was sickened at the thought of Horsa's fate. All that vitality and joy had gone into the earth before time had decreed that he should perish, so even Hengist's gruesome justice had a grim aptness. But the thought of lying under the rotting corpse of an enemy, while breathing in the crumbling earth and straining to find any isolated pocket of air, was almost more than Myrddion could bear.

"Go home, Finn ap Finnbarr," Vortigern ordered, his face almost gentle as he looked at the broken man before him. "Go home until I have need of you. And you, woman," he added, pointing to Annwynn. "You may now return to Segontium with my thanks. My steward will release three gold coins to you in payment for your services." He smiled enigmatically. "But your apprentice rides with me."

"But, lord, I am needed with my family in Segontium," Myrddion protested, rising to his feet and preparing to accompany his mistress. "I cannot accompany you anywhere."

"You will comply with my wishes or, by the goddess, I'll tie you to a horse and take you with me anyway. I am going into the south to gather my levies and take back my throne before my traitorous son has a chance to beg more troops from Ambrosius. At the very least, I expect to win back Rowena and secure my kingdom. If you fail to do your duty, many men will die needlessly, so gather together whatever men and women you believe will be adequate as servants during my campaign. I'd not rob Segontium of both its healers, but by the gods I'll have one of you. For what it's worth, if you serve me well, perhaps I'll tell you the name of your father."

Myrddion surged to his feet with unexpected speed, leaving Vortigern's guards flat-footed and gaping. Annwynn stopped at the entrance flap of the tent and turned back, her mouth framing a soundless cry of warning.

"What do you know of my father?" Myrddion cried, his voice hoarse with passion. "How could you know anything of him, when I don't even know who he was?"

"I realize now that you have your father's eyes, healer, though why

I am bothering to explain this to you surprises me. I have puzzled over those eyes for weeks, and I have finally remembered."

"Tell me!" Myrddion howled, as two guards gripped his elbows and bodily picked him up.

"Not yet," Vortigern retorted dismissively. "Serve me, and I may change my mind. But, for now, get out of my sight."

Somehow, Myrddion found himself in the open air with Annwynn pressing his hand, promising him that she'd take care of everything at home, but saying that he must obey Vortigern, who was capable of any violence imaginable.

Somehow, he found himself leading Finn Truthteller back through the camp, which was starting to stir like a disturbed ants' nest. He went to Cadoc and three widows who had become his assistants in the weeks since he had first arrived at Vortigern's camp, and heard himself ordering that the tents be struck and packed in the wagon along with all their supplies. Annwynn was already at work organizing warriors to move the last of the wounded into one of Vortigern's wagons to travel with her to Segontium.

The afternoon was long and bleak, and Myrddion walked through his duties like a man asleep. He was dazed and angry by turn, his mind stretched by Finn Truthteller's recollections of horror, Vortigern's unreasonable demands, and his imminent parting from Annwynn.

"Everybody I love goes away," he whispered, as he packed containers of herbs into large wicker baskets. Annwynn heard his despairing voice, turned and saw her apprentice's heartbroken face, and enfolded him in her warm arms.

"Oh, my darling boy, what am I going to do without you?" She pulled back from his embrace and looked up into his moist eyes. "You're so dear to me, Myrddion—you are my son of the heart. I never bore a child, for I never had the time or the man, but had I been so fortunate, I would have wanted my son to be exactly like you. Be brave, darling boy, and take very great care of yourself until you return to Segontium once again. I'll be waiting for you, no matter how long you are away or how many miles you travel."

"Vortigern will harm you, or Cadoc, or Tegwen, if I don't obey. But I don't want to serve him, Annwynn, and I don't know how I can bear to be near him, especially if you're not with me."

Annwynn drew him close to her once more. If she could have done so, she would have pressed his warm flesh into the essence of her being and held him there, but regretfully she pulled herself away from him.

"I will watch over Eddius and his boys, I promise. And I'll take Tegwen with me as well. The poor girl has only briefly known a family, and now she's distraught at the fracturing of her new security. Don't fear for her—I'll find her someone she can work for, someone who'll be kind and care for her."

Myrddion's eyes clouded and he passed one hand over his face. He had forgotten his assistant and her fire-red hair.

"Tegwen! I must explain to her."

"Aye, Myrddion. Calm her fears and explain that she must be ready in the morning to join me on the wagon. It's not so far to Segontium, but I want to start at dawn or I'll never be able to leave you."

"I'll talk to her, Annwynn. I'm feeling the loneliness already."

Annwynn patted the boy's face and shooed him away so she could continue her packing.

Nervously, Myrddion went searching for Tegwen. The afternoon light was dim and clouds had obscured the sun, adding to the gloom of the young healer's mood. Beyond Tomen-y-mur, a thunderhead was building, and Myrddion smelled the tang of the sea brought to him by the ocean breezes. When he had thoroughly searched the camp, he walked down a long slope of lightly wooded ground, calling Tegwen's name. Despite himself, the misty trees with their delicate traces of skeletal branches, the golden gorse, and the long dry grasses did something to calm his angry spirit.

In the dense sky above, a storm bird called its eerie, repetitive warning. Myrddion stood and turned in a full circle so he could survey the wild and beautiful scene, and caught a flash of bright red right at the periphery of his vision. Then he saw her, a twist of red rag holding back her vivid curls as she sat against a sun-warmed rock and stared out towards the distant sea.

"What are you doing out here by yourself, Tegwen? I've been calling for you."

Tegwen turned towards him, surreptitiously wiping her eyes with the knuckles of her hand and snuffling endearingly in distress. Most women look terrible when they've been weeping, but Tegwen was one of those rare few who appear softer and more feminine with a red nose and puffy eyes. Myrddion felt an irrational urge to kiss her swollen lids.

"I'm sorry, master. I was searching for somewhere quiet where I could cry in peace, because I really don't want to leave this place. How will I find my Gartnait's grave after the army has gone and the passage of time makes the grass grow tall?"

Her eyes began to fill again, so Myrddion dropped down to sit beside her on the grassy slope. Although the day was dim and the breeze was cool, Myrddion pointed out a black and white butterfly that had found a small cluster of daisies which were still flowering in a protected hollow. Affectionately, Myrddion watched Tegwen's face lighten as she watched the insect flutter amid the white stars of petals.

"Gartnait will always be with you, Tegwen, because he lives in your heart and in your memory. What does a grave matter? He's done with his body now."

Tegwen stared across at him through the veil of her tears.

"We're like that butterfly," Myrddion continued. "We seek out the flowers for their sweet honey, even though the storms will come and smash our wings."

"If that is true, our lives are pointless," Tegwen muttered.

Something about her trembling lips and the tear that clung to the edge of a curled lower lash tore at Myrddion's heart and he found himself kissing her swollen mouth and reveling in the sweetness of her lips and tongue. Without conscious thought or effort, he found himself undressing her until all of Tegwen's hard muscular body was exposed to his gaze.

Her flesh was imperfect, with scars, ridged muscle, calluses, and a scattering of freckles across her chest that matched the sprinkling across her nose. Unaccountably, the blemishes on her white skin moved him, and he felt a tide of affection building inside him spurred by the courage and travail that had been written on her flesh. Something within him wanted to weep for the sadness of those who are crushed by life, yet live on because life is precious and a butterfly on a daisy can move them to tears.

How long he luxuriated in Tegwen's flesh, Myrddion would never be able to say. An hour? A day? She was generous and sweet, and gave her body freely and with a bitter joy, until Myrddion knew that he didn't love this woman as she needed, yet loved her sufficiently to give a small part of himself.

Untutored in the arts of the body, Myrddion had no expectations, but he discovered that the fleshy pads on his fingers had a new purpose besides the sensitivity that helped him to heal ruined flesh. Now his hands could give pleasure, and accept pleasure in turn, so that their brief idyll was more than his first stumbling steps towards sexual awareness. He was learning about the souls of women and would be grateful to Tegwen all his life long for her generous warmth and the openness that permitted him to see into her wounded heart.

No, Myrddion didn't love her, but perhaps the feelings he held for her were better and cleaner than physical desire. He gave her knowledge of himself, naked and defenseless, which was the greatest concession he could make.

Half-dressed, he used the daisies to build a crown for her head and stole a kiss when he placed it on her curls. She smiled up at him with eyes that were painfully young, so that he wanted to protect and cherish her, although he knew that their time together was over.

"Master?" she asked. Her eyes were deep and mysterious, and he found it difficult to meet her gaze squarely. The Mother lived in those eyes. "We will never meet again—but I have loved you! Remember me when you are a great lord and the world bows at your feet. Remember that I loved the man, and not the power."

"We will meet again, Tegwen, I promise you."

His mind was filled with daydreams of his own cottage, Tegwen beside the fire, and children squirming like puppies on his hearth. She saw his dreams clearly in his shining black eyes.

"No, my lord, we shall not. I know that one day you will marry another woman, one who is better, cleverer, and more powerful than I could ever be. But remember me just a little when the daisies bloom, and I'll be happy."

"You're sentimental, girl," he chided her, and kissed her like a brother, for his mind had begun to consider the journey and the wonders that would start on the morrow. So quickly, Tegwen became his past, and although he felt a momentary guilt to relegate her so, he was still a young man with youth's enthusiasm. As they walked companionably back to the tents, Tegwen watched the man once again become the Demon Seed, and was quietly sad.

Ah, lord of light, she thought, as he pressed her fingers. I will never be truly happy again, because you will be far away. You'll forget me, she thought, and that is how it should be.

The sky was still winter grey, the sea was still the color of polished metal, and the winds still blew with sharp teeth of cold. But Myrddion felt and saw little of the breaking of camp that day. Even through a haze of happiness and the weary satiation of his body's desires, an incredible, impossible refrain repeated through his mind as he considered Vortigern's words over and over again.

"If you serve me well, perhaps I'll tell you the name of your father."

Chapter XIX

CIVIL WAR

Sabrina Aest gleamed like a silver mirror in the watery, pallid sunshine. The great channel was near its narrowest point, just below the valley where two great rivers embraced and ran together into the sea. The fabled Roman port, ancient and protected gateway to the sea for generations before the Romans came, hunkered at the far side of the channel where the river swept into the shallows in mud, detritus, and dirty sand.

From his vantage point above, Myrddion looked down at a scene that was both grand and a little frightening in its vast scope.

"I can believe that the Father dug a great ditch into the land and all the rivers poured their waters gratefully into the salt, just so that the great ones could drink fresh water while they carved this land out of the ocean."

At his shoulder, Cadoc snorted and Finn shuddered. Myrddion cursed himself for his thoughtlessness, for Finn was unable to sleep for thinking of buried men and, every night, he dreamed of being interred alive with rotting corpses. Each morning, he awoke with a throat seared from silent screaming. Unable to go home, Finn had sat in Vortigern's camp in a profound despair that seemed to rob him of the will to eat and drink. Myrddion had taken Finn as his responsibility, perhaps out

The Battle of Glevum between Vortigern and Vortimer

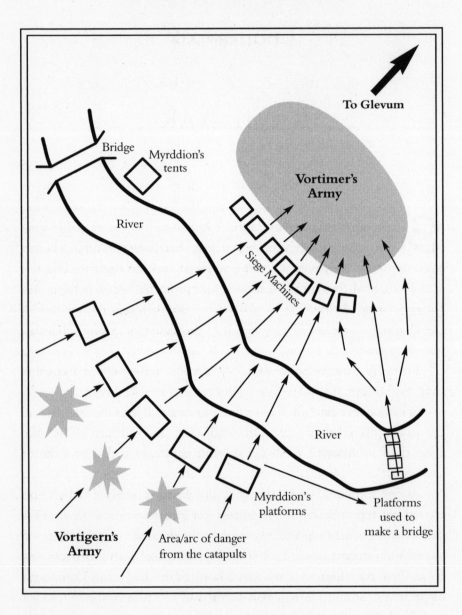

To Glevum

Bridge

Myrddion's tents

Vortimer's Army

River

Siege Machines

River

Myrddion's platforms

Platforms used to make a bridge

Vortigern's Army

Area/arc of danger from the catapults

of a sense of guilt. After all, Myrddion had survived his own collection of dead and was relatively unscathed. And so Finn Truthteller, the name the warrior insisted on using, became an assistant in the tents of the healer.

Vortigern had raged through Powys, Gwent, and the petty kingdoms of the south, demanding troops and provisions with the high-handed fury of a much younger man. With persuasion and outright threat, he terrified the princelings into stripping their kingdoms bare. The old, neurotically frightened High King of the past was gone, vanished with the news of the death of his bastard son, and the princelings cowered in the wake of Vortigern's furious energy.

And so they had marched, thousands of men and wains groaning with supplies, heading for the south where Vortimer was harrying and begging Ambrosius in turn, so that two great forces could meet, touch, and tear each other to pieces for the sake of transitory power. Myrddion was swept along in the train of Vortigern's war machine, so he had ample opportunity to ponder how some men live lives of quiet ordinariness while others rise and rise, crushing life's spear carriers and bannermen to seize the golden prize, a crown or a lasting monument.

"I'll have none of it," Myrddion whispered, looking down towards Abone across the fast-flowing river, and up towards Glevum, situated inland and pregnant with power. "I'll remain just a simple healer, and keep my soul."

"Healer you may be, Master Myrddion, and I've the scars to prove your skills, but *just* a healer? Don't make me laugh, master. You're little more than a boy, but I can feel the power in you, like a fish swimming in your blood. Up here, we can watch and feel separate from what is going to happen, but we'll still be up to our elbows in shite soon enough. You're a healer, perhaps, but you'll be something else as well. You draw us to you, you see."

And no matter how Myrddion tried to force Cadoc to expand on his words, the sharp, scarred ex-warrior professed to know nothing more.

The hill rose out of the Forest of Dean, high above dense wood-

341

land and ancient oaks, beech, ash, and alder. Vortigern had amassed his army during the depths of winter, breaking with tradition and moving huge numbers of men through snow and the icy cold. Myrddion looked behind him at the wide Roman road that ran from Burrium, skirting the forest to eventually reach Glevum. From that great town it traveled as straight as the landscape permitted to Corinium and Calleva Atrebatum where the road divided. One road headed south to Ambrosius's capital, Venta Belgarum, while another branched to the southwest, terminating at Durnovaria and the coast. The last branch headed eastwards to reach Londinium, the city where all roads terminated. At Corinium, another branch moved south to Aquae Sulis, Lindinis, and Isca Dumnoniorum, while to the northwest the Fosse Way, as the Romans had called it, plunged into the mountain spine, linking Venonae, Ratae, Lindum, and onward to the pivotal fortresses of the north.

"He who rules the roads owns the land," Myrddion said quietly, as he withdrew a piece of vellum from his tunic. He made charcoal marks upon it that could be transposed into a more permanent form in the hours after the evening meal, when he had the time to concentrate on the task of mapmaking.

Charts and maps consumed Myrddion's thoughts, almost supplanting his study of the healers' scrolls. He had already recorded Vortigern's movements throughout the entire campaign, including details of the villages, natural formations, and peculiarities of the countryside through which they had passed. The young man had no idea why he felt compelled to keep a record of his journeys, but he imagined that, like all pastimes, he would find a use for it eventually.

"Vortigern is clever, Cadoc. Vortimer must come to him now, and join battle before Vortigern reaches Glevum, because from there the old man controls all movements along the Roman road, both north and south."

The irreverent warrior grinned like the young man he still was, despite the ugly burn scars that turned one side of his face into a puckered travesty. "Vortimer and Ambrosius will be shitting themselves, for the old wolf is back with a vengeance. Vortigern may have taken the throne by treason and invited the Saxons into Dyfed but, by Ban's balls, he is magnificent when he's determining a fighting strategy."

"Where do you think Vortimer will meet him?" Myrddion asked, but it was Finn who answered.

"My master Vortimer will wait outside Glevum. I know it. He thinks to force his father to come to him so he can crush our men without having to depend on long supply lines. Glevum will follow Vortimer's standard because they know him, and he brings wealth to the town fathers through southern trade links with Ambrosius. He'll choose his ground on the plains northwest of the town and hope to crush his father in one final battle."

Myrddion looked towards the east. Behind them, the Roman road was crowded with levied peasants on the march. The men of Dyfed, Powys, Gwynedd, Glywising, and the petty kingdoms moved along the rock-hard gravel and cobblestone road with the type of workmanlike march that was out of step, but disciplined and purposeful. From the point of view of the farmers and artisans of Glywising, Vortimer had allied himself with a southern king who had sent the prince to resolve his problems in the east. The death of Prince Catigern, regardless of the rumors that surrounded the circumstances, was laid at the door of Ambrosius. If he had wanted the Saxons gone from his lands, then Ambrosius should have done the fighting and the removing.

"Vortimer's a right fool, sucked in by lust for his father's throne before the old bastard dies," one grizzled old warrior from Dyfed told a brother soldier from Caer Fyrddin as they marched over the cold stones. "The prince doesn't really understand us, nor care much for what we want. Why couldn't he chase the Saxons out of Dyfed, if he's so determined to free the land of that lot?"

"Shite, this road's still slippery with ice. It's a damned stupid time to march into battle, if you ask me. But old Vortigern's cunning as a starving wolf and his back is to the wall, if you take my meaning. Gods, but it's cold!"

"Stop whining," one of the men from Glywising muttered in the rank behind them. Vortigern had mixed the troops to avoid any problems with divided loyalties and the strategy created a variety of viewpoints that never had the opportunity to grow into insuperable differences. "Vortimer's a decent king, but he's not able to fill his father's boots. Sometimes that's a good thing, especially when Vortigern's pissed off with the world. That old wolf has been known to kill a whole village because the headman didn't bow low enough. On the other hand, Vortimer fiddles around like a girl with a new ribbon for her hair when he's trying to make up his mind. I'm not saying he's not mostly right in what he does—but what are we doing here? He always looks to someone like his father to tell him what to do."

The Dyfed foot soldier snorted with incredulity. "You're full of shite, man! Why would Vortimer want someone like his father to bolster him up if there's so much hate between them? It don't make sense to me."

"March, you sons of bitches!" A tall sergeant ranged up behind them. "Who said any of this mess makes sense? We'll be fighting people who're neighbors, maybe even friends. Just do what you're told to do and pray that we all get to go home."

When the army settled into bivouac that evening, the men had a good supply of firewood from the Forest of Dean. As the light faded, the healer and his two assistants had ridden down the hill and out of the forest to the smell of rabbit stew that wafted on the breeze from the direction of their wagon.

"Those widows are truly good cooks and they're dab hands at finding meat as well," Cadoc said, his voice warm with anticipation. "They're not too bad to look at, either."

"In the dark," Finn grumbled irascibly. As usual, Truthteller was very tired.

"Did you hear that, Master Myrddion? Our glum friend made a joke. There's hope for you yet, Finn."

Finn stared at his boots and made nervous circles with his soles in the mud. "I doubt that, Cadoc."

Myrddion smiled and said nothing, but after hobbling the horses he clapped both men on the back before breaking into a brisk walk to sample the stew. The night appeared to be free of rain and a tasty, filling meal awaited. What more could a young man desire? For a moment, he thought of the faraway Tegwen and he felt an unfamiliar ache in his loins, but he put all thoughts of her away from him, into the past with the other women he had lost, where she would remain safe with his blessed Olwyn.

However, Myrddion had barely started his rough pottery bowl of stew when he was interrupted apologetically by one of King Vortigern's guards. The High King of the north required his presence— immediately! Myrddion stared at his slightly greasy but well-salted stew with a child's anticipation, and reluctantly put it aside. Another reason to hate Vortigern's guts.

"Very well, I'll come immediately. I'll have my satchel, please, Cadoc."

Armed with his tools of trade, Myrddion followed the guard at a brisk trot across the bivouac. Vortigern had replaced his vast, gaudy leather tent with a smaller version that could be packed and moved quite quickly, expressing his intention to pound his son into the dust more clearly than any angry words. Seated on a folding chair, he brooded over a series of simple drawings on vellum from his forward scouts, which described the landscape to the west of Glevum.

"Well met, healer. I trust you're prepared for action without your herb mistress?"

"Aye, lord king. I had a fresh supply of herbs sent to me by courier while we traveled, and my assistants have stripped the villages and forests of anything we might need while we were on the road. I'm certain we can save as many of your men as possible."

"I've asked you here to discuss some of my concerns about this campaign, Myrddion of Segontium. I'd be a poor commander if I were to sacrifice any of my warriors through poor communication and a wanton lack of forward planning. Can you read a map?"

"Of course, my lord." Myrddion's confusion showed on his face. Vortigern's proximity, as usual, made him feel sick.

"See?" Vortigern stabbed the vellum with one sword-calloused forefinger. "The higher land and forest almost meet before Glevum. Only the river and a small area of flat land on each bank separate the town from the last fringes of the Forest of Dean."

"Aye, lord, I understand. The road runs straight and true over the flat lands directly to Glevum." But why are you telling me? Myrddion thought.

"Yes," Vortigern agreed. "The geography is against us, especially if we were to cross the river and risk getting caught between the water and Glevum. Vortimer could trap us there and smash our army, but I don't think he will. Knowing my son's need to be certain before he moves, I think he'll prefer to bring his forces to our side of the river to give himself room to maneuver."

Myrddion was mystified. He could imagine the devastating cost for any army that was left with no room to retreat if such a tactic became necessary. If Vortimer were as timid as his father described, he might never cross the river.

"Lord, no one would deliberately place deep water at his back. They must have a reason." As you do, you son of a whore.

Vortigern grinned wolfishly. "As you so rightly point out, only a fool would expect his enemy to place himself in such a vulnerable position. And my eldest son is not a fool. You needn't fear to say it, as I would be the first to admit that he's bested me strategically once before. But Vortimer is nervous, and slow to make up his mind. He likes to consider all possible problems before he makes a move, as eventually he must, from the security of Glevum."

Myrddion shrugged. What else was there to say, except to ask why the High King would discuss strategy with a mere healer, but he was not so foolish as to broach that question. He waited for the High King to explain himself in his own good time.

"Ambrosius has provided Vortimer with Roman-trained engineers from Gaul. He has rebuilt the old Roman bridge upstream with a series of rafts that allow him to cross and recross at will. He has fortified this bridge and my scouts tell me that he has ballistas, catapults, and other engines of war on the far riverbank. These machines could pound us into oblivion if we allow them to be used against us. We would never reach the river, let alone cross it. Then, at a time when my son was certain we were mortally wounded, he would come to us."

"But such machines of war can be destroyed by determined men. They can be burned or sabotaged, and then Vortimer's edge is lost," Myrddion suggested hesitantly, trying to imagine such deliverers of long-range death. "They can be captured and turned against the prince, just as the Greeks turned the Trojan Horse against Troy in days long gone."

"I've no idea what you're talking about, lad," Vortigern snapped. He was ill pleased to be at a disadvantage with a boy of just fifteen years.

Quickly, Myrddion explained the role of the Trojan Horse and how the Greeks became famous for their innovations in warfare.

"How do you know all this?" Vortigern asked, stroking his beard reflectively.

"My grandmother procured tutors to instruct me in Latin. My tutor loved the writings of the blind philosopher, Homer, so I learned to read Latin translations of his *Iliad* and *Odyssey*."

Vortigern's eyes flickered briefly and Myrddion could tell that the High King was filing away evidence of Myrddion's learning against some future time when it would become useful. Then, as if his face was wiped clean, Vortigern returned to the problem at hand.

"Our only way to the river is across the open land, so it seems we will have to face Greek fire and huge boulders that my son will cast down among us. The loss of life will be hellish until our warriors are in close contact with Vortimer's army. Then his engineers would be killing their own friends as well as their foes. It would seem that catapults would be most effective against a stationary target."

Myrddion's mind was racing. For catapults to work effectively, they would need to hold very large rocks, or huge piles of waste metal and smaller stones designed to break open on impact and kill or maim all the men within a wide radius. Loading and winching such a machine, if such was the means of operation, would take some time. But burning oil? Myrddion shuddered at the thought of such a thing inside breastplates or armor.

"Will your healers be able to cope with the number of injured in the opening salvo of the battle? Do you need more materials? I need men on the front line who can fight on, even with injuries, which is where you come in."

"I can prepare a large supply of unguents for burns and small projectile wounds, but surely the foot soldiers can protect themselves as well." Myrddion's brain, like a thing of cogs and wheels itself, was planning how to treat the injuries likely to be caused by Vortimer's war machines. Even as he stood close to the man he hated most on earth, he was seeking workable solutions for the sheer love of solving the problem.

"Explain!" The flat tone of Vortigern's voice should have warned Myrddion that the king was unsettled by the healer's unsolicited suggestion.

"If fire and missiles come from above, the first line of attackers should use some kind of movable platform to provide shelter and protection. We have good carpenters among the levies, don't we?"

The king nodded, his eyes suddenly brighter.

Myrddion removed a strip of vellum from inside his tunic and a piece of charcoal from the pouch on his belt. He began to sketch a large, flat-topped structure, higher than a man, and fitted with large wooden wheels. Shafts, under cover behind the front wheels, permitted the structure to be pushed by men or slaves. The High King peered over his healer's shoulder, the glitter in his eyes feral and charged with menace. He returned to his chair and stared hard at Myrddion with an ambivalent expression.

"Good. I'll hold you to your word that you and your assistants can handle most injuries, and you will return the warriors to the field if they are only slightly wounded."

Myrddion bowed and prepared to leave, but Vortigern halted him with a gesture. Myrddion felt strangely light-headed, as if his fits were returning after many years of absence, but fortunately the spasm passed quickly.

"We'll remain in this bivouac for four days. In that time, I want as many of these contraptions built as possible while we still have access to trees. You'll be in charge of their construction."

"My lord, I'm a healer, not an engineer," Myrddion protested, his face a little pale and pleading. He was appalled at the notion that a casual idea of his could be used in a real battle, even though it might pave the way to victory.

"You are your father's son, damn the man! He was skilled in every element of warfare, which was why I needed his advice in the first place. I was . . . but no. You still have to fulfill your part of the bargain, boy."

"But . . ." Myrddion's voice trailed away.

"Be content with the knowledge that he was Roman and skilled in warfare," Vortigern replied with a smirk that was both smug and resentful. "You'll have to earn more information."

Shite, Myrddion thought. Vortigern is playing me like a fish on a line. He lets me run by telling me a few, meager details about my father, but then he stops me by cutting off the flow of information until I've completed some task for him. He's a hateful, clever man. But Myrddion knew, even during these times when his thoughts ran hot with resentment, that he would continue to play at Vortigern's game, for, ultimately, he was determined to learn the details that would make sense of his life.

When he spoke, he was careful to keep his voice neutral and passionless. The less Vortigern knew of his eagerness, the better. "As you wish, King Vortigern. I will do my best."

The king nodded absently, picked up a dried apple, and began to eat, leaving Myrddion to stand like a fool—ignored and confused. The healer bowed, put away his sketch, and backed out of the tent.

"What am I to do now, Grandmother?" Myrddion whispered to the night sky as he strolled away. "What do I know about war machines?"

But the stars were distant and cold, and Olwyn was lost in death.

Learn, a voice whispered in his brain, and Myrddion set his face towards the section of the camp where the carpenters kept their wagons.

BEHIND ITS WALLS, Glevum was still and dark, its cobbled streets laid out in a grid pattern that was typically Roman in the newer parts of the town. There, in an old villa of particular magnificence, Vortimer had installed his household.

Rowena sat in the most opulent room in the house, with only a single maidservant to attend her. The girl was a slave, but she had been taken as a child and had lost all her original language, so Rowena had no way of discovering her parentage. The girl's pale, brown-blond hair and light eyes marked her as a northerner, as did her golden skin and her unusual height. As if like called to like, the girl was only comfortable with Rowena, and the queen with her.

Rowena's superb hair was loose and the maidservant, Willow, was combing the long, tangled locks with exquisite care. Under the gentle, long strokes of the ivory comb, Rowena's tense shoulder muscles began to relax and the ache in her heart eased just a little.

"I miss my sons." Rowena spoke aloud, knowing that Willow wouldn't betray a single word that the queen spoke in her hearing. "But my husband will have secured their safety."

"Aye, madam," the maidservant replied in a rich contralto voice that the queen found very soothing. The ivory slid with a soft susurration and untangled the hair with ease, although Rowena's tresses had never been cut and hung almost to her knees.

"Where is Vortimer?" The queen's hands clenched together until her knuckles shone white with strain. "Where is my stepson?"

"The master is closeted with his captains. The servants whisper that they plan a war."

"Then Vortigern is coming. Freya and the Mother are still with me. Soon, very soon, I shall be free again."

But Rowena suspected that she would never be free as long as Vortimer remained alive, and probably not even then. Initially, she had not been concerned for her safety when Vortigern's son had captured the baggage train, the queen's servants, and her person. The boy was her stepson and she had watched him grow from a shy, nervous ten-year-old into the man he had become. She had been a fool.

Directly after his father had surrendered and fled from his ambush, Vortimer had entered Rowena's tent. He was bloody, sweaty, and white around his usually rational eyes. She had hoped to be able to calm him, for she had tried to be a mother to him from the time when she had married an ageing despot as a girl of fourteen, and since she had borne her first son, supplanting the illegitimate Catigern within the family, relations between them had been civilized, if not warm.

Although less than five years separated Rowena and Vortimer in age, the queen had never considered the boy as anything but a step-son who might disapprove of her but at least treated her like another human being. But on that first night of captivity, when Vortimer stank of blood and fear, she looked into his eyes and saw that he was no longer a boy. She had tried to escape, had attempted to fight, but he had struck her on the temple with his gloved fist and she had lost consciousness. Unfortunately, she had awoken while he was still grunting over her body, his eyes blind to any mercy or reason, so she had rammed her fist in her mouth to silence her screams. He had finished with her, straightened his clothing, and stared down at her naked, spread-eagled legs before stalking out of the tent.

"What the father possesses, the son longs to defile," Rowena sighed as, reflected in the silver mirror, she saw Willow's eyes, hooded and sad, their clear depths marred by something primal.

Because she had recalled that first night, repeated often whenever Vortimer was not in Venta Belgarum or in battle, Rowena suddenly felt the pain of the deep-seated bruises, contusions, and wrenched tendons that had resulted from their last encounter. Her beautiful face revealed her bodily ills as her brows furrowed. Usually Rowena was able to mask her distress.

"Wait, mistress," Willow whispered, her feet padding away on the cold tiles. When she returned, she was carrying a simple pottery bowl containing a dark, foul-smelling unguent.

"What's that, Willow? It stinks like old boots taken from an excessively dirty old man."

Willow almost smiled. "It's good for aches and bruises, my lady. The smell is a little . . . ripe, but it works."

Willow was already drawing aside Rowena's embroidered robe to expose her thighs, belly, and breasts, covered with new black contusions and others that indicated their age by the purples and ugly yellows that marred the queen's smooth, golden skin. As gently as a mother soothes her babe, Willow began to massage the mud-colored, greasy substance into her mistress's flesh.

"It hurts, my lady," Willow whispered and turned her face away from her ministrations for a moment. Rowena looked down at her maid's silken head and saw the gentle curve of a downy cheek, then sighed as she felt a pleasing heat begin to ease the tightness in her abused muscles.

"Thank you, Willow; your salve helps. The smell may even be useful if Lord Vortimer should visit me. Especially if I breathe through my mouth."

Her wry humor prompted a quick, shared smile of amusement between the two women, as Willow continued to massage the salve into Rowena's side where large, rough hands had recently left fingermarks.

"Men don't notice such things, my lady. We are only objects in their minds, possessions to play with, or break, depending on their mood. But the salve does help, doesn't it?"

Rowena nodded, her throat suddenly constricted. "You're so young, yet so wise, Willow. Who taught you the nature of the other sex, child? You can't be more than fourteen."

"I am sixteen, my lady, and I have borne two living sons."

The girl's voice was muffled, for Rowena could see only the top of her silken, pale head. She gripped the clever, deft fingers that worked on her flesh so gently.

"Where are your boys now?"

"Gone, mistress. Lord Vortimer has no patience with babies, and no use for a maidservant who has a child to care for."

Willow's voice was quite flat and emotionless, but Rowena could feel something hard, cold, and hungry emanating from the maidservant's slender fingers.

"Are they still alive?"

The queen tried to imagine how she would feel if her newborn sons had been wrenched from her arms at birth. Her blue, northern eyes hardened into chips of ice as she decided that she would kill anyone who attempted to harm her children.

"I don't know, my lady. They were taken from me and given to other women in Glywising. I couldn't find my boys after all this time, even if I was able to try. They are three and four now, you see."

The hopelessness in Willow's voice made Rowena's heart ache. Perhaps that sense of impotence was even worse than the initial loss. Willow's despair was realistic, for she would never find her children again.

"I'm in your debt, Willow. I've been feeling sorry for myself, because I've been stolen from my children and I've been raped—but my boys are still safe. I'm fed well and cared for better than many women are. All I need do is tolerate the touch of my stepson, and many poorer women would readily change places with me for the sake of a full belly. Even my husband, King Vortigern, is too free with his fists, so the bruises are not unexpected. My only cause for complaint, really, is shame."

Willow tied a simple square of flaxen cloth over the lid of the unguent jar and rose to her feet. "Thank you, mistress. We are all really the same, we women. Queen or slave, some man owns us. So the world goes on, and there's no help for it."

Rowena's eyes were reflective and cold. She chewed on Willow's words as she dismissed the maidservant and changed into a sleeping robe. Although she readied herself for the likelihood of Vortimer's unpleasant attentions, her mind dissected her situation and she concluded that she had the means at hand to salvage her honor.

But not yet. She could endure a little longer, until the battle between the two kings was joined and her husband won or lost on the field. Her future hung on a mortal struggle to be fought by strong, thoughtless, and eternally childish men.

No, not yet. But soon.

MYRDDION REQUISITIONED EVERY man that he could find with experience in carpentry. As in the past, Cadoc was invaluable. The amiable, sardonic young man seemed capable of producing tools, men, or coin for supplies at will. Nothing that Myrddion desired was too difficult for Cadoc to purchase or, more usually, purloin. Even the foot soldiers who were ordered into the Forest of Dean to cut lumber treated the task like a holiday, setting off with axes, saws, and carthorses into the dim, green mysteries of the forest with whistles and songs. Each band of warriors brought back long, straight tree trunks, dragged by the heavy workhorses once the smaller limbs had been trimmed off.

The logs were roughly sawn in half or quarters over pits, while blacksmiths used the plentiful waste wood to fire their forges as they produced long iron spikes to nail the sawn logs together. Myrddion's tall platforms weren't pretty, but they were strong, even though rope was used where necessary to lash the timbers together. Speed was essential.

Over the course of a single week, five tall platforms of wood were built, with walls at the front to protect up to five men in each line, standing shoulder to shoulder, and protected by the roof overhead so that ten lines of men could shelter under the unseasoned oak beams. Huge circular wheels were also constructed, although Myrddion decided that time didn't permit the manufacture of iron collars to strengthen the rims. The platforms wouldn't be able to travel very far, nor would there be a need once they had served their purpose. However, he insisted that the long axles should be made of iron, and that these should be fixed to the main frame by interlocking collars and pins of the same metal. Because of the size and weight of the platforms, chains would be attached that allowed them to be dragged into position by teams of carthorses. With the judicious use of heavy grease between axles and wheels, the landlocked leviathans would soon be ready to move.

Myrddion gazed at his creations with satisfaction, and Cadoc slapped a tall wheel with one calloused hand.

"What shall we call these beauties, Master Myrddion?" He grinned cheekily. "The men want to paint their names on the front panels, but they asked me to consult you first. None of them know how to write, so they want you to make the letters for them."

"Why not just paint a figure to represent a name?"

"You could use a drawing of a stag's head to represent Cernunnos," Finn Truthteller suggested, and Cadoc clutched his amulet at the very thought of the Horned God who led the Wild Hunt.

"Thank you, Finn." Myrddion stroked his chin. "I like that. And, even though it gives me the shudders, you're right. If a stag's horn on a wooden machine could cause me concern, it'll scare Vortimer's scum shiteless."

Soon after, Cadoc wandered off to give the carpenters Myrddion's suggestions.

So, a week and a day after he first sketched the outlines of a war machine for Vortigern, the children of his brain set out for the lowlands by the river, drawn by teams of horses and oxen. One sported the stag-headed god, while another displayed a running horse for Rhiannon. The owl was inscribed crudely on another, and a hawk for Llew Llaw Gyffes, son of Gwydion, the trickster god, who was represented by a self-satisfied pig in a field of mushrooms. Myrddion's only contribution was a serpent for the Mother, which frightened the foot soldiers a little, but, as Cadoc explained, "My master's a demon seed, so if I was in the front line with him, I'd want to shelter behind his symbol."

What Vortimer's scouts made of the boxy structures that came trundling and crawling down into the river valley and stopped a safe distance from his war machines was unknown. His engineers probably divined their purpose, but even they must have laughed at such ungainly means of defense.

"They'll be aiming their catapults at our platforms, that's for sure," Cadoc told Myrddion as they stared across the river where the huge wooden siege machines towered among the vast army that Vortimer had raised to pursue the conflict with his father. Each catapult sat on a boxlike framework with four wooden wheels. The front of the machine was a braced rectangle of heavy timber that supported a slightly curved, notched beam that ran from front to back, from the top at the front to the bottom at the rear. While he concentrated on interpreting the workings of this insectlike wooden structure, Myrddion was already imagining its graduated notches and how a long wooden pole could be ratcheted into the throwing position and then released with incredible force. Even now, with its huge iron pot empty and dangling from the end of the pole, Myrddion could visualize hot coals, burning oil, rocks, pieces of metal, and even nasty spikes of wood hurled from the pot when the tension was released and the firing pole sprang back into the upright position.

"The Romans were clever," he murmured. "A hail of death—and all from a safe distance. I wonder what the range is?"

"We'll soon know, for there seems to be activity around the catapults and the ballistas."

"Now we'll see who can hold their nerve longest," Myrddion whispered as Vortigern's platforms were pushed to the fore and began to move at the head of his army. Fifty men stood within each structure, with at least another fifty warriors following close behind. The front and side rows of men inside the machine provided the muscle power to move the cumbersome carts.

Once again, the army came to a halt. Myrddion paused before ordering his medical tents to be raised by a crew of servants. He looked back towards the valley, and heard a strange sizzling noise as a flaming ball of fire soared over the river, trailing a pall of smoke through the still air. The burning object spun as it streaked across the space between the two armies, as if thrown by a giant hand. The projectile hit the ground with a dull thud and blazing oil splashed outwards in burning droplets for a radius of well over twelve feet. Hot metal fell like fiery, red ice, and the men on the hillock imagined how those small pieces of hot iron would burn through leather, flesh, and bone.

"We don't seem to be in range yet," Cadoc said cheerfully. "From now on, it'll become a pissing contest between father and son."

Myrddion issued a list of rapid orders and servants began cutting swathes of long grass for pallets and setting up the folding tables that were necessary for amputations and wound care. The female assistants unpacked the many pottery jars of herbs and curatives, rags for swabs, bandages, and Myrddion's tools of trade. Cadoc took himself off to oversee the process, a task he completed with a type of genius peculiar only to himself, until the healer's tents were humming with organization and ready for patients when the two opposing armies chose to engage.

From his vantage point high above the massed ranks of foot soldiers, the healer was aware of the silence, as if even nature held its breath and waited upon some terrible event. The sky was pale blue with a promise of spring, while the waters of Sabrina Aest could be seen to the right of the battlefield, blue-grey in the hesitant sunshine. In a nearby thicket, a bird warbled sweetly.

Then, as if determined to shatter this fragile peace, the platforms began to rumble forward again, powered by the men who sheltered behind the thick planks. At this distance, Myrddion couldn't hear the groan of timbers or the grunting of straining men as they forced the platforms closer and closer to the burned field where the dried grass still sizzled. Behind them, the bulk of the army waited, poised like a bowman with an arrow nocked and ready to fire. Myrddion could almost feel the tense anticipation that ran through hundreds of legs as they waited to be released, like the arrow flying towards its target.

"He's a wily old fox," Finn murmured.

Myrddion had almost forgotten that Truthteller still stood beside him. "Who? Vortigern? Yes, he is. The platforms will become the targets for the catapults and the ballistas. Meanwhile, Vortigern will count. Those machines take time to rearm and the king is hoping that Vortimer will set all his long-distance weaponry firing in unison to smash the platforms in one swift bombardment. It's a risky strategy, for the platforms will probably have to withstand at least two salvos, so they must keep moving steadily towards the river. If Vortigern's calculations are correct, he should be able to move his army up to a point where the catapults will have to be repositioned and recalibrated if they are to retain any accuracy. With luck, our warriors will move very quickly while Vortimer's engineers are preparing for their next assault. Hopefully, our foot soldiers will be so afraid of the burning oil that they'll have wings on their heels. If so, the army could be out of range before Vortimer can bring his weapons to bear again. Meanwhile, the bulk of our army will cross the valley with only minor casualties."

In the greening valley below, the slow, inexorable trundle of the platforms had generated a mad flurry of activity around the catapults.

"They're loading—and all at once," Myrddion whispered. "I've read that those machines work best when the target stands still, as in sieges. But an experienced commander can pull the catapults back and reposition them to keep their enemy within the firing arc."

"But if he does, he'll leave his own warriors in the line of fire, so he'll have to pull them back as well," Finn shouted. "Look! The platforms are within range now, so we're about to see a particularly Roman kind of orderly killing!"

The noise of catapults releasing their deadly loads was clearly audible on the hillock. Suddenly, flame bloomed on the roof and front of the central platform, but although the huge wooden structure faltered for a moment it slowly resumed its forward movement, blazing dully as it continued to trundle along. Another platform was struck by a salvo of rocks, but the platform scarcely shuddered at the impact.

The ballista fired and a vast bolt struck the much-targeted central platform with enormous force. On the hillock, Myrddion felt the sudden backward force that its soldiers experienced as their feet were literally swept from under them. Yet, slowly and painfully, trailing plumes of black smoke and wearing the bolt of the ballista like an insect antenna, the platform resumed its lurch into forward movement—albeit a little crookedly. Now, the leviathan left a small pile of crumpled bodies behind as it continued its march towards Vortimer's lines.

"Again!" Finn screamed, his voice hoarse with excitement and emotion. "The engineers are loading again."

But Myrddion was counting and assessing the time needed for the war machines to fire their second salvos, just as he knew the old king was, while making mental preparations to welcome the maimed and injured once they had been collected by the bearers. The minutes stretched out as small, ant-sized men scurried around the catapults in a flurry of mad activity while they reloaded the iron pots with deadly missiles.

Then the second salvo was fired, but now the platforms were closer to the firing point so the rocks, fire, and shrapnel overshot their targets and barely clipped the roof of the central platform. However, as the platforms continued to move forward unscathed, the warriors sheltering at the rear of the machines were caught on the edges of the strike. Their screams chilled Myrddion's blood, but, seen from above and freed from its stink and blood, the battlefield appeared like a giant chessboard where the gods moved the pieces.

"Prepare for wounded!" Myrddion shouted, and both men turned away from the spectacle of war to take up their positions in the tents where the fruits of war were soon to be brought home to them in all their filth and squalor.

The healer missed Vortigern's attack orders. The moment the second salvo was fired, the old king ordered the body of the army to cross the killing fields before the next hail of death could be rained down on his warriors. At full stretch, men ran as if Death itself was trying to outpace them and scythe them down. The platforms stood below the arc of fire of the catapults, their movement slowed as they waited for the bulk of the army to catch up with them.

Vortigern again called a halt so the rearguard didn't move. Burned earth, with small piles of dead and wounded, was all that was left to show the path of the catapult missiles. The salvo was repeated, but the range was too long now and the rocks fell on those Celts who were already dead and dying. The screams sounded as insubstantial as the cries of the birds in the thicket, but Myrddion was no longer on the hillock to hear them. Then, on a signal from Vortigern, the rearguard charged and the platforms began to move once more.

Vortimer realized that the deadly effectiveness of his war machines was over, and they were now so much useless timber. The angle of the catapult could be changed to shorten the range, but with each readjustment Vortigern's army drew closer to the river under the protection of the platforms. They were damaged—but were mostly intact.

What to do? What to do?

Vortimer didn't dare to utter his fears aloud, but the calm brain that had visualized the piles of his father's dead, stacked like cordwood where the catapults left them, was now confused and indecisive. If Vortigern's warriors were allowed to cross the river, could he crush them without his machines, or would his father prevail?

What to do? What to do?

When in doubt, do nothing. How the Romans would have laughed at Vortimer's inability to act. And how Vortigern *did* laugh!

As his son hunkered down on the riverbank, his war machines spent, Vortigern's army reached the opposite bank. Shouted insults from Vortigern's warriors made Vortimer quail in a shell of inadequacy that increased his indecision. He had always hated and feared his father, as is so often the case with weak men.

Meanwhile, Vortigern was hard at work.

The platforms were dragged to the rear and disassembled by the carpenters and a large team of laboring warriors. The ten large panels that remained after the carpenters had sawn off the wheels and heavy frames were dragged downstream along the riverbank to a spot where the old king intended to establish a new crossing point. There, those Celts who could swim took long lengths of strong rope across the river, secured them to trees along the opposite riverbank and then towed each of the platforms into place to form a makeshift bridge.

Piece by piece, the heavy beams were maneuvered into position before being anchored to each bank by a network of heavy ropes. In the deeper waters, the shaky rafts were lashed together to minimize the exposure of nonswimmers to the currents.

Myrddion would have approved the design, had he had the luxury of time to watch the activity that was taking place beyond the bend in the river. As the stream was wide, the platforms couldn't hope to span the whole distance from shore to shore, but the long ropes created linkages so that warriors could drag themselves to the platforms, make their way across the deeper waters in relative safety, and then finish the crossing to the other side along further rope linkages.

Compared with Vortimer's bridge upstream, Vortigern's span was primitive, but it was effective. Vortigern knew that the bridge controlled by the prince would be under constant guard, and any attempt at crossing by his army would necessitate a bloody, preliminary battle for control of that structure.

As soon as the makeshift bridge was created, Vortigern's scouts crossed to the far side and began to hunt for sentries and enemy outposts. At the same time, other warriors undertook the crossing to form a defensive perimeter on the far side that would protect the bridgehead.

Like the wily, ancient fox he was, Vortigern sent over a third of his army under cover of darkness without any obvious movement of his forces. Myrddion only discovered the ruse for himself when the old king called for his healer to join him on the riverbank.

Once Myrddion reached the front line, he found the king pacing on a small mound in a full-length body shield of toughened leather. The original campfires had been allowed to die to mere glowing coals, so Myrddion failed to realize that the ranks of soldiers had thinned until he asked a guard where the platforms were set.

"Gone, healer," the guard answered. "They've all gone."

Vortigern turned to face Myrddion. "Can you move all your equipment to the far bank before dawn?"

"Aye, lord, I could do it. But healers have no place in the middle of a battle, for we can't guarantee the safety of our patients or ourselves. I'm unable to defend myself while I'm cutting off a man's leg and I'm bound by Hippocrates to do no harm to my patients. We'll set up on this side of the river, at the foot of your bridge."

"How old are you, Myrddion?" Vortigern asked, bringing his face down to the level of the young healer's.

"Fifteen, I think, my lord."

"Fifteen! If I didn't know better, I'd swear you *were* a demon seed. So young and yet so old. Yes, you are your father's son."

"What do you mean, lord? What does my father have to do with moving my tents over the river?"

Vortigern smiled broadly. Even in the low, ruddy light, Myrddion could see the gaps in the yellowed teeth and the king suddenly looked every day of his age.

"By dawn, half my army will have crossed the river downstream and reached the far bank, courtesy of your excellent platforms. The rest of my army will swim across. Yes, there'll be losses, not just from the carnage I expect on the far bank, but also from drowning accidents, although I have kept back my strongest swimmers to carry lines with them as they cross. I expect the death toll to be high, but Vortimer's warriors are already nervous and they doubt his power to defeat me in open battle, so I can promise you that the little turd has no chance. I should never have married a Roman woman in the first place."

Myrddion's mind raced. He could see the effectiveness of Vortigern's plan and he smiled ironically at the brilliant use to which the king had put his platforms. As he listened, he began to understand why Vortigern had held his throne for so long—for only clever, unscrupulous, and totally flexible rulers live to be old men.

A picture of his great-grandfather Melvig flashed briefly through Myrddion's mind.

"I'll move a tent downriver and we'll prepare for the kind of injuries you describe. I have ample servants."

"Why only one tent?"

362

"Men are dying in the other tent, my lord. And I'll not leave them exposed to the elements. Rain is coming. I can smell it in the air."

Vortigern looked up, but he could see nothing but stars out in the deepest reaches of the night. Clearly, if he hadn't been aware of Myrddion's prescience, the king would have laughed aloud. Instead, he immediately factored the likelihood of mud and rain into his battle plans.

"Get to it then, healer. We'll meet again after the battle, at which time I'll tell you a little more about your father."

Before dawn, the force that had crossed the river during the night fell on Vortimer's unsuspecting warriors like ravenous wolves. Vortigern's men were desperate, for they were fighting a better equipped, superior force and they could easily be defeated without the element of surprise, good leadership, and perfect timing for their attack.

And then the rain came, just as Myrddion had predicted. A heavy downpour fell from a bank of thick cloud that at times reduced visibility to less than fifty feet and caused Vortimer's sentries to huddle in any available shelter.

A hundred of Vortigern's finest warriors hid patiently in the willows on the shore and shivered in their wet clothes as reinforcements dragged themselves through the swiftly running current to join them. Had Vortimer's sentries not been wholly absorbed by the sudden attack on their left flank and the opening of the heavens, they would have seen that the river was alive with the heads of men dragging themselves along heavy ropes that had been tethered between the trees on both sides of the river.

As soon as Vortigern joined his men on the eastern bank, he ordered the two hundred men with him to prepare for a frontal attack. Before even half the rearguard had reached Vortimer's army, battle was joined on two fronts.

Myrddion peered across the swiftly flowing stream, and through the sheets of rain that lashed friend and foe alike the healer watched a dim sunrise reveal the desperate struggle to determine who held the crown. Foot soldiers were still swimming across the river while a small group of warriors protected the rope lines at the willow trees.

From Myrddion's restricted view of the battlefield, it was impossible to untangle the struggling melee of men or to ascertain which side had the advantage. Vortimer had the initial advantage through sheer weight of numbers, but every moment that passed meant that fresh enemy warriors arrived from the river crossing to redress the numerical imbalance. Besides, against all odds, Vortigern retained the element of surprise, so the attack on the enemy's flank, which ought to have been a failure, had penetrated deeply into Vortimer's defensive line through sheer audacity.

Gradually, and inexorably, Vortimer's warriors were forced into an unplanned retreat.

When the main elements of Vortigern's fighting force had all crossed the river, Myrddion ordered half of his team to accompany him to the far side, where they would establish a dressing station to treat the walking wounded who made it back to the rope bridge. But within minutes of observing the suffering of the injured, Myrddion changed his mind.

"Finn! You and Cadoc, get back to the tent! I want all our equipment repacked into the wagons and brought over the upstream bridge so we can set up on this side of the river. I don't care how much time it takes, as long as you're over here in two hours. No excuses, for Vortimer's guards will have deserted their posts by now. Get to it!"

Cadoc was back in the water before Myrddion had finished speaking.

At least the wounds can be cleaned and kept dry now the dressing station is over here, Myrddion thought irritably. Let's hope no one bleeds to death while I wait for Cadoc to arrive.

The grey rain continued to fall; men died in bloody individual combats while, inexorably, Vortimer continued to give ground.

Cadoc and Finn returned in less than the stipulated two hours with the tent, plus all the supplies that Cadoc considered would be crucial to Myrddion during the coming day. As he dealt with hideous slash and stab wounds, cleaning, stitching, and bandaging where possible, the healer had ample opportunity to assess the crushing weight of the rain as it caused the leather tent to balloon under the weight.

Myrddion feared it would collapse, so Cadoc pushed upwards with a long pole, allowing cold water to cascade down the sides of the heavy leather, where it crept in under the flaps and turned the earth into a slurry of mud that soon reddened with blood. The cold began to seep up through Myrddion's boots until his legs were chilled, but he pushed the discomfort away from his conscious thoughts so that he could concentrate on the work to be performed by his busy, deft fingers.

Finn Truthteller provided hot water in a constant supply, although his master had no idea how the warrior conjured up a fire in such impossible conditions. In fact, a scavenger at heart, Finn had found an abandoned fisherman's hut close to the river. Inside, he found a supply of dry timber suitable for burning and, amazingly, recovered a large metal pot that he washed and dried thoroughly. Removing his finds to the dressing station, he built his fire under the large cauldron.

As the stream of wounded began to slow to a trickle, Myrddion sent Cadoc to discover what was happening to Vortigern's forces as they continued their advance.

Cadoc soon returned, his face creased in a wide grin.

"Good news, master! Vortimer's army seems to have vanished. If the prince was winning the battle, his warriors would be on top of us by now."

"What are you saying, Cadoc?" Myrddion asked, as he cleaned an ugly sword cut across the chest of a warrior. Fortunately, the patient was unconscious, so Myrddion was able to draw together the gaping edges of the deep wound and begin to stitch them without causing undue pain to the wounded man.

"The warriors I spoke to told me that Vortimer has retreated to Glevum. Somehow, against all the odds, Vortigern has won and, as a bonus, he has captured the catapults and the siege machines. Glevum will be shaken to its roots."

"There'll be a siege now," Myrddion muttered, and then his fingers resumed their stitching. "God help us all!"

Chapter XX

AN UNTIMELY END

To reap a field ere it is ripe,
Is it right, O stars' High King?
It is eating ere the hour
Flower of hazel, white with spring.

—An early anonymous Celtic poet

Vortimer raged through the villa like a crazed bull that has been stung to madness by a hive of bees. Furniture, cloth hangings, and precious alabaster jars were smashed, torn, and powdered underfoot as he made his way towards the sleeping chamber of the queen. Rowena heard him coming and seated herself on a stool with some of Willow's mending in her hands to quiet her trembling fingers. The glide of the needle through coarse wool was sweet, soothing, and useful as she hid herself within the calm center of her mind.

The door crashed open on its hinges as Vortimer struck it with his shoulder. It swung inwards and hit the wall so hard that plaster cracked and fell in shards onto the tiled floor.

Rowena kept the needle sliding through the rough wool—in and out, then pull tight, in and out, and then pull tight—like a mantra or a prayer.

"Lord Vortimer, why are you so out of temper? What is amiss?"

"Look at me, you bitch. Stop that . . . that rubbish, and look at me!"

"Of course, Lord Vortimer." Rowena laid down the coarse tunic, neatly pushed the needle through the cloth, and placed her sewing on the floor. Her eyes rose and she forced herself to face Vortimer as calmly as she could, folding her graceful hands in her lap.

Her stepson's face was congested and red with impotent fury, his eyes were almost inhuman in the lamplight, and a streak of his own blood marked his knuckles from where he had struck out blindly at a wall while rampaging through the villa.

"You bleed, Vortimer," she murmured. "Allow me to clean the split on your knuckles."

Her body was submissively tender, but her gaze was direct, fearless, and chill. Vortimer couldn't see the terror she hid so successfully.

"Your fucking husband is already encircling Glevum, Stepmother. He's captured my own siege machines, so he'll start battering down my walls with the arrival of the dawn."

In defiance of all the established rules of war, a whistling noise shattered the still of the night, as if on cue. It was followed by a dull thud.

The earth shuddered under their feet.

"Shite! Shite! Shite!" Vortimer continued to swear and added several epithets that described his father's parentage and courage.

"You think it's funny, don't you, Saxon whore! You sit there, like a prim Christian saint, but you spread your legs for an old man willingly enough, to turn him against his own sons. You caused the death of Catigern, and you found a way to send spies to my father, didn't you?"

Vortimer's voice had risen to a scream and he leaned over the queen, his face only inches from her own. Every fiber of Rowena's being urged her to spit into his twisted, beet-red face, but she kept her features calm and reasonable although it required a concentrated strength of will.

"The walls of Glevum are strong, lord, and the men of Dyfed are unlikely to bow their heads in submission to Vortigern. My husband will have to fight for every street and every filthy back alley before this city surrenders. I didn't spy for my husband. What could I have told him, Vortimer? I am not permitted to stir from this room. I am unaware of anything that occurs in the world outside."

Her stepson's shoulders had begun to relax as her reasonable voice soothed him, but her final words caused him to raise his fist and strike her, for the first time, across her face where the blow would show. Rowena felt her nose break and she cursed her stupidity even as she began to fall. She had been critical and Vortimer was very sensitive.

"You bitch! You wanted me, you led me into sin, and you seduced me. You sit there, all innocence, with your long hair unbound, inviting any man with red blood in his veins to fuck you."

He kicked out at her ribs, and Rowena tried to curl into a ball to protect herself. Her cheek brushed the discarded mending and the needle scratched her cheek. As her stepson continued to kick at her, she ripped the tiny weapon out of the cloth and hid it in her fist.

"Don't!" she gasped as she felt a rib break. She knew beyond doubt that he would kill her if she couldn't calm him. "I'm your stepmother!"

From the moment the words left her mouth, she realized that she had unwittingly inflamed him again.

Vortimer pulled her up onto her faltering legs by her unbound hair and struck her face until her senses swam and she could taste the blood of her split lips. Even as he prepared to hit her again, Rowena went for his eyes with both hands, until he, too, screamed shrilly and reeled away from her.

Her left hand had clawed Vortimer's face from forehead to chin on his right side, leaving deep scores in his cheek from her long, sharp nails. But his left eye began to bleed immediately, for she had driven the needle deeply into his enlarged pupil. A scrap of thread hung down from his eye like an obscene tail.

One hand rose to cover his blinded eye, while the other arm swept her away from him so that she stumbled over the plaster shards littering the floor until she crumpled in the corner of the room like a broken doll. Tears of blood, serum, and water streamed down his face as he turned on his heel and ran from the apartments.

His parting words were dreadfully audible, even as she lost consciousness.

"I'll be back, *Mother,* and then I'll take great pleasure in killing you. Vortigern will never see his precious Saxon whore again."

THE NIGHT WAS aflame as the circular huts that clustered outside Glevum's walls burned to the ground. Against his will, Myrddion had been summoned from his patients at Vortigern's express command, to divine the workings of the catapults and ballistas. No pleas or reasoning made an iota of difference to the king. He planned to bring Glevum to its knees, so he refused to be deflected by a lowly healer who might hold the answer to the secret mechanisms within his agile brain.

The tide of battle had swung against Vortimer with such speed that his engineers had been forced to abandon their weapons. Normally, they would have sabotaged them so they couldn't be used against their original owners, but the speed of the retreat was too great. Loyal to Ambrosius rather than Vortimer, the engineers had run for their lives to the shelter of the old Roman walls encircling Glevum. Now, as the flames lit the night with a hideous, bloody tint, the war machines of King Ambrosius were drawn into position to attack the central gates of Vortimer's refuge.

But before they could be aimed against his enemy, Vortigern had to learn how to use them. Myrddion clambered all over the catapult with a child's flexibility and a man's curiosity. He understood the gears and levers that permitted the great pole to be ratcheted down and locked into position, ready for firing. He found the long iron handle used to lower the bucket to be filled with the ordnance that would rain down on their targets, and found the release mechanism just as easily.

But how was the arc of the strike calibrated? How was the elevation changed?

"I'll need to load a catapult and practice until I understand how to aim it. Do I have your permission to fire at the gates of Glevum until I know what I'm doing?"

"Pound them into oblivion if you want." Vortigern snorted with laughter. "But you don't return to your patients until my men know how to use these infernal machines."

"But your wounded warriors will die if they remain untreated, King Vortigern," Myrddion warned. "You may need every fighting man you have if the siege of Glevum stretches out over weeks or months."

"If the gods will it, my warriors must be sacrificed. Unfortunately, I require those catapults far more urgently than I need a few extra men."

In his displeasure, Myrddion's lips twisted and he recalled, belatedly, the hatred he still felt towards the old king. For a few weeks, the healer had found himself seduced by Vortigern's energy, his swift intellect, and his ferocious recuperative powers. Even now, as the king's eyes bored into his, Myrddion could feel the man's charm, a trait possessed by all great men who entice others to follow them to the death.

Myrddion masked his sudden upsurge of hatred so that nothing reached his black, glistening eyes, but the healer knew that the king had divined the edges of his thoughts.

So Myrddion was allotted a group of lightly wounded men who had volunteered to work the *infernal machines.* Captured peasants were impressed into collecting rocks and other ordnance and placing them in large piles, ready for the bombardment that would soon take place. Fortunately, Vortimer's men had obligingly gathered a significant store of boulders that were just light enough for men to lift, with difficulty, into the iron buckets.

Carefully, and using a practical man's language, Myrddion explained the purpose of each part of the catapult before ordering two huge ex-farmers from Dyfed to turn the winch handle that would lower the bucket. With one hand on the great shaft of the catapult,

Myrddion could feel the tension in the timbers as they strained for release.

"Fill the bucket with rocks, as many as possible," Myrddion ordered, and his grinning laborers hurried to obey. With much grunting and effort, the dangling bucket was filled to the top.

Myrddion grinned at his makeshift engineers. "I have no idea if this is going to work, or if we'll hit anything at all." And before he could dwell on the subject, or change his mind, he released the firing mechanism.

The noise, and the thudding of missiles into stone, made a very satisfying explosion of powdered rock, dislodging a large section from the top of the wall. On the far side, within the township, other missiles struck buildings and dust rose in a pall thick enough to be visible in the darkness. Unfortunately, the catapult salvo had overshot the target and missed the gates entirely.

"This machine must be moved back to lower the trajectory. I have no other ideas on how to achieve the required result. We must also line up the raised pole on the gate. The other machines can be moved forward a little to send their loads of boulders over the walls and into the town itself."

As the men set to work to reposition the machines, Myrddion deciphered the workings of the ballistas, fired one to make a range calculation, and then set their crews about the same task. However, before he was allowed to trot back to the healer's tent, the High King called Myrddion over and took him to one side so they could speak privately.

"I'm a plain man at heart, healer, and I keep my word," Vortigern began. "You have done what I asked, so I'll tell you that your father said he came from Ravenna, where he claimed to be an aristocrat. I have no idea if he spoke the truth, because the man was as crooked as a willow branch. I trusted him so little that I ordered him thrown overboard during a sea voyage from the port of Deva into the Seteia Aest. As usual, the devil survived. It was near enough to make me convert to the Christian god."

"What was his name?" Myrddion asked in a voice suddenly hoarse with emotion.

"I think I'll save that information for another day," Vortigern replied with a nasty smile. "I'm sure I'll need your services at some time in the future."

Rowena struggled back to consciousness through a vortex of pain and terror. Both eyes struggled to open, but the swellings around her cheekbone and temple glued her right eyelid shut. Every bone and muscle screamed their protest at these abuses, while her broken ribs made every breath painful.

"Madam! Madam! Please wake up, madam," Willow whispered, as she gently shook Rowena's arm. "The master has gone berserk and is ordering his troops to arms. He swears he'll burn Glevum to ashes, with everyone within its walls, before he permits Vortigern to set foot in the town."

Disoriented and dizzy, Rowena saw the vague, misty face of Willow, and could feel the ministrations of another, old woman, who had been smearing ointment on her wounds. The crone was in the process of binding her ribs with lengths of coarse linen, and it was the agony of being touched that had dragged the queen back from the mercy of unconsciousness.

"Let me rise." Rowena blinked her one good eye until the edges of the room came back into focus and she could see her servant girl clearly. "I must try to stop him."

The old woman cackled her opinion of Rowena's chances more clearly than words. "Fathers and sons! Sons and fathers! There's no peace in a household when they live together, aye?"

"Aye," Rowena replied softly, and sighed. "But to weep and suffer needlessly is stupid, especially when innocent people will perish with us. Could you find some belladonna from the roots of the nightshade, Grannie? I have a desperate need for it. We all have need of it, for Glevum will be destroyed unless Vortimer is stopped."

"Old Grannie Edda has a small supply of the distilled juice of the berries, my lady, and other potions that kill, but I doubt that he'll drink anything from the hands that blinded his eye."

Rowena swung her legs over the side of her sleeping couch and winced as her head spun crazily. With Willow's assistance, she finally managed to stand, although she was hunched over like an old woman.

"Get me the belladonna nevertheless, and anything else you think will help. I'll find some way to put it into his drink. Believe me, the abstemious Vortimer *does* drink, when he thinks no one is looking."

Willow smiled fleetingly, for she also knew the master's habits, the cautious, strategic mind torn by the insecurities that caused him to bully weaker, less well protected souls. Before the queen had been taken as the booty of war, Willow had known the bite of Prince Vortimer's inadequacy. Now, mercifully, the prince was obsessed with Rowena, and Willow was both relieved and shamed by her feelings, especially when she tended to the marks that her master left on the queen's beautiful flesh.

"You must not go near him, mistress. His eye has been blinded permanently, for Grannie Edda was called to draw the needle from his pupil. She was unable to cure the damage, even with her knowledge, so he must go through life crippled. Please, Mistress Rowena, listen to me. He has vowed that he'll hurt you when next you meet."

Grannie Edda cackled again, her wise, tortoise-wrinkled eyes shining brightly in her ancient face. A streak of irony learned through a lifetime of watching human nature twisted her lopsided smile. To Grannie Edda, the world was a simple place, albeit one where amusing quirks of human nature added seasoning to its plain taste. We are born, we live, and then we die.

"No, madam, you must stay away from him," she agreed. "The scratches on his face are nothing, but his eye looks like a raw oyster. The pupil is curdled." Then Edda cackled gleefully once again, while Rowena shuddered at what she had done to the prince in her extremity.

"I shall wait until he comes to me. Yes, I know he will come. I cannot understand why he needs to possess me, but he does, so he'll seek me out when he is most afraid. He will probably kill me then, especially if Vortigern has already taken his precious Glevum. I cannot guess why the master needs to shame my honor—but he *will* come."

"Fathers and sons!" Edda laughed her crone's broken giggle, full of wicked, sardonic understanding.

"Bring me the belladonna, Edda. As much as you have. To beguile and poison Vortimer will be my allotted task, so pray to your goddess for me."

"I'll fetch it now, mistress." Grannie Edda grinned, exposing gaping holes where her teeth had once been. Only brown and rotting canines remained to give some shape to her seamed mouth. "I still need to stitch your foot when I return, for you've cut it almost to the bone."

The queen looked towards her right foot, which was loosely bandaged, but was beginning to ooze blood onto the floor. The wound on her sole suddenly hurt fiercely, so she sat down before she lost her balance and fell.

"Hurry, Grannie," Rowena whispered urgently. Outside, the dawn was coming quickly and a bird chirped outside her single window. The early morning air had the close stillness of summer, although winter had barely relinquished its hold on the city. "Hurry, for the barrage could begin very soon if Vortigern wishes to smash Glevum."

As Edda pattered away, the first boulders began to fall on the city, accompanied by the eerie, whistling sound that always warned of another approaching salvo. The impact of the boulders caused the earth to shake below Willow's feet, and although she knew they were far from the walls of the city, the maidservant glanced fearfully towards the window.

Distant screams and the keening of wounded citizens disturbed the quiet after the missiles had fallen. Dust from the roof floated down onto Rowena's hair.

"I pray that my husband is not so ruthless that he uses fire," Rowena whispered softly, as she lifted her feet onto the couch and lay back with a little sigh of pain. She closed her eyes, and both women waited quietly as the catapults continued their grim bombardment.

After a few minutes, Rowena opened her one good eye and turned to speak to Willow.

"Fetch wine, water, and glasses, Willow. No pottery, do you hear? Just fine glass goblets, the best you can find, so the contents seduce the eye. And platters of sweetmeats. Scour the kitchens for anything that is even remotely tempting." As the maidservant rose to obey, Rowena added, "Hurry, Willow. The city can't take too much pounding and I can smell smoke already."

Willow ran.

Rowena dozed briefly, despite the pounding of her head and the persistent ache of abused flesh. A gentle hand shaking her shoulder brought her back to consciousness.

Willow had found two precious Roman decanters, and goblets decorated with rims of pure gold. In one decanter, the maidservant had poured a rich, ruby-colored wine. In the other, cold water caused condensation to film the glass and trickle temptingly down the sides. A platter of small pieces of well-cooked meat jostled for attention with another covered with cubes of sugared rose petals in a jelly that was dusted with powdered almond and drenched in honey.

Reflectively, Rowena popped a sweet delicacy into her mouth and licked her fingers clean of the sticky amber treat.

"It's good. Vortimer will find these morsels difficult to resist, no matter how angry and frightened he is. And he'll guzzle the wine for sure. Now, a goblet of water, Willow, if you would."

The maidservant was in the process of obeying her mistress when Grannie Edda returned, bringing the faint reek of smoke into the room with her. The barrage continued with a sickening stink of fire and brick dust.

"We must hurry," Rowena warned them both. "Who knows when the situation inside the city will become grave?"

Grannie Edda held up two vials of a liquid that looked like slightly dirty water. "Belladonna," she stated.

"Fine. Now poison the wine and the water, and then sprinkle a few droplets on every item on the platters. Oh, and poison the water in my goblet as well."

"Mistress!" Willow protested. "You can't!"

"I must, so don't be afraid. I don't plan to kill myself, but Vortimer trusts nobody. He could insist that he'd prefer to drink my goblet of water rather than his own wine. I must be prepared for any foolishness on his part."

As Edda went to work, Rowena noticed a plate of fruit that had survived the carnage of the previous evening.

"Can the fruit be poisoned?" she asked Edda, who exposed the last of her teeth in an ugly, clever grin. Her wrinkled brown hands darted into a pouch at her waist and came out with a powder sealed inside a twist of cloth.

"This dust comes from grave mummy, apricot kernels, and certain berries. Every grain of this powder kills those who handle it, so beware that it doesn't touch your fingers. Even when it is burned, it gives off noxious fumes that will kill. I'll dust the fruit myself, so we can be certain that he will die if he even touches the rinds."

"I would poison my own flesh if I thought it would work on him. Please stitch my foot now, Grannie Edda, and then you should both depart until such time as he comes to have his way with me. The sun is rising and the city is on fire, so Vortimer will come for me soon."

MYRDDION WATCHED HIS handiwork rain death on the city of Glevum with a grim mix of guilt and relief. Vortigern's army was safe, while Death was abroad and hungry in the narrow streets and damaged buildings of Glevum.

The air was thick with smoke above the city, for the breezes were gentle and the flames spread so slowly that the army inside the besieged walls was able to extinguish all but the most persistent blazes. Myrddion could readily imagine soot-blackened warriors forming bucket lines to kill any burgeoning fire, or digging desperately through collapsed walls of brick, plaster, and timber to find buried comrades. He saw thatched roofs blaze like oil lamps, and imagined the bubbling, burning skin of children and infants with the sickened knowledge of a healer. Closing his eyes momentarily, he reassured himself that the city could choose to surrender, so he could put his guilt behind him.

Vortimer was the only man who could change the fate of Glevum, but Myrddion feared that the son would be as ruthless as the father. Cruelty was a learned skill.

The catapults continued to batter the city. The gates should have been smashed hours earlier, but the old oak timbers were heavily braced with thick iron bands and the inhabitants of Glevum had piled many weighty objects against them to absorb the punishing blows. Still, nothing can stand repeated blows indefinitely, and Myrddion could see that the wood was beginning to splinter around the hinges, although a heavy iron bar still held the gates closed.

"It won't be long now," Cadoc said cheerfully from behind Myrddion. The assistant rocked cheerfully back and forth on his heels, his hands hooked over a leather belt as he surveyed the suffering township. "Sieges can be long, drawn-out affairs without catapults, so Vortimer would have been better off if he'd never accepted Ambrosius's gifts."

Myrddion grunted his agreement. Now that the rigid surface of the gate was breached, its fall was only a matter of time. Then Vortigern would order his men to attack and the healer would soon have new wounded to treat.

ROWENA HAD DRESSED herself with painstaking care so that the worst of the swellings and contusions were covered. She lay on her sleeping couch with her hair demurely braided while she waited for Vortimer to decide that his position was so difficult that the queen must pay.

In the late afternoon, she heard the sounds of his approach: the slam of doors, a dropped amphora of oil on the hard tiles, and a single moaned protest as Willow was slapped away from outside the queen's room. Rowena prepared herself for pain, torment, and argument.

Vortimer entered without the violence of the previous evening, for the door remained unrepaired. His demeanor was colder, harder, and more fixed, as if the well of his softer emotions had been emptied, leaving a hungry void. His wounded eye was covered with a stained bandage that was tied around his head at a rakish angle, but he was disheveled as if he had spent time fighting the blazes in the town, as indeed he had.

"Madam, Glevum will belong to your husband by morning, by which time I expect to be dead. If my father thinks to enjoy my surrender, he will be sadly disappointed. I'll not give him the satisfaction of ordering my death."

Rowena raised herself so she was almost sitting upright on her pillows. Inadvertently, one white shoulder was bared as her gown fell away. A livid bruise caused by his boot was clearly visible on her naked flesh. Vortimer felt his manhood become aroused with shamed excitement.

"You choose to die then, Vortimer? Surely there are hidden routes out of Glevum? I can't believe that you have left yourself with no means of escape."

As a clever planner with an eye for the main chance, Vortimer had already determined the route of his retreat. His histrionic tale of imminent death was a ploy to divert her attention from his planned desertion of the citadel. He had no intention of leaving her alive, because every throb of his wounded eye that pulsed through his brain convinced him that his plan to strangle her was all she deserved. But he wanted her to be compliant. He desired her body one more time, although he trusted her words even less than he trusted his father.

"There are no means of retreat for men of honor. Do not insult me, Stepmother. We both know what Father will do to me if I am captured alive. After all, you have provided him with other legitimate sons."

Rowena read the craftiness in Vortimer's eye and knew that he lied. She veiled her own eyes and lied in turn.

"I should be sorry to learn of your death, stepson. Prior to my captivity, I always believed you to be a man of honor."

Cursing ferociously, he gripped her bruised shoulder until she cried out with the pain of his clasp. He felt a surge of pleasure and rising tumescence. Whenever he forced this proud, contained woman to bend to his desires, Vortimer experienced an exhilaration that fulfilled some dark need in him—as if he was inflicting her dishonor upon his father.

He stroked her swollen cheek, forcing her to close her good eye so he shouldn't see her revulsion. Stroking her and pinching her by turns, he spread her legs with scant concern for the bandages that were mute proof of his recent assault. When he entered her, he sighed a deep, shuddering breath and luxuriated in her agony as he deliberately let his full weight press onto her abused body.

Once again, she moaned in pain. But, unlike the night before, she was unable to resist him. Callously, he leaned on her cracked ribs until tears spilled down her cheeks and she bit her split lip until blood filled her mouth. But still she refused to fight, knowing that any resistance would give him pleasure. Once the rape was over, Vortimer slumped onto her, breathing heavily against her wounded face until Rowena thought she would vomit with disgust.

Eventually, the prince lifted his body away from hers, straightened his clothing, and stared down at her supine form. He felt no pity or shame, only emptiness. He was done with her and knew, instinctively, that he could endure his life only if she were to stop breathing.

Standing idly over her, he picked up her long braids and absently played with the heavy hair. He considered strangling her with her own plaits, an apt symbol of his freedom from her charms, but rejected the idea as quickly as he thought of it. The vision of her congested face and protruding tongue caused him a thrill of sexual pleasure, so he toyed with the desire to strangle her during another rape.

She reached out her hand for her goblet of water, but he took the precious glass out of her hand and placed it back on the table. He shivered at the immediate physical response he felt at his proximity to her.

"You don't need water, Rowena. You don't need anything." He looked around the clean, well-lit room and his eyes fell on the wine, the water, and the platters of food. "You're a clever bitch, aren't you? Do you think to poison me?"

"I'd be poisoning myself if I did," she whispered. Her realization of impending failure made her shoulders droop, for his gaze told her that she had been too obvious in her entrapment.

"Yes, I know. But I'll still reject your offerings, just in case."

He eyed the fruit, which seemed a little past its best, and remembered that the same platter had been in the room on the previous night. He recalled that he had eaten an apple when he first entered the apartments, and had suffered no ill effects. Absently, he picked up a costly orange, but rejected the fruit because the skin was split. Instead, he took up a handful of black berries, rolled them around in his palms and then popped them into his mouth, one by one.

Sure of himself, Vortimer failed to notice the sheen of dust on the bloom of the fruit. Nor did he notice that not all the berries were the same, for the cunning Edda was thorough and had added ripe belladonna berries to the bowl.

Rowena closed her good eye and prayed to Freya that he would succumb to the poison before he killed her. His intent was crystal clear, as obvious as the continual barrage of the catapults that maintained their earthshaking salvos, or the sound of muffled footsteps outside her broken door, where Willow waited, her breath held, listening for some sign of disaster from within.

Vortimer selected another handful of berries, and once more he ignored their dustiness while concentrating on the sweetness that burst inside his mouth with each bite.

"Willow!" he called suddenly. "Come here, girl. I need you."

Willow slipped into the room and bent her head in obeisance.

"Bring me some wine. I want a flagon, not this muck. I'm very thirsty and I can't trust your mistress not to poison me."

Willow disappeared to obey his demands, while Rowena watched Vortimer covertly out of her good eye. So far, beyond a sudden thirst, he showed no ill effects from the poison provided by Grannie Edda. He began to stroke her thighs under her robe and the queen realized, finally, that she would die. She tried to smile, but the promise of pain turned her conciliatory gesture into a grimace.

"My sons," she whispered to herself. "At least my sons are safe."

The sadness in her voice affected Vortimer more potently than any seductive glance or touch could have done. He would have stroked the golden column of her throat, preparatory to throttling her, but Willow entered with a tray on which rested one goblet of water and another of wine. Without thinking, Vortimer gulped the water down.

"Out," he roared, unaware that his voice had subtly changed. "And don't come back."

He staggered a little as he returned to Rowena, but she hardly dared to hope. Careless of her injuries, she swung her legs to the floor tiles and stood before him.

Vortimer reached out a hand to restrain her, but his vision was oddly blurred and she evaded him easily. With an odd detachment, he noticed that he seemed to be wading through thick honey, while the room was tilting alarmingly. Suddenly, he was drenched in sweat and his limbs began to twitch. He staggered towards Rowena and gripped the sleeve of her robe, almost dragging her down with him before the delicate fabric tore and freed her, half-naked, from his rigid, clenched hands.

Clutching the folds of her torn dress, Vortimer fell onto knees that had suddenly lost the power to lock his legs in an upright position. He reached one hand towards her pleadingly, so that she imagined she saw the face of a frightened boy superimposed over the snarling features of the man.

"What's wrong with me?" Vortimer's voice was slurred and barely clear enough to understand.

Naked, Rowena stood tall like a slim golden column marred only by the marks, scars, and bandages that told of his assaults. Her braids had come undone so that her hair fell down her back. She should have looked either seductive or pathetic, but instead her cold, impassive face gave her a regal dignity that seemed to judge him as he looked up at her.

"You are dying, stepson," she said.

"That filthy little cow poisoned the water," Vortimer panted. He was having trouble getting a full breath of air into his lungs.

"You're wrong, Vortimer, as always. I poisoned the berries. I poisoned all the fruit. In fact, everything in this room is tainted. I'd have poisoned my own skin if I could have done so and lived. I left your punishment to the fates, Vortimer, and you chose to eat."

"Slut! Whore! Saxon cow! Why have you done . . . this . . . to me? Surely you couldn't . . . want an old man?"

For all his curses, he looked at her pleadingly, as if she could stop the sweat that drenched his body or the pains that had begun inside his head.

"What would I want with *any* man? So he can do *this* to me?" Her hands stroked the cuts and bruises on her body. "I do what I must to save my sons."

Vortimer laughed painfully, trying to keep her form in focus with his one eye. His laughter sounded grating, ugly, and sad. "My father has no idea what a monster you are. You'll be the death of him as well."

"Not me, Vortimer! I've never raised my hand against any of you. I was sold, paid for with red gold when I was just a little girl, and put into an old man's bed. No one asked me what I wanted. You took me just to thumb your nose at your father and to prove you were the better man. What should I care for men? You break what you possess, no matter how much you value it, because it's yours and because you can. Are you surprised that your toys can stand back and watch as you kill yourselves?"

Vortimer fell onto his back and felt every muscle start to spasm until his body arched like a bow.

Rowena turned away, shamed and weak despite the iron truth in her words. We are betrayed by our own natures, which are made for love rather than hate, the queen thought sadly as her unraveling hair fell like a curtain over her swollen face to hide the evidence of her injuries. But try as she might, she couldn't avoid the snuffling sounds, the grinding of teeth, and the drumming of Vortimer's heels on the floor.

"I loved you . . . in my way. You were the only . . . mother . . . I remembered."

The convulsion had ended and Vortimer forced the words out through his numbed lips and tongue. A tear snaked down from his eye.

A small bundle of fury exploded through the door and stamped on his face with one sandaled foot. The queen watched the sudden violence with horror. Vortimer was unable to avoid Willow's blows, because another convulsion was beginning to stretch his mouth into a rictus of terror.

"He's lying! He's lying, mistress. He threw away his own sons without love or thought," Willow panted as she aimed another kick at the prince's genitals with all the strength at her disposal. "His idea of love is to take what he wants because he's the son of a king. He took my boys away and then ordered my breasts to be bound so their shape wouldn't be ruined—or so he said. He wants what he wants when he wants it."

"He's a man," Rowena replied, straightening her spine and putting aside her sympathy for her stepson. "He's not dead yet. Send for his captains as fast as you can, but find me a decent robe before you go. Men are dying as we chatter about the motives that impel a rapist, and I'll not waste more lives. All that remains is to convince Glevum to surrender to Vortigern's army."

With one last, vicious grinding of her sandaled heel into Vortimer's contorted face, Willow complied. She brought a warmed robe to her mistress and wrapped it round Rowena's trembling body.

"Send for Grannie Edda and a manservant first, to move this carrion to a place where he can be left until he dies. But no torture, hear? Then I want everything harmful removed from this room with great care and burned to ensure that no danger threatens other innocents. No one else should have to suffer so filthy a death, especially by accident."

From somewhere, the queen in Rowena's nature had rediscovered its voice. Surprised, Willow scurried away to obey her orders. Shortly afterwards, two large men entered the room, picked up the still convulsing Vortimer and carried him out of sight. Grannie Edda, who had accompanied them, would have followed, but was stopped by a single peremptory gesture. She looked up, a little nervously, at the tall woman who wore her injuries as if they were jewels.

"Make my stepson comfortable, Mistress Edda. To kill is one matter, especially to save many lives. But to deny the comfort of poppy juice to a dying human being would be a stain on my honor. Do not disobey me, and send word to me when the prince has succumbed to the illness that afflicts him."

"Aye, Queen Rowena," Grannie Edda replied respectfully. "As you wish."

Shortly afterwards, Willow returned with three maids who were instructed to remove all contaminated objects, replace all linen, scrub the floors, and make the apartments as clean as possible. Despite the probability that rumors would swiftly follow, the servants were told to use tongs, gloves, and rags to remove every trace of food and drink. Fully aware of the perils associated with the task, the servants were scrupulously careful in their disposal of the contaminated food and drink.

While the cleaning women toiled, Rowena sat and observed their labors with folded hands and a serene face that hid the turmoil of her thoughts. She had killed and she could never be the same again.

Five minutes later, two bearded warriors were admitted through the ruined door, and their eyes widened as they noted the injuries to the queen's face. They had seen the blinded eye and scratched cheek of their master, but now they could see with their own eyes the indignities that the prince had inflicted on his stepmother. Both soldiers successfully hid their revulsion.

"You asked to see us, your highness?" the older man asked. A senior officer, his eyes roved around the apartment and his mind recorded every tiny sign of violence on the couch, the walls, and the door.

"My stepson, Prince Vortimer, is dying. As there is no clear successor, I am making it your responsibility to assume interim command of his army. I order you to protect the innocent citizens of Glevum from King Vortigern's wrath by ending this siege as quickly as possible. There must be no further damage to the town. Nor will any harm be inflicted on the citizenry of this place by neighbor fighting against neighbor. You will send a message to King Vortigern immediately to acquaint him with what has taken place on this day and advise him that you will petition for peace."

The grizzled commander contrived to look grave and relieved at the same time. He nodded his acquiescence and the two men backed away from the queen, bowing low as they did so. They knew that Vortigern's rage would be explosive when he saw the injuries that had been inflicted upon his wife, and both warriors were terrified at the possibility of being blamed for any perceived failure to protect her. With heartfelt sighs of relief, they left the room and its regal occupant. Outside, the air seemed sweeter and easier to breathe.

"What are your orders, sir?" the younger man asked his commander as they strode along the colonnade of the villa and out into the dusty air. The night was lit by the reflection of fires from burning buildings and Glevum was like a disturbed ant heap as it struggled to survive.

"So it's going to be like that, is it, Collen Blackhair? As the commander, I am to face Vortigern's wrath!"

"The risks of command, Aelwyn, the risks of command! Still, Vortigern will be pleased to take Glevum with so little loss of life, so we must act quickly and preempt his revenge."

Aelwyn sighed with resignation. In Collen's place, he would have acted in the same manner. "I will send a messenger to Vortigern and open the gates before the damned things fall down. Timing is everything at the moment. What a mess!" he added under his breath. "The day was cursed when Vortigern's sons decided to supplant their father on the throne. Ambrosius has successfully undermined the northwest, so he'll be the only winner who survives this fiasco."

"What?"

"Nothing. Get to it, Blackhair. We have a town to save, and our own skins, if it's at all possible."

WHEN THE GATES of Glevum were opened during the second evening of the siege, Vortigern's troops were taken completely by surprise. The army was in a festive mood and the foot soldiers were already counting the spoils they would loot from Glevum when the city fell, so the sudden emergence of an unarmed officer under a flag of truce was not entirely welcome. However, no man was quite brave enough to stand between King Vortigern and Glevum's emissary, although some stones were thrown as the enemy officer was taken into custody.

Soon, bleeding from superficial cuts and bruises, Collen Blackhair was ushered into the presence of King Vortigern. The young officer had decided that to volunteer for such a perilous mission offered him the best chance of survival.

"Does Glevum surrender, young man?" Vortigern asked without preamble. "If so, why?" He, too, was irritated, for he clearly relished the prospect of besting his son in the coming battle for control of the town.

"The commander of the troops of Glevum, Aelwyn ap Beynon, surrenders the town to you without reservation. He begs that you welcome those men of Glywising and Dyfed who followed your son into battle without the luxury of choice. He begs your forgiveness for the sins committed by Prince Vortimer and Prince Catigern in their attempt to wrest power from the legitimate High King."

"Aelwyn is to be congratulated, for he has sent you with a very compelling apology for the treachery committed by my sons. But I am not an idiot, Collen Blackhair. Where is my son?"

Collen bit his lip and Myrddion, who had been ordered to the king's tent in order to learn the status of Glevum, knew at once that Prince Vortimer had been swept off the chessboard.

"Your son was near to death when I left Glevum, my lord. I do not know the full details, but Queen Rowena ordered us to surrender the city to your forces, and Aelwyn obeyed her without question."

Vortigern's brows lowered dangerously. "What has the queen to do with the siege of Glevum?"

"I am here at her express command, my lord, through the orders of Commander Aelwyn. The queen is concerned that the innocent people of Glevum should not be forced to suffer for the sins of your son."

Vortigern rose so suddenly that his seat crashed to the ground behind him. "What sins? Is the queen well?"

Collen's face paled a little, but he squared his shoulders and continued manfully. "The queen has been badly beaten, and has been under the care of one of the healers of Glevum. She is well, but eagerly awaits being reunited with her lord and master."

"Who laid hands upon the person of the queen?" Vortigern demanded in a quiet, expressionless voice. Myrddion immediately recognized the threat in those quiet words and prayed that Prince Vortimer was safely dead.

"The prince attacked the queen and beat her." Collen coughed awkwardly. "I believe he may have forced himself upon her."

"Where is my son now?"

Vortigern's expression was impossible to read, but Collen Blackhair visibly shrank away from the old man in an attempt to remain out of the reach of his sword.

"Your son is probably dead by now. He has been poisoned."

Vortigern pressed his lips together, but he said nothing more other than to order his men to prepare for the occupation of Glevum. As for Collen, he was ordered to return to his commander with instructions to ready his warriors for the entrance of the High King into the city.

So, on a morning that promised the arrival of another spring, when the distant Sabrina Aest shone blue and the sky was pale and clean with weak sunshine, the siege of Glevum was lifted. Slowly, and with due ceremony, Vortigern and a guard of several hundred men rode and marched through the splintered gates of the city. Aelwyn ap

Beynon and the city fathers awaited the High King's arrival on bended knees, their weapons laid out ceremoniously before them in total surrender.

"Hail, Vortigern, rightful High King of the Britons," Aelwyn roared, and the voices of Vortimer's foot soldiers shouted the greeting in turn, frightening the carrion birds that had been drawn to the battlefield outside the walls, causing them to rise in great spirals towards the sun.

Dressed in the palest of bleached-white wool, Queen Rowena came forward, her bruises worn proudly on her golden throat and face, to abase herself on the cobblestones before her husband. When Vortigern assisted his queen to her feet, she kissed the palm of his hand in gratitude. As she bent over her master's hand, Myrddion wondered just how sincere her passive, loving expression actually was. A collective, sentimental sigh rippled through the ranks as the king kissed his wife on her blackening cheek.

"And so another war ends," Myrddion whispered to Cadoc, who grinned irrepressibly back at his master. "The north is at peace once more."

"You've forgotten that King Ambrosius is still alive and well, master. He's lost nothing during the past year, but Vortigern has been deeply wounded and his resources have been sorely tested and wasted. Surely, the Roman waits for a propitious sign to demonstrate that he can safely remove Vortigern, and our autonomy, once and for all."

"Your vocabulary is improving," Myrddion hissed back at his cheerful companion, his eyes torn between the last fingers of smoke rising over Glevum's walls and the squabbling crows and ravens in the sky. His thoughts were as bleak as the freshening wind that threatened to scour away the warmth of the morning. "Vortigern is a dangerous man, so Ambrosius will not permit him to live. We will remember today because it offered us foolish hope for the future."

Cadoc grinned to show his understanding, and Myrddion looked down into the scarred, stretched skin around his servant's eyes, eyes that saw humor in the foibles of weaker humans.

"Men like us are carrion birds, Myrddion, for we follow the scent of fresh blood. We'll have new patients soon enough."

"Aye, soon enough," Myrddion replied, and the day was suddenly cold. The sunshine wavered as cloud cover sent Glevum into shadow, while the queen shivered within her husband's embrace.

Chapter XXI

ENDINGS AND
BEGINNINGS

Like a long chain of irregular beads, Vortigern's army had been strung out along the Roman road for nearly two weeks. Eager to be home, the marching foot soldiers were progressively discharged from their duties at Caerleon, Venta Silurum, and Caer Fyrddin as the levies returned to their farms, their forges, and their safe, ordinary lives. Men had died, but not so many that the spring planting would be compromised. The world rolled on irrevocably for the towns and hamlets of the west, just as it always had.

Myrddion was describing the promise of their new life in Segontium to Cadoc and Finn Truthteller when a warrior thrust his head into their tent to deliver a message that Vortigern demanded his presence. The three men were preparing to devour a stew made of lamb that had been purchased from a local farmer, and was now simmering in a broth of vegetables. Myrddion could almost taste the tender nettles, new carrots, and sweet, greasy flesh, so he sighed with impatience as he excused himself from his companions.

"Some days I'm convinced I was born to be Vortigern's dog," the fifteen-year-old complained grumpily, while the messenger escorting him to the king's tent darted a horrified look at the young man for speaking such blasphemy. "Hades knows that Vortigern expects me to jump through whatever hoop he has found for his amusement— usually when I'm about to eat."

"No, lord! There's been a courier come from the north," the warrior protested, shaking the long braids that marked his status as a man and as a master of weapons. "I believe the message is for you. Indeed, the High King does his duty by you."

"Why didn't you say so?" Myrddion snapped, breaking into a run that left the shorter, heavier warrior far in his wake. When he reached the gaudy tent of the High King, he skidded to a halt, straightened his long black hair, and slid through the flap.

Vortigern was seated with his wife and his two remaining sons, Vengis and Katigern. The boys were close in age to Myrddion and eyed the famed healer with nervous, admiring eyes. Both were strong, deep-chested lads, taking their features from their mother rather than the High King, but Myrddion perceived a streak of willfulness and recklessness in the elder boy's eyes. Vengis was passionate, clever, and, in his manly way, quite beautiful.

"You required my presence, my lord?" Myrddion asked, carefully hiding his irritation.

"A very odd message has come from Canovium, via your kin at Segontium. I'm sorry to inform you that Melvig ap Melwy has died, but he breathed his last in his sleep so his death was a gentle one. Your great-grandfather was very old, I believe—almost a Methuselah, as the Christian priests would say."

"He was nearly seventy years," Myrddion replied with a frisson of pride.

"Venerable." Vortigern sighed with approval, as if reaching a great age was a sign of considerable virtue. Myrddion remembered his great-grandfather's sharp, vindictive eyes and sardonic grin. He considered the old man's prideful, arrogant ways and then concluded that virtue was one character flaw that Melvig would never have accused himself of. The old man had been far too pragmatic for virtue and loved life far too passionately.

"The message was sent to you by the old king when he realized that his health was failing. He reminds you of a promise you made to him that his head should part company with his shoulders under your blade. I have no idea what Melvig means by such a message, but some kin of yours . . . Eddius? . . . yes, Eddius . . . seems to think that you will understand."

"Aye, your majesty, I do. My great-grandfather followed the ancient customs of his people, so he commanded me to strike his head from his body after his death to allow his soul to be set free. He believed that I would carry out his instructions properly."

"How very strange!" Queen Rowena murmured, her blue eyes blank and almost doll-like in the light of the perfumed oil lamps. Myrddion shivered when he glanced into those lambent eyes, which no longer possessed any trace of the proud queen of Dinas Emrys or Glevum. Something had changed in her, or had been forcibly removed.

"A barbaric custom, my dear," Vortigern explained. "Long discarded by most of our people, especially by those cautious men who are nervous about being beheaded while they are still alive. Not all of us have a noted healer as a kinsman."

"I will need to leave at once, my king. Melvyn ap Melvig will be eager to lay his father to rest. He has ruled in all but name for several years."

Vortigern examined Myrddion's face for any sign of regret or sorrow and was surprised to discover that Myrddion seemed almost cheerful. Suspicious as always, he shot a narrow glance in the direction of his healer. Vortigern rarely allowed the smallest inconsistency to pass his notice.

"I'm astonished that you don't appear to mourn the passing of your liege lord and kinsman."

"I liked King Melvig, both as a man and as a kinsman. After all, he permitted me, a bastard, to live in his daughter's house where I was loved and nurtured. Whatever I desired, he allowed me to have, so I will remember him with great fondness. But how could I mourn the passing of a man who has lived for the full span of his life and had only a slow decline into feebleness before him? I pray that if I should live so long I also might die gracefully and without regret, like my great-grandfather."

Queen Rowena roused herself from the torpor that had seemed to consume her since the siege of Glevum had been lifted.

"I understand, healer. We don't weep for our heroes either. Nor for the elderly who have drunk their full measure from the cup of life. Any tears we shed are for ourselves."

Vortigern coughed to cover the awkward little gap in the conversation caused by Rowena's odd comment. Her elder son moved a little closer to her and placed one arm protectively round her shoulders.

"Then you'd better be off, healer. But don't think to leave my employ, not until after the summer campaign in the south. I fully expect Ambrosius to come knocking at my door in the next few months."

Myrddion merely nodded. Even the promise of his father's name was insufficient incentive to bring him back to King Vortigern's side once he had broken free.

"In case you choose to stay at home rather than rejoin me at Dinas Emrys, I will be keeping your assistants, your servants, and your scrolls with me as hostage. Never fear, for I'll ensure that your possessions are safe. If the High King cannot guarantee the protection of your property, who can? I'll be waiting for you at my fortress. I'm sure you remember the way."

Then Vortigern laughed in that patronizing, sneering fashion that Myrddion hated with all his heart. The cruel humor caused Queen Rowena to flinch and the healer wondered what was amiss. What else could he do but bow his head and back away from the High King and his family? He seethed with disappointment and chagrin at Vortigern's high-handedness, but there was nothing he could say to change the king's mind. Better he should save his breath.

The next morning, on a swift bay horse he could barely control,

Myrddion rode away from Caer Fyrddin without even the time to seek out his great-aunt or his other kin. As he gave the dancing horse its head with some misgiving, the beast heaved its way up the steep track leading from the river towards the old Roman fortress. Thick forest furred the hills before the road veered away towards the northwest, and Vortigern's encampment became a small flutter of colored banners and antlike activity around smaller squares of tents. With one last backward glance, Myrddion turned his face towards the long, arduous journey home.

The young man reached Tomen-y-mur on a hot day when the sight of the sea in the distance made him hungry for home, so it was with regret that he bypassed Segontium and took the direct route through the mountains to Canovium, arriving via a poorly maintained track that wound through the close, flinty foothills. Myrddion's horse had ceased to fight him for ascendancy once they reached the mountains, and the gelding now plodded along the ill-defined track with its head held low and every line of its body speaking of resignation and weariness. Tired, stiff in the flanks, and sore in the backside from the beast's spine, Myrddion almost fell off the bay when he reached the king's hall.

Melvig ap Melwy had lived in some state in a wooden structure that served the multiple purpose of palace, judgment hall, and warrior accommodation. In the town, the doors of the simple conical cottages were firmly shut. Although night had not yet come, the lintels were festooned with bunches of herbs, amulets, and other charms to propitiate the powerful spirit of the dead king. No one in Canovium would feel completely safe until the old king's spirit was sent to the Otherworld, no matter how great the respect and the love that had been accorded to Melvig during his lifetime.

Myrddion handed his reins to an ostler, giving instructions that the gelding should be stabled and cared for after its long labors. During the journey, Myrddion had developed an odd affection for the horse, which he had named Vulcan after the Roman god of the forge fires, a name that suited its temperament. Once the bay was led away to be watered and fed, Myrddion squared his shoulders and mounted the three stone steps leading to Melvig's judgment hall at the top of the broad, flagged forecourt.

The hall had been decorated and beautified during Melvig ap Melwy's long reign. The great slabs of wood that formed the doorposts, and the massive lintel across them, had been heavily carved with serpentine interlace, and even Myrddion's quick eyes couldn't discern either the beginning or the end of the complex patterns. Melvig had loved brightly colored displays, so the complex, incised designs were colored with red ocher, yellow pigment, and even the deep blue of woad. Some craftsman had touched up the paintwork when Melvig died, so the design stood forth from the weathered wood of the hall in a brave display of defiance. Even from the shadows of death, the old king continued to thumb his nose at time and fate.

Myrddion paused at the doors and traced the interlacing pattern. A serpent, a wormlike dragon, a ribbon of light—all the symbols swam together in the healer's mind and each image reflected an aspect of Melvig's personality. With one hand resting on the carving, Myrddion paused and remembered his great-grandfather. As complex as the decoration, Melvig had been fair, irascible, joyous, stern, and prone to fits of rage. Yet Myrddion remembered the old man with affection and was proud that he shared bloodlines with such a redoubtable character. Sadness tugged at his chest and constricted his breathing, although he accepted Melvig's easy death as a cause for rejoicing.

He struck the doors with the palms of both hands and the heavy wood swung silently inwards. With one part of his mind, Myrddion noticed that the large bronze hinges had been freshly oiled, another mark of respect by nameless servants. Inside, darkness enfolded him, relieved only by strategic oil lamps that burned precious oils giving off no trace of the fishy smell that Melvig had detested. The few narrow windows had been covered with brightly colored woolen hangings so that no natural light disturbed the rest of the king of the Deceangli.

The body had been placed on a cloth-draped table. The king's remains had been dressed in his finest armor and a cloak of exceptional magnificence that had been woven by Olwyn during her youth. As Myrddion approached his kinsman, he remembered Olwyn's loom and the brilliant reds and greens that she had used to dye spun wool. He felt tears form in his eyes and brushed them away impatiently.

So much had been lost in the inevitable passage of the years. Even these sharp, painful memories would pass.

A shadowy figure waited in the darkness at the back of the judgment hall, and Myrddion moved forward to pay his last respects to the man who had decided every major event in his young life.

Melvig had been dead for over a week, so the many flowers and scented oils were needed to mask the sweet, cloying smell of corruption. Inside the hall, darkened and cooled by the stone floors, and ventilated by the open windows behind the hangings, his grandfather's body had not swelled into gross, rotting ugliness. Rather, the strong face had fallen in and the waxy skin shone tightly over the powerful bones at his forehead, his cheekbones, and the beak of his nose. Melvig's mouth had sunk and his strong jaw was thrust forward so that his face was a study in light and shade, as inhuman as the carvings on his doorway. The face spoke of strength, power, and pride, and Myrddion marveled once more how death smoothed away the lines of a long and autocratic life.

Moved, he bent and kissed Melvig's hand, noting that the king's great ruby ring had been taken from his finger. Then the healer lifted a fold of Olwyn's cloak and kissed the fine weaving, trying to inhale some trace of his grandmother's perfume from the material. But it was gone, lost in the lonely years since her death.

Unsettled and saddened, Myrddion backed away from the body and walked respectfully towards the shadowy figure at the rear of the room. A warrior dressed in full battle gear stepped out of the darkness and bowed his head very low, as if to a king.

"The family awaits you in the dining chamber, Lord Myrddion. Please follow me."

They passed through a door concealed by another hanging and Myrddion's eyes were dazzled by light that flooded the colonnade leading to the king's private apartments. A hazel tree had grown from seed beside a fountain that had not worked for fifty years, yet such was Melvig's piety that every day its basin was filled with clear, pure water so that the tree shed its nuts directly into the standing pool. Strange shapes seemed to stir in the shallow depths as Myrddion paused to trail his fingers through the water, and then plunged his tired face into its coolness. Despite his skepticism, he felt the weariness of his journey drain away with the runnels of water that poured off his skin. Unconsciously, he chose not to drink a drop of the holy water, not yet.

Melvig's eldest son, Melvyn, greeted Myrddion at the entrance to the dining hall. Melvyn was old, nearly as ancient as his father had been when Myrddion was born, but he was smaller than his sire and much darker, although his hair was almost white. Enfolded in his great-uncle's arms, Myrddion felt the pull of kinship.

When he had made his obeisance to the new king, Myrddion looked round the massed crowd of kinfolk and mourners. Branwyn turned her face away from him, but even in profile her features were pinched, sallow, and old, although she had lived for barely twenty-nine years. Her body had thickened with childbirth, and no trace of her lithe, childhood fecklessness remained. Myrddion felt old and sad at her obvious, unrelenting enmity.

Then, from out of the press of women, a small, plump form rushed at him and embraced him with pleasure and affection. All he could really see of her was her long braided hair, but he dimly remembered her smell, composed of newly baked bread, milk, and sweet earth. A man with a balding head and one ragged ear stood proudly watching the small tableau of welcome, and Myrddion recognized him with a rush of affection.

"Aunt Fillagh and Uncle Cletus! How wonderful to see you again. I still wear your amulet, Cletus, with pride and gratitude. I had hoped to meet you again when I was at Caer Fyrddin, but news of our king's death called me north."

"Let me look at you, boy," Fillagh enthused. "So young and so fair! And so tall! How the young ladies will love you—if they don't already.

Hasn't he grown tall, Cletus? Why, I swear he'll be far more impressive than even Melvig, our lord, who was a man of exceptional height. And your beautiful hair! I am jealous, indeed I am!"

Cletus stepped forward, extricated Myrddion from his wife's stranglehold, and gripped his hand firmly.

"We've heard of your learning and your position in the court of High King Vortigern. It is said that he depends on your skills as a healer and will not stir without you. We always knew that you were marked for greatness when the sun god claimed you and the snakes of the Mother embraced you as well. We have been proud of your achievements, but dear Olwyn would have burst with love and admiration if she had lived to see your triumph."

Myrddion blushed scarlet at the admiration in the eyes of his kin. As a demon seed, he had spent much of his childhood alone and shunned, so this accolade both warmed and unnerved him.

"And yet I serve her murderer."

From the corner of his eye, Myrddion saw Branwyn nod before she turned her face and body away from him. He sighed with disappointment.

Then Eddius was with him, enfolding the healer in his still-strong arms, and Myrddion felt the older man's tears as they ran down his cheek.

"Look at you, boy! She would have been so happy. Do not be shamed that you serve the regicide. You do what you must, as will I."

Myrddion felt his breath catch in his throat with Eddius's final words, while a presentiment of danger made his skin crawl.

"What do you mean, Eddius? What do you plan?"

"Nothing, son. Nothing at all. Now, let me look at you properly."

Eddius saw a changed Myrddion, something other than the boy apprentice who had been torn away from his family by King Vortigern, the cursed tyrant who slew his beloved Olwyn. Myrddion had grown tall, over six foot, a remarkable height for a Celt who had hill dwellers in his ancestry. The boy's face was almost inhuman in its comeliness, yet Eddius could recognize traces of both Olwyn and Branwyn. Each had bequeathed fragments of her features to Myrddion in a new composition that was both manly and beautiful.

His mobile hands and feet were narrow and fine, and his body, although slender and elegant, was also strong, with clearly defined muscles in the arms, chest, and abdomen that even a heavy healer's robe could not disguise. Only Myrddion's eyes marred the lyricism of body and face, for they were alien in their blackness and measuring in their expression. Even Fillagh was surprised by her great-nephew's cool, rational appraisal and the control that masked his emotions.

He is a young man to be reckoned with, and will make a better friend than enemy during the years to come, Melvyn thought as he presented his kinsman with a goblet of fine wine. Father would have been impressed that one so young had grown so tall and so strong.

By contrast, Eddius had aged in the year since they had last met. Sorrow sat heavily on his muscular shoulders and bent his spine as if he was middle-aged already. Grey threads dulled his hair and care had scored deep lines on his handsome, tanned face. Even his wide, guileless eyes were now secretive and shuttered. Myrddion felt terrible regret that he had permitted Vortigern to live, something that continued to hurt Eddius, but the young man had had very little choice.

"I'm so glad to see you, boy. So glad! When we leave Canovium, you must come to Segontium and see the boys. I swear that Erikk is the image of my dear Olwyn, and Melwy has waited for your return with impatience. Your servant Tegwen has told them so many stories about you that you've become quite a hero in their eyes."

Myrddion laughed at the thought. "Aye, I'll come to visit. So Tegwen has found a home with you and the boys at Segontium?"

"She's a wonder, Myrddion. I'm amazed that you could bear to lose her. She serves the boys and has been a wonderful influence on their characters. Not only does she help Annwynn with any outbreaks of disease, but she also treats any small injuries that any of us suffer at the villa. I am quite relieved that she has come, as her presence lifts a heavy load off my shoulders. I can see my way clearly at last."

"I'm glad, Eddius, truly. Tegwen is a good woman—and very intelligent albeit she has never been educated."

Privately, Myrddion stared into Eddius's closed face and worried. What did Eddius see so clearly? And where did his way lead?

During the long evening, Myrddion was welcomed into the heart of his extended family. Nothing was said of the final duty he would perform for Melvig ap Melwy, but Myrddion felt the weight of his promise behind every warm gesture and joyous reunion. He ate and drank, described the far places that he had seen and the famous and mighty personages who had utilized his talents. His kin were especially taken with the death of Horsa, while Hengist's fearsome revenge, a tale told faithfully from the recollections of Finn Truthteller, elicited gasps from his audience. Melvyn, in particular, found the story intriguing.

"You speak of these Saxon interlopers as if they are noble characters. How can this be? The Saxons are barbarians, and they threaten us from across Litus Saxonicum even as we speak."

Myrddion considered his response carefully before he answered.

"I knew them, both Hengist and Horsa, and I discovered that they were the scions of kings. We should beware of the word *Saxon,* for it is as deceiving as the description Frisian or Briton. Both Hengist and Horsa were noble, living exemplary lives of duty to their people as well as giving loyalty to their masters. They adopted honor as a personal code. To my mind, they represented the best that the northern races have to offer."

"You seem to admire them, Myrddion," King Melvyn said, his face drawn down in an expression of disapproval.

"Admiration and liking are two different things, my king. The Saxons can be far crueler than we can imagine, for they have been shaped by violence and landlessness. But Hengist is not our problem. The other Saxons who follow him into our isles are the true threat. From what the brothers told me, the ports of the Frankish lands and the kingdoms to the north are full of landless northerners who will do anything to carve out a place for their families. They lack Hengist's nobility and reason, so they are dangerous. These invaders look at our shores through envious and calculating eyes now that the Romans have gone. But there is no need to worry, my lord Melvyn. The Saxons will not venture so far into the northwest for centuries, by which time all that we now know will have been powdered into the dust and our people will have lost control of their lands. Even then, in the twilight of the Celts, your kingdom will remain unscathed, although your descendants will be forced to welcome refugees into this quiet land where the past will retain its potency through the old stories and songs. Fear not, my lord, for you will sleep with your ancestors for many, many years before those dark days come."

Melvyn's shoulders straightened and he smiled with relief. "Does your intelligence tell you what the fates will bring?" he asked cautiously. "Or something else?"

Myrddion thought carefully again, and when he spoke his voice was quiet and sincere. "Both, my king. Both senses tell me what to say, but I cannot give guarantees of their accuracy."

"The bastard—the Demon Seed—speaks the lies that he is told from the darkness of the evil ones," Branwyn interrupted with such vindictiveness in her voice that her kinfolk drew away from her. "Beware the tainted words he speaks."

"Silence, Branwyn! You are tolerated in this hall for the sake of your holy mother, so don't force me to send you away. I'll not have Myrddion insulted when he has promised to fulfill my father's wishes in a way that I could never do."

Melvyn spoke with such contempt that Branwyn's husband dragged her away from the family group to their quiet sleeping chamber where she was free from prying eyes.

"My apologies, Myrddion, for your mother is demented and she grows worse and worse. Sooner or later I will be forced to intervene for the sake of her children, who are no longer safe in her presence. Her husband often bears the marks of her attacks on his person and I fear that tragedy will end this particular family nightmare. Avoid her while you remain in Canovium, for your safety and for hers."

Myrddion waved away the apologies of his king, for he was accustomed to his mother's murderous impulses when she was around him. There were times, however, when he wondered how Branwyn's life would have progressed if she had never found her beautiful man on the shoreline of Segontium. But he reasoned that the seeds of madness had always waited inside the mind of the child, dormant but poised to emerge if she ever suffered a major blow to her vision of the world. Myrddion's father had been the spark that lit the latent madness in her nature. He could see that fire as it blazed behind her eyes.

Without Branwyn's awkward presence, the evening continued pleasantly. Melvyn explained the ceremonies associated with Melvig's interment. The old autocrat had decided to be inhumed and had chosen a slab of mountain granite to mark his final resting place. Even now, the great slab was being polished and carved and would be finished within the week.

"The last of the great druids are coming to Canovium from Mona, from the forests of Arden and Sherwood and from Melandra in the north. They are gathering to witness the freeing of my father's soul and will be with us in two days when the ceremony will take place. Are you prepared to fulfill your promise, Myrddion?"

"Aye, lord. I promised Melvig, and I keep my word."

"My father instructed me to give you his sword to sever his head, fearing that any other blade would lack the weight to cut cleanly through the neck. Are you prepared to obey his wishes?"

"Aye, my lord. But I will need some practice to determine the weight and feel of the blade."

"Of course," Melvyn responded. "Melvig left his sword, which he called Blood Bringer, to you as payment for carrying out your promise. His ruby ring, your grandmother's necklace, and an armlet with cabochon gems are also left to you absolutely. My father believed that you were born for greatness, Myrddion."

"The ruby ring should be on your finger rather than mine," Myrddion protested. "The ring always symbolized the king's power, so I cannot imagine his hand without it. When all is said and done, I am the bastard child of the female family line, of little worth to either the Deceangli people or the Ordovice tribe. That ring should not grace my hand."

Melvyn's face softened and relaxed. Myrddion had passed the test of treasonous ambition.

When his father had ordered the disposition of his worldly goods, Melvyn had made the same arguments against the bequest of the ring. Now, Melvyn used Melvig's arguments to convince the healer that he should comply with the old king's wishes.

"Melvig's sword was his own to give as he chose. And so is this ring. I already possess the thumb ring and the great torc of the Deceangli tribe. The fish necklace was never mine, but belonged to Olwyn and the Mother. Why shouldn't you accept these familiar daily gems that he wore on finger and wrist? He always saw something to be admired in you, and once he grew to know you better he desired to go with you on your long journeys, even if only in spirit."

Myrddion assessed Melvyn's true feelings about the bequests with a strange detachment. The young man hardly needed more enemies at his back. Finally, he came to a decision.

"Melvig flatters me, but I will accept my great-grandfather's gifts in the spirit in which they were given. While I live, I will wear your father's ring with pride."

"So the week of ceremony and interment may now begin." Melvyn smiled his acceptance. "We shall pray for the soul of Melvig ap Melwy, king of the Deceangli, and for those of us who are the poorer for his loss."

THE NEXT MORNING dawned with the same kind of oppressive, muggy heat that had welcomed Myrddion to Canovium. The healer snatched a fast meal of warmed stew and two apples from the kitchens, where servants were already hard at work preparing the feasts that would accompany the festivities surrounding both the funeral and the coronation of the new king. Eating one of his apples, he strolled out into the forecourt and looked down at Canovium and towards the sea beyond.

The river valley was fertile and the soil was deep, allowing the township to be encircled by farms right up to the foothills where the land began to rise steeply. Sheep grazed on the lower slopes while plots of vegetables, fruit, and grains turned the rich soil into a patchwork quilt of color. Canovium had possessed many names over the years and many different peoples had come to this narrow, fertile strip of land where the river soil provided food, water, and links with the ocean and fishing.

Far away, in the mountains where the stream was fed by melted snow from great escarpments of granite, Vortigern might by now be looking down on the same river from his sanctuary at Dinas Emrys, Myrddion thought. This burgeoning land that fed Canovium relied on the High King's fortress in the mountains for its security.

"How predictable we are," he murmured. "We cluster where the land is good and only the wild people or the strange ones seek out the distant, harsh places where rivers don't run."

"Your maternal ancestors were therefore wild or strange," a voice replied from behind him. Melvyn had approached in silence, and Myrddion had been unaware of the older man's presence. "Your great-grandmother's sister has been cared for on my father's strict instructions for the past twenty years. She comes from the hill country, as did Olwyn's mother, and she is very, very old. She should have passed into the shadows long ago, but her spirit is fierce and strong. She would like to see you."

Myrddion's brow furrowed.

The previous night, he had been surrounded by kinfolk, which had been a strange experience for a young man who had spent a large portion of his life alone. Why would an ancient hill woman wish to meet him, even if they were distant kin? However, he was far too courteous to ask impolite questions.

"Of course, uncle, I would be happy to meet the venerable lady. I will wait upon her at a time of your choosing."

Melvyn laughed softly and clapped the healer on the back with relief. "There's no time like the present. Aunt Rhyll will give me no peace until she sees you. I warn you, she's a frightening woman for someone who barely reaches my shoulder if she stands upright which, unfortunately, she cannot do."

Myrddion shrugged good-naturedly and crunched into his second apple. "The morning is bright, my lord. I have a day of leisure before me, except to pray for the soul of the king and to renew my acquaintance with Eddius, so I am at your disposal."

"Good, good."

Melvyn turned on his heel and led Myrddion back into the rambling building, down narrow corridors, and through a rabbit warren of smaller and smaller rooms until he reached the back of the palace, if such a word could be used to describe such a patchwork of intertwined buildings.

The new king stopped before a simple door, knocked, then entered a small room that opened onto a little courtyard hard against the side of the cliff. Sheltered from the sea breezes, and in a rare pocket of clear sunshine, the courtyard was a mass of color from large troughs of porous stone or fired clay pots filled with hardy daisies, roses, herbs, and an ancient vine that bore brilliant purple flowers. The mix of color was so surprising against a backdrop of grey, rocky hillside that Myrddion almost missed the tiny, wizened creature who sat on a soft stool amid the riot of flowers, for she was huddled in a heavy shawl of vividly dyed wool so that only a small, brown face and a pair of inquisitive hazel eyes peered out to survey her visitors.

"Well done, Melvyn. I take it that you have brought Olwyn's lad to visit with me, for I see a young beanpole standing behind you." She smiled up at her young visitor before turning towards a door at the rear of her rooms. "Lindon?" she bellowed with surprising strength. "Where are you, you lazy baggage? The new king has come calling with a young visitor. Bring me heated wine and fruit, for I can see my kinsman is fond of apples."

Embarrassed, Myrddion crunched the last of the core with his sharp white teeth. He bowed, in considerable respect, and smiled as engagingly as he knew how.

A plump, middle-aged woman with a weather-beaten face came bustling out through the folded shutters that separated the tiny sleeping chamber from the courtyard. Her work-roughened hands already held a pitcher on a wooden tray with several beakers made of horn that had been polished to the sheen and color of amber.

"Very well, you old besom. Always nagging a body, though I slave from sunrise to sunset to keep your scrawny body comfortable and well. Here's the honeyed wine you demanded, warmed as you like it, but I'll have to find some fruit, if you still want it."

Myrddion was surprised by the maidservant's tone and manner, until he realized that such talk was familiar and pleasurable to both women. Auntie Rhyll swore like a soldier, grunted, and then waved Lindon away to fetch apples, pears, and berries.

"This young man is Myrddion, Auntie, and he is Olwyn's grandson. As I've told you, he is a healer of renown, even at this very young age. He serves Vortigern, the High King, on his campaigns and has traveled to far-off places since his childhood. He has come to Canovium to fulfill my father's last wish."

"This nonsense about beheading, I take it. Never mind. There's nothing so strange in this world that some moon-mad fool won't believe it and adopt its customs. Still, it does no real harm, I suppose, for Melvig is already dead. The Mother save us, it might even work." Then old Rhyll cackled away merrily as if she had made a particularly amusing joke. Both men were too polite to respond.

"Well? Drink, then! And you, boy, pour a cup for me. I'm not so old that I've forgotten the taste of sweet, honeyed wine. And if my lazy maid ever returns, we'll enjoy the fruit of the season as well. I do love a ripe, juicy peach."

Myrddion wondered how Rhyll could eat any fruit, since her sunken, seamed mouth suggested that she lacked a single tooth in her head. However, as soon as Lindon returned, the old woman made a gesture that ordered haste more powerfully than words, and the servant cut a blushing peach in half, removing the stone. Toothless or not, Rhyll speedily demolished the fruit, without any thought for the juice that ran down her face and her scrawny neck.

As Lindon washed the tiny face with a clean scrap of linen, the old autocrat ordered Melvig to be about his business. Meekly, the new king obeyed.

"I'm terrified of you, Kinswoman Rhyll," Myrddion began in the comfortable silence. He softened the edges of his abrupt words with a smile that reached his eyes. "What can you want of a nameless bastard who is not yet a grown man?" He was fully aware that Rhyll was examining him closely.

"Ah, but you're a beautiful boy, kinsman. Just like my roses."

Her hand plucked a red rose, full blown and blowsy with a perfume that was almost too sweet. Myrddion wondered at the strength in the skeletal fingers that could snap a stem with such ease. She sought out another rose, as pale as the first was red. Even opened, the petals were tighter and the smell less heady, but the stamens at the heart of the rose were golden.

Wordlessly, Rhyll offered the roses to Myrddion, who took them with a frown.

"Your heart is closed. Love will not touch you until three women come into your life. Of these, a woman with red hair will break your heart and freeze it to solid ice, but another woman with white hair will make it whole again. I will not discuss the third for I am only a poor seer from the hill country and I am not permitted to do so. All of them will cause you to suffer, kinsman, but the worst blows won't come from the hands of women, but from beloved men."

"Are you truly a seer, Auntie Rhyll? Do you see the pictures of the future in your head, or in your dreams?"

Rhyll's wizened face split into a broad, gummy grin. "You test me, boy! I have the sight, waking and sleeping, as did my mother before me. My sister and her daughter Olwyn never knew the curse, so they were free to marry without seeing the fate of their offspring in their dreams. You have the sight, boy, but it is a man's gift that is entangled with power, swords, and kings uncrowned. Beware of hubris, Myrddion, for you will rise very high and you will come to dictate the lives and the decisions of kings."

Even though he shuddered inside, Myrddion forced himself to laugh. "I am a healer, Auntie Rhyll. Short of healing wounds and caring for noble patients, I can think of no situation where a healer could influence the actions of great men."

"You are a healer, but you are much more," Rhyll retorted, repeating Cadoc's words. "But I'll speak no further of these things. Go, child. You must win your name from a man with black eyes, but I wonder if you'll believe it was worth the blood, the pain, and the weary miles that you will be forced to travel. But you will learn many more skills on the journey, not the least being the nature of your own soul. I will be long dead when you return to Canovium, but you will understand my warnings one day. Beware of hubris, as I have already said."

Rhyll would say nothing more of his future, regardless of how sweetly Myrddion smiled or how long they conversed in the quiet arbor built into the side of the hill. When the long afternoon began to darken, Myrddion kissed Rhyll's withered cheek and left her to her roses and the night.

THE AIR WAS thrumming within the dark hall as if random breezes were plucking an invisible harp. Myrddion knew that the strange, internal noise had its origins in the power of the men who stood around the bier and waited for the healer's arrival.

Before he had entered the Great Hall, he had washed himself carefully in the bowl of water under the hazel tree, having first stripped to his loincloth. Once he had dressed in the silent courtyard, he had pushed Melvig's ring onto his left hand, closest to his heart. Snapping open the old, stiff clasp of his bulla, he removed the birth gift from the lord of light and thrust the sunstone ring onto the index finger of his right hand. Then, holding Melvig's sword across his palms, he entered the Great Hall.

The air was close, and the floral scent failed to mask the smell of corruption that left Myrddion feeling light-headed and nauseous. The druids were imposing figures, their long robes of homespun wool in black, brown, and a raw, undyed cream elongating their bodies until they seemed taller and thinner than they were even in natural sunlight. Within the hall, lit by the flames of oil lamps and crossed by wavering shadows in the uneven light, their cowled faces took on an eerie, otherworld quality. The bridge of an aquiline nose, a pointed chin, the strands of a flowing beard, or high cheekbones caught the flame and gave the druids the insubstantiality of grave wights or spirits.

As if they knew the effect of their presence on the male kin of Melvig ap Melwy, the druids began to chant in the old language. The voices melded together imperfectly, for one of the druids was a castrato, but the solemnity of the ritual could not be doubted. The weight of Melvig's ceremonial sword dragged at Myrddion's still-developing muscles.

The day before, at Melvyn's bidding, he had examined the blade that he'd been given in order to perform his grisly duty. Like his great-grandfather, the sword was crudely powerful and utilitarian. The blade had been forged over a hundred years earlier, so Myrddion was unable to tell if it had been made with the benefit of Celtic workmanship. It was shorter than the usual warrior's sword, but Melvig had a long reach and had never found any lack in it. Perhaps a long-dead Roman smith had made it for an officer. No man could know, for time had washed over its origins and left nothing that could be used for comparison with other blades.

Its hilt lacked a crosspiece and was covered with fish skin to improve the grip, but the plain iron pommel had been beautified with gold and a single stone of brilliant red that had been carved with an intaglio of a hunting bird. In the early morning sunshine, Myrddion hefted the blade, felt its excellent balance, and enjoyed the weight of the weapon as it sat in his hand.

Now, with the ceremony of beheading about to begin, something had caught his attention on the silken texture of the blade. He had been trying to decipher the worn inscription when Melvyn had opened the rear door of the hall and ushered him in.

As the druids chanted, Myrddion moved forward to stand by Melvig's corpse. The blade was raised, but at rest, between his open palms.

At the foot of Melvig's bier, Melvyn ap Melvig's shadow seemed huge, menacing, and patient. Only when the druids ceased to chant did the uncrowned king raise both hands, turn, and speak to the assembly of male kin, Deceangli dignitaries, and various friends, including King Bryn of the Ordovice and his son, Prince Llanwith.

"Rejoice, kinsmen and citizens, friends and allies, for Melvig ap Melwy prepares to journey to the shadows where he will feast in glory with his illustrious ancestors. While he drew breath, Melvig ruled this land with courage, dignity, and justice. He raised his children in security, and served his tribe with honesty and a fine sense of duty. The gods rewarded him with a long and peaceful life, so we should not mourn his death, but honor his passage from this world to the next."

A chorus of agreement broke the silence, but then the stifling darkness and the power emanating from the bier withered the words of affirmation on the tongues of the guests.

"The Sword Bearer, Myrddion, has been asked to free Melvig's soul from his body in the ancient way. Only kin or a druid may wield a blade for such a purpose, and Healer Myrddion is a direct descendant of our deceased king. Stand forth, witnesses and masters of the groves, while Myrddion, healer of Segontium, frees the soul of our lord."

The tallest druid approached Myrddion, who stood at attention, with the sword placed at rest across his naked hands. Three other druids flanked him, carrying the religious artifacts necessary for their part in the ceremony.

The master took a handful of soil from a bowl of sandy loam carried by the first druid and, with due ceremony, sprinkled it along the length of the blade, which Myrddion turned so that both sides could be blessed.

"By the power of the earth!" the priest intoned solemnly.

The second druid, clad in brown, stepped forward bearing a large oil lamp that the priest took in both hands. Slowly, he anointed the blade with liquid fire so that the steel surface flickered with scarlet and sanguine light.

"By the power of fire!"

The last druid bore a basin of water that was liberally sprinkled over the shining blade and hissed as it struck the heated metal.

"By the power of water!" The priest turned to one side to face the witnesses. "Let the soul of King Melvig ap Melwy soar forth with the eagles until he reaches our Father, the Sun, who is your namesake and the master of us all."

In the stillness, Myrddion moved to the side of the bier as the druid freed the robes that enclosed the old man's withered and wrinkled throat. Moved by the ceremony despite his skepticism, Myrddion raised the sword above his head with both hands so it caught the flames of the lamps and condensed them into a single focus of light. Then he permitted the blade to fall swiftly, but with minimal force. Honed to razor sharpness by Melvig's whetstone, the blade sheared through skin and bone to strike the wooden bier with a dull thud.

The blow was clean and well aimed.

As the master raised Melvig's head, now noble with age, the watchers sighed long exhalations of breath as if the old king's spirit was rising, rising, towards the roof of the hall, through it, and onwards into a sun that now stood high over the eaves of the building. A sudden gust of wind from outside stirred the woolen hangings and caused the flames from the oil lamps to dance. Then, with due reverence, Melvig's decapitated head was placed beside his torso and the ceremony was over.

Later, surrounded by his family and yet alone in the sanctity of the deed, Myrddion examined the sword that now belonged to him for life. The inscription on the blade was very faint, but as he played light along its smooth surface he was able to read a single line of Latin that gave the weapon its name.

Truth lies in Death.

Myrddion thought of the name, Blood Bringer, that had been bestowed on it by its owner, Melvig ap Melwy, who had never learned to read.

"Truth and Death! Such an ambiguous marriage of words," Myrddion murmured softly. Eddius heard his mutterings, and asked what he meant, so Myrddion was forced to explain his comments to those kinfolk present.

"Perhaps the sword should be renamed," Eddius said thoughtfully. "Only Melvig could ever wield Blood Bringer with the true courage and nobility that the name requires."

"I'll think on it," Myrddion replied. "Still, it's strange to find a Roman sword among the weaponry of a Deceangli king. If I believed in omens, I would be hesitant to accept this weapon."

"Do you still dream, Myrddion? Do you still suffer your waking fits?" Eddius asked eagerly. "Have you ever seen my Olwyn? If Death could be defeated, I know she would come to you."

Regretfully, Myrddion shook his head. "No. I wish I could intercede with Death and give you a message from her, but that skill was taken from me when my mother brained me with a rock."

An uncomfortable pause followed.

"Do you ever think of killing Vortigern, Myrddion? I've often wondered how you could bear to serve him, when Olwyn's blood stains his hands."

"I wish him dead every day, but I can't risk the lives of my servants to wash away my guilt. Whether I succeeded or not, Vortigern's kin would slay everyone close to me to discourage other men from regicide." The conversation was beginning to worry Myrddion. What was Eddius struggling to say? "Why do you ask, Eddius? You don't plan to raise your own sword against Vortigern, do you? It would be a foolish venture. He is very careful, so he has decreed that no one who is armed is permitted to come near him. You would surely perish in any attempt at murder, as would your boys, while your death could plunge the Deceangli tribe into an unwinnable war."

Eddius smiled a little recklessly, and Myrddion felt sick with anxiety. "Don't fret, Myrddion. I won't attack anyone, so my sons and my kinsmen will remain safe."

Myrddion wasn't comforted, even when Eddius embraced him warmly. When he looked away for a moment, Eddius slid into the crowd and made a hurried departure.

In the days of mourning that followed, Myrddion thought about the sword, the mystery of its origin and the names that he might bestow on it. No wiser than before, he ate and drank as was required and, a week later, he watched Melvyn ap Melvig's coronation with pleasure. He dawdled away the last warm days of summer, luxuriating in the unfamiliar embrace of family, although Eddius made an excuse to return to Segontium early and Myrddion sincerely missed the most important male in his upbringing.

Before Eddius departed from Canovium, he drew Myrddion into the colonnade where the hazel tree danced in a faint breeze and ruffled the waters in the basin. Eddius's face was twisted with a strong emotion that Myrddion initially failed to recognize.

"Can I trust you, Myrddion?"

"Aye, Eddius, you can trust me with your life. Why do you ask?"

"I have been considering my mortality, son of my heart, and I beg you to care for my children should the gods call me to the shadows before they have grown to manhood."

Myrddion's winged brows drew down with concern. "You are still young, Eddius. Why should the gods call you into the Valley of Death?"

Eddius shrugged, but his face was blank with unshared secrets. "Promise me, Myrddion. I cannot trust them to the mercies of Branwyn and her husband."

"I swear that I will carry out your wishes, Eddius, but you'll make old bones. Olwyn would never forgive me if I allowed anything to trouble you."

Eddius grinned in his old carefree fashion, but under the flash of teeth and warm, brown eyes, Myrddion sensed a great sadness and a flood of unshed tears. He stirred awkwardly.

"Good!" Eddius exclaimed gruffly, and they spoke no more.

He was gone by morning.

Finally, after several weeks, Myrddion knew that he could tarry at Canovium no longer. Vortigern would be vexed and might take it into his head to punish Myrddion's servants for his tardiness. With a man as unpredictable as the High King, all things were possible. With regret, Myrddion took his leave of King Melvyn ap Melvig, of Auntie Rhyll with her fierce lust for life, of Fillagh and Cletus One Ear, all faithful, loving, and devoted kinsmen and -women who warmed the healer's lonely heart.

All that Myrddion needed now was to breathe the salty air of Segontium and the villa by the sea. He would sit on Olwyn's bier and tell her all the wondrous and terrible things he had seen and done since her death. As the gulls wheeled overhead and the sea crept up the sand like white lace, he would look over towards Mona and wonder about his father. Perhaps Olwyn would have an answer that Myrddion could clutch to his heart. He hungered for his grandmother, but her abrupt, untimely death had stilled that warm communication forever. Still, in the villa by the sea, he could remember the past.

The young healer told himself that he needed to borrow supplies from Annwynn, which was a reason for tardiness that Vortigern would understand, but he recognized that the smiles of his family had been seductive during his sojourn in Canovium. Segontium would renew his faith in himself and would wash away the accumulation of human vices and agonies that he had seen. At the very least, he would see Tegwen again and prove her odd prophecy was wrong.

He had only to ride those few extra miles and, perhaps, his path to the future might become clear.

Chapter XXII

THE BURNING MAN

Dinas Emrys sulked over the river valley that lay within a shell of great mountains. To the northwest, snow was already gleaming whitely on the highest mountains and Myrddion felt claustrophobic under their beetling, overpowering shoulders. The brief sojourn at Segontium had been unsatisfactory, for Eddius had not returned from Canovium, although the children had remembered their young kinsman and had climbed all over him with enthusiasm and affection.

Nor was Tegwen present, having been sent to Tomen-y-mur to mind Branwyn's children during her absence at the funerary celebrations.

Without the calming good humor of Eddius or Olwyn, the villa by the sea was empty and echoing. Myrddion imagined that the beloved old building was being buried by shifting sand as the winds constantly scoured away the cliffs and the sharp sea grasses. For relief from his sorrow and disappointment, he had gone to Annwynn's cottage.

With ease, Myrddion slipped back into the familiar role of apprentice. Boudicca was long dead, but the starving mongrel he had rescued years earlier had a new litter of pups and Myrddion luxuriated in proof that the life force in all things was strong and vigorous. Annwynn had welcomed him as if he had only left Segontium the day before, and had set him to work at once, collecting herbs and preparing her ointments, tisanes, and unguents. Myrddion was quietly happy through that golden morning, as if he could return to the first days of his apprenticeship when his world was joyous. Eventually, laden down with supplies, and kissed again and again by Annwynn in farewell, Myrddion began the return journey into his unholy captivity as the healer for Vortigern's army.

They had parted with many tears. Annwynn kissed the rings on his adult fingers and tried to find words that were adequate to express her pride in him. Unlike her usual voluble self, she was almost mute with the fullness of her heart, but her inability to express her feelings didn't matter to Myrddion. He had known what his old mistress felt. He could read her eyes with empathy that was newly sharpened by his experiences at Canovium. On their parting, she had wept.

"You've become a man, Myrddion, so you are free of your apprenticeship. Be the greatest healer in the world, but remember Hippocrates's rule always. The world will tempt you because you are so able, but you'll never fail as long as you remain true to yourself." She smiled up at the young man she had raised so well. "Now, get you gone, my dear one. Ride safely and believe that I'll be here when you next return."

Myrddion had ridden away with packed panniers, a full heart, and an uneasy feeling that Eddius was in serious trouble.

After riding Vulcan all over the north, Myrddion had become a competent horseman by default, so the journey to Dinas Emrys was relatively uneventful in spite of the ghosts from his past whom he met on the journey. Hengist and the dead, cheerful Horsa seemed to share the road with his younger self, and where the track plunged off into the underbrush he remembered the cart in which Olwyn's body had been returned to the bosom of her family. Dark in mood and assailed by the flail of memory, Myrddion was already sunk in gloom before he reached the glowering fortress.

Dinas Emrys was as bleak and as grey as it had been when he first saw it. The ruined tower still stood like a weathered, broken fang while a new structure had been erected at the other end of the fortress. Evidence of further construction was clearly visible in flagging, new stables, and the many facilities that were essential to a functioning community. A working blacksmith, a commissary, storerooms, and separate stone kitchens to guard against fire had all been raised around the skirts of Dinas Emrys.

Myrddion was a familiar and welcome face in Vortigern's service, so he was ushered to the healers' tents at the rear of the fortress with many friendly greetings from the king's guard. The tents were raised on a ragged plateau at the base of a small incline, so that Myrddion was forced to look upwards towards the brooding walls of Dinas Emrys. Still, he relished what space there was between his tents and the fortress, for after his previous exposure to those grim, ugly walls Myrddion hated and feared the brooding, ancient citadel. His other sense whispered that dead things had left their imprints on Dinas Emrys, like the deathless malice that had sealed the stones of its foundations. Perhaps his prophecy was true, spoken aloud when he was only a boy, and dragons really battled under the fortress. Perhaps he simply loathed the place that had borne the stain of Olwyn's blood.

Once he had greeted Cadoc, Finn, and the widows who were the nucleus of his nursing circle, Myrddion sluiced his whole body in clean water to wash off the dust of the road. He dressed his hair and donned a new tunic preparatory to renewing his acquaintance with Vortigern after his long absence. His ruby shone on his forefinger like a single drop of blood, while his sunstone caught the last rays of the lord of light with the sunset's brilliance. Fortified by these tangible proofs of family and love, he decided to confront the High King with an open face.

"Take your satchel with you, master," Cadoc warned. "Queen Rowena has become gravely ill during your absence and is like to die. We've given her purgative drugs, but nothing seems to work, so I'm convinced that she's been poisoned. Be sure that Vortigern will expect you to return her to health, especially as you've been away and cannot be suspected of an attempt on her life."

Myrddion felt as if a weight had suddenly settled on his widening shoulders, and his hopeful mood evaporated.

Vortigern must have been informed of Myrddion's return, for a large warrior materialized outside the healer's tent and summoned him to the presence of the king.

"Don't forget your satchel!" Cadoc shouted, as he scooped up the leather bag and scrambled after his master. "Take care, for Vortigern is a madman, and he grows more irrational and bad-tempered every day."

This last warning was whispered in his ear, and Myrddion nodded briefly in understanding, for he was fully aware of the streak of ruthless cruelty that dominated his master's character. Who better to know Vortigern than a young man who had been offered in sacrifice to the High King's power and hubris?

The king's hall had barely changed, except for the addition of hangings and bench seating of the crudest kind. After the sun-drenched comfort of Canovium, the fortress was cheerless, cold, and threatening, as if Dinas Emrys had taken on the spartan nature of its mountain location. No ornamentation softened the hard rock walls, while unprotected window openings let in the skirling autumn winds.

Surrounded by his guard, the king awaited him in the cold, grey space of the hall.

"You've been overlong, healer, considering all you had to do was to remove a head. By the gods, I could have done it for you in a few seconds."

Myrddion was vaguely alarmed by Vortigern's nasty smile, which was obviously designed to threaten. He was certain that the High King had no intention of harming him personally, but would have no qualms about avenging himself on Cadoc or Finn. Myrddion smiled placably, and explained that the ceremonies associated with the death and coronation of the kings at Canovium had taken a considerable length of time.

"Hmf! I have had need of you, healer. Queen Rowena is gravely ill and I fear for her life. You must use your powers to make her well again."

"I will give you my opinion as soon as I have examined her, my lord."

Vortigern's eyes were feral. They swiveled to impale the healer with a malignant glance of suspicion. "You cannot examine the queen. You are a man, so such an examination would destroy her honor."

Myrddion showed his impatience in a frown of scorn that he quickly tried to hide. As reasonably and as calmly as he could, he tried to explain his needs.

"I cannot treat her if I cannot examine her, my lord. You cannot have it both ways. Surely your wife can be chaperoned by her sons or her maidservants? How could I treat a warrior on the battlefield if I wasn't permitted to see him or to touch him?"

Vortigern grumbled into his beard. The High King would have denied that any changes in his circumstances had affected his attitudes, but Myrddion sensed that some necessary vitality had been leached out of Vortigern's spirit with the deaths of Vortimer and Catigern. Although he had been a vigorous man of fifty when Myrddion had first met him, something within the autocrat had weakened, if not broken. His decisiveness had fled, as had the zest that fueled him during the campaign against Vortimer at Glevum.

This place is cursed, Myrddion thought, as Vortigern considered his options. It sucks the will from all those it touches.

"You are the High King and what you decide is law," Myrddion added, pandering shamelessly to the High King's arrogance. "But I cannot sit by if someone needs my assistance."

The king shook his greying head and threw up both hands in unwilling submission. "Very well, healer, but I will show you the way."

Given no real choice if he wished his wife to be treated, Vortigern rose to his feet and stalked off into the gloom of the hall with Myrddion trotting at his heels. The fortress was a simple structure, so the queen's bedchamber was separated from the hall by only a few rooms and a narrow stairway. Its proportions were quite small, and when Myrddion followed Vortigern through the doorway the space seemed even more claustrophobic. A narrow bed with a large coffered clothes chest at its foot filled over half the room. The queen's two sons sat on stools on her right side, the older boy stroking her forehead with a damp cloth. A maidservant with a clean bowl in her hands bustled around.

Rowena was very pale and her skin was clammy. When Myrddion gently laid his hand upon her forehead, she opened her eyes wearily. Her extraordinary blue eyes were blurred and her skin was folded with pain.

"What is amiss, my queen? Tell me of your ailment."

Myrddion had learned to speak quietly and confidently to patients to counteract the impact of his clean-shaven youth. He had also learned to smile, not only with his pale, well-shaped lips but also with his alien, brilliant eyes.

"I know you," Rowena whispered. "My husband thought to sacrifice you. Oh, Freya, do you hate me too? I tried to pay the blood price. I gave Hengist the best cloth I owned to use as a shroud that would wrap your kinswoman during her journey to the shadows. I prayed and prayed to Freya that no stain would defile my sons. If I have to die, I don't care, but my sons shouldn't be punished for my sins. There's been too much blood spilt and, may the gods help me, I have killed as well, so my soul is tainted also. But I swear—I swear— that I was left with no choice at Glevum. Too many innocent people would have perished if I'd done nothing. I swear I wasn't thinking only of myself."

She shivered, as if she was freezing under the heavy blankets on her narrow bed. Myrddion watched as an old horror rose in her eyes like a pike out of deep water.

"Glevum was so warm! So warm! But it's cold here."

"Hush, my queen. I don't hate you. Indeed, I was grateful for the regal gift you gave to my dear grandmother. Nor would she ever have demanded payment in blood for her death. And certainly not from you! I was at Glevum, madam, so you need say nothing more, for the innocent foot soldiers and citizens you saved in that town owe you a debt for raising the siege. The least said, the greater the peace. I can tell that you have a fever, but I must know what other symptoms you have if I am to return you to good health."

"Thank you," Rowena whispered and gripped her son's hand. Her eyes were sunk into the fine bones of her skull and her mouth was cracked and dry. Myrddion saw a flagon of water on a nearby table and went to pour some for her.

"No. No. I cannot drink, for everything here tastes strange. I'll not touch it." The queen turned her face into the pillow and sobbed out her distress.

"Look at me, my lady," Myrddion ordered compellingly. "I won't give you any water from this room. I have my own water bottle here with me, so I will drink from it first, if you will then take some of mine for yourself. See?"

Myrddion drank from his wooden bottle, and then filled a beaker and handed it to the queen.

She was so weak that the goblet shook in her hand, but Katigern, her younger, cupped his strong, golden fingers around hers to steady them. Myrddion held her while she eagerly gulped down the water.

"From now on, your sons will collect water directly from the well, just for you. They will drink the water first so you can be sure that it is pure."

The queen nodded mutely, as did her sons, while Vortigern drew his brows together at the obvious implication of the healer's words.

"You must tell me your symptoms now, my lady. Don't be embarrassed. There's very little about the human body that I have yet to see, so I promise not to be shocked."

Myrddion smiled engagingly, and Rowena responded, albeit tremulously.

"I can keep nothing in my stomach. The very smell of food sickens me. I'm afraid that I have . . . soiled myself as well, and I have felt such pain in my stomach, my legs, and my joints that I can barely stir. Nothing helps. If anything, I grow worse and worse."

The queen's eyes welled with tears as she revealed her embarrassment and shame, but Myrddion took her hand and ran his sensitive fingers over it. He felt the deep ridges in the almond-shaped nails and his brows twitched with concern and suspicion.

"I think I understand what I am dealing with, my lady, and I hope to return you to health. But I must depend on your sons and my lord to care for you—and on them only. No servant may give you anything to eat or drink, no matter how trusted they might be."

"Speak freely, healer, and don't try to spare our feelings," Vortigern demanded roughly. "What is amiss with my queen?"

With a sigh, Myrddion acknowledged that he must tell the plain, unvarnished truth if Vortigern and his sons were to take his orders seriously.

"The queen has been poisoned—and for some time, sufficient for the toxin to be present in her fingernails. The body stores some poisons within the nails, body fat, and hair, so, while I can detect the presence of the toxins, I cannot tell how much damage has been done to my lady's health. But strict precautions must be taken, starting immediately. No food must come into this room that has not been prepared by persons you absolutely trust. If necessary, the boys must learn to cook." He turned his head slightly to address Vengis and Katigern directly. "No salt, no dressing, no fruit, no fluid of any kind can be trusted, unless innocent and loving hands have prepared it. No meat must be eaten for some time. Eggs can be boiled and mashed, as their shells cannot easily be breached. Better that food be tasteless than dangerous. Any milk you use should be taken from the cow yourself, and should be stored in a clean container. Then, and only then, may it be given to your mother." He looked around at the shocked faces in the small room. "Someone has the hidden desire that the queen should die in agony."

Rowena began to weep in earnest at the thought that some nameless person would wish her such harm.

At this inauspicious moment, the serving woman returned with a bowl of thin gruel and a foaming glass of milk. Vortigern would have dashed the whole tray to the ground, but Myrddion stopped him with a peremptory gesture.

"May I speak to you outside this room, my lord?" As the king nodded in agreement, the healer turned to Rowena's sons. "Boys, keep the tray safe. Let no one touch it in my absence." He turned his attention to the serving woman, who showed the whites of her eyes in fear. "You, woman, will wait in the kitchens till I come to you."

The servant blanched, but quickly excused herself and slipped out of the room, while Katigern took the tray and placed it gingerly on his stool as if it contained live serpents.

Once outside the confines of the room, Vortigern turned toward his healer with a thunderous face.

"Who has done this thing, Myrddion? Who would *dare*? This is *my* fortress, so the guilty person must be very confident to risk my revenge."

"Or very frightened. But I believe that I can discover who the culprit is, if you will allow me to conduct an experiment. Will you remain silent until I discover who the traitor might be?"

"Of course, healer! I want this traitor caught and killed, but I also need to know who has ordered such a cowardly act to be committed within my house."

Myrddion grimaced at Vortigern's immediate assumption that another, more powerful personage was behind Rowena's illness. "You are already guessing, my lord, that the perpetrator isn't acting alone in these treasonous deeds. But, for now, we must order every servant and cook involved in the preparation of food within the fortress to gather together in your kitchens. We shall see who's willing to eat the gruel and drink the milk."

Vortigern grinned savagely, then strode away to issue the necessary orders. Myrddion returned to the sickroom, collected the tray and issued his final instructions to the queen's sons.

"You, Katigern, will go to the warriors' bivouac and find the healer's tent. There, you will remain with my servant, Cadoc, and watch while he boils two hen's eggs for the queen to eat. The eggs must be finely mashed, and you may use a little of my own store of salt to add taste to them. After that, you will observe one of my assistants as he milks a cow. Hear my words, and watch closely. I trust my servants absolutely, but you must take no chances. As for you, Vengis, stay with your mother. Here is my water bottle, for your mother must have clean water to drink. Use the cleanest cup you can find, and you mustn't leave her for a moment. Trust no one except for your brother, not even me. Do you understand?"

"Aye!" the young man answered, determination clearly written in his pale eyes. "Everything shall be done as you have instructed."

"I killed Vortimer with poison, Myrddion," Rowena interrupted. "Perhaps I deserve no better than the dreadful fate I gave to him."

"I didn't hear the words you just spoke, my queen. Nor have your sons heard them. I saw the marks on your face and on your body when you returned from your captivity. I saw the women of Glevum, and the children, all of whom live because you caused the death of Vortimer. If the Mother is kind to us, perhaps she will allow you to survive this illness. Whatever happens, my queen, I will do everything I can for you, for I owe you a debt for your kindness to my grandmother."

Myrddion opened his satchel to find a small piece of oilcloth containing a white powder.

"Vengis, take this powder and mix it with water. It's a harmless herbal remedy that will cleanse the blood. I don't know if the purgative will be powerful enough for our purposes, but it cannot hurt your mother. I will taste it myself, to assure you of its safety. Then, once I've ascertained what toxin has been used, I can treat your mother's illness with more aggression."

He bent over the queen, although he knew that Vortigern was waiting impatiently.

"Have courage, my lady. The goddess rules us, regardless of what names we give her. She hasn't deserted you. Your illness is the cruel result of human vice and I will find a way to ease your pain, if such a remedy exists."

"Thank you, Master Myrddion. Whatever happens to me, I have absolved you from all guilt. But do your best for my sons, I beg of you."

The last sentence was whispered so that only the healer could hear her. Myrddion sighed. Friendless, child of a hated race, and completely without power, the queen lay in her simple bed and fretted over the possible fates of her sons. Even Branwyn, in her madness, was more free than the High Queen of the Britons.

As Myrddion left the room, he heard Rowena begin to vomit weakly as her body was racked in a convulsion of pain. He sighed as he saw Vengis place a basin at the ready and support his mother's twisted torso. She is gravely ill, he thought with regret. Great malice is at work in this place, and I doubt she will survive.

He found the kitchens and with a heavy heart entered the stone structure with its large fireplaces. He was already sickened at what he would be required to do if he was to isolate the culprit.

Vortigern and two warriors stood threateningly near the doorless entrance and faced two cooks, a kitchen boy who cut wood and cleaned the dishes and pots, two kitchen maids, and two older house slaves.

"These servants are the only people who have been near the queen's food and drink since we returned to Dinas Emrys," Vortigern explained. "The only servant still to arrive is Willow, my queen's personal maid, who has been with her since Glevum. She has been collecting feverwort for the queen's heated flesh."

Myrddion vaguely remembered Willow as the pretty child with a serious face who had stood behind her mistress at the gates of Glevum.

"Instruct your servants to wait outside under the close watch of one of your warriors," he told the king.

Vortigern bridled slightly at Myrddion's presumption, but gave the order to his guard. No one spoke until the kitchen was empty except for the High King, the healer, and one burly warrior.

An unnatural silence stretched out in the simple room, where only the crackling and spitting of burning wood in the fires broke the stillness. Myrddion placed the tray upon a crude scrubbed table and the eyes of everyone present fixed themselves on the simple earthenware bowl and beaker.

Ten minutes later, Willow joined the servants. A large warrior carrying a basket full of freshly picked herbs accompanied her. Her face initially registered confusion, but it was soon followed by fear.

Myrddion left the kitchens and addressed the assembled servants.

"You first," he told the cook. "Come into your kitchen and obey your king."

When the man had crossed the threshold and the entry had been barred, Myrddion explained the situation, stressing that the queen had been deliberately poisoned.

The cook paled a little.

"It's not me! I know I must be the first person suspected, but I will stand by the food I have prepared. My meals are always sound and wholesome when they leave my hands."

Myrddion silenced him with a glance of his basilisk-black eyes and a swift gesture of command. "Then prove your innocence," he said. "Eat a little gruel and drink a little milk."

"Gladly," the cook replied. "I made the gruel with my own hands and I'll happily taste it." He ate a small portion of the soup and drank a mouthful of the milk.

One by one, and protesting their innocence, each servant entered the room and did the same. No one showed any outward evidence of reluctance when forced to eat the gruel.

Myrddion's brow furrowed. The murderous culprit had either called his bluff or the meal was safe to eat.

"Now each person will taste a pinch of salt from the bowl on the table and eat some more."

Once again, each servant complied, frowning at the taste, but no one seemed alarmed or disturbed by Myrddion's demands. Myrddion's thoughts raced. What is the answer? The poison must have been introduced somehow!

He turned his attention to Willow, who was standing to one

side of the main group. "Where is your feverwort concoction, Willow?" he demanded. "The queen has been using it for some time, I imagine."

"It's in my room, my lord," she answered evenly, although her mouth appeared to be a little pinched. "I will fetch it, if you wish."

Myrddion's quick eyes spotted a tiny, telltale quiver of her pale, well-shaped lips.

"No. This young warrior will gather all the potions and unguents in your room and bring them here. You will wait with us. Do you sleep with the other servant girls?"

"Yes, master, I do," she replied, showing no obvious sign of concern.

"Search the room diligently and bring everything," Myrddion ordered the warrior, who glanced at Vortigern for confirmation.

"Do it!" Vortigern ordered peremptorily. "Everything! Hear me?"

"Aye, lord," the warrior answered, and left at a run.

"Now we wait," Myrddion said evenly and sat on the side of the table with one foot swinging idly. To the gathered servants, he seemed totally at ease, although his thoughts scurried feverishly as he sought an answer that would save his mistress.

Some time elapsed, during which the servants rolled their eyes and gave every indication of natural nervousness. They knew that even innocence might not save them from a terrible death, not with a master like Vortigern.

After the best part of an hour, the warrior returned. He was accompanied by a man-at-arms bearing a large collection of unguents, a hide bottle containing liquid, various powders, and a small jar of dark glass that immediately aroused Myrddion's suspicion. What was a servant girl doing with such a precious material?

"What is in the bottle, Willow?" he asked quietly.

"I distill the dried feverwort with a little wine to ease the queen's fever," she replied, slightly too quickly. "It's harmless."

"Then drink some for me, for feverwort will do you no harm."

With her eyes darting from one person to another in the prosaic surroundings, Willow made her decision. With a swagger of bravado and injured innocence, she filled the empty beaker that had held the milk and swallowed the concoction defiantly.

"And what is this cream, Willow?" Myrddion picked up the glass jar with its cloth stopper.

"It is a beauty preparation that the queen uses on her skin to soften her hands and face."

"Then it will do you no harm, will it? Put some on your hands and face, Willow."

"The cream is expensive and isn't mine to use," Willow responded quickly.

"Are you refusing, Willow? Must this warrior hold you down while I don gloves and smear it all over you?"

Willow took the jar and removed the stopper. Her fingers trembled above what appeared to be an almost full jar containing an innocent, colorless cream. Then, defiantly, she threw the container into the fire so quickly that the watching warrior had no chance to stop her.

"Hold her!" Vortigern ordered, his face thunderous.

Meanwhile Myrddion had opened a square of oilcloth to reveal a small amount of white powder. He smelled it, but it had no odor. "And what is this, Willow?"

"I don't know," she replied, and Myrddion was sure that she spoke the truth.

"And this?" He opened each unguent bottle.

"The queen's cosmetics," she whispered.

"No doubt you'd prefer these in the fire as well," Myrddion responded softly. "How long, Willow? How long have you used this white powder in the queen's lip rouge and face powders? A week? A month? Or longer?"

"Longer," she replied in a whisper. Her eyes were downcast, almost in shame.

"Then your fate is sealed, Willow. The reasons for your attempt to kill your mistress will be extracted from you by King Vortigern, but perhaps he will show some mercy if you reveal them quickly and with repentance."

Vortigern cut in, as Myrddion knew he would. The king's face was congested and red, demonstrating that he could barely contain his temper. Any treacherous blow against the queen was also treason against the High King, as far as he was concerned.

"Bring her!" he snapped to his two warrior escorts. "You too, healer, since you've given this traitor to me. I don't want her to die before I know the whole breadth of this plot. Your job will be to keep this bitch alive until I have finished with her."

Myrddion was appalled. To use his medical skills in such a situation was gruesome and contrary to all the ethics that he held dear. And the idea of being a party to torture caused his gorge to rise.

"I cannot obey you in this matter, my lord."

"But you *will* obey me, healer, or you will regret your refusal. As will your assistants! How can I be certain that they haven't been a part of a treasonous plot? After all, you have little reason to love me." He turned to the warriors. "Escort him!"

One of the warriors approached Myrddion cautiously, obviously determined to obey his master's orders and physically drag the healer in the High King's wake if it should prove necessary. With a grimace of distaste, Myrddion waved him away.

"I'll come with you, but I won't act dishonorably. I was the one who discovered Willow's involvement in this matter, Vortigern. Is this how you intend to thank me?"

Vortigern merely snorted in response and strode back into the fortress.

Willow and Myrddion were led to the newly built tower, where steps led up to an elevated room that was bare except for rings fixed to the rock walls, a brazier which waited to be lit and a table on which were arrayed a collection of pincers, knives, and lengths of rope. Quickly and efficiently, Willow's arms were attached to the rings. Then, with a sharp pull on the neck of her robe, Vortigern tore the frail material from neck to hem, exposing her pale, childish body.

"Tell him what he wants to know, Willow," Myrddion begged softly. "He will kill you anyway, but you can earn a quick death if you comply with his wishes." He turned to the High King. "For the sake of the gods, Lord Vortigern, she is barely more than a child. She cannot be more than sixteen years old. Willow could never have plotted this treason, or found such an obscure poison. She has been the tool of very powerful men."

Without acknowledging Myrddion's pleas, Vortigern smiled across at the terrified girl. "The queen has told me how you helped her at Glevum." His voice was very soft and Myrddion knew that the king had passed into the cold, controlled rage that made him one of the most dangerous men in the tribal lands. "She convinced me to bring you with us to Dinas Emrys as her personal maid, because she believed she owed you something. So why have you done this thing? Why have you tried to kill a woman who never did you any harm?"

Wordlessly, the healer prayed that Willow would not provoke Vortigern any further.

"I know you'll not understand, but I had no choice," Willow gasped as the manacles cut deeply into her wrists. "I know you'll not forgive me, but perhaps the mistress will. Please, tell her I'm sorry and that I never wished her ill. The man came, gave me the powder, and told me what I had to do. He explained that his master had a long reach and that my sons would die if I didn't obey, but if I were to succeed, my little boys would be returned to me. So I agreed to poison the queen. I had no choice."

"What are you maundering about, woman? What children?"

Vortigern had no softness in him and he accompanied his question with a vicious punch to the woman's soft belly. Myrddion remembered how a single blow from that gloved fist had killed his grandmother.

Willow groaned and gasped for breath. A string of saliva drooled from her mouth and Myrddion thought that she would vomit, but somehow the girl managed to control herself.

"I bore two living children to your son. He gave them away because he couldn't be bothered with the bastard children of a servant girl. Ask the queen! She knows how I felt and why I helped her to kill your son."

Vortigern slapped her again with the back of his hand, a gentler blow on the jaw, but Myrddion heard her teeth break.

"Who has the power to find your lost sons? Who was your master in this plot?"

"I never met him before Glevum—how could I? He stands high in your regard and he watches me closely, even here in this horrible place. But he told me that Ambrosius himself wanted the queen dead."

Willow spat out a gobbet of blood and broken teeth, but she saw Vortigern's hand begin to rise and hurried back into speech.

"The queen's death is designed to send a message to you that there is no safe refuge for you in these lands. Besides, my mistress killed Vortimer, Ambrosius's ally, and the Roman would never let such an insult pass. For him, the death of my mistress serves a double duty."

"Who approached you? Who gave you the poison?"

Willow bit her bleeding lip. "He said he'd kill me if I told you," she whispered. "But I suppose that doesn't matter now, for it's more likely that you will kill us both."

Then, making her last decision, Willow gave Vortigern a long, aristocratic name that Myrddion didn't recognize. The healer watched with interest as Vortigern's face paled with mingled chagrin and fury.

"I trusted that bastard, Ban rot his soul. He'll regret this treason," Vortigern muttered spitefully. He turned to one of his warriors. "As for this slut, strangle her and get rid of the body." He glanced across at Myrddion. "Go back to your patient, healer, and leave me to deal with these treasonous dogs."

Myrddion left, but a sick curiosity caused him to turn back at the top of the ladder that would take him out of the tower. The strangler had looped a rope around Willow's neck and her face was already purpling. Taking pity on her, the warrior snapped her neck with a quick jerk of his wrists, killing her instantly. As Willow's body voided in a stink of loosened bowels, Myrddion turned away and fled the gruesome scene.

In his absence, Rowena had been encouraged to swallow a little mashed egg and milk, but she had vomited up the contents of her stomach not long after. White, shaken, and pallid with pain, Vortigern's once beautiful wife lay on her pillows in a state of physical and mental exhaustion. Myrddion mixed a little poppy juice and induced her to swallow it. Once it had taken effect, she drowsed quietly, and Myrddion advised her sons to wait a few minutes before trying to feed her again.

"She must eat or she will die," he told them softly. "The poison has built up in her skin, her blood, and her organs, which is why she continues to be sick. We must try to leach the toxins out so that she can gradually return to health. Unless her strength increases, she will not have the will to fight. My lady," he whispered, and the queen responded weakly. "It was Willow who poisoned your cosmetics, on the orders of Ambrosius. But before you judge her too harshly, the Roman threatened her lost children and promised to return them to her if she succeeded in killing you. Before she died, she begged your pardon and hoped that you would understand."

As if his voice had come from a great distance, Rowena nodded sadly. "I do understand, for women will do almost anything for their children. For this, Freya must judge her, for I cannot do so."

Myrddion stroked Rowena's forehead and then departed from the sickroom to search for a remedy in the scrolls. To his later shame, he gave no further thought to the fate of Rowena's servant, or the refusal by her puppetmasters to see her as a human being. She was only an expendable tool in a much larger game.

"Damn Ambrosius, that he must attack Vortigern by using one innocent woman to kill another. Neither of them matter a tinker's curse to Ambrosius, or even to Vortigern. To these great men, women are of lesser importance than the toys of children."

For a brief, poignant moment, Myrddion placed himself in his mother's shoes when, at twelve, she had found herself raped, pregnant, and powerless. He felt a surge of vitriolic rage so visceral that it almost closed his throat. For the first time, he felt truly sorry for Branwyn. At last, he understood her as a fierce soul transformed into an unnatural and perverted creature by the casual cruelties of proud men.

ROWENA, SAXON WOMAN and queen of the Britons, died before sunrise at that time of night when the human spirit is at its weakest and Death comes out of his dark corner and smothers the failing spirit. Her sons were with her at the end, one on each side of her threshing body, and they saw the suddenly flaccid hands and loosened mouth and heard her last deep, shuddering breath. She had been unconscious since midnight, so Myrddion feared the worst when Vengis screamed for help. The healer moved to the queen's side, raised her limp hand, and found that the great vein in her neck was still. When he shook his head, Katigern began to weep.

Myrddion patted the boy's shoulder awkwardly, but Katigern pulled away with a muffled curse. The healer allowed his hand to drop. Meanwhile, after kissing his mother's face, Vengis rounded on Myrddion as if he was the enemy who had caused Rowena's death.

"How could you let her die? Aren't you supposed to be some miraculous healer, a demon who can even bring the dead back to life? Well, bring *her* back to life!"

"No one can recall the dead, Vengis. I couldn't change the flow of the tides or set your mother's heart to beating even if I *was* a demon."

Vengis's face twisted with grief and frustration. The child and the man within him warred in his mutinous eyes.

"Ambrosius did this. Ambrosius—and my father! Damn them both! Damn you too, if you can't bring her back. What good are any of you?"

Myrddion studied the two youths before him—blond, golden, and blue-eyed with little of their father in their high-cheekboned faces. He sighed with genuine regret.

"Be careful, Vengis, for your father is an angry man and he is not above killing sons who rise against him. If you truly don't wish to be Vortigern's sons, and if you decide to dwell in the northern lands once your father is dead, you must choose the path you will follow—Saxon or Celt. Should you choose to follow the Saxon way, I advise you to run far and fast after your mother goes to the fire. Ambrosius will be after your blood too, for he cannot permit either of you to live if he wishes to rule all the Britons. You are Vortigern's only sons, so I suggest that you go to Thane Hengist at his encampment beyond the Abus Flood at Petuaria. I have heard whispers that the thane has returned, and out of loyalty to your mother he will take you into his house and give you sanctuary. You may use my name, for I have some acquaintance with Thane Hengist and I can attest that he is a brave and honorable man. But keep your faces still and your voices quiet, just as your mother was forced to do. Poor lady! She suffered at the hands of men who should have cared for her."

He watched the boys' faces twist with grief, regret, and apprehension. "Katigern, your name will be a stumbling block, for Thane Hengist hated Catigern, your half brother, who was responsible for the death of Horsa. You have heard the stories, so you will understand my concern. What possessed your father to burden two sons with similar names?"

Katigern grinned with such bitter irony that Myrddion wondered how a lad of fourteen years could feel such anger.

"He put Catigern Major in his place by giving his grandfather's name to a lesser son. I was a warning to my older brother that he wasn't legitimate and that my father could put him aside any time he chose."

Myrddion smiled sadly, for the explanation was entirely consistent with Vortigern's sardonic nature. "So Catigern became twisted and cruel, and died because of these failings. Let your father be a warning to you, Katigern. You must find a name for yourself."

THE NIGHT BEFORE Rowena's burning was oddly stifling, for wild storms circled ominously around the high mountains, almost as if summer had returned. Myrddion sensed the portents of danger in the air, so he prayed that he would survive whatever punishment the goddess inflicted on Vortigern for his hubris. The healer paced his tent and refused the stew offered by Cadoc, as he brooded on the violence promised by the coming tempest.

He was almost relieved when, later in the evening, Vortigern sent for him.

The fortress was dark and oppressive in the threatening air. Only a few warriors were awake. They were guarding the entrance to the hall, and Myrddion saw an oil lamp flickering in the upper room where Rowena's body lay in preparation for the following day's ritual cremation. Myrddion nodded to the guards and passed through the heavy oaken doors, cursing as the hinges complained loudly.

The darkness in the hall was almost absolute. A single oil lamp lit the High King's face from below as he lifted a crude goblet to his lips, splashing a little of the scarlet wine on his tunic as he did so. As Myrddion approached, he realized that Vortigern was drunk. The great, greying head was weaving back and forth and Myrddion doubted that the old man could stand, but when he spoke his words were carefully articulated.

"Sit and drink with me, Myrddion. I'm offering you more than I'd have given to your father. He would have had my head in the blinking of an eye if I had given him an opportunity like this. Now his son comes knocking, just when I'm nearing my end."

Unwillingly, Myrddion accepted a pottery mug of raw red wine that Vortigern had attempted to fill. He spilt most of the contents on the floor as he owlishly tried to focus on his task.

"My thanks, lord," Myrddion replied, and almost gagged on the sharp sourness of the liquor.

"It's bad, isn't it? Still, it would be a pity to waste it."

Vortigern emptied his cup and refilled it with the last dregs in the jug. Throughout this careful operation, Myrddion stared at the puddle of spilt wine on the floor and watched the single oil lamp leap and dance in its reflection. He felt sick and dizzy, as if one of his prophetic fits had come to trouble him again.

"I'm a fair man, healer. I promised you a name, so I'll give it to you. The gods alone know how long Ambrosius will leave me alone, now that he knows how to reach me and touch me. Incidentally, I have killed the bastard who forced the maidservant to poison Rowena. But there are many other Celts who'd happily revenge themselves on me, including yourself."

"I should like to retain my head, my lord, so I have no intention of seeking revenge on you."

Vortigern snickered drunkenly. "Yes! And the trickster god, Gwydion, sold horses that turned into mushrooms. Or was it pigs? Doesn't matter!"

Myrddion waited quietly. He knew better than to interrupt the maunderings of the ageing king. Drunk he might be, but Vortigern was still a vicious man, capable of striking out if he was of a mind to do it. The king would tell Myrddion what he wanted his healer to know, when he finally made the decision for himself.

"Your father's name was Flavius," Vortigern slurred, his speech finally succumbing to the wine. "Flavius—a pretty name for a bird of ill omen! Birds. Now, birds he loved—your father—the hunting birds in particular. Oddly, they loved him back, so they would fly to his glove when he called. They killed for him too. Like the women! Ban only knows why, but they'd fight over him like sluts—good women, too. Even Rowena looked at him like . . . well, no matter!"

Once again, Myrddion waited for the king to resume his tale. He now had a name, and a dim picture of the man he sought to understand, or hate. Vortigern seemed almost asleep, or in a trance of memory, but the healer continued to stand patiently in front of the huddled figure on the wooden throne.

Then the king reopened his blurred eyes and noticed Myrddion's presence once again.

"You're still here?" Vortigern peered through the fog of wine towards his healer. "What was I saying? Yes. Flavius, the bastard! Bastard Flavius! Bastard Myrddion! That's the whole problem, isn't it? I hated him, with his damned birds and women fawning all over him. Didn't ever hear his given name, not even from his women—everyone called him Raven to his face and Storm Bird behind his back. He had black eyes, you know. And a black heart! He was after the main chance, even if he claimed to be an aristocrat. We suited each other at the time, especially when he did messy work for me . . . but he was only a mercenary who gave himself airs." He paused, musing over old wrongs. "Do you know he threatened me? *Me?* So I took action first. But he survived, of course. *He's* the demon seed, not you." Vortigern stood up shakily, staggered forward, and tapped Myrddion's chest. "A word of advice, healer. If you want something done . . . do it yourself. Do it yourself."

Vortigern's legs were beginning to fail, so Myrddion gripped the king under the shoulders and held him upright. He called for the guards, who supported the king between them while he continued to mumble.

"Put your lord to bed. Tomorrow will be a difficult day."

As Myrddion watched the guards half carry the High King down the narrow corridor behind the hall to his sleeping chamber, he caught a glimpse of the shadowy figure of a servant waiting in the darkness, his face a blur of white features. For a moment, Myrddion thought he recognized the slouching silhouette, but then he put the notion aside. Vortigern's servants were rarely seen and never trusted, so Myrddion knew none of them, except by sight. Silent, cat-footed men completed their assigned tasks and fitted into the landscape of the fortress, as unnoticed as the furniture.

When Myrddion returned to the leather tent that was his home, his own servants were already asleep. Even the horses dozed at their picket lines, their harness bells tinkling sweetly in the darkness.

Myrddion sat quietly on his pallet in the still heat and thought hard about the king's revelations. Vortigern had told him all that he was ever likely to reveal. Perhaps, if Myrddion asked careful questions, Vortigern might still remember some details of dress or appearance, but Flavius had chosen to be a flamboyant character, using dramatic devices to hide his true self. Myrddion saw through Vortigern's drunken euphemisms and realized that, to a king, *messy work* could well describe murder.

"The great ones never learn. Ambrosius has spies who suborn young girls to murder queens, while Vortigern uses a Roman nobleman to bring the northern tribal kings into line. They throw their tools away when the tasks are done, so innocents like my mother suffer for the sins of others."

"What?" a drowsy voice responded, as Cadoc emerged from his blanket like a disgruntled tortoise from its shell. With his hair awry and his eyes blurred with sleep, Cadoc sniffled, groaned, and rose to his feet, taking his blanket with him.

"Where are you going?"

"Taking a piss, master. I don't think I need your help with it."

Cadoc shuffled out of the tent, and after a brief interval he returned looking far more awake and alert. As he tumbled down on his pallet, Myrddion came to a decision.

"Get up again, Cadoc. We're leaving! After you've woken the rest of the assistants, pack everything onto the wagons so we can be on our way long before dawn. Be as quiet as possible, for I'd rather Vortigern didn't become aware that we're running away in the dead of night."

"Why, master? Wouldn't it be sensible to leave in the morning when we can pack in comfort?" Cadoc ran his fingers through his wild red hair and yawned with jaw-cracking broadness.

Myrddion restrained the urge to put Cadoc in his place, remembering that his servant was a grown man and a warrior, and that he, for all his status, was a sixteen-year-old with few fighting skills. He thought of Melvig's sword in his scroll chest, still unnamed, and how he had no idea of how to use it.

"Don't make me order you to get moving, Cadoc. Vortigern is drunk and half-crazy, the queen is dead, and I'm certain that his last two sons plan to escape his clutches before her ashes are cold. He'll be a raging bull in this fortress and I for one don't plan to be his scapegoat. Hop to it, my friend, and let's leave this wicked place."

"Why didn't you explain? We'd have to be crazy to stay here an extra day more than we have to. Leave it to me."

So Myrddion did, but first he warned his servant to avoid lights and noise. Dinas Emrys had very sharp ears.

Stealthily, the healer's assistants packed up their possessions within the tent and loaded the two wagons that had become Myrddion's world. The tent was the last item tackled, for it was large and excessively heavy, requiring all hands to strike it. As the final roof support came down, Myrddion looked up the rise in the land towards the fortress and, with a sudden pang of fear in his heart, saw a flickering light.

At first, he thought that someone was moving through the lower rooms of the fortress with a lantern. The light flickered and bobbed, but the flame seemed too red and too random. Then his intelligence caught up with his eyes and he realized that the right side of the fortress was on fire as someone ran through the rooms with a lit torch.

"Cadoc!" he yelled. "The fortress is on fire! Get that tent folded and packed. The wains must be ready when I return. Come with me, Finn. Run!"

As he scrambled up the incline, lightning from the approaching storms flashed around the silhouette of the fortress, searing the sky and setting the earth to trembling. "Fire! Fire in the fortress!" Myrddion screamed, his young voice traveling some distance before a long roll of thunder obliterated his yells. "The king, his sons, and their servants could be trapped inside. Hurry!"

Gasping and bent double with his exertions, Myrddion found himself inside the smoke-filled hall along with a gaggle of bewildered, half-dressed warriors. "Open the doors to let out the smoke," he ordered. "Don't stand there like logs. Where are your master and his sons?" This last exhortation was aimed at a servant who stood numbly in a corner of the hall. Smoke wreathed in long tendrils around his face and he began to cough weakly.

Once again, Myrddion experienced a flash of recognition. This time, he thrust his face towards the slack-jawed servant and put both hands up to shake the broad shoulders and force the man to pay attention. Then, as the stranger swatted the healer's hands away from his body, Myrddion knew who he was.

"Eddius?" he hissed. "Eddius? What in Hades are you doing here? Why aren't you in Segontium?"

"I had to do it! How could I let my lovely Olwyn rot in the ground while the bastard king remained unscathed? With Melvig dead I was free of my oath to him, so the goddess demanded that the High King should feel her wrath. Can't you hear her footsteps over the mountains? She's coming for Vortigern."

Myrddion wrapped one hand round Eddius's mouth to shut off the rambling, betraying words that would have them all killed. Eddius's face was blistered along the jaw and Myrddion's free hand could feel burns along the right hand and lower arm, almost to the elbow. The widower had been careless with his own safety when he set the fortress alight.

"How long have you been at Dinas Emrys?" Myrddion whispered in his ear. "How long, Eddius?"

Eddius mumbled a response through the fingers of Myrddion's hand, but the words were muffled and the healer eventually released his hold on the older man's mouth.

"It was easy. Too easy. I've been here for over a month, working in the village to cover my presence. Vortigern's no fool, but he's contemptuous of ordinary men. He never even noticed that I was a stranger within his fortress." Eddius hiccuped with shock, and then began to weep.

"Finn! Finn! I need you, Finn!" Myrddion called through the thick smoke as he forced Eddius to move on unsteady legs towards the open door and the clean air. Finn appeared out of a press of milling warriors, and Myrddion pulled his assistant closer to ensure that no others overheard his words.

"Take this man to the wains, dress his burns, and give him poppy juice," Myrddion hissed into the ears of his assistant. "Sufficient poppy juice to induce unconsciousness. Hear me? Then cover him with blankets so his face is concealed—but shut him up! He's my kinsman and he's set on some crazy, suicidal mission of revenge against Vortigern. He must be saved, for the sake of his children."

Finn led the weeping man away to the safety of the wagons, while Myrddion began issuing orders to rescue those whose lives could still be saved.

"Open all the doors and evacuate the building. Get everybody out, or they'll die from the smoke and the flames."

The rear door to the hall was opened to allow the warriors to reach the king's apartments. A huge gout of smoke billowed out and the warriors reeled away, coughing and choking. Overhead, the lightning from the storm lit the sky and the flagging began to tremble as rolls of thunder shook the mountains with paroxysms of noise.

From somewhere in the hell of fire and smoke, a hoarse voice yelled in sudden pain.

"To me!" the voice roared. "To me! To me!"

Myrddion could see that sheets of flame were following the smoke along the main timbers of the roof, fed by the new supply of oxygen that was sucked into the inferno through the opened doors. As the fire began to spread along the corridor and the interior walls, the voice beyond the maelstrom of fire was stilled, while the flames began to lick eagerly along the roof of the hall like some ravening, hungry beast. Myrddion assessed the situation with a quick upward glance and abandoned Vortigern to his fate.

"Back! Get back! Everybody back! The roof is afire, and will soon collapse. The smoke will choke us if we remain here, so get out of this place while you can."

As the warriors began to retreat away from the flames, a black human shape, wreathed in yellow, red, and white twisting coils of heat, suddenly ran out of the corridor and into the smoke-filled hall. The mouth of the burning man gaped with an illusion of fire within, and its legs and arms windmilled in a vain attempt to escape the agony of burning. The onlookers stepped aside from the blinded, hairless thing that ran and keened from fire-blasted lungs, permitting it to break free into the open forecourt. It twisted and turned horribly, and then fell into its own fiery shroud.

Myrddion was the first to break out of the hideous spell of Vortigern's burning.

"Keep him down! Use blankets! Anything at all that will beat out the flames. It's the king!"

The warriors only needed direction. The fire that consumed the blackened figure was smothered with cloaks, hangings, and anything else to hand. As the flames regretfully relinquished their hold on the sizzling flesh, the storm above the fortress intensified so that the sky appeared to be split open by jagged streams of light until, with a great roar, the roof of the building gave way with a crash that rivaled the sound of thunder in the heavens.

Then, after the fire had done its worst, the rain came in buffeting sheets that fell out of the lightning-rent sky to extinguish the conflagration with a great hissing and huge gouts of steam. Water ran down the fire-cracked stone and drenched the onlookers.

The body on the forecourt paving was sluiced by driving rain that cleansed the charred flesh, the fused fists raised to assault the black skies, and the rictus on a face that had melted into the visage of a beast. When the rain stopped, as quickly as it had begun, all that was recognizable as Vortigern, High King of the Britons, had been washed away.

The warriors began to keen as they sensed the passing of their world and the beginning of something dangerous and strange.

Myrddion turned away from the corpse of his master, but it would be years before Vortigern ceased to run, in a cloak of fire, through the healer's dreams.

Vengis and Katigern had finally relinquished their watch over their mother's body, and had climbed out through the slit window with the agility of boys to reach the ground and safety. They were unscathed, except for scraped knuckles and bruised knees. Myrddion found them in the stables, helping themselves to the best of their father's horses.

"Where will you go?" he asked them. Vengis twisted his mouth bitterly, and it was Katigern who finally answered.

"We travel the Saxon path, healer. I pray we do not meet again, for we will certainly have chosen different sides."

"Then fare you well, sons of Vortigern. Your mother was a fine woman with great courage, and her burning was worthy of a hero out of legend. This cursed place served as her funeral pyre and I pray that no stones are raised again where so much wickedness has lived. I wish you freedom from your father's blood."

He watched the boys leap onto their horses and slap their mounts' rumps with the reins. Then Myrddion set off at a run towards his own wagons, where his assistants waited impatiently, ready to depart at speed.

"Master?" Cadoc asked with a twitch of his one good eyebrow.

"We are leaving, Cadoc, before Dinas Emrys finally discovers a way to take my life and revenge itself on me. Pray for us all in the dark days ahead, now that Ambrosius is our new master."

The wains jerked wildly as they rolled down the rutted track that led to the river valley.

"Home," Myrddion whispered. Then, as his voice gained strength, he shouted the word out again, so that the clusters of warriors beside the ruined towers stared out into the darkness with bleak, lost eyes.

"Home, Cadoc, should we deserve such a blessing. We have promises to keep."

Behind them, a single sheet of flame burst into transitory life within a tumble of fallen stones. For one short moment, Myrddion imagined that a figure stood within the fire, and, as the healers fled down the hill, he imagined that it shook its fist at him.

EPILOGUE

Far away from Dinas Emrys, and the hurried burial of Vortigern with the gathered, fragmented bones of his wife, the wind blew bleakly from the ocean with ice in its teeth. Within the stone fortress of Tintagel, Ygerne and her daughters enjoyed the snug comfort of a blazing fire and warm rugs that covered the floor and walls. Curled together, mother and daughters presented a picture of idyllic beauty when Gorlois entered the tower room, brushing snow off his traveling cloak and shedding his wet boots.

Like slim, dark dryads, his daughters crawled all over his burly form as he bent to kiss his wife. The Boar of Cornwall was the jest of the western lands, for he loved his wife with a passion and depth normally reserved for mistresses. As for his lissome, dark-haired daughters, he was a man completely obsessed. Not even a son could have eclipsed their places in his heart.

With the sleet buffeting the wooden shutters, Gorlois raised his wife's flower-frail face and kissed the tip of her nose. Ygerne smiled and nestled into his shoulder. "I'm glad you're home," she whispered. "Tintagel is cheerless without you."

"I would be happy anywhere as long as I'm with my three girls." Gorlois bit his lip. "The war is over, and change is coming. Ambrosius has swept the board clear, now that Vortigern is dead and his young sons have fled. He has sent out spies to hunt the boys down, so I pray he doesn't find them. Uther is also traveling the Roman roads, for he searches for the boys to serve his own ends."

"Why?" Ygerne asked seriously.

Gorlois shrugged. Uther was a law unto himself, and no sane man could gauge his motives.

"I love your innocence, little one. Ambrosius won't tolerate any threat to his position as High King, so he must kill all of Vortigern's kin. I know it's an ugly practice, and I wish the world were a kinder place, but the children of rulers have died after their fathers for thousands of years. At any rate, rumor has it that the boys have fled into the north, to Hengist and their Saxon kinfolk. They'll be safe there."

"We needn't go to Venta Belgarum, need we?" Ygerne whispered, hiding her face in her husband's shoulder. "I don't care for our new High King, and his brother Uther seems cruel and harsh. I want our daughters to be happy and safe, far from courts and kings."

She raised her face so that her mouth and eyes seemed enormous. As always, Gorlois was drawn into her wide pupils and felt as if he was falling into the soul of his beloved. In Ygerne's arms he knew true happiness, and, like any sensible man, he was determined to hold his joy to his breast as tightly as he could. Sometimes, he feared that the gods would become jealous of his felicity and take Ygerne away.

"You need go nowhere that upsets you, beloved. If you wish to avoid the High King and his younger brother, then you may stay away from them all. I am the Boar of Cornwall and my word is law in these lands, so my queen can go where she wills, without hindrance or coercion."

Relieved, Ygerne sighed contentedly, for the tale of Vortigern's sons had pierced her tender heart.

As GORLOIS's FAMILY enjoyed the security of strong walls and love, Myrddion and his assistants faced the wind, the snow, and the freezing rain on the open road. They had left the seaside villa as the storms began to build over Mona and had been pursued by wild weather ever since.

After Vortigern's death, Eddius had been returned to his happy children and the care of Plautenes. Myrddion had dressed his wounds, and had ascertained that Eddius would carry the scars of Dinas Emrys on his body, and in his soul, for the rest of his life.

"Why, Eddius? You have always been a peaceable man and sensible in your actions. How could you be sure that innocent men and women wouldn't die as a consequence of your actions? Revenge is such a pointless action, and Olwyn would have been horrified if her children had been left alone in the world had you perished in the conflagration."

Shocked and in agony from his burns, Eddius had been sufficiently alert to lower his eyes in shame. Eventually, his tortured face rose to meet that clear, puzzled stare.

"I was a little mad, I suppose. At Canovium, surrounded by Olwyn's kinfolk, I felt her loss so greatly that I imagined I heard her speaking to me about the life that had been taken from her. I can't explain how the feeling rose in me, along with the need to see Vortigern's face and understand what breed of man took someone I loved so much away from me. But grow it did, like an ulcer in my heart. I couldn't stay in Canovium, or return to Segontium with its memories of the past. Going to Dinas Emrys seemed to be the only way I could gain peace."

Myrddion tried to understand, but he had never experienced the loss of a lover or the contentment of total trust in a life partner.

"Didn't Vortigern ask why you came to work for him? He was notoriously suspicious of everyone and everything, especially strangers."

Eddius laughed sardonically, but Myrddion detected only self-mockery in his mirth. "Not he. Or at least, his distrust didn't extend to servants, for they were just tools in his thinking. He needed more servants, so he took them from the village where I'd gone to work as a laborer. The villagers were suspicious of me, but they had no cause to love Vortigern, and if I was impressed into slaving for no wages at the fortress, then one of their sons would be left in peace. Consequently, I had no difficulty in becoming his servant.

"I was practiced at being invisible and I was a diligent worker. No task was too humiliating for me. I watched Vortigern, day and night, and I realized that he loved nothing—neither his wife nor his children, who were simply useful possessions. The longer I watched him, the more I hated him, and my darling's face was everywhere I looked, so pale and damaged by his cruel fist. In the end, I had to stop him before you recognized me, so I laid a fuse of oil through the rooms and the corridor. I wanted to see him burn and I needed to hear him beg for his life. But, in the end, you discovered me and I never saw him take his final breath."

"Be grateful for that mercy, Eddius. Even Vortigern couldn't have imagined such a death, although his penchant for cruelty was honed. He died hard."

Myrddion watched Eddius's face crumple with guilt. Away from the poisonous atmosphere of Dinas Emrys, the older man had reverted to his gentler self, but Myrddion was still at a loss to understand the streak of violence that the fortress had exposed in the nature of his old friend.

In the end, Myrddion couldn't bear the silences that lay at the heart of the villa by the sea. Something had gone from his beloved home and he feared that he would never find it again. Perhaps he had simply grown beyond the quiet life of domestic pleasure. Vortigern's final conversation with Myrddion also resonated through both his waking and sleeping hours, so that his desire to find his father, either living or dead, was growing in him like an itch that he couldn't scratch. Also, as an added temptation, the healer longed to see, with his own eyes, the lands where his scrolls had been written and to learn the sophisticated skills of medicine that still eluded him.

The fever rose in him, and he discovered his course of action when he visited Olwyn's grave on the windswept headland. He felt her presence, as warm and as supportive as she had been in life, and his plans were finally set in motion. Never one to dawdle over decisions, he had informed his family and his assistants that he planned to travel, and given Cadoc, Finn, and the widows the opportunity to part company with him. In the warm villa, Myrddion's proposals had seemed exciting and challenging, so the widows never hesitated, for their lives outside the healer's tents were likely to be fraught with danger and the threat of poverty.

As for Cadoc and Finn, their allegiance to Myrddion ran so deep that if their master had proposed that they should journey to Tartarus, the seventh ring of Hades, they would have happily agreed. So now, in the teeth of a snowstorm, the troop was following the Roman road beyond Aquae Sulis, bound for Londinium and the coast. The wains groaned, and there was no escape from the inclement weather as the wind insinuated itself into the leather protective shelters.

"A mare's nest, master!" Cadoc shivered inside a fur-lined hood that failed to warm his reddened nose and streaming eyes. "Whatever you're looking for, couldn't we wait until spring? Londinium will still be there, and we'll be warmer." He sneezed wetly, but his skillful hands held the struggling team in check. Ice on the roadway gave the horses little purchase, and the wooden wheels of the wagons skidded and slid on the uneven ground, testing Cadoc's expertise to the limit. Altogether, Myrddion and his assistants were miserable, cold, and bad-tempered.

"Don't you want to see the world, Cadoc? You'll soon warm up if you think of the women to be wooed and the gold to be won. These isles are at the farthest tip of civilization, so don't you hunger to see richer, older lands that are far from these freezing winds? Where we are going, there is a great need for our particular skills, while the year-round weather is much warmer. Where's your sense of adventure?"

"Lost in the last storm! I pray to the gods every day that we can't take ship until spring. I've never been on a boat and I'd rather not start in the winter gales."

Amused despite his irritation, Myrddion grinned inside his many cloaks and blankets, his own aquiline nose turning a little red from the cold. "Whine, whine, whine. I've never been on a ship either, Cadoc, so think of it as a challenge."

"Hmf!"

As the wagons creaked and his companions tried to find a warm corner away from the wind and the unpleasant conditions, Myrddion's thoughts ranged ahead. Truly, the world was very wide and strange, and to find one man among the uncounted millions who lived around the Middle Sea was a virtual impossibility. But something in Myrddion's extra sense told him that Flavius was alive and could be found. A man called Storm Bird, with a sense of drama and lethal habits, would leave large footprints that his son could follow. Myrddion knew that his decision to leave everything he had achieved behind him was illogical, but he hungered to learn the truth about his conception. Like many sons before him, he was happy to wager the safety of his servants and his friends on the substance of a dream.

After all this time, I finally have a chance to find him, Myrddion decided, although he was a little apprehensive at the thought of the wooden ship that would take them over the Litus Saxonicum. But he comforted himself with the thought of the new scrolls he could read and the knowledge he would accumulate. His excitement gave a sparkle to his black eyes and he set Vulcan to pirouetting on the slick roadway.

He stared into the swirling whiteness that obliterated the borders between day and night. Out there, in the wilds, his destiny awaited him. Beyond a sea that he had never seen, adventure beckoned. He prayed to the Mother that she would guide his footsteps through the alien and dangerous lands that they would traverse.

"Wait for me," he whispered. "I'm coming!"

But the wind blew Myrddion's words away and filled his mouth with snow.

ACKNOWLEDGMENTS

I am aware that few readers bother with acknowledgments, which is rather sad as authors have few opportunities to thank the many people who make our creations possible. Family members sacrifice their routines so that authors can have the luxury of time in which to write. For the garden untended, the maintenance undone, the carpets unbeaten, and the tidying that is ignored, I thank you!

Thank you to Michael, who keeps saying "What's next?" or, more often, "What does this crap mean?" Every writer needs an honest, fiercely partisan critic who expresses his views constructively, so I am fortunate that Mike has always guarded my back and challenged my preconceived ideas.

My thanks also extend to Damian, who struggles on through illness and debilitation with his passion for history and his curious lateral thinking. Sometimes, with a simple observation, he sharpens my viewpoint or sets me off on a new path. We both love the darkness, the bizarre, the uncomfortable, and the uncompromising nature of truth, all of which have a place in this work.

To Pamela Guy, a distant relative and very true friend, thank you for your big heart, your unquestioning support, and your almond flour cake during long conversations over what to do next. As a "chalkie," which is teacher talk for a fellow educator, she has seen firsthand my passion for history, literature, and the sheer beauty of knowing and searching. Love you, Pam!

Then there's my management crew in London. Dorie Simmonds,

my agent, asked for the first ten chapters of this novel, and then bullied me into a plan of where I was going with the trilogy. Bless her! Like Michael, she is a charming and elfin spur who always says exactly the right thing. I depend on her sound professionalism, and I appreciate her great talents.

I would especially like to thank Judith Curr, publisher of Atria Books; my editor, Johanna Castillo; and the wonderful team at Atria Books. The extraordinary speed, efficiency, and professionalism that the company has shown in the production of the first book of the Merlin trilogy amazes me. You have created the tangible manifestations of a dream by bringing my Merlin and my King Arthur to the public.

There are no words to express my earnest hope that our relationship will be long and fruitful.

M. K. Hume

DRAMATIS PERSONAE

Agricola	The Roman commander who, in the first century AD, was responsible for most of the conquest of Britain. He ordered the murder of the last of the druid population on the island of Mona off the coast of Gwynedd.
Ambrosius	Also called Ambrosius Aurelianus, he was the son of Constantine III and the brother of Constans II and Uther Pendragon, all High Kings of the Britons. Constans II was murdered and succeeded by Vortigern, who was eventually succeeded by Ambrosius. Ambrosius returned to Britain after many years of exile and reclaimed the throne in his own right. He was to be the last of the Roman kings.
Annwynn	A female healer who lives in Segontium. She is well versed in herb lore and takes Myrddion Merlinus as an apprentice.
Apollonius	A Greek magician in the employ of Vortigern, High King of the Britons.
Artorex/Artor	Legitimate son of Uther Pendragon, High King of the Britons, and Ygerne, wife of Gorlois, the King of Cornwall.
Balbas	An incompetent Roman surgeon who serves in Vortigern's army.

Baldur	A Saxon warrior who serves under Hengist's command. He is named after the Norse god of light and beauty.
Bors	Nephew of King Gorlois of Cornwall.
Boudicca	Iceni queen who led a revolt against the Romans in the region surrounding Londinium. Also the name given to Annwynn's pet hound.
Branwyn	Daughter of Olwyn and Godric, and granddaughter of Melvig ap Melwy, king of the Deceangli tribe.
Bryn	King Bryn ap Synnel, father of Llanwith pen Bryn, later to become mentor to King Arthur.
Cadoc	A warrior in Vortigern's service who comes from the Forest of Dean, and becomes Myrddion's assistant.
Catigern	Illegitimate son of Vortigern and a servant girl. He is the younger half brother of Vortimer, and the elder half brother of Vengis and Katigern, the sons of Rowena.
Ceolfrith	A Celtic warrior in Vortigern's army. His family lives in Deva.
Ceridwen	A Celtic enchantress. She possesses the Cauldron of Poetic Inspiration.
Cletus One Ear	Husband of Fillagh, and brother-in-law of Olwyn. He is a successful farmer, and lives with Fillagh on a farm near Caer Fyrddin.
Collen Blackhair	A junior officer in Vortigern's army.
Constans	A king of the Britons. He is the older brother of King Ambrosius, and the son of King Constantine.
Crispus	An incompetent surgeon who serves as a healer in Vortigern's army.
Crusus	A Greek servant who is the chief cook in Olwyn's household. He is the lover of Plautenes.

Democritus	A Greek scribe employed by Melvig ap Melwy. He lusts after Myrddion's scrolls.
Don	Celtic goddess representing the Mother. Her name is rarely spoken aloud.
Eddius	Second husband of Olwyn. He becomes mentor to the young Myrddion.
Erasistratus	A noted Alexandrian physician.
Erikk	Eldest son of Eddius and Olwyn.
Fillagh	Sister of Olwyn, daughter of Melvig ap Melwy.
Finn Truthteller	A forward scout with Vortigern's army, who becomes one of Myrddion's assistants.
Fortuna	Goddess of chance or luck.
Freya	Norse goddess of love and fertility. She is the most beautiful and propitious of the goddesses, and is called upon in matters of love.
Galen	A Roman philosopher and physician.
Geoffrey	Geoffrey of Monmouth wrote a number of works, including *The History of the Kings of Britain* and the *Vita Merlini*. His writings are influential for they are believed to be copies of earlier works lost in the mists of time.
Godric	An aristocrat of the Ordovice tribe who owns a villa by the sea at Segontium. He is the first husband of Olwyn and father of Branwyn.
Gorlois	The Boar of Cornwall who is king of the Dumnonii tribe. He is married to Ygerne, and is the father of Morgan and Morgause.
Hengist	A Saxon aristocrat who serves under Vortigern as a mercenary for a number of years before leaving to rejoin the Saxon invaders. He eventually becomes the thane of the Kentish Saxons.
Herophilus	A famed Greek philosopher and physician.
Hippocrates	A famed Greek philosopher and physician.
Hnaef	King of Jutland.

Horsa Brother of Hengist and a mercenary in Vortigern's forces.

Katigern Son of Vortigern and Rowena, and brother to Vengis; half brother to Vortimer and Catigern.

Lindon Aunt Rhyll's serving woman.

Llanwith pen Bryn Son of Bryn ap Synnel. He eventually becomes a mentor to Arthur, king of the Britons.

Lupus An incompetent healer who serves in Vortigern's army.

Magnus Maximus Legendary Roman ruler of Britain. He was the grandfather of Ambrosius.

Maelgwn Husband of Branwyn, in an arranged marriage.

Maelgwr Brother of Maelgwn, and his steward until his death. He becomes Branwyn's second husband.

Mark Nephew of Melvig ap Melwy. He becomes King Mark of the Deceangli.

Melvig ap Melwy King of the Deceangli tribe. He is the father of Olwyn, grandfather of Branwyn, and great-grandfather of Myrddion Merlinus.

Melvyn ap Melvig He is the son of Melvig, and succeeds him on the throne.

Melwy Younger son of Eddius and Olwyn.

Mithras An obscure deity in Zoroastrianism. He represents the father figure and was adopted as the warrior god of the Roman soldiery.

Morgan Eldest daughter of Gorlois and Ygerne, sister to Morgause and half sister to Arthur, who becomes High King of the Britons.

Morgause Daughter of Gorlois and Ygerne, younger sister to Morgan and half sister to Arthur, king of the Britons.

Myrddion Merlinus   He is named after the sun, and his Merlinus name means Lord of Light. He is Merlin.

Odin   Scandinavian god of war.

Olwyn   Daughter of Melvig ap Melwy, mother of Branwyn and grandmother of Myrddion.

Otha   A warrior/scout in Hengist's army.

Paulinus   Roman ruler of Britain in the first century AD who commanded the legions that first exterminated the druid enclaves on Mona.

Plautenes   A Greek steward in Olwyn's household.

Pridenow   Father of Queen Ygerne.

Rhun   A Greek magician in the service of Vortigern.

Rhyll   A venerable old lady who is the sister of Myrddion's great-grandmother.

Rowena   Second wife of King Vortigern. She is of Saxon descent and is the mother of Vengis and Katigern.

Selwyn   A town councillor from Segontium. He is a grain merchant.

Severa   Widow of Constantine III and the mother of Constans, Ambrosius, and Uther Pendragon. As was so often the case in the ancient world, Vortigern married Severa to legitimize his rule after he assassinated Constans. Vortimer is also Severa's son.

Tegwen   A grief-stricken widow.

Uictgils   Son of Uitta Finn, father of Hengist.

Uitta   Son of Finn, King of Saxaland, and the grandfather of Hengist.

Uitta Finn   One of the early kings of Saxaland (Frisia). He was Hengist's grandfather.

Uther Pendragon   Younger brother of Ambrosius and the father of King Arthur. He succeeds Ambrosius as High King of the Britons.

Vengis

Son of Vortigern and Rowena, brother to Katigern and half brother to Vortimer and Catigern.

Vortigern

High King of the northern Britons of Cymru some generations before the emergence of King Arthur. He is remembered as the first monarch to welcome the Saxons into his realm to appease his Saxon queen, Rowena.

Vortimer

Eldest son of King Vortigern and half brother of Catigern. Votimer and Catigern are both half brothers of Vengis and Katigern.

Willow

A handmaiden and servant to Vortigern's queen, Rowena.

Ygerne

Wife of Gorlois, the Boar of Cornwall. After his death, she marries Uther Pendragon. She is the natural mother of King Arthur.

GLOSSARY OF PLACE NAMES

The following is a list of place names in post-Roman Britain with their present-day equivalents.

Abone	Sea Mills, Bristol
Abus Flood	River Humber
Anderida	Pevensey, East Sussex
Aquae	Buxton, Derbyshire
Aquae Sulis	Bath, Somerset
Bravoniacum	Kirkby Thore, Cumbria
Bravonium	Leintwardine, Herefordshire
Bremenium	High Rochester, Northumberland
Bremetennacum	Ribchester, Lancashire
Burrium	Usk, Monmouthshire
Cadbury	Cadbury, Devon
Caer Fyrddin	Carmarthen, Wales
Caer Gai	Llanuwchllyn, Gwynedd
Calleva Atrebatum	Silchester, Hampshire
Camulodunum	Colchester, Essex
Canovium	Caerhun, Gwynedd
Causennae	Saltersford, Lincolnshire
Corinium	Cirencester, Gloucestershire
Cymru	The ancient name for Wales.
Deva	Chester, Cheshire
Dinas Emrys	Blaenau Ffestiniog, Snowdonia, Gwynedd

Durnovaria	Dorchester, Dorset
Durobrivae	Water Newton, Cambridgeshire
Durobrivae	Rochester, Medway
Durovernum	Canterbury, Kent
Dyfed	Pembrokeshire, Wales
Eburacum	York, Yorkshire
Forden	Welshpool, Powys
Gelligaer	Caerphilly, Wales
Gesoriacum	Boulogne, France
Glastonbury	Glastonbury, Somerset
Glevum	Gloucester, Gloucestershire
Hengistdun	Cornwall
Isarium	Aldborough, N Yorkshire
Isca	Caerleon, Newport
Isca Dumnoniorum	Exeter, Devon
Lavatrae	Bowes, Durham
Lindinis	Ilchester, Somerset
Lindum	Lincoln, Lincolnshire
Litus Saxonicum	English Channel
Llandowery	Llandow, Vale of Glamorgan
Llanio	Bremia Llanio, Cardiganshire
Londinium	London
Magnis	Kenchester, Herefordshire
Mamucium	Manchester, Greater Manchester
Melandra	Glossop, Derbyshire
Metaris Aest	The Wash
Mona	The Isle of Anglesey
Moridunum	Carmarthen, Wales
Nidum	Neath, West Glamorgan
Noviomagus	Chichester, W Sussex
Onnum	Halton, Northumberland
Pennal	Machynlleth, Powys
Petuaria	Brough-on-Humber, East Yorkshire
Portus Dubris	Dover, Kent

Portus Lemanis	Lympne, Kent
Ratae	Leicester, Leicestershire
Rutupiae	Richborough Port, Kent
Sabrina Aest	Bristol Channel and the River Severn
Salinae	Droitwich Spa, Worcestershire
Segontium	Caernarfon, Gwynedd
Seteia Aest	Dee and Mersey rivers
Sorviodonum	Old Sarum, Wiltshire
Tamesis River	River Thames
Thanet Island	The Isle of Thanet, eastern Kent (now part of the mainland)
Tintagel	Tintagel, Cornwall
Tomen-y-mur	Trawsfynydd, Gwynedd
Trimontium	Newstead, Borders
Vectis	The Isle of Wight
Venonae	High Cross, Leicestershire
Venta Belgarum	Winchester, Hampshire
Venta Silurum	Caerwent, Monmouthshire
Verterae	Brough, Cumbria
Verulamium	St. Albans, Hertfordshire
Viroconium	Wroxeter, Shropshire
Y Gaer	Brecon, southern Powys, mid-Wales

AUTHOR'S NOTES

Initially, I had no intention of returning to the Arthurian legends once my trilogy on the life and times of King Arthur of Britain was completed. However, a number of people kept asking questions about my interpretation of the characters in the novel, especially about my Merlin, Myrddion Merlinus, causing me to return to my research and hunt out the obscure strands of the legends of that enigmatic figure. Prior to writing my own books, I had believed that Mary Stewart's magnificent trilogy (*The Crystal Cave, The Hollow Hills, The Last Enchantment*) was the definitive, realistic description of Merlin's early life.

Then, as I considered the comparisons between them, I realized that my vision was quite different from Mary Stewart's masterly seer and prophet. My Myrddion is an erudite, driven individual, a man born to be a scientist or a medical researcher in a kinder age, but also a scholar possessing an intellect that was not content to stay within the narrow parameters of his age. Maps, engines of war, architecture, in fact all the sciences, would have appealed to a man so interested in how the world worked.

The legends gave me vital pieces of information, so I was challenged to make sense out of a series of superstitious incidents, several of them tied to Dinas Emrys. I opted for a dramatic, but physically possible, conception for Myrddion, just as I tried to construct a realistic environment for his upbringing. Branwyn became my villain, as did

Vortigern, but as all the legends described him as a wicked man, his character was relatively easy to construct.

Poor Branwyn! In Myrddion's era, children of aristocratic birth were carefully raised, because they were classed as property and had the potential to bring wealth to the family through marriage. If a willful, rather spoiled girl should be raped and become pregnant, I reasoned that she would have tried to ignore her condition rather than face the repercussions of the physical assault. If she was unable to avoid discovery, she could be killed because she had cost the family a great deal of money. Likewise, any child of the rape would be treated as a bastard and considered worthless to the family because of its uncertain parentage.

This explanation underlines the position of women, even in the more female-friendly culture of the Celts. If they were a part of the aristocracy, girls were property and their worth was tainted if they were spoiled by the loss of their virginity and pregnancy. Branwyn was not a compliant girl. Today we would consider that she had spirit but was unable to move past her rape, a condition that is now accepted as post–traumatic stress disorder. In short, I couldn't paint her as black as she could have been made as a woman who attempted infanticide. Nor were Melvig or Olwyn to blame for her treatment—it was the times in which she lived that made some kind of character flaw inevitable.

The name, Myrddion, for the lord of light, or the sun god, is derived from research carried out by John Rhys. As he is also called Myrddion Emrys, the Merlin I chose owes much to Rhys's interpretations of Welsh folktales, for it seemed logical to me that Merlin would have been given a name that possessed the stature to counteract his illegitimacy. The name Myrddion Emrys resonates with power rather than any magical connotations.

Dinas Emrys itself is the supposed fortress where Vortigern tried to sacrifice the Demon Seed. Some versions of the legends put it at the site where Vortigern was struck by lightning, a death that seems unlikely. Whatever the legends may say, Dinas Emrys is a rather dreary and grim place, and I constructed my tale around it because Vortigern, when under attack, would have almost certainly holed up in a citadel where he felt safe.

Certainly, the sources suggest that Vortigern died by lightning or fire, close to Segontium, so I chose Dinas Emrys as the site for the events I have described. It seemed appropriate that Vortigern should die at the place where he made his most famous mistake, the attempt to sacrifice Merlin.

As for the perpetrator of Rowena's death, it is accepted that she was murdered on the orders of Ambrosius, although Vortigern is said to have died with his wives. My version is a solution to the contradictions that exist within the legends.

As I worked on my characters, I became convinced that Rowena, Hengist, and Horsa couldn't possibly be as black as they were painted in the legends. All Saxons were demonized in the years that followed the initial migration into Britain. I took the facts that were known, and tried to show the possible motivations beneath the violence and the savagery of their reputations. I also realized that these three characters represented the best of the Saxon and northerner migratory waves into Britain. Often noble in background, the best of the northerners weren't barbarians, simply uneducated by Celtic or Roman standards. The invaders that followed the first wave were probably of a different ilk, and would have sought plunder rather than settlement. They were almost certainly as cruel, as destructive, and as ruthless as their reputations paint them.

Rowena, in particular, suffers demonizing in the legends, which is hardly consistent with her enforced marriage when she was little more than a child. Many sources refer to her as the daughter of Hengist, but I rejected this version, although I make them kin. Basically, I wanted to rehabilitate her, and I can't believe that Hengist would leave a daughter to die without taking immediate revenge. Strangely, one early version claims that she was of Jute descent rather than Saxon.

Many versions fail to mention the children that resulted from her marriage, yet her son is reputed to have poisoned Ambrosius out of revenge at a later date. I used the name of Catigern/Katigern twice, to solve the persistent problem of the repeated use of this name in the legends and to try to sort out the later Saxon thanes and kings who would claim legitimacy in the wars against King Arthur. A son or grandson of King Vortigern would be able to make a legitimate claim of a dual right to the British throne.

The entire invasion of Britain must be seen in the context of the European situation. All the old boundaries, alliances, and kingdoms were in states of flux, but the great void left by the departure of the Romans was filled by the tribes who poured out of northern and central Europe in search of a secure homeland. Every wave of migratory tribes created groups of dispossessed and refugee peoples who must have longed for land, security, and the peace necessary to raise their families.

According to the legends, Myrddion was in a position to judge both Vortigern and the shadowy figure of Ambrosius, who might be seen as representatives of the old ways. I have deliberately concentrated on the pragmatism and use of power of these men, who are involved in their own struggle with each other and a rejection of the changes occurring in Europe. Vortigern stole a throne held by Roman aristocrats; Ambrosius and Uther tried to re-create the days of their father and grandfather, so the behaviors of these kings were blurred by personal desires for revenge. The fact that, in my version of the legends, innocent people were the primary victims of this tug-of-war over a crown is my reading of human nature and the motives that impelled these great men.

In time, Uther's son, Arthur, would rise as a new man who attempts to preserve the old ways, a feat that was manifestly impossible. That challenge was his curse and his nemesis, and is one of the themes I used when writing the three volumes of the Arthurian trilogy.

Ultimately, I have chosen to follow the strands of the legends that separate the Merlin figure into two distinct personalities. The Merlin who is the confidant of kings has always seemed at odds with Merlin Sylvestris, the hermit who is driven mad by the death of his family. Geoffrey of Monmouth wrote his *Vita Merlini* about this prophet and madman, while the adviser of kings in *The History of the Kings of Britain* seems to be a completely different man in motivation, power, and *dignitas*. Merlin as seer and dweller in the wild places is not my Myrddion. I have chosen to utilize the Merlin who becomes a statesman.

As for Merlin's reputed sorcery, shape-changing skills, and almost godlike ability to create, as his reputed building of Stonehenge attests, I accept the importance of the belief in magic in Celtic society, but acknowledge that I didn't create a Merlin who is fantastical. I am prepared to believe in the possibility that some people have extrasensory perception, such as the ability to prophesy. Merlin is acknowledged as having this skill, so I used this talent as a part of my Myrddion's special nature. The fact that this skill comes and goes is my testament to the complex nature of Myrddion, who I believe would have disliked losing his senses and making rambling statements about the future. The war between the seer and the scientist is one of the features of my Myrddion Merlinus's character.

Because of his childhood experiences of shunning, being rejected by his mother, and almost being sacrificed by the High King, Merlin is not a perfect person and sometimes he throws his sense of justice away, if it suits him. My Merlin is no saint. But he adheres to the healer's code as his governing morality, and this character trait makes him a rarity in his world.

Because he is literate in a society that is predominantly composed of uneducated persons, Myrddion would have possessed significant status, given the reverence attached to written documents. It is entirely possible that the female healer, Annwynn, would have kept her old master's scrolls when he died, even though she was unable to read them. Similarly, since Myrddion could read, it is logical that she would give the scrolls to her apprentice with the proviso that he imparted the contents of the scrolls to her. However, his thirst for knowledge sometimes causes Myrddion to seem cold and unemotional, because *things* can be more important to him than people.

Incidentally, beheading after death was an ancient Celtic practice tied to their worship of the head, and Myrddion would certainly have obliged his great-grandfather, if asked, by carrying out this gruesome task.

In an age of some ignorance caused by rapid social change, Myrddion is both an anachronism and a new man because of his curiosity. I would like to think that intellectual innovation is not confined to any age and that the description of Myrddion's time as the "Dark Ages" is a misnomer. In fact, I sometimes fear that we are far more barbaric in our miraculous cities of glass and steel than were the great enemy, the Saxons.

I wonder what Myrddion would have made of the present-day health system in Western countries, or the political institutions of our time. I believe he would have teetered between disgust and humor, and would have decried our ignorance and our superstition.